PENGUIN BOOKS

RED DWARF OMNIBUS

Grant Naylor is a gestalt entity occupying two bodies, one of which lives in north London, the other in south London. The product of a horribly botched genetic-engineering experiment, which took place in Manchester in the late fifties, they try to eke out two existences with only one mind. They attended the same school and the same university, but, for tax reasons, have completely different wives.

The first body is called Rob Grant, the second Doug Naylor. Among other things, they spent three years in the mid-eighties as head writers of *Spitting Image*; wrote Radio Four's award-winning series *Son of Cliché*; penned the lyrics to a number one single; and created and wrote *Red Dwarf* for BBC Television.

They have made a living variously by being ice-cream salesmen, shoe-shop assistants and by attempting to sell dodgy life-assurance policies to close friends. They also spent almost two years on the night shift loading paper into computer printers at a mail-order factory in Ardwick. They can still taste the cheese 'n' onion toasties.

Their favourite colour is orange. Red Dwarf was an enormous best-seller when published as a Penguin paperback in 1989. *Better Than Life* was the not-very-long-awaited sequel. Penguin also publish *Primordial Soup: Red Dwarf Scripts*.

RED DWARF OMNIBUS

RED DWARF:
INFINITY WELCOMES CAREFUL DRIVERS

BETTER THAN LIFE

GRANT NAYLOR

PENGUIN BOOKS

PENGUIN BOOKS

Published by the Penguin Group
Penguin Books Ltd, 27 Wrights Lane, London W8 5TZ, England
Penguin Books USA Inc., 375 Hudson Street, New York, New York 10014, USA
Penguin Books Australia Ltd, Ringwood, Victoria, Australia
Penguin Books Canada Ltd, 10 Alcorn Avenue, Toronto, Ontario, Canada M4V 3B2
Penguin Books (NZ) Ltd, 182–190 Wairau Road, Auckland 10, New Zealand

Penguin Books Ltd, Registered Offices: Harmondsworth, Middlesex, England

Red Dwarf first published in Penguin Books 1989
Copyright © Rob Grant and Doug Naylor 1989

Better Than Life first published by Viking 1990
Published in Penguin Books 1991

Copyright © Rob Grant and Doug Naylor 1990

15 17 19 20 18 16 14

This omnibus edition published with a Backword, 'The Beer Mat',
Dave Hollins – Space Cadet and *Red Dwarf Pilot Script* in Penguin Books 1992
Copyright © Rob Grant and Doug Naylor, 1992

Typeset by Datix International Limited, Bungay Suffolk
Printed in England by Clays Ltd, St Ives plc

CONTENTS

RED DWARF

Infinity Welcomes Careful Drivers

To Kath and Linda

Special thanks to Paul Jackson
for everything, to Ed Bye for
everything else and to Chris Barrie,
Craig Charles, Danny John-Jules,
Norman Lovett, Peter Risdale-Scott,
Roger Bolton, Peter Wragg and all the
Red Dwarf backstage crew.

Part One

Your own death,
and how to cope
with it

ONE

'DESCRIBE, USING DIAGRAMS WHERE APPROPRIATE, THE EXACT CIRCUM-STANCES LEADING TO YOUR DEATH.'

Saunders had been dead for almost two weeks now and, so far, he hadn't enjoyed a minute of it. What he wasn't enjoying at this particular moment was having to wade through the morass of forms and legal papers he'd been sent to complete by the Department of Death and Deceaseds' Rights.

It was all very well receiving a five-page booklet entitled: *Your Own Death and How To Cope With It*. It was all very well attending counselling sessions with the ship's metaphysical psychiatrist, and being told about the nature of Being and Non-Being, and some other gunk about this guy who was in a cave, but didn't know it was a cave until he left. The thing was, Saunders was an engineer, not a philosopher – and the way he saw it, you were either dead or you were alive. And if you were dead, you shouldn't be forced to fill in endless incomprehensible forms, and other related nonsensica.

You shouldn't have to return your birth certificate, to have it invalidated. You shouldn't have to send off your completed death certificate, accompanied by a passport-size photograph of your corpse, signed on the back by your coroner. When you're dead, you should be dead. The bastards should leave you alone.

If Saunders could have picked something up, he would

have picked something up and hurled it across the grey metal room. But he couldn't.

Saunders was a hologram. He was just a computer-generated simulation of his former self; he couldn't actually *touch* anything, except for his own hologramatic body. He was a phantom made of light. A software ghost.

Quite honestly, he'd had enough.

Saunders got up, walked silently across the metal-grilled floor of his sleeping quarters and stared out of the viewport window.

Far away to his right was the bright multi-coloured ball of Saturn, captured by its rainbow rings like a prize in a gigantic stellar hoop-la game. Twelve miles below him, under the plexiglass dome of the terraformed colony of Mimas, half the ship's crew were on planet leave.

No planet leave for Saunders.

No R & R for the dead.

He caressed his eyelids with the rough balls of his fingers, then glanced back at the pile: the mind-bogglingly complicated Hologramatic Status application form; accident claims; pension funds; bank transfers; house deeds. They all had to be completed so his wife, Carole – no, his *widow*, Carole – could start a new life without him.

When he'd first signed up, they both understood he would be away from Earth for months on end, and, obviously, things could happen; mining in space was dangerous. That was why the money was so good.

'If anything happens to me,' he'd always said, 'I don't want you to sit around, mourning.' Protests. 'I want you to meet someone else, someone terrific, and start a new life without me.'

What a stupid, fat, dumb thing to say! The kind of stupid, fat, dumb thing only a living person would ever dream of saying.

Because that's what she was going to do now.

Start a new life – without him.

Fine, if he was *dead* dead. If he'd just taken delivery of his shiny new ephemeral body and was wafting around in the ether on the next plane of existence – fine.

Even if there was no life after death, and he totally ceased to be – then again, absolutely fine.

But this was different. He was dead, but he was still here. His personality had been stored on disc, and the computer had reproduced him down to the tiniest detail; down to his innermost thoughts.

This wasn't the deal. He wanted her to start a new life when he was gone, not while he was still here. But of course, that's what she'd do. That's what she *had* to do. You can't stay married to a dead man. So even though she loved him dearly, she would, eventually, have to start looking for someone else.

And . . . she would sleep with him.

She would go to bed with him. And, hell, she would probably enjoy it.

Even though she still loved Saunders.

She would, wouldn't she? She would meet Mr Terrific and have a physical relationship.

Probably in his bed.

His bed! Their marital bed. His bed!

Probably using the three condoms he knew for a fact he had left in the bedside cabinet.

The ones he'd bought for a joke.

The flavoured ones.

His mind ran amok, picturing a line of lovers standing, strawberry-sheathed, outside his wife's bedroom.

'No!' screamed Saunders, involuntarily. '*Noooooo!*'

Holographic tears of rage and frustration welled up in Saunders' eyes and rolled holographically down his cheeks. He smashed his fist down onto the table.

The fist passed soundlessly through the grey metal desk top, and crashed with astonishing force into his testicles.

As he lay in a foetal position, squealing on the floor, he wished he were dead. Then he remembered he already was.

Saunders didn't know it but, twelve miles below, on the Saturnian moon of Mimas, Flight Co-ordinator George McIntyre was about to solve all his problems.

TWO

George McIntyre sat in the Salvador Dali Coffee Lounge of the Mimas Hilton, and stared at a painting of melting clocks while he waited for the tall, immaculately-dressed mechanoid to return with his double Bloody Mary, no ice. He couldn't stand Bloody Mary without ice, but he didn't want his shaking hand to set the cubes clanking around in the glass, advertising his nervousness when his visitors arrived.

Five minutes later they did arrive, and McIntyre wished they hadn't. When he turned and caught sight of them, the heat left his body as quickly as people leave a Broadway first night party when the bad reviews come in.

There were three of them. Big men. They each had the kind of build that looks stupid in a suit. Shoulders tiered from the neck. Thighs like rolls of carpet. Biceps and triceps screaming to be released from the fetters of the finely-tailored lounge suits. The kind of bodies that only look right and natural in posing pouches. In suits, no matter how expensive – and these were expensive – they looked like kids who'd been forced into their Sunday best, all starched and itching. McIntyre couldn't shake the feeling that they were yearning, aching to get nude and start oiling-up.

They didn't say 'hello' and sat down at his table. One of them took up both spaces on the pink sofa, while the other two drew up chairs from a nearby table and squeezed into them. The armrests were forced out into a tired Vee, to the accompaniment of an uneasy creaking sound.

McIntyre just sat there, smiling. He felt as if he was sitting in the middle of a huge barrel of sweating muscle. He was convinced that if he shook hands with any of the three, he would immediately die from an overdose of steroid poisoning.

He wondered, though not too hard, why one of them was carrying a pair of industrial bolt clippers.

The tall, immaculately-dressed mechanoid came up and served McIntyre his Bloody Mary. All three of the men ordered decaff coffee. While they waited for it to arrive, they chatted with McIntyre. Small talk: difficulties parking; the decor; the irritating muzak.

When the coffee came, McIntyre pretended not to notice that they couldn't get their fingers through the cup handles.

The man on the sofa lifted up a briefcase and fiddled clumsily with the lock. For a moment McIntyre found himself feeling sorry for the man – everything was too small for him: the briefcase, the coffee cup, the suit. Then he remembered the bolt clippers, and stopped feeling sorry for the man and started feeling sorry for himself again. The case eventually sprang open and the man took out a fold-out, three-page document and handed it to McIntyre with a pen.

McIntyre explained, apologetically, that it was impossible for him to sign the document.

The three men were upset.

George McIntyre left the Salvador Dali Coffee Lounge of the Mimas Hilton, carrying his nose in a Mimas Hilton Coffee Lounge napkin.

THREE

The four astros paid the fare, leaving the smallest of small tips, and staggered through the jabbering crowd and up the steps into the Los Americanos Casino.

Lister flicked on the 'For Hire' sign, and decided to take the hopper down Central and back towards Mimas docks. He slipped the gear into jump, and braced himself. The hopper leapt into the air, and landed with a spine-juddering crunch two hundred yards down Eastern Avenue. The hopper's rear legs retracted into the engine housing, then hammered into the ground, propelling him another two hundred yards. As it smacked into the tarmacadamed three-lane highway, Lister's neck was forced into the hollow at the base of his skull, further aggravating an already angry headache. The hopper's suspension was completely shot to hell.

Lister began to wish he'd never stolen it.

Hoppers had been introduced to Mimas thirty years previously, to combat the ludicrous congestion which had blocked the small moon's road system so badly that an average Mimian traffic jam could last anything up to three weeks. People had been known to die of starvation in particularly bad ones. Hoppers, which could leapfrog over obstructions, and spend most of their time in the air, helped ease the problem. True, there were a fair number of mid-air collisions, and there was always the possibility of being landed on by a drunk-driven hopper, but, by and large, you reached your destination in the same season you set off.

Lister watched with envy as another hopper overtook him with the easy grace of a frolicking deer. The next landing was the worst. The hopper hit a metal drain cover with such violence that Lister bit his cigarette in half, and the glowing tip fell between his thighs and rolled under the seat of his pants. Frantically, he arched his body out of the seat and tried to sweep the butt onto the floor as the hopper leapt madly down the busy highway, like a sick metallic kangaroo.

Something was burning.

It smelled like hair. And since he was the only thing in the hopper that had hair, it was fairly safe to assume some part of him was on fire. Some part of him that had hair. He liked all the parts of him that had hair. They were his favourite bits.

His eyes searched desperately for a place to park. Forget it.

In London people parked wherever it was possible. In Paris people parked even where it *wasn't* possible. On Mimas people parked on *top* of the people who'd parked where it wasn't possible. Stacks of hoppers, three, sometimes four high, lined the avenue on both sides.

A typical Saturday night on Mimas.

The thick air hung heavy with the smells and noises of a hundred mingling cultures. The trotters, Mimian slang for 'pavements', were obscured by giant serpents of human flesh as people wrested their way past the blinking neons of casinos and restaurants, the on-off glare of bars and clubs; shouting, screaming, laughing, vomiting. Astros and miners on planet leave going wallet-bulging crazy, desperate for a good time after months of incarceration in the giant space freighters that now hung over the moon's shuttle port.

The Earth had long been purged of all its valuable mineral resources. Humankind had emptied its home planet like an enema, then turned its rapacious appetite to the rest of the solar system. The Spanish-owned Saturnian satellite of Mimas was a supply centre and stop-off point for the thousands of mining vessels which plundered the smaller planets and the larger moons and asteroids.

Smoke began to plume from between Lister's legs.

Still nowhere to park.

Traffic blared and leapfrogged over him as he skewed across lanes, fighting to keep control.

In desperation he grabbed the thermos flask lying on the passenger seat, struggled with the unfamiliar cap, and poured the contents into his smouldering lap.

A hiss signalled the end of the cigarette. There was a second of delicious relief.

Then he smelled coffee. Hot coffee. Piping-hot coffee . . . Piping-hot coffee that covered his loins. The pain had already hit him by the time he poured the bottle of upholstery cleaner he found in the glove compartment over his thighs.

The hopper, now madly out of control, caromed off the Mutual Life Assurance building, taking a large chunk out of the neon sign before Lister wrestled it back under control, and, still whimpering in pain, headed towards the docks.

The man in the navy-blue officer's coat and the blatantly false moustache flagged down Lister's hopper and got in.

'A hundred-and-fifty-second and third,' he said curtly, and pressed the tash, which was hanging down on the right-hand side, back into place.

'Going to a brothel?' asked Lister amiably.

'Absolutely not,' said the man in the blue officer's coat; 'I'm an officer in the Space Corps' – he tapped the gold bars on his lapel – 'and I do not frequent brothels.'

'I just thought, what with hundred-and-fifty-second and third being slap bang in the middle of the red light area . . .'

'Well, you're not paid to think. You're paid to drive.'

Lister flicked on the 'Hired' sign, slipped the hopper into jump and bounced off to the district the locals affectionately called 'Shag Town'.

On the first landing, the officer's moustache was jolted almost clear of his face.

'What the smeg's wrong with the suspen–' his head disappeared into the soft felting of the cab's roof '–sion . . .!?' He bounced back down into the seat.

'It's the roads,' Lister lied.

They stopped at a blue light. At right angles to them, thirty hoppers sprang forward like a herd of erratic gazelles pursued by a pack of wolves.

'What's it like?'

'What's what like?' said the man, feeling his jaw, convinced a tooth had been loosened in the last landing.

'Being in the Space Corps? Being an astro? I was sort of thinking of signing up.'

'Were you really?' Contempt.

'D'you need any qualifications?'

'Well, not exactly. But they don't just accept any old body, I doubt whether you'd get in.'

Lister felt for the fare-enhancer button he'd found concealed under the dashboard of the taxi, and added a few dollarpounds to the fare. The lights changed and they lurched off, conversation impossible.

Lister had been trying to get off Mimas for nearly six months now. How he'd got there was still something of a mystery.

The last thing he really remembered with any decent clarity was celebrating his birthday back on Earth. He, and six of his very closest friends, decided to usher in his twenty-fifth year by going on a Monopoly board pub-crawl around London. They'd hitched a ride in a frozen-meat truck from Liverpool, and arrived at lunchtime in the Old Kent Road. A drink at each of the squares was the plan. They started with hot toddies to revive them from the ride. In Whitechapel they had pina coladas. King's Cross station, double vodkas. In Euston Road, pints of Guinness. The Angel Islington, mezcals. Pentonville Road, bitter laced with rum and black-currant. And so they continued around the board. By the time they'd got to Oxford Street, only four of them remained. And only two of the four still had the power of speech.

His last real memory was of telling the others he was going to buy a Monopoly board, because no one could remember what the next square was, and stepping out into the cold night air clutching two-thirds of a bottle of saké.

There was a vague, very vague, poorly-lit memory of an advert on the back of a cab seat; something about cheap space travel on Virgin's new batch of demi-light-speed zippers. Something about Saturn being in the heart of the solar system, and businesses were uprooting all the time. Something about it being nearer than you think, at half the speed of light. Something about two hours and ten minutes. And then a thick, black, gunky fog.

He'd woken up slumped across a table in a McDonald's burger bar on Mimas, wearing a lady's pink crimplene hat and a pair of yellow fishing waders, with no money and a passport in the name of 'Emily Berkenstein'. What was more, he had a worrying rash.

He was broke, diseased and 793 million miles from Liverpool.

When Lister got drunk, he really got *drrrrr-unk*.

He brought the hopper to a crunching halt on the corner of hundred-and-fifty-second and third, outside a garish neon sign promising 'Girls, Girls, Girls' and 'Sex, Sex, Sex'.

'I understand,' said the man in the navy-blue officer's coat, surreptitiously re-gluing his moustache, 'there are some excellent restaurants in this area, offering authentic Mimian cuisine.'

'Look,' said Lister as he short-changed the officer, 'd'you want me to pick you up?' He really didn't feel like cruising around in the bone-juddering hopper for another fare. 'I don't mind waiting.'

The officer glanced down the street at the various pimpy types with poorly-concealed weaponry under their coats.

'Fine. Wait round the corner.'

'How long will you be?'

'Well, I'm led to believe the Mimian bladderfish is particularly exquisite, and I would be insane if I didn't at least try the legendary inky squid soup. Plus, of course, pudding, brandy and cigars. Say . . . ten minutes? Call it twenty to be on the safe side.'

Lister took the hopper round the corner, and saw his fare stride purposefully towards a Mimian restaurant, pause outside, studying the menu, then turn and walk straight into the building with the neon sign boasting 'Girls, Girls, Girls' and 'Sex, Sex, Sex.'

Lister locked the door of the hopper. He wasn't totally crazy about this area, safety-wise. He poured what remained of the coffee into the flask lid, and lit a cigarette. What could be nicer, he thought, than smoking Spanish tobacco and drinking real Spanish coffee? Except, possibly, having your whole body vigorously rubbed by a man with a cheese grater.

He was sick of this armpit of a moon.

He'd spent the last six months trying to get the eight hundred dollarpounds he needed to buy a shuttle ticket home. So far he'd saved fifty-three. And he was probably going to blow that tonight.

Making money on Mimas wasn't easy. For a start you needed a work permit, and Lister didn't have a work permit because, officially, he didn't exist. Officially, Lister wasn't here. Officially, he was a space bag lady called Emily Berkenstein. Hence his problem. Which he attempted to solve by stealing taxi hoppers.

Each evening, or at least each evening he felt in the mood, which turned out to be about one evening in four, he'd hang around taxi hopper ranks and wait for the drivers to converge for warmth and conversation in a single cab. When he was convinced it was safe, he'd steal the rear-most hopper and bounce around the seedier districts of the colony, where few taxi cabs and absolutely no police ever went, and pocket the night's takings before abandoning the hopper at a busy rank back at Mimas Central.

If he'd set about his hopper scam in a slightly more business-like way, the chances are he'd have been off Mimas within a month. Unfortunately, he found Mimas so deeply depressing – quite the most hideous place he'd ever been; worse, even than Wolverhampton – that quite regularly he felt compelled to hit the bars and drinking clubs, and blow every single pennycent he'd saved. In some half-assed, subconscious way, he felt, if only he could get drunk enough he was sure to wake up back outside the Marie Lloyd public house, off Regent Street in London, trying to hail a cab to get a Monopoly board.

Sadly, the price of alcohol on Mimas was so outrageously prohibitive, he could only ever buy enough Mimian sangria to get him in the mood to start drinking seriously, before his money ran out and he'd have to slope back to the shuttle port, where he'd hire a left-luggage locker, and sleep in it.

'Life,' thought Lister, 'sucks.'

Outside the hopper two pimps were having a minor disagreement about a girl named Sandra. It was brief and, for the most part, friendly. It ended when the severed ear of the taller pimp landed with a soft, wet plop on the hopper's windscreen.

Lister double-checked the door locks, and suddenly found it important to read the *A to Z* of Mimas with fierce concentration. He was only half-aware of the hopper rocking gently from side to side as the two men rolled on its bonnet.

Suddenly there was another soft, wet plop, and a second, slightly smaller, ear joined the first on his windscreen.

What the hell's happening? thought Lister. *It's raining ears on my windscreen*. He turned on the wipers, and used his window wash. When the windscreen cleared, the ears had gone, and so had the pimps.

Saturday nights on Mimas were wild. So wild, in fact, the Mimians had instigated an eight-day calendar, so that everybody could have two Sundays to recover from Saturday night. Sunday one and Sunday two, then back to work on Monday.

Lister looked at the hopper clock. Forty minutes since the man in the blue officer's coat had gone for his 'meal'. He slipped his taxi-driver's night stick up the arm of his jacket, stepped over the body of a dead, one-eared pimp, and dashed across the trotter towards the building with the 'Girls, Girls, Girls' sign.

FOUR

Denis and Josie were lovers. Not that they actually *made* love. Not any more. They hadn't made love for the last four years; neither of them had been capable of it. Denis was into Bliss, and Josie was a Game head.

Denis huddled in the shop doorway, tugging the remnants of his plastic mackintosh around his knees for warmth, his hangdog eyes searching the busy Mimian street for a 'roll'. Even though it was cold, he was sweating. His stomach had bunched itself into a fist and was trying to punch its way out of his body. He hadn't eaten for two days; his last meal had been a slice of pizza he'd stolen off a drunken astro. But it was a different kind of hunger that was gnawing at him now. He took out a long-empty polythene bag, and licked pathetically at its already well-licked insides. Denis had a second-class degree in Biochemistry. Though, if you asked him now, he probably couldn't even spell Biochemistry.

Josie was sitting by his side, laughing. She'd been laughing for nearly an hour. Her long, once-blonde hair was matted into a series of whips which lashed at her pale, grimy face as she tossed her head, giggling idiotically. Of the two, she was the really smart one. Josie had a first-class degree in Pure Mathematics. Only, right now she couldn't even have counted her legs.

They'd met at the New Zodiac Festival six years earlier, when the Earth's polar star had changed and the entire zodiac had to be realigned. Everybody shifted one star sign forward.

Josie had moved from Libra to Scorpio, and Denis had changed from Sagittarius to Capricorn. It was a turning-point in both their lives: they both felt so much happier with their new star signs and, along with the other five thousand-or-so space beatniks who'd gathered for the four-day festival in the Sea of Tranquillity, they'd taken many, many drugs, and talked about how profoundly the shifting constellations had changed them, and how maybe the druids were the only dudes who'd ever really got it right.

Now they were on their way to Neptune, for Pluto's solstice, when Pluto took over from Neptune as the outermost planet of the solar system. They'd been travelling for five years, and so far they'd only managed to bum their way up to Saturn. Still, they weren't in a particular hurry – the solstice wasn't going to happen for another fifty years.

So Denis scanned the street for a roll while Josie sat beside him, laughing. Across her brow gleamed the metal band of a Game head. Underneath it, needle-thin electrodes punctured the skull and burrowed into her frontal lobes and hypo-thalamus.

The Game started out actually as a game. It was intended to be the zenith of computer game technology. Tiny computer chips in the electrodes transmitted signals directly to the brain. No screens, no joysticks – you were really there, wherever you wanted to be. Inside your head, your fantasies were fulfilled. The Game had been marketed as 'Better Than Life'. It was only a month after its release that people realized it was addictive. 'Better Than Life' was withdrawn from the market, but illicit electronic labs began to make copies.

It was the ultimate hallucinogen, with only one real major drawback.

It killed you.

Once you entered 'Better Than Life', once you put on the headband and the needles wormed into your mind, it was almost impossible to get out.

This was partly because you weren't even aware you were in 'Better Than Life' in the first place. The Game protected itself, hid itself from your memory. Your conscious mind was totally subverted, while your body slowly withered and died. At first, well-meaning friends tried to rescue Game heads by yanking the headset out of the skull, but this always resulted in instant death from shock. The only way out of the Game was to want to leave it. But no one ever wanted to leave.

Most Game heads, unable to look after themselves, died very quickly. But Josie had Denis. And Denis at least shared his food with her, and kept her alive. When Josie first bought the headset from a South African Game dealer on Callisto, she'd urged Denis to get a set too. She wanted to try 'multi-using', when two or more headsets were connected together, so the users could share the same fantasy.

But Denis was into Bliss.

Bliss was a unique designer drug. Unique for two reasons. The first was that you could get addicted to Bliss just by looking at it. Which made it very hard for the police to carry out drug busts. The second was its effect. It made you believe you were God. It made you feel as if you were all-seeing, all-knowing, eternal and omnipotent. Which was laughable, really, because when you were on Bliss you couldn't even lace your shoes. The Bliss high lasted fifteen minutes; after coming down, the resulting depression lasted twenty-five years. Few people could live with it, so they had to take another belt.

Denis took off his boot, unrolled a second polythene bag, which contained a teaspoonful of the soil-coloured substance, and toyed with it pensively. He always saved a final belt for when he needed to roll someone for money. Which is what he was going to do right now.

Lister should have known better. He'd been on Mimas long

enough to know not to turn round when he heard the voice. He should have put his head down and run. But he didn't. And by the time he worked out what was happening, it was too late.

'Stop, my son!' the voice bellowed, and Lister twisted to see the Bliss freak in the plastic mackintosh swaggering towards him in a Mysterious Way.

'Dost thou knoweth who I am?'

Lister's eyes darted from side to side, looking for an exit, but the Bliss freak edged him into a doorway, and there was nowhere to go.

'Dost thou knoweth who I am?' he repeated.

Yes, thought Lister, *you're a smegging Bliss freak.*

'Yes,' he said aloud, 'you're God, right?'

Denis beamed and nodded sagely. The mortal had recognized Him. Not everybody did.

'That's right. I am God. And I have cometh to thee for a mighty purpose. I need some of your mortal money.'

Lister nodded. 'Look, I'm completely strapped, man. I've got absolutely nothing on me. Not a bean.'

The Bliss freak sighed heavily, trying to contain His wrath. 'Would you like Me to call down a mighty plague, and lay waste this entire world?'

'No.' Lister shook his head.

'Would you like to be turned into a pillar of salt?'

'No.' Lister shook his head again.

'Then give Me some money.'

'Look, I've told you. I'm broke.'

The Bliss freak stuck his right hand into the pocket of his ragged raincoat. 'I've got something in here that can hurt you.'

Lister eyed him up and down. He wasn't that big, actually. And what did he have in his raincoat pocket that could hurt him? A lightning bolt? He decided to stand his ground.

'I don't believe you,' he said, smiling pleasantly.

The Bliss freak took his hand out of his pocket and showed Lister what he had in there that could hurt him.

It was his fist.

He swung it round, hitting Lister on the side of his face. The punch had no strength, but it took Lister by surprise. He banged his head against the edge of the doorframe, and went down.

When he came to, barely thirty seconds later, his fifty-three dollarpounds had gone, and so had God.

FIVE

Lister made his way shakily down the brothel's dusky staircase and stepped onto the red, thick-pile carpet of the main reception area. Plastic palm trees encircled a vast, artificial, heart-shaped lagoon in pink tile. Phallus-shaped diving boards cast frightening shadows onto the softly gurgling water, while Chinese chimes, bedecked with glass erotica, tinkled in the strawberry-scented breeze of the air conditioner. A black, fake marble staircase led up to a mezzanine level, where twenty-odd clam-shaped doors marked 'Love Suites' circled the room. Music, which sounded as if all its charm and energy had been surgically removed, trickled out of a number of breast-shaped speakers. Various fat men of various nationalities sat around the lagoon in white towels, sipping fake champagne cocktails.

In front of Lister a small red-haired man, with a porky roll of flesh above his towel-top, was examining a line of girls.

'This one's face . . .'

'Jeanette's face . . .' The Madame followed behind him, taking notes.

'This one's breasts . . .'

'Candy's bosom. An excellent and most popular choice.'

'Legs: I'll have the right one from her, and the left one from her.'

The Madame scribbled furiously.

'Barbie's right . . . Tina's left. And what would sir like, bottom-wise?'

'Uh . . . I think this one.'

'Mandy's derrière.'

The Madame clapped her hands, and two engineers began dismantling the android girls then re-assembling them according to the client's order.

Lister watched, trying to keep his lunch in his stomach, as limbs were changed and buttocks swapped, much to the apparent excitement of the small red-haired man.

The Madame turned to Lister. 'Sorry to keep you waiting, sir. Would you like a pick'n'mix or an off-the-peg?'

'No, I don't want a girl . . .'

'That's absolutely no problem at all, sir – we have some beautiful boy-droids.'

'No, – uh, this is kind of, uh, embarrassing . . .'

'I understand.' She smiled. Before Lister could stop her, the Madame clapped her hands and a flock of android sheep baa-ed their way noisly into the reception area.

'No, look . . . listen . . .'

'Baa.'

'Yes, sir?'

'Baaaaaaaaa.'

'You don't understand . . .'

One of the sheep turned, winked at him coquettishly, and wiggled off, hips swaying provocatively, towards the marble staircase.

'Oh my God, no. I'm looking for someone. I'm supposed to collect him.'

Lister described his fare, and the Madame led him through to a rest room.

The man with the false moustache was sitting in a Jacuzzi, having a heated conversation with a member of staff.

'I want my money back.'

'Absolutely sir. This has never happened before.'

'She nearly pulled the damned thing off.'

'There was a slight circuitry problem . . .'

'She wouldn't stop. It was like being trapped in a milking machine.'

'Well, if sir would care to make another choice, at the expense of the management —'

'Are you insane? It'll be out of commission for at least twelve months! If you hadn't heard my screams . . .' He looked up and saw Lister for the first time. There was an extraordinarily long pause.

'You know,' he continued, pretending he hadn't seen Lister, 'I don't think this is a restaurant at all. I haven't seen so much as a *soupçon* of the spicy bladderfish for which Mimas enjoys such a splendid reputation. I thought it was a bit strange the way you insisted I take off my clothes and wear this skimpy towel. In fact, if you want to know what I think: I don't think this *is* a small bijou eaterie. I think it's a smegging brothel.'

The officer continued his protestations of innocence all the way back to the docks.

The hopper lurched to a halt outside the shuttleport hopper rank. Lister's fare climbed painfully from the cab, paid up, and leaned conspiratorially into Lister's window.

'Look,' said the officer, his moustache still skew-whiff and curling at the edges from the heat of the Turkish bath, 'Space Corps-wise, I'm pretty much a high-flier; and career-wise' – he looked around – 'it might not be such an A1 wonderful idea if this little adventure were to go any further.'

Lister held out his hand, and the man pressed one dollar-pound into his palm and winked.

'Go on,' he said, 'enjoy yourself on me.'

Lister let him limp up to the automatic doors in the docking port before he leaned out of the window and shouted. 'Hey, whoremonger!'

The man raced back. 'Keep your voice down, for mercy's sake – people can hear.'

'You made a mistake. Instead of a hundred dollarpound tip, you've only given me a one dollarpound tip.'

'Right,' said the officer, loosening the buckle on his money belt and extracting a brown leather purse, 'it's a dirty world, and I suppose I'm going to have a pay the toll.' He handed over a stale-smelling note.

'You're very kind.' Lister took the note and stuck it behind the upturned earmuffs of his leather deerstalker. 'Very kind.'

'Just provided we understand: this is the end of the matter.'

'Sure.'

'Don't try coming back for more. Don't cross me, O K?'

'Sure.'

'Nobody crosses Christopher Todhunter and gets away with it.'

He closed his purse, which was monogrammed: 'Arnold J. Rimmer, B Sc, S Sc', and walked back across the forecourt.

Lister leaned out of the window. 'See you, Rimmer.'

'Yeah. 'Bye,' said Rimmer, absently.

SIX

George McIntyre placed the antique Smith and Wesson in his mouth and pulled the trigger. His last thought was: *I bet this doesn't work*. But he was wrong.

The bullet passed through the back of his head, killing him instantly, before it sailed through his rubber plant and ended its brief but eventful journey in the wall of his office.

The rubber plant was surprised. If the rubber plant could have spoken, it wouldn't have said anything. That's how surprised the rubber plant was. Over the last few weeks it had witnessed the gradual deterioration of McIntyre's mental health, but if the rubber plant had had a name it would have said: 'George McIntyre is not the kind of guy to commit suicide, or my name's not . . .' – whatever its name would have been, had it had one.

Three medical orderlies duly arrived, followed by two doctors, the Captain, the Morale Officer, and the ship's Head of Security. They put McIntyre's body on a stretcher and took him away.

Eight people in all passed through McIntyre's room, and not one of them, the rubber plant reflected rather bitterly, had expressed the slightest interest in the gaping bullet hole which went straight through the middle of his favourite leaf. His biggest and greenest leaf. The only leaf he was truly one hundred per cent happy with.

The humans muttered darkly about why McIntyre would

have done such a thing. The rubber plant knew, but it wouldn't have told them, even if it could have.

Saunders lay on the brown leather couch in the medical unit. Or so it appeared to the naked eye. In actuality, he was suspended half a millimetre or so above it. The hologramatic illusion of Saunders' body was provided by a light bee. The light bee, a minute projection device the size of a pin head, hovered in the middle of his body receiving data from the Hologram Simulation Suite, which it then transmitted into a 3-D form.

The effect was so convincing, so real, that all holograms bore a two-inch high, metallic-looking 'H' on their foreheads, so they could never be mistaken for living people. The stigma of the Dead. Not the mark of Cain, the killer, but the mark of Abel, the slain.

And so Saunders lay suspended an infinitesimal distance above the brown leather couch in the medical unit, trying to fend off a vision of his wife's seduction of the entire offensive line of the London Jets' Zero-Gee football team.

'There was a Being,' the metaphysical psychiatrist was saying, 'and this Being was called "Frank Saunders". Now, that Being died.'

'Yes,' said Saunders, 'he was hit on the head by a four thousand kilogram demolition ball. He couldn't be deader.'

The good doctor shifted in his seat, re-crossed his thin legs, and tugged thoughtfully on his long nose. 'Frank,' he said eventually, 'let me ask you a question. Do you believe man has an eternal soul?'

'I don't know,' Saunders said, wide-eyed with exasperation. 'I'm from Sidcup. I'm an engineer.'

'I do, Frank.'

'Do you?'

'Yes, I do. And I believe, as we speak, Frank, your eternal soul has passed on to the next plane of existence, where it's very happy.'

'The point is,' Saunders said, 'if you have an eternal soul, then there's got to be something badly wrong when it's having a lot more fun than you.'

'Look,' the metaphysical psychiatrist continued unabashed; 'you are *not* the Being called Frank Saunders. The Being called Frank Saunders no longer exists in this dimension.'

'So, who's lying on this brown leather couch talking to you, then?'

'You, Frank, are a simulation of Frank Saunders. You act in the way the computer estimates Frank Saunders would probably have acted. You are a simulation of a *possible* Frank Saunders, or, rather more accurately, a *probable* Frank Saunders.' He said this very slowly, as if he were talking to a small baby who'd splattered mashed apple and apricot dessert over the jacket of his father's new suit.

So Saunders was a computer simulation of a probability of a possible person. He didn't *feel* like a computer simulation of a probability of a possible person. He also didn't feel like listening to another philosophical discussion about the nature of Reality.

What he *did* feel like doing was taking a small ball-peen hammer and tapping it several times on top of the balding pate of the metaphysical psychiatrist who was now twittering on about tables – in particular, tables which had a quality of 'tableness'. And then, when Saunders was completely lost, the balding counsellor asked him if he was familiar with 'The Cartesian Principle'.

'Yes,' Saunders nodded. 'Didn't they get to number five with *Baby, I want your Love Thing*?'

'No, Frank. The Cartesian Principle is: "I think, therefore I am." And although you're not thinking, the computer is just making you think you're thinking; nevertheless, you think you're thinking, therefore you possibly are.'

'I possibly are?'

'Yes, Frank.' The psychiatrist smiled, believing Saunders had grasped the concept at last.

For a short time Saunders listened to the relentless clicking of the clock in the corner.

'I possibly are what?'

'You possibly *are*!'

'Ah! I possibly are!'

'Yes!' The Counsellor beamed.

'Well, thank you for all your help.' Saunders got up and made his way to the exit hatch. 'If I have any other little difficulties, any other little problems I don't understand, rest assured I'll be round in a shot.'

'I really have been of help?'

'None at all.' Saunders smiled for the first time in two weeks. 'You're a useless big-nosed goit.'

As Saunders turned to go, Weiner raced through his holo-gramatic body, and into the medical unit.

'Sorry, Frank,' she said, turning to Saunders.

'Doesn't matter. It's not as if I *am* – I only possibly are, anyway.'

Weiner crossed into the room, her face flushed from run-ning.

'I've got some bad news, Frank. You'd better sit down.'

Saunders was a little bemused as to what could possibly constitute bad news for a dead man.

As Weiner relayed the news of McIntyre's suicide, the consequences began to dawn on Saunders. McIntyre was a flight co-ordinator. He outranked Saunders. Hologram sim-ulation of a full human personality took up forty per cent of the computer's run-time, and burned up enough energy per second to illuminate Paris for three years, which was why *Red Dwarf* was only able to sustain one hologram at a time. With his superior rank, McIntyre would take precedence over Saunders and become the ship hologram.

'So,' he said, slowly, 'I'm going to be turned off.'

'Maybe not,' said the psychiatrist. 'He committed suicide. Maybe he's unstable; not suitable for revival.'

'Of course he is,' Saunders said firmly. 'I'm going to be turned off. I'm going to die for a second time in a fortnight.' He gave the air a celebratory uppercut and danced a little jig of joy. 'Smegging great!'

SEVEN

'Surname?'

'David.'

'First name?'

'I told you: David.'

'Your name's David David?'

'No, it's David Lister.'

Caldicott sighed and reached for the Tipp-Ex.

Lister gazed out onto the busy Mimian street and tried to read the sign on the window: 'ERTNEC TNEM-TIURCER NOITAROPROC GNINIM RE-TIPUJ'.

On a poster on the wall of the newly-painted office, two crisply uniformed officers, male and female, linked arms and smilingly invited all and sundry to 'Join the Corps and see Space'.

Caldicott Tipp-Exed out 'David' from the surname box on the recruitment form and, in his meticulously neat hand-writing, replaced it with 'Lister'.

'Date of birth?'

'Unknown.'

'What d'you mean, unknown?'

'I was found.'

'In what way "found"?'

'In a pub. Under the pool table.' Lister paused. 'In a cardboard box.'

Caldicott eyed him dubiously. Caldicott spent his entire

working day sitting in his immaculate white uniform in the window of the recruitment centre, projecting the Space Corps' corporate image. Which was white and brave, strong and smiling. Once the suckers had signed up, they'd learn the truth soon enough. In the meantime, it was his job to be white and brave, strong and smiling.

He looked at the object sitting opposite him, presently working some unspeakable substances from the tracks on the soles of his boots with one of Caldicott's pencils. Four or five gangly, matted plaits dangled from under the fur-rimmed leather deerstalker atop a podgy face built for a perpetual smile. Short, fat fingers, the nails blotched white from zinc deficiency, scratched at the gap between the top of green, multi-stained combat trousers and the bottom of a T-shirt, whose original colour was long lost in the mists of time. He looked like a casualty in a catering war: as if all the world's chefs had had a gigantic food fight, and somehow he'd got caught in the middle. If his daughter had brought home this specimen, Caldicott reflected, he would have shot them both without a second's reflection.

'Do you know when you were found?' He smiled whitely.

'Some time in November. 'Fifty-five.'

'Well, I need a date of birth for the form. When do you celebrate your birthday?'

'Most of the time, actually.'

'I'll put 1st November, 2155.'

'Not November. I was about six weeks old then. It was probably some time in October.'

Caldicott reached for the Tipp-Ex again.

'How about 14th October?'

'Brutal.'

'Why do you want to join the Space Corps?'

Lister thought for a moment. 'I want,' he said, 'to visit strange new worlds, to seek out new life and new civilizations. To boldly go where no person has gone before.'

Caldicott smiled wanly and wrote: 'Possible Attitude Problem' in the comments box.

'Qualifications?'

'Technical Drawing.'

'What level?'

'What d'you mean?'

'Master's degree, perhaps?' said Caldicott, almost imperceptibly raising his left eyebrow. 'Ph.D., maybe?'

'GCSE.'

Caldicott wrote '1 GCSE, Technical Drawing'.

'It doesn't really count, though, that, does it?' Lister picked at a flap of rubber hanging from the sole of his boot.

'Why not?'

'I failed.'

Caldicott took out the Tipp-Ex again and obliterated the word 'Possible'.

'If you'd just like to read through this, and sign where I've indicated.' Caldicott pushed over the application papers, picked up the phone and stabbed in a ten-digit number.

Lister cast his eyes over the conditions of employment. He was signing up for five years. Five long years. When he got out, he'd be pushing thirty. An old man.

Ha! Want to bet?

He wondered why he hadn't thought of this before. Join the Space Corps, get on an Earth-bound ship, and as soon as he got home: thank you, goodnight. Lister, David, AWOL.

He signed and pocketed the pen, including its metal chain and holder.

'OK,' said Caldicott, putting down the phone, 'the situation is this: there are fourteen ships in dock, but no vacancies for anyone with your . . . abilities.'

'What are my abilities?'

'You haven't got any. You'll have to enter at third technician level.'

'Technician?' repeated Lister, impressed.

'That's right,' said Caldicott, smiling.

A third technician's duties basically consisted of making sure the vending machines didn't run out of chicken soup, mopping floors, and a thousand-and-one other tasks considered too menial for the service droids. Caldicott didn't feel this was absolutely the best time to put Lister in the picture.

'Tech-nishern,' said Lister, putting on a pseudo-swanky voice. He glanced up at the white uniformed officer with the Burt Lancaster smile in the poster. 'I'm a bleeding technishern, don't yew know.'

'As soon as something crops up, we'll let you know. Leave your address.'

'Address?' Lister wondered what to put.

He settled on: 'Luggage locker 4179, Mimas Central Shuttle Station.'

EIGHT

'Shuttle Flight JMC159 for *White Giant* now boarding at gate number five,' the tannoy announced, and proceeded to make the same announcement in Esperanto, German and three different dialects of Chinese.

A group of miners stubbed out their cigarettes and finished their beers, then reluctantly swung their kit-bags over their shoulders before joining a group of white-suited officers and some grey-suited technicians in the queue to gate five.

Two Shore Patrol officers strode through the milling crowds, casually swinging their argument-settlers. People pretended not to look at them. You didn't mess with the Shore Patrol. Not unless you wanted your skull rearranged to resemble a relief map of Mars, canals and all.

'This has got to be a joke.'

'This is the address we were given,' said the blonde.

They stopped at the huge bank of luggage lockers and looked around, searching for number 4179. The dark-haired one banged on the door.

'This has got to be a joke,' she repeated.

Lister was awakened from a dream about a pickle sandwich that spoke fluent Italian by the deafening metallic clanging, as Shore Patrolwoman Henderson beat the luggage locker door with her steel truncheon.

'It's a joke. I'm telling you.'

'Hang on,' called Lister. 'Let me get dressed.' In the

confined space of the locker, which was designed to accommodate two smallish suitcases, he groped around in the
blackness, located his clothes, and pulled on his coffee-
and-upholstery polish-stained trousers. 'Who is it?'

'Shore Patrol. We're looking for a guy called "Lister".'

'I'll see if he's in,' called out Lister, stalling for time. 'Uh
. . . why d'you want him?'

'He's been assigned. They've found him a ship.'

The door opened and Lister jumped the six feet down to
the ground. He cupped his chin in one hand, placed the
other on the back of his neck and snapped his head to one
side, to the accompaniment of a series of stomach-churning
cracks.

'Your papers have come through,' said Henderson, 'and –'

'Wait a minute,' said Lister; 'I can't see yet. Give me a
minute.'

He blinked a few times and rubbed his eyes. Slowly, the
two Shore Patrolwomen came into focus.

'Hi,' said Lister. 'I'd invite you in, but it's a bit of a mess.
It's more of a bachelor luggage-locker than –'

'How long have you been sleeping in there?' Henderson
interrupted.

'Since my second night on Mimas. I tried sleeping on a
park bench, but I woke up in the middle of the night
completely naked, and this old Chinese guy was licking my
foot. So, compared with that, this is the Mimas Hilton.'

'No work permit, right?'

'I have, actually, but it belongs to a woman called Emily
Berkenstein. It's a long story.'

'Get your stuff together.'

'I've got my stuff together.'

'Where is it?'

'In my pocket.'

They walked back across the shuttle lounge towards the
departure gates.

'We've got to deliver you to gate nine.'

'Time for breakfast?'

'If you make it quick.'

Lister peeled off from his escort and, without ever stopping, walked through the Nice'n'Noodly Kwik-Food bar, picking up a half-eaten soya sandwich and a three-quarter finished noodle burger that people with weaker constitutions had left behind.

'You're probably thinking I'm a slob,' said Lister, finishing off a quintuple-thick milkshake and hoovering around the base with the straw. 'But I'm not – I'm just hungry, O K?'

'Hey, it's a real pity you've got to go on this ship, and everything,' said Henderson; 'because, otherwise, you could maybe have taken me out for dinner. You know, a couple of half-eaten egg rolls. Maybe root through a bin for the remnants of a Kentucky Fried Chicken. Then back to your place for half a bottle of paraffin. It could have been so romantic.'

'Well, listen,' said Lister, totally missing the irony, 'I'm not exactly married to this spaceship idea. Why don't we do it? Just promise not to bring your steel truncheon.'

> *'To Ganymede and Titan,*
> *Yes, sir, I've been around,*
> *But there ain't no place*
> *In the whole of Space,*
> *Like that good ol' toddlin' town . . .*
>
> *Lunar City Seven,*
> *You're my idea of heaven.*
> *Out of ten, you score eleven,*
> *You good ol' artificial terra-formed*
> *settlement . . .'*

Through the shuttle's tinny sound system Perry N'Kwomo,

the African ballad singer, was crooning one of the many 'easy listening' hits from his best-selling album, *Nice 'n' Nauseating*.

Lister sat in the packed shuttle with the rest of the new recruits on the twenty-five minute jag up to their assigned ship, gazing out from his window seat as Mimas dropped away below him like a bad taste he'd spat into the night.

He thumbed through the shuttle's in-flight magazine, *Up, Up, And Away!* He stared for a brief moment at the blisteringly unpromising contents page: 'Salt – An Epicure's Delight'; 'Classic Wines of Estonia'; and 'Weaving the Traditional Way' were just some of the more fascinating articles. How is it possible, Lister wondered, to fill a hundred-and-twenty-page magazine without actually including anything remotely readable? He tucked it back into the netting of the seat in front of him, and decided to read the plastic card containing the crash-landing instructions for the second time.

The shuttle buzzed slowly through the groups of gargantuan space freighters that bobbed in orbit like a bunch of clumsy balloons.

Aerodynamics was never a consideration in starship design. All the ships were constructed in orbit, designed never to land, never to encounter wind resistance or gravity, and were consequently, a variety of bizarre and outlandish shapes.

For five full minutes the shuttle ran alongside a supply ship called the *Arthur C. Clarke*: a two-mile length of dirty grey steel, orange lights dotting the huge, bulbous cargo hold, out of which sprang a long, thick, tubular nose section, curling and twisting like the stem of an oriental hookah.

Eventually the shuttle reached the cusp of the star freighter's bulb, and turned.

Lister's window was filled with red.

And red.

And red.

He couldn't see where it started and he couldn't see where it finished. But it was big. No, it was *BIG*.

A big, red, red, big clenched fist of metal.

As the shuttle accelerated towards the redness, details slowly emerged through the thick gloom of space. Gradually, Lister made out the thousands of tiny pin-pricks of windows and a tooth floss-thin line of light ringing the ship: the vessel's metro system.

A huge, shadowy carbuncle jutted out a mile or so from the red monster's belly – a small moon, torn out of orbit, had flung itself into the ship's solar plexus and was now embedded in the hull, hanging there like a giant stone leech.

As the shuttle swung out to align itself for docking, the red ship's nose-cone loomed into view – six half-mile steel poles, bound by magnetic cable, as if the fist were clutching a huge shuttlecock. This was the scoop. The scoop sucked hydrogen from the currents of space and converted it into fuel, theoretically making the ship capable of travelling forever.

Lister was aware of the hot whisky breath of the burly astro beside him, who was now leaning over him to share his window.

'The *Dwarf*,' he said in a Danish accent, ripping open another can of Glen Fujiyama.

'The what?' Lister tried not to inhale.

'*Red Dwarf*.'

'How *big* is it?'

'It could eat Copenhagen,' said the Dane, 'and have Helsingør for afters.'

Lister accepted a belt from the whisky can, and they swapped names.

'It's got to be five miles long.'

'Something like that,' said Petersen.

Lister squinted out of the window again. 'And God, is it ugly!'

'Ugly as my mother.' Petersen smiled through bar-brawl broken teeth. 'First trip?'

Lister nodded.

Petersen belched, crumpled up the whisky can, tossed it into the aisle, and fished in his knapsack for another. 'I'd offer you one,' he said apologetically, 'but I have only twelve left. Been on Mimas long?'

'Six months.'

'It's a bit of a dump, right?'

'It's a lot of a dump.'

'Wait till we get to Triton. Triton's OK.'

'Triton?' Lister's brow furrowed. 'We're going to Earth.'

'Sure, we're going to Earth. But first we've got to go to Triton to get the ore to take to Earth.'

Lister closed his eyes. 'Where's Triton?'

'Round Neptune.'

'Oh,' said Lister. 'Neptune. Right.' He took a swig from Petersen's nearly-empty whisky can. 'Where's Neptune?'

'From here?' Petersen took out a calculator. 'I'll tell you exactly.' He punched a lot of numbers into the machine. 'It's two billion, seven hundred and seven million miles away.'

Lister sighed like a burst tyre. 'How long is that going to take?'

'Say, eighteen months,' said Petersen. 'Eighteen months, not counting Customs. And Triton Immigration Control is a son-of-a-bitch. It's worse than New York.'

'Eighteen months?'

'Then twelve months' mining,'

'Twelve months' *mining*?'

'Then two more years to get back to Earth.'

'Four-and-a-half-years?'

'It's an old ship. It only does two hundred thousand miles an hour.'

'Four-and-a-half-years,' Lister repeated like a mantra, 'Four-and-a-half-years.'

He turned and looked out of the window as the shuttle ducked into the trench cut deep into *Red Dwarf*'s back. On either side, buildings flitted past: skyscrapers, tower blocks a hundred storeys high; monoliths of steel and glass. One minute it was as if they were flying through Manhattan; then without warning the architecture changed, and it looked like Moscow; then fluted pillars and elaborate neo-classic arches, and they could have been in New Athens: a tasteless mish-mash of styles from the decades upon decades the vast mining ship had taken to build.

For a tantalizing moment, between a huge mosque-shaped dome and a line of industrial chimneys, the tiny blue light that was Earth winked and flickered invitingly in the glow of the distant Sun, then just as suddenly was gone, as they swooped towards the yawning doors of the docking bay.

'Four-and-a-half-years,' said Lister catatonically.

NINE

Lister pushed through the crowded docking bay, fighting his way to the Intake Clearance Zone, a now moronically drunk Petersen in tow. They'd been stopped at *Red Dwarf* customs and Petersen had been bag-searched. His possessions had comprised a toothbrush, one pair of underpants, three socks and eleven cans of whisky. Informed that he couldn't bring the liquor aboard without paying duty, he had stood in the green channel and downed all eleven cans, one after the other, offering Lister a sip a can.

Now Petersen was walking sideways, his head cocked at a curious angle, singing a lewd Danish folk song, punctuated with appropriate gestures and slobbering leers, as Lister dragged him by his lapel towards the moving walkway.

High above, dominating the ship's shuttle port, was a monitor screen the size of a football pitch, from which a disembodied head was lugubriously dispensing information. The head was a digitalized reproduction of a balding forty-year-old man, with a voice that had a slight East London twang.

'The floor's stopped moving,' said Petersen as they reached the end of the walkway; 'that's a very good thing.'

Lister scanned the various name-cards that *Red Dwarf* induction staff were holding above the heads of the jostling crowd.

'Hi, I'm Chomsky.'

'Chomsky? Pierre, right?' Rogerson ticked his clipboard.

'OK stand there a second. We're still looking for a Burroughs, a Petersen, a Schmidt and a Lister.'

'I'm a Lister,' said Lister.

'I'm going to be sick,' said Petersen. And he was. Exorcist sick.

'Yerrrrrrrrgh.

'YAAAAAAAAAAAAAAAAAAAARGHHHHHH.'

A pause. A sigh.

'Yuuuuuuuuuuuuuuuuuuuuuuuuuuuuuuuuuuuuuuurh.

'Yurgh.' Petersen smacked his lips and wiped his face with the back of his sleeve. 'That's better.'

Two skutters, claw-headed service droids which looked like miniature amputee giraffes on motorized bases, swept into view and cleaned up the mess. Petersen tried to tip them.

'We're still looking for a Burroughs and a Schmidt,' Rogerson said, trying to disguise his disgust.

'What's that thing?' asked Lister, pointing up to the disembodied head on the monitor screen.

'Holly, the ship's computer. He's got an IQ of six thousand. You want to ask him a question?'

'Like what?'

'Like anything at all.' Rogerson called up to the ceiling; 'Hey, Holly – this is Lister . . .'

The huge eyes rolled down in their direction. 'I know. Lister, David. Date of birth, 14th October, 2155. Qualifications: GCSE, Technical Drawing, failed. Rank: Technician, Third Class. Ambitions: to visit strange new worlds, to seek out new life and new civilizations: to boldly go where no person has gone before. All right, Dave?' A huge eyelid rolled over the digital eye and winked at Lister.

'Ask him something,' Rogerson urged.

'Who holds the all-time record for three-dimensional yardage in a single Zero-Gee football season?'

'Jim Bexley Speed, London Jets Roof Attack, season '74–

'75. Four thousand, six hundred and thirty-six square yards in the regular season.'

'And what colour tie was he wearing when he was interviewed by Mark Matheson after Megabowl 102?'

'Aquamarine, with a diagonal lemon stripe.'

'Brutal.' Lister grinned.

Chomsky chipped in: 'Who was the Chinese Emperor of the Ming dynasty in 1620?'

'T'ai-ch'ang,' Holly replied immediately; 'also known as Chu Ch'ang-lo Kuang Tsung. Born 1582.'

They all began shouting questions: 'Who was the . . .?' 'How many . . .?' 'When did . . .?' and, one by one, Holly got them right.

Finally Petersen asked a question. 'Why is the room going round and round?'

'Because you're drunk,' said Holly.

'That's *riiiiight!*' Petersen clapped, delighted.

Burroughs and Schmidt finally arrived, and the ten of them were herded onto the *Red Dwarf*'s Northern Line, one of a network of tube trains which criss-crossed the length and breadth of the ship. Spread evenly throughout the carriage were more monitors displaying the genius computer, who was capable of conducting several thousand conversations simultaneously, ranging from what was on the ship's movie channel that night to discussing the melding of quantum mechanics and general relativity.

Some thirty minutes later they boarded the Xpress super lift, which whisked them up to Floor 9,172, where they were met by a ship rover – a three wheel electric buggy-bus – and driven down two miles of corridors towards the sleeping quarter, Area P.

'OK,' said Rogerson, showing Lister into his sleeping quarters. 'Make yourself at home. I'll just go and fix up the other guys.'

Lister looked round the room which was going to be his

home for the next four-and-a-half years. Dull, gunmetal grey walls reflected his mood. Neon strips around the walls simulated the time of day. Dirty yellow at the moment signalled the middle of the afternoon. A dirty orange would signal early evening, and a dirty blue would indicate night.

Two bunk cubicles were carved into recesses in the wall, one above the other. To the right stood a simple pedestal wash basin and mirror, which, when voice-activated, swivelled on its base to reveal an antiquated chemical toilet bearing the legend: 'Now please irradiate your hands'. Lister began to wish he was in his nice, cosy luggage locker back at Mimas Central.

Behind him was a bank of fitted aluminium wardrobes, and two steps led down to what was laughingly sign-posted 'Lounge Area'. The lounge area was about two metres square, with a three-seater reinforced steel settee, and a tiny coffee table welded to the floor.

Nice, thought Lister. *Very homely*.

The other occupant of the room left very little evidence of his existence. Whatever he did possess was meticulously tidied away. On the wall of his bunk, the lower one, hung a home-made revision timetable in worryingly neat handwriting, and an array of startlingly complex colour codes. Beside it were a number of certificates, neatly framed, and a series of cut-out newspaper headlines, all along the lines of: 'Arnie Does It Best'; 'Arnie Comes Out On Top'; and 'Arnold – A Living Legend'.

Lister scanned the titles in the bookcase built into a recess above the video screen: *Astronavigation and Invisible Number Theory Made Simple*; *Conceptual Foundations of Quantum Mechanics Made Simple*; *Heisenberg's Uncertainty Principle for Beginners*; *An Introduction to the Liar Paradox and the Non-Mechanizability of Mathematics;* and *How to Get More Girls by Hypnosis*.

He opened his bunk-mate's wardrobe and peered in.

Twenty pairs of identical, military blue underpants hung on coat hangers in protective cellophane sheaths, next to seven pairs of pale blue pyjamas, with dry-cleaning tags pinned to the collars. Lister was disturbed to see that the pockets of the pyjamas bore an insignia of rank. Brightly polished boots stared unblinkingly in rows on the floor. A pair of monogrammed slippers on the shoe-trees stood beside them.

Lister closed the wardrobe, struck a match on the 'No Smoking' sign, lit up, and sat down on the metal settee.

'Nice. Very, very nice.'

Rogerson came back in. 'Oh, David, meet your bunk-mate . . .'

Lister looked up. Behind Rogerson stood a grey-suited technician; tall and rangy, flared nostrils and wide, slightly manic eyes and a hyperactive, constantly jiggling right leg that always seemed to want to be somewhere else. Even without his false moustache, there was no mistaking the 'officer' who'd hired his hopper.

'He's also your shift leader, so he's the guy who'll be showing you the ropes. Lister, this is First Technician –'

'Arnold Rimmer,' said Lister. 'We've already met.'

'No, we haven't,' said Rimmer, smiling too much.

'You're a technician,' said Lister, surprised. 'I thought you said you were an officer.'

'Shut up,' said Rimmer, pumping his hand and smiling even harder.

TEN

On the first morning into space, Lister sat in the lecture theatre, with the other eleven members of Z Shift, in his brand new technician's uniform which made him itch in nineteen different places, while his left arm and his right buttock competed for the title 'Most Painful Appendage', following his twelve inoculation jabs.

The rest of the previous morning and the whole of the afternoon had been a long process of multifarious humiliations: hours standing around in backless surgical gowns (*Why* backless? When did a surgeon ever need to get to your bottom in a hurry?) giving various bodily fluid samples – Petersen had, in fact, delivered rather more bodily fluid samples than was absolutely necessary, and nobody was pleased; IQ tests; genetic fingerprinting; hand-to-eye co-ordination work; centrifugal weightlessness simulation; then, finally, they'd all been marched like a serpent of school children down to the computer decks, where they each had their personalities recorded for storage in the hologram library. Lister had sat in the suite, a metal skull-cap bolted to his head, while his every memory and personality trait had been logged onto a depressingly small computer slug. His entire life; his whole personality copied and duplicated on a piece of computer hardware the size of a suppository. Petersen's recording had crashed three times, with an error-message which read 'Non-Human Lifeform'. In the end, they had to drip-feed him coffee and subject him to several very cold showers before his brain was functioning sufficiently well to be recorded. If, in the highly unlikely circumstance of Petersen achieving the status of 'Indispensable Personnel', and then dying, he would be retrieved as a hologram with the mater and pater of all hangovers.

The lecture theatre hatchway breezed open, and Rimmer clicked up to the podium in boots so brightly polished you could see infinity in them.

The previous evening in the sleeping quarters, no mention had been made of the incident in the brothel. In fact, Rimmer had played the part of a man who'd never met Lister before very credibly indeed. He was, he had declared, not exactly in love with the idea of bunking out with a subordinate, but it was something that they both had to put up with.

'There's just one rule,' he'd maintained, polishing his boots for the third time, 'and that rule is K-I-T. D'you know what K.I.T. stands for?'

'Ken Is a Transvestite?' Lister had offered.

'Keep It Tidy. And if you K.I.T., then we'll G.O.J.F.' He'd left this hanging in the air for effect before translating: 'Get On Just Famously.'

Lister spent the rest of the evening trying to take advantage of the fact that he now had a proper bed, of sorts, for the first time in six months. Though, curiously, he'd discovered he couldn't drop off to sleep until he sat up in bed and wrapped both arms around his knees, luggage locker-style. Meanwhile, Rimmer sat at his slanting architect's desk and whiled away the time until Lights Out reading a book called: *How to Overcome Your Fear of Speaking in Public*.

Rimmer gripped the podium tightly, the inside of his wrists pointing out towards the new intake, a trick which, his book told him, would make his audience trust him, and began his speech to Z Shift.

'My name,' he said, 'is Arnold J. Rimmer. You will call me "sir" or "First Technician". I am your shift leader. This is my very first command, and I don't intend it to be my last. What I do intend is for Z Shift to become the best, the fastest, the tightest, the most efficient Routine Maintenance, Cleaning and Sanitation Unit this ship, or any other ship in the Space Corps, has ever seen.' He paused.

Silence. The book said silence could be as effective as speech, if used judiciously. Use silence, it urged. Rimmer stood there, being silent. Enough silence, he decided. More speech.

'When we do something, we do it fast and we do it right.'

More silence.

Still more silence.

No, this was a dumb place to have silence. It just made him look like he'd forgotten what he was saying.

'This ship is three miles wide, four miles deep, and nearly six miles long. But . . .' he paused again – a most excellent and petite silence, he congratulated himself. Very telling. '. . . if anywhere on it a vending machine so much as runs out of chicken soup, I want a member of Z Shift to be there within four minutes.'

More silence. The best silence yet.

'You used to think your mother was your best friend. Not any more. From now on, your best friend is this . . .' he held aloft a three-foot-long metallic tube, with a vari-twist grip and seven detachable heads. 'It's called a sonic super mop. It washes, it steam-cleans, it mops and it vacuums. And from now on, it never leaves your side. Wherever you go, the SSM goes with you. You work with it, you eat with it, you sleep with it.'

The new members of Z Shift exchanged glances.

Rimmer gave them another shot of silence. It had gone well, he thought. Nice, pointy speech. Some good silences. No! Some *great* silences. And he was especially proud of the macho bit at the end about the sonic super mop, which he'd lifted shamelessly from his favourite movie, *God, I Love This War*.

Lister stood up and snapped a salute. 'Sir, permission to speak, sir!'

Sloppy salute, Rimmer thought. He'd have to teach them all his own salute – the one he'd invented. The one he'd drawn diagrams of and sent off to the Space Ministry, in the hope that it would replace the passé, old-fashioned standard one. It was a great salute, and one day it would make him famous. It went thus: from the standard attention pose, the saluter brought his right arm sharply out in front of him, at a perfect angle with his body. He then twirled his wrist in five circles, to symbolize the five arms of the Space Corps, then snapped his arm back, fingers rigid, to form an equilateral triangle with his forehead; he then straightened the elbow, so the arm was pointing sideways from the body, from which position it was snapped smartly back down to his side. There were also variants: the 'Double-Rimmer', for dress occasions, where the salute was performed with both arms simultaneously, and the 'Half-Rimmer', with only one arm, and only three circles for emergency situations, when there wasn't time to carry out the 'Full-Rimmer'.

'Permission granted,' said Rimmer, returning Lister's salute with a five-loop Full-Rimmer.

'Sir . . .'

'Yes, Lister?'

'Is it possible to get a transfer to another shift, sir?'

'Why?'

'Well, with respect, sir, I think you're mentally unstable.'

'Sit down.' Rimmer shook his head. 'There's always one, isn't there? One wag. One clown. One imbecile.'

'Yes, sir,' Lister agreed, 'but he's not usually in charge, sir.'

Laughter.

This was a tricky situation. Rebellion, a loss of respect. It had to be stamped on, it had to be crushed. His book on 'Poweramics' was quite clear on that. To crush a minor mutiny, you choose the leader: the toughest, the biggest, the strongest; and you humiliate him. And the rest follow like lambs.

Don't look angry. Smile. Real power, true power, is unspoken – understated.

Rimmer smiled. Slowly they stopped laughing.

Excellent. Time to strike.

Without warning he wheeled round and pointed. 'You! On your feet!'

A man with a face like moon rock hauled his two hundred and fifty pound frame onto its feet. Rimmer climbed down from the podium and slowly, casually, strolled over to face him. He looked up at the small black shark eyes, the bald bullet head, the long, matted nostril hair. He was a good eighteen inches taller than Rimmer. And Rimmer was tall.

'What are you chewing?' Rimmer said, after a suitable amount of silence.

'Tobacco.'

'Tobacco?' A grin.

'Yeah.' Defiance.

Rimmer smiled and nodded, looking around the lecture theatre.

'Well, I hope you brought enough along for all of us.' The others laughed. On Rimmer's side. 'Well?'

'Nope.' Slightly nonplussed.

'Nope, *sir*.' Victory! 'Get rid of it.'

The big man chewed thoughtfully for a few seconds. Then, suddenly, a long plume of brown sputum plopped onto the polished toe-cap of Rimmer's left boot.

Rimmer looked at his left boot, then slowly raised his head.

'Some people's respect I've won already. I can see with you it's going to take a little longer. Now, get on the floor and give me fifty, mister.'

'Ppt,' said the big man, and a second stream of half-chewed tobacco arrived on Rimmer's right boot.

Rimmer rocked back and forth on his heels, nodding his head and still smiling.

'Right. OK,' he said, pleasantly, 'I think that's about everything. Shift dismiss.'

Slowly, Z Shift began to meander out of the lecture theatre.

'Oh, by the way . . .' Rimmer called after the tobacco chewer. As the man half-turned, Rimmer leapt through the air and, with a kamikaze scream, wrapped his arms and legs round the big man's frame, and they crashed into a row of chairs.

As Lister left the theatre, Rimmer was having his head rhythmically beaten against one of the desk tops.

BONK.

'Fine,' Rimmer was saying.

BONK.

'There's nothing wrong . . .'

BONK.

'. . . with your reactions.'

BONK.

'Just checking.'

BONK.

'So you like chewing tobacco, eh?'

BONK.

'Well, that's absolutely fine and dandy.'

BONK.

'Perhaps you'd like me to run down to Supplies and buy you some more.'

BONK.

'I think I'm going to lose consciousness now.'

BONK.

BONK.

BONK.

ELEVEN

Everyone agreed it was a splendid funeral, but no one enjoyed it more than the deceased himself.

'I can't tell you how great it is, being dead,' he told everyone who would listen. 'It's solved all my problems.'

Every off-duty member of the eleven thousand, one hundred-and-sixty-nine-strong crew had packed into the vast ship canteen.

McIntyre sat at the top table, a huge coffin-shaped cake containing his own effigy in marzipan before him, and listened, his ego aglow, while his fellow officers sang his praises.

Saunders, much to his own personal delight, had finally been turned off, and although initially there had been some concern about hologramatically reviving a man who had killed himself, those doubts were allayed when the reasons for McIntyre's suicide were discovered.

McIntyre rose to the sound of tumultuous applause, and fingered the 'H' emblazoned on his hologramatic forehead, as over eight thousand people stamped on the floor and banged wine glasses with forks and spoons.

'Well, first I want to thank the Captain for the beautiful eulogy – uh, it was very flattering and deeply moving, and it was well worth all that time I spent writing it.'

A huge laugh echoed round the canteen, and McIntyre smiled happily.

'On a serious note, I know there's a rumour going round

that I committed suicide. I'd like to try and explain why I did it . . .'

McIntyre started to talk about his gambling debts. Debts he'd incurred during his ship leave in bars on Phoebe, Dione and Rhea playing 'Toot'.

'Toot' was a banned bloodsport, involving a fight to the death between two specially-bred Venusian fighting snails. The ferocious gastropods, with hand-sharpened horns, would meet in a six-foot square pit, and bets would be taken on the eventual victor. 'Eventual' was the word; a single butt from a Venusian fighting snail could take upwards of three hours to deliver, and the whole combat often took days. Meanwhile, the baying spectators got drunker and drunker, placing bets of wilder and wilder proportions. You could lose a lot of money playing 'Toot'. And McIntyre had. McIntyre admitted it was a cruel and pointless sport, which said much about man's inhumanity to just about everything to which he could be inhuman. But the buzz from watching two killer snails charging about slowly in the concrete pit; the roaring of the crowd as one snail drew blood, and the other retreated into its shell for hours on end . . . well, you had to be there to believe it.

Before he knew it, McIntyre had debts amounting to almost five times his annual salary. In desperation to pay off the Ganymedian Mafia who ran the snail pits, he'd taken a massive loan from the Golden Assurance Friendly and Caring Loan Society, which, as it turned out, was also run by the Ganymedian Mafia. He didn't know it when he signed, but they charged an annual percentage rate (APR) of nine thousand eight hundred per cent.

The clause in the contract which specified this took the term 'small print' into a whole new dimension.

The clause was concealed in a microdot, occupying the dot of the 'i' on page three of the loan agreement, in the phrase: 'Welcome, you are now a member of the Golden Assurance family.'

Startled to discover his first monthly instalment was some seven times more than the original loan, he gambled what was left, and lost that, too.

McIntyre wrote to the Society, explaining the situation, and a number of increasingly anxious letters were exchanged during *Red Dwarf*'s tour of the Saturnian satellites. Eventually, McIntyre agreed to meet a representative from the company's head office when the ship docked over Mimas, to discuss a repayment plan.

Duly, on the first evening in orbit round Mimas, McIntyre donned his dress uniform and went to the coffee lounge of the Mimas Hilton, where he met three gentlemen, representatives of the Golden Assurance Friendly and Caring Loan Society who arrived in Mimas's one and only five star hotel brandishing a pair of industrial cable clippers.

There, before the eyes of hotel guests casually taking coffee and scones with clotted cream, McIntyre was force-fed his own nose.

He needed little further persuasion before deciding to try a new repayment plan, and finally plumped for the Golden Assurance Friendly and Caring Loan Society's Pay-By-This-Evening-And-Don't-Get-Murdered Super Discount Scheme.

Half-crazed with fear, he staggered back to his office aboard *Red Dwarf*, briefly explained his predicament to his rubber plant, and killed himself.

The beauty part of this scheme was of course that, as a hologram, he was now safe from reprisals. He could continue his life, dead and untroubled. Which is why he was telling everyone who would listen how great it was to be dead, and how it had solved all his problems.

McIntyre finished his speech by thanking everyone for their understanding, and kind words, and concluded by paraphrasing Mark Twain. 'Rumours of my death,' he said, 'have been greatly understated.' Out of the eight thousand assembled, only five people got this joke, and none of them laughed. McIntyre didn't even understand it himself; he'd been told to say it by the ship's metaphysical psychiatrist who assured him it would get a 'big laugh'.

After the toast, the Captain, a short, dumpy American woman who'd had the misfortune to be born with the surname 'Kirk', made a short yet very boring speech welcoming the new intake aboard and outlining the schedule for the jag to and from Triton, before sitting down and thus signalling the beginning of McIntyre's death disco.

The huge sound system vibrated and shook as it pumped out a Hip-hop-a-Billy reggae number from a band which had been red hot for two weeks, five years previously.

Two thousand crew members stood on the dance floor, swaying and sweating, while the rest sat around tables, drinking and sweating.

Though they'd been aboard less than two days, all the low-lifes, ne'er-do-wells and slobs in general had somehow found each other, kindred spirits, and were sitting around in noisy, moronic pockets having drinking competitions. Equally, all the ambitious career-types had somehow been sucked together, and were drinking low alcohol white wine, or slimline mineral water, and talking intensely about work.

Except for Phil.

For some reason, Phil Burroughs had accidentally got himself attached to Lister's group. Phil was a serious-minded academy undergrad on a two-year attachment. It would be a full twenty-four hours before he realized he had joined the wrong group, and had absolutely nothing in common with any of the people with whom he was presently sharing his evening. In the meantime, Petersen was pouring a pint of beer into his jacket pocket.

'That's my beer! What the hell are you doing?' screamed Phil.

'It's just my way,' Petersen beamed charmingly, 'of saying it's your round, pal.'

Phil got up and staggered to the bar. Although there were only five of them at the table, Lister, Petersen, Chen, Selby and himself, he'd been told to order twenty pints of beer. For some reason he couldn't understand, every round consisted of four pints each. 'Saves on shoe leather,' Petersen had pointed out. It didn't seem to matter whether or not you wanted them, either. Each round Phil had requested a low alcohol white wine, and each round he'd been delivered four pints of foaming Japanese lager. He knew for a fact Chen and Petersen were filching at least two of his four pints, but that was absolutely fine with him; his top limit was three pints a night, and he'd had seven already.

Three identical barmen asked for his order. He asked for twenty pints, laid his head in a beery pool on the bar, and promptly fell asleep.

Back at the table, Lister finished his story about how he'd been shanghaied aboard. He'd embellished it only slightly. In his version, for instance, both the Shore Patrolwomen had seduced him in a Photo-U-Kwik booth, and that's why he had that slightly shocked expression on his passport photograph.

Petersen took his turn. He'd arrived on Mimas on a nuclear waste dump ship called *Pax Vert*, which had ejected its putrid load on the Saturnian moon of Tethys, and was now returning to Earth. He was trying to work his passage across the solar system to Triton, where he'd bought a house. As he explained, since Triton was on the very edge of the solar system, being over two-and-a-half billion miles away from Earth, house prices there were really reasonable. For just two thousand dollarpounds, Petersen had bought a twenty-five bedroom home dome, with twelve en-suite bathrooms and a zero-gee squash court.

'At first I thought there was something wrong with it,' he

said, showing Lister a sketch he'd been sent by the estate agent, 'but look, it's beautiful.'

'They didn't send you a photograph?' said Lister, his eyes narrowing.

'No, you can't photograph in a methane atmosphere.'

'You're telling me they haven't installed an oxygen atmosphere yet?'

'No. I'll have to wander around my house in a spacesuit. But that's why it's so cheap!' He quickly downed two pints. 'You ought to move there. There's a plot of about two thousand miles right next door to me. I'm telling you – it's a great investment. Ten, twelve years, they have plans to install oxygen. Can you imagine what will happen to house prices once the atmosphere's breathable? They'll rocket, baby!'

Lister looked at him. Was he *serious*? Yes, he was.

'No, listen,' Petersen continued. 'Do you know Triton is the only moon in the whole solar system which rotates in the opposite direction to the planet it's orbiting?' Petersen demonstrated the scientific principle by rotating his head and swooshing his beer glass around it the other way. Thin, fizzy lager cascaded onto the already sodden table.

'Maybe,' said Lister, who was seriously beginning to wonder whether Petersen was brain-damaged, 'but that's no reason to buy a house there.'

'True,' agreed Petersen, 'but if ever you have guests, it's a nice talking point.'

The music changed; a Johnny Cologne number: *Press Your Lumps Against Mine*. It was smooch time.

There was a loud scraping of chairs as people stood up and guided their partners onto the already packed dance floor. A huge, multi-limbed beast rippled, ebbing and flowing, contracting and expanding to the gentle sway of the music.

Lister suddenly found himself alone at the table, the others lost in the undulating, pulsating mass of smooching bodies. He squinted drunkenly around the vast disco. So many people. People dancing, people touching, people laughing, people talking, people kissing.

So many people.

In just over seven months, every one of them would be dead.

TWELVE

Five months later, Lister stared out of the sleeping quarters' viewport window and saw nothing. Just a few, very distant stars, and an awful lot of black. It was pretty much the same view he'd had for the past twenty-one weeks. At first he'd found it awe-inspiring. Then, slowly, that had given way to just plain dull. Then very dull. Then deeply dull. And now it was something below deeply dull, and even below deeply, hideously dull; a word for which had yet to be devised. It was, he thought, even more mind-numbingly, deeply, hideously dull than an all-nighter at the Scala, watching a twelve-hour season of back-to-back Peter Greenaway movies.

If you went to the British Library and changed every word in every single book to the word 'dull', and then read out all the books in a boring monotone, you would come pretty close to describing Lister's life on board *Red Dwarf*.

He looked at his watch. 19.50, ship time. He was waiting for Petersen to show up, and they were going to go down to the Copacabana Hawaiian Cocktail Bar to spend the evening exacly in the same way they'd spent one hundred and thirty-three of the last one hundred and forty-seven evenings: drinking hugely elaborate San Francisco Earthquakes from plastic coconuts, with Chen and Selby, and failing to meet any interesting women. Or, more to the point, any interesting women who were interested in them.

Dull and gruesomely monotonous as his social life was, Lister knew for a fact it was at least four hundred and seventy-four times more interesting than his working life on Z Shift under Rimmer.

Rimmer was sitting at his slanting architect's desk, under the pink glow of his study lamp, with a tray of watercolours, making out a revision timetable in preparation for his astro-navigation exam.

In all, he'd taken the exam eleven times. Nine times, he'd got an 'F' for fail, and on two occasions he'd got an 'X' for unclassified.

But he persevered. Each night he persevered, under the pink glow. Each night he nibbled away at his skyscraper-high stack of files which stored his loose-leaf revision notes. He nibbled away, trying to digest little morsels of knowledge. Little morsels that stuck in his gullet, that wouldn't go down. It was like trying to eat wads of cotton wool. But he persevered. Rimmer wanted to become an officer. He ached for it. He yearned for it. It wasn't the *most* important thing in his life. It *was* his life.

Given the opportunity, he would gladly have had his eyes scooped out if it meant he could become an officer. He would happily have inserted two red hot needles simultaneously through both his ears so they met in the middle of his brain, and tap-danced the title song from *42nd Street* barefoot on a bed of molten lava while giving oral sex to a male orang-utan with dubious personal hygiene, if only it meant attaining that single, elusive golden bar of an Astronavigation Officer, Fourth Class.

But he had to do something much more demanding, much more impossible, and much more unpleasant. He had to pass the astronavigation exam.

Born on Io, one of Jupiter's moons, thirty-one years earlier, he was the youngest of four brothers. Frank was a gnat's wing away from becoming the youngest captain in the Space Corps. John was the youngest captain in the Space Corps. Howard had graduated third in his class at the academy and was now a test pilot for the new generation of demi-light speed Zippers at Houston, Earth.

'*My boys,*' his mother would say, '*my clever, clever boys. Johnny the Captain, Frankie the First Officer, Howie the Test Pilot, and Arnold . . . Arnold, the chicken soup machine cleaner. If you could sue sperm, I'd sue the sperm that made you.*'

'*I'll do it, Mother. One day, I will become an officer.*'

'*And on that day,*' his mother would say, '*Satan will be going to work in a snow plough.*'

If Rimmer hadn't been such a dedicated anal retentive, he would have realized the simple truth: he wasn't cut out for Space.

He wasn't cut *out* for it.

He would have realized he wasn't the slightest bit interested in astronavigation. Or quantum mechanics. Or any of the things he needed to be interested in to pass the exams and become an officer.

Three times he'd failed the entrance exam to the Academy. And so, one night after reading the life story of Horatio Nelson, he'd signed up with a merchant vessel as a lowly Third Technician, with the object of quickly working his way through the ranks and sitting the astronavigation exam independently, and thereby earning his commission: the glimmering gold bar of officerhood.

That had been six years ago. Six long years on *Red Dwarf*, during which he'd leapt from being a lowly Third Technician to being a lowly First Technician. In the meantime, his brothers went for ever onward, up the ziggurat of command. Their success filled him with such bitterness, such bile, that even a Christmas card from one of them – just the reminder that they were alive, and *successful* – would reduce him to tears of jealousy.

And now he sat there, under the pink glow of his student's table lamp ('Reduces eye-strain! Promotes concentration! Aids retention!' was the lamp manufacturer's proud boast), preparing to sit the astronavigation exam for the thirteenth time.

He found the process of revising so gruellingly unpleasant, so galling, so noxious, that, like most people faced with tasks they find hateful, he devised more and more elaborate ways of not doing it in a 'doing it' kind of way.

In fact, it was now possible for Rimmer to revise solidly for three months and not learn anything at all.

The first week of study, he would always devote to the construction of a revision timetable. At school Rimmer was always at his happiest colouring in geography maps: under his loving hand, the ice-fields of Europa would be shaded a delicate blue, the subterranean silica deposits of Ganymede would be rendered, centimetre by painstaking centimetre, a bright and powerful yellow, and the regions of frozen methane on Pluto slowly became a luscious, inviting green. Up until the age of thirteen, he was constantly head of the class in geography. After this point, it became necessary to know and understand the subject, and Rimmer's marks plunged to the murky depths of 'F' for fail.

He brought his love of cartography to the making of revision timetables. Weeks of patient effort would be spent planning, designing and creating a revision schedule which, when finished, were minor works of art.

Every hour of every day was subdivided into different study periods, each labelled in his lovely, tiny copperplate hand; then painted over in watercolours, a different colour for each subject, the colours gradually becoming bolder and more urgent shades as the exam time approached. The effect was as if a myriad tiny rainbows had splintered and sprinkled across the poster-sized sheet of creamwove card.

The only problem was this: because the timetables often took seven or eight weeks, and sometimes more, to complete, by the time Rimmer had finished them the exam was almost on him. He'd then have to cram three months of astronavigation revision into a single week. Gripped by an almost deranging panic, he'd then decide to sacrifice the first two days of that final week to the making of another timetable. This time for someone who had to pack three months of revision into five days.

Because five days now had to accommodate three months' work, the first thing that had to go was sleep. To prepare for an unrelenting twenty-four hours a day sleep-free schedule, Rimmer would spend the whole of the first remaining day in bed – to be extra, ultra fresh, so he would be able to squeeze three whole months of revision into four short days.

Within an hour of getting up the next morning, he would feel inexplicably exhausted, and start early on his supply of Go-Double-Plus caffeine tablets. By lunchtime he'd overdose, and have to make the journey down to the ship's medical unit for a sedative to help him calm down. The sedative usually sent him off to sleep, and he'd wake up the following morning with only three days left, and an anxiety that was so crippling he could scarcely move. A month of revision to be crammed into each day.

At this point he would start smoking. A lifelong non-smoker, he'd become a forty-a-day man. He'd spend the whole day pacing up and down his room, smoking three or four cigarettes at a time, stopping occasionally to stare at the titles in his bookcase, not knowing which one to read first, and popping twice the recommended dosage of dog-worming tablets, which he erroneously believed to contain amphetamine.

Realizing he was getting nowhere, he'd try to get rid of his soul-bending tension by treating himself to an evening in one of *Red Dwarf*'s quieter bars. There he would sit, in the plastic oak-beamed 'Happy Astro' pub, nursing a small beer, grimly trying to be light-hearted and totally relaxed. Two small beers and three hours of stomach-knotting relaxation later, he would go back to his bunk and spend half the night awake, praying to a God he didn't believe in for a miracle that couldn't happen.

Two days to go, and ravaged by the combination of anxiety, nicotine, caffeine tablets, alcohol he wasn't used to, dog-worming pills, and overall exhaustion, he would sleep in till mid-afternoon.

After a long scream, he would rationalize that the day was a total write-off, and the rest of the afternoon would be spent shopping for the three best alarm clocks money could buy. This would often take five or six hours, and he would arrive back at his sleeping quarters exhausted, but knowing he was fully prepared for the final day's revision before his exam.

Waking at four-thirty in the morning, after exercising, showering and breakfasting, he would sit down to prepare a final, final revision timetable, which would condense three months of revision into twelve short hours. This done, he would give up and go back to bed. Maybe he didn't know a single thing about astronavigation, but at least he'd be fresh for the exam the next day.

Which is why Rimmer failed exams.

Which is why he'd received nine 'F's for fail and two 'X's for unclassified. The first 'X' he'd achieved when he'd actually managed to get hold of some real amphetamines, gone into spasm and collapsed two minutes into the exam; and the second when anxiety got so much the better of him his subconscious forced him to deny his own existence, and he had written 'I am a fish' five hundred times on every single answer sheet. He'd even gone out for extra paper. What was more shocking than anything was that he'd thought he'd done quite well.

Well, this time it was going to be different, he thought, as he sat carefully colouring all the quantum mechanics revision periods in diagonal lines of Prussian blue on a yellow ochre background, while Lister stared out of the viewport window.

Petersen clumped noisily into the room and did his trational parody of the full Double-Rimmer salute, which ended with him slapping his face several times and throwing himself onto the floor. The first time Lister had seen it, it was funny. This was the two hundred and fifty-second time, and it was beginning to lose its appeal.

Lister and Petersen then went down to the Copacabana Hawaiian Cocktain Bar for the hundred and thirty-fourth time. Only, this time Lister did something incredibly stupid.

He fell in love.

Hopelessly and helplessly in love.

THIRTEEN

Third Console Officer Kristine Kochanski had a face. That was the first thing Lister noticed about her. It wasn't a beautiful face. But it was a nice face. It wasn't a face that could launch a thousand ships. Maybe two ships and a small yacht. That was, until she smiled. When she smiled, her eyes lit up like a pinball machine when you win a bonus game. And she smiled a lot.

Lister could perhaps have survived the smile. But it was when he found the smile was attached to a sense of humour that he became irretrievably lost.

They were both standing at the bar, queuing to get a drink, and Lister was looking at her in a not-looking-at-her kind of way: in the bar mirror, in the reflection in his beer glass, over his shoulder, pretending to look at Petersen, at the ceiling just above her head, and occasionally, because it was permitted, directly at her. His heart sank when a tanned, white-uniformed officer, who obviously knew her, came up and touched her on the shoulder. Touched her on the shoulder – just like she was some kind of ordinary person. It really made Lister mad.

The tanned, white-uniformed officer noticed a book sticking out of her black jacket pocket. Lister had noticed it too. It was called *Learn Japanese*, by Dr P. Brewis.

'"Learn Japanese"?' the officer snorted. 'Talk about pretentious!'

What she said next tipped Lister over the edge.

'Pretentious?' she placed her palm on her chest, 'Watashi?'

Lister didn't know any Japanese but he guessed, rightly, that it was an adaptation of the 'Pretentious? Moi?' joke.

The officer just looked at her blankly.

She got her drinks and went back to her seat, while Lister was still trying to think of something to say which would start a conversation.

For the next hour Petersen droned on about the supply station at the Uranian moon, Miranda, where *Red Dwarf* was due to stop off for supplies in seven weeks. It was to be their only shore leave between Saturn and Triton, and Petersen was telling him what a great time they were going to have. But Lister wasn't listening. He was looking across the crowded cocktail bar, trying to calculate the amount of drink left in the glasses of the girl with the pinball smile and her female companion, so he could be at the bar just as she arrived, and casually offer to buy her a drink.

Who was he kidding? How do you casually offer to buy someone a drink, without making it sound like 'I want you to have my babies'? If he hadn't been crazy about her, it wouldn't have been a problem. Lister never had any trouble asking women for a date, provided he wasn't too keen on them. When he was, which didn't happen too often, he had all the charm, wit, and self-possession of an Alsatian dog after a head-swap operation.

She got up to go to the bar. Lister got up, too. They exchanged smiles, ordered drinks and went back to their separate tables.

Damn. Smeg. Blew it.

She got up again.

'My round,' said Petersen, rising. Lister thrust him back in his chair and went to the bar. They exchanged smiles and 'Hi's this time, ordered their drinks, and went back to their separate tables.

Damn. Smeg. Blew it again.

She'd hardly sat down before she was getting up again. The two girls' glasses were full.

She's going for peanuts, thought Lister.

'You want some peanuts?' he asked Petersen.

'No, thanks.'

'I'll go and get some.'

They stood at the bar again. They exchanged smiles again. Then she introduced herself and asked him out for a date.

And so it began.

Lister became a walking cliché. His senses were heightened, so even the foul, recycled air of the ship tasted crisp and spring-like. He went off his food. He stopped drinking. Pop lyrics started to mean something to him. Magically, he became better-looking; he'd heard that this happened, but he'd never really believed it. He got out of bed before his alarm clock went off – unheard of. He started to marvel at the view out of the viewport window.

And his face acquired three new expressions. Three expressions which he'd stolen from her. Three expressions which, on her, he found adorable. He wasn't aware of even copying them, and he certainly wasn't aware how stupid he looked when he pulled them. And even if he had been aware, he wouldn't have cared. Because Third Console Officer, Kristine Kochanski, a.k.a. 'Babes', a.k.a. 'Ange' (short for Angel), a.k.a. 'Krissie', a.k.a. 'K.K.', 'Sweetpea', and a host of others too nauseating to recount, was madly, electrically in love with him.

Lister's all-time favourite movie was Frank Capra's *It's A Wonderful Life*, and, just to make things totally perfect, it happened to be Kochanski's too. They sat in bed – Kochanski's bunk-mate, Barbara, had been chased away to the ship's cinema yet again – eating hot dogs doused in mustard, and watching, for the third consecutive night, *It's A Wonderful Life* on the sleeping quarters' vid-screen.

Suddenly, in the middle of the scene where Jimmy Stewart's father dies, Lister found himself for the first time in his life talking about his own father's death.

It wasn't, of course, his real father, but he was only six at the time and he didn't know then that he'd been adopted. It had been a gloriously hot day in mid-summer, and the six-year-old Lister was given toys and presents by everyone. It was better than Christmas. He remembered wishing at the time that a few more people would die, so he could complete his Lego set.

She held his hand and listened.

'My grandmother tried to explain. She said he'd gone away, and he wasn't coming back. So I wanted to know where, and she told me he was very happy, and he'd gone to the same place as my goldfish.' Lister toyed absently with his plaited locks. 'I thought they'd flushed him down the bog. I used to stand with my head down the loo, and talk to him. I thought he was just round the U-bend. In the end, they had to take me to a child psychologist, because they found me with my head down the pan, reading him the football scores.'

This had never stuck Lister as being funny. But when Kochanski started roaring with laughter, he started laughing too. It was like a geyser going off. Something was exorcized. And as they lay in the crumb-laden sheets, wrapped in each other's arms, giggling like idiots – and even though they'd only been dating for three-and-a-half short weeks – Lister knew more certainly than he'd ever known anything in his life before that they'd be together, forever.

FOURTEEN

Seven months out into space, while Rimmer sat at his slanting architect's desk under the pink glow of his study lamp, Lister stared out of the sleeping quarters' viewport window, longing to be bored again.

He'd been not going out with Kochanski now for three weeks.

The whole affair, the glorious 'forever' he'd imagined, had lasted just over a month. Then one evening in her sleeping quarters, as Lister arrived to take her to a movie, she'd told him she wanted to break it off. He'd laughed. He thought it was a joke. But it wasn't.

She'd been seeing 'Tom' (or was it 'Tim'?), a Flight Navigation Officer, for almost two years. Tom or Tim (it may have been Tony) had left her for a fling with some brunette in Catering. And Lister had been a rebound thing. She hadn't realized it at first, but when Tom, Tim, Tony or Terry, or whatever the smeg he was called, had turned up at her door, having dumped the brunette in Catering, she'd gone scurrying back.

There were tears, there were apologies, and pathetic clichéd platitudes: they could still be friends; if he met Trevor, he'd really like him; she wished she were two people, so she could love both of them; ad nauseum.

She'd returned the blue jumper he'd left. She'd returned his DAT tapes, and offered to give back the necklace he'd bought her, which, of course, he'd declined.

And that was that.

Except it wasn't. Because now she was everywhere. Everything he did, he did *without* her. Everywhere he went, he went *without* her. When he went shopping, he didn't go shopping, he went shopping without Kochanski. When he went to the bar, he didn't go to the bar, he went to the bar without Kochanski. She'd infected every part of his life. His mental map of the ship now judged all distances in relation to her sleeping quarters, or the Drive Room, where she worked. He wasn't walking on such-and-such a corridor, he was walking on such-and-such a corridor which was n floors above or n floors below where she was at that precise moment.

So he lay on his bunk, staring out of the viewport window, longing for the anaesthetic of the stupifying monotony which he used to feel two short months earlier.

His only relief from the Kochanski blues had been three days' planet leave on the alcohol-dry Uranian moon, Miranda, when *Red Dwarf* had docked for supplies. Three days drinking cola and playing video machines with Petersen. Petersen, who'd got drunk every night of his life since he was twelve, was so thrilled with the benefits of being sober, he'd gone teetotal overnight. So their excursions down to the Copacabana were a thing of the past, denying Lister his one last refuge.

He sighed like a senile dog and looked down at Rimmer, hard at work.

'Do you fancy going for a drink?' he asked, knowing the answer would be 'No' even before he'd finished saying the word 'Do'.

'No,' said Rimmer, without looking up.

'That's a surprise.'

'As it happens, I am going out tonight. Just not with you.'

'What about your revision?'

Rimmer had decided to change.

His latest three-month revision timetable had been constructed within two hours. And four hours a day, come what may, he read his course books, made notes, and revised in a sensible way. And revising in a sensible way obviously meant an adequate provision for leisure time.

'Well, where are you going, then?'

'Out.'

'Where?'

Rimmer ignored him. He was going to spend the evening not getting any older. He was going to spend it in a stasis booth.

Red Dwarf, like most of the older ships, was equipped with stasis booths for interstellar travel. A hundred years earlier, travelling to other star systems had been considered economically and philosophically interesting. But not any more.

To travel the vast distances involved, even with craft which could achieve demi-lightspeed, took decades. Necessity being the mother of invention, the stasis booth was duly invented. Basically, it was a fool-proof form of suspended animation, but instead of freezing the body cryogenically, and having all the attendant revival problems, the stasis booth simply froze time.

Once activated, the booth created a static field of Time; in the same way X-rays can't penetrate lead, Time couldn't penetrate a stasis field. An object caught within the field became a non-event mass with a quantum probability of zero.

In other words, the object remained in exactly the same state, at exactly the same age, until it was released. Most of the important groundwork for Time-freezing and stasis theory had been done by Einstein in the 1950s. Unfortunately, just as he was on the verge of a breakthrough, he started dating Marilyn Monroe, and basically lost interest in the project. Even after their short affair was over, he found it difficult to concentrate on quantum theory, and spent much of the rest of his life taking cold showers.

His notes on the theory were later discovered and developed – and the stasis booth was born.

For a period, ships full of astros in stasis booths were hurled out of our solar system, and interstellar travel enjoyed its golden age. The big hope, of course, was that they'd contact intelligent life.

They didn't.

Not even a moderately intelligent plant. Not even a stupid plant.

Nothing.

And it was surmised correctly, although it wasn't confirmed for a further two thousand years, that Mankind was completely and totally and inexplicably alone.

In all of the universe.

In all of the universe, the planet Earth was the only planet with any life forms.

That's all there was.

Interstellar travel was abandoned as a total waste of time. And the returning stellarnauts tried to reintegrate into society and cope with the fact that many of them were now fifty years younger than their own children. This led to curious generation gap problems, of which the greetings cards industry took full advantage.

Rimmer had a keycard to one of *Red Dwarf*'s stasis booths, which he used whenever he could.

While morons like Lister and Petersen were urinating their lives down the gutter in the Copacabana Hawaiian Cocktail Bar, he was in a stasis booth, not existing, not getting any older.

It made great good sense to Rimmer. Take tonight. There was nothing he particularly wanted to do. He'd achieved all the aims on his daily goal list, and under normal circumstances he'd just lounge around, doing not very much, and eventually go to bed. As it was, when they took to their bunks that night, Rimmer would be three hours less older than Lister. Because he wouldn't have lived those three hours: he'd have saved them. Saved them for when he really needed them.

True, technically, he wouldn't be living.

But he didn't particularly want to live tonight. He wasn't in the mood.

It was just like a bank, only, instead of saving up money, he was saving up time. He'd been doing it, on and off, for about five years, and in this way he used up most of his free leisure time. Most Sundays were spent boothing. And then, usually, three evenings a week, for three hours or so. And obviously, if there were any bank holidays, he'd take full advantage of the facility not to exist, and pinch back a few hours from Father Time.

In just five years he'd saved three hundred and sixty-nine full days. Over a full Earth year. In five years, he'd only lived for four. Although his birth certificate said he was thirty-one, technically he was still only thirty.

Occasionally Rimmer reflected that his boothing could possibly be the reason why he didn't have any friends, but, as he pointed out to himself, if having friends meant having to hang around and get older with them, then he wasn't sure he wanted any. Especially since the perks were so astonishing. He often looked in the full-length mirror, when Lister wasn't there, and reflected that, although he was thirty-one, he still had the body of a thirty-year-old. If he could maintain this routine, by the time his birth certificate said he was ninety he'd actually only be a very sprightly seventy-eight-year-old. Pretty a-smegging-mazing, eh?

Lister slumped off to try and persuade Peterson to go for a drink. Rimmer watched him go, then showered and changed, treated himself to a little aftershave, and went off to spend the very last evening of his life not existing.

FIFTEEN

On the very last morning of his life, Rimmer strode into the lecture theatre to give Z Shift their work schedule for the day.

'OK, men,' he said as always, 'Listen up.'

As always the whole of Z Shift inclined their heads to one side and pointed their ears at the ceiling. But, as always, Rimmer missed this as he turned his back to pull down the blackboard he'd prepared the day before. As always his schedule wasn't there. What was there was a crudely-drawn cartoon of a man making love to a kangaroo, wearing hugely exaggerated footwear covered in brown spit, and underneath, in the same crude hand, 'Old Tobacco Boots goes down under!'

Nobody laughed. Rimmer looked round at a sea of blank faces. He'd long since given up referring to the blackboard insults.

'OK,' he said, consulting his notes, 'Today's schedule. Turner, Wilkinson: we've had a number of reports that machine 15455 is dispensing blackcurrant juice instead of chicken soup. While you're down there, Corridor 14: alpha 12 needs new Crunchie bars. Thereafter, I want you to go down to the reference library and hygienize all the headsets in the language lab. Saxon and Burroughs: continue painting the engineers' mess. And I want that finished today. McHullock, Schmidt, Palmer: as yesterday. Burd, Dooley, Pixon: laundrettes on East alpha 555 report no less than twenty-four driers out of commission. I want them up and drying by nightfall. Also, there's an unconfirmed rumour that the cigar machine in the officers' club is nearly empty. Now, it may be nothing, but just in case: for pity's sake, stay by a phone.'

A paper dart whistled past his head.

'OK, roll out. Lister, you're with me today.'

The men began to shuffle out.

'Why me?' Lister moaned.

'Because it's your turn.'

As always, just before the first man reached the door, Rimmer called out his team chant, which he hoped would catch on.

'Hey, and remember: "We are tough, and we are mean – Rimmer's Z Shift gets things clean".'

Z Shift shuffled out silently.

Two of the three worst things that ever happened to Rimmer happened to Rimmer on this day.

The worst thing that ever happened was, of course, his death. But that was a clear twelve hours away.

The second worst thing that ever happened had happened thirteen months earlier and it was so horrible his subconscious had created a new sub-department to hide it from his waking thoughts. It involved a bowl of soup.

The third worst thing that ever happened to Rimmer happened to Rimmer shortly after ten o'clock, as he and Lister made their way towards Corridor 1: gamma 755, to check, just to put Rimmer's mind at ease, that there was enough shower gel in the women's wash-room.

At first it was Lister who had a horrible thing happen to him, as he pushed his squeaky four-wheel hygiene truck along the steel mesh floor. First Technician Petrovitch rounded the corner.

Rimmer didn't like Petrovitch. Petrovitch, three years his junior, was his equal in rank, and leader of A Shift – the best shift. A Shift got all the plum jobs, the serious, technical work, repairing porous circuits, and, if that weren't bad enough, Petrovitch had taken and passed the astronavigation exam the exact same time Rimmer had made his claims to fishhood, and was now merely waiting for his orders to be processed before he got his gold bar and took up the rank of Astronavigation Officer, Fourth Class. Also, he was good-looking, popular, charming and amiable. All in all, as far as Rimmer could see, there wasn't a single thing *to* like about Petrovitch.

There'd been a wild rumour some months back that Petro-vitch was a drug dealer. And Rimmer did whatever he could to spread it. He didn't know whether it was true, but, God, he hoped it was. Whenever he was feeling low, he entertained himself with visions of Petrovitch having his badges of rank ripped from his uniform, and being led away in manacles. Still, there was no evidence that it was true, so all Rimmer could do was keep spreading those malicious rumours, and hoping.

'What the smeg is wrong with your bleepers? I've been trying to get hold of you for an hour,' said Petrovitch. 'Lister, the Captain wants to see you.'

Rimmer looked dumbfounded. Why should the Captain want to see Lister? In the ordinary course of things, Lister, being a lowly Third Technician, should go the whole trip without ever meeting the Captain.

Unless, thought Rimmer, brightening, *he's in very, very deep smegola indeed*. And by the slightly sick look of Lister's smile, Rimmer confidently surmised the very same thought had occurred to him.

'Why does she want to see *me*?'

'I think you know why,' said Petrovitch, his usual geniality completely absent.

Lister dragged himself off towards the Xpress lift.

'Oh dear,' said Rimmer, breezily. 'Oh dear, oh dear, oh

dear.' He tutted and shook his head. 'Dearie me. Dearie, dearie, dearie me.'

Petrovitch didn't smile; he made to follow Lister, but then stopped and turned. 'What are you doing with Lister, anyway? It's five past ten.'

'So?' said Rimmer.

'I thought you were taking the astronavigation exam.'

'That's November the twenty-seventh, you square-jawed chump,' said Rimmer, with naked contempt.

'No, it's October the twenty-seventh.'

'I think, Petrovitch, I know when my own exam is, thank you so very, very much.'

'My bunk-mate is taking it today.'

'Hollerbach?'

'Yeah. He went up at ten.'

Rimmer's smile remained exactly where it was, while the rest of his face sagged like a bloodhound's. He looked at his watch, 10.07. He tapped it a couple of times, and walked off without saying anything.

Rimmer arrived, breathless, back at the sleeping quarters. He skidded to a halt in front of his timetable. His eyes scanned the chart for an error. He couldn't find one. He couldn't find one for a whole two minutes. Then he froze. In his haste not to dwell on the construction of the chart, somehow he'd included two Septembers.

'August, September, September, October, November', ran the new Rimmerian calendar.

How could I have included September twice, and not noticed? thought Rimmer, sucking on his fist. *This is what happens when you spend most of your social life not existing.*

He looked at his watch. 10.35. He'd missed thirty-five minutes of a three-hour exam.

A strange calmness overtook him.

Well, he could still get to the exam by, say, 10.45.

If he kept his answers short and pertinent, it was still more than possible to pass. So far, so good. What would be slightly trickier was cramming a whole month's revision into minus thirty-five minutes. Thirty-five minutes was hard enough, but minus thirty-five minutes – well, you'd have to be Dr Who.

As always at crisis times in his life, Rimmer asked himself the question: 'What would Napoleon do?'

Something French, he thought. *Probably munch on a croissant, and decide to invade Russia. Not really relevant*, he decided, *in this particular scenario. What, then . . . what, then?*

The seconds ticked away. Then it came to him. He knew exactly what he must do.

Cheat.

Rimmer took out a black felt tip pen, stripped off his shirt and trousers, and began work. He had, he estimated, twenty minutes to copy as much of his textbooks onto his body as humanly possible.

SIXTEEN

Lister had never been up to the Drive Room before.

It was enormous.

Hundreds of people scurried along the network of gantries stretching above him. Banks of programmers in white officers' uniforms clacked away at computer keyboards, in front of multi-coloured flashing screens arranged in a series of horseshoe shapes around the massive chamber. Skutters, the small service droids with three-fingered clawed heads, joined to their motorized bases by triple-jointed necks, whizzed between the various computer terminals, transporting sheets of data.

Occasionally a voice could be heard above the unrelenting jabber of hundreds of people talking at once.

'Stop-start oA3! Stop-start oA3! Thank you! At *last*! Stop-start oA4! Is anybody *listening* to me?!'

Lister followed Petrovitch as he zigzagged through a maze of towering columns of identical hard disc drives and people pushed past them, desperate to get back to wherever they had to get back to.

Up above them, Holly's bald-headed digitalized face dominated the whole of the ceiling, patiently answering questions and solving quandaries, while dispensing relevant data updates from other areas of the ship.

Through the computer hardware Lister caught sight of Kochanski, expertly clicking away at a computer keyboard, happily going about her business, just as if nothing had happened. Lister didn't exactly expect her to be sobbing guiltily onto her keyboard. But smiling? Actively smiling? It was obscene. Lister remembered reading in one of Rimmer's *Strange Science* mags that an Earth biochemist claimed he'd isolated the virus which caused Love. According to him, it was an infectious germ which was particularly virulent for the first few weeks, but then, gradually, the body recovered.

Looking at Kochanski merrily tippy-tapping away, Lister was inclined to believe the biochemist had a point. She'd shrugged him off like a bout of dysentery. She'd recovered from him like he was a dose of 'flu. She was fine and dandy. Back to normal.

They climbed the gantry steps to the Admin level, where glass-fronted offices wound round the entire chamber, like the private boxes which skirted the London Jets Zero-Gee football stadium.

Five minutes later they arrived outside the Captain's office. Petrovitch knocked, and they went in.

'Lister, sir,' said Petrovitch, and left.

The office looked like it had been newly-burgled and freshly-bombed. The Captain was mumbling into a phone buried beneath gigantic reams of computer print-out, surrounded by open ledgers and piles of memoranda.

Lister shifted uncomfortably and waited for her to finish her call.

'Well, you see he does exactly that,' finished the Captain, and before the phone had even hit its holder, and without looking up, she said: 'Where's the cat?'

'What?' said Lister.

'Where's the cat?' repeated the Captain.

'What cat?'

'I'm going to ask you one last time,' she said, finally looking up: 'Where is the cat?'

'Let me get this straight,' said Lister. 'You think I know something about a cat, right?'

'Don't be smart.' The Captain was actually smiling with anger. 'Where is it?'

'I don't know what you're talking about.'

'Lister, not only are you so stupid you bring an unquarantined animal aboard. Not only that,' she paused, 'you have your photograph taken with the cat, and send it to be processed in the developing lab. So, let's make this the last chorus. Where's the cat?'

'What cat?'

'This one,' she shouted, pushing a photograph into Lister's face. 'This goddam cat!'

Lister looked at the photograph of himself sitting in what were unmistakably his sleeping quarters, holding what was unmistakably a small black cat.

'Oh, *that* cat.'

'Where'd you get it? Mimas?'

'Miranda. When we stopped for supplies.'

'Don't you realize it could be carrying anything? Anything. What were you thinking of?'

'I just felt sorry for her. She was wandering the streets. Her fur was all hanging off . . .'

'Her fur was hanging off? Oh, this gets better and better.' Two of the Captain's phones were ringing, but she didn't answer them.

'And she had this limp, and she'd walk a few steps, then let out this scream, then walk a few more steps and scream again.'

'Well, now *I'm* screaming, Lister. I want that cat, and I want it now! D'you think we have quarantine regulations just for the hell of it? Just to make life a bit more unbearable? Well, we don't. We have them to safeguard the crew. A spaceship is a closed system. A contagious disease has nowhere else to go. Everybody gets it.'

'She's better now. Fur's grown back, I've fixed her leg. She's fine.'

'It's impossible to tell. You got the cat from a space colony. There are diseases out there, new diseases. The locals develop an immunity. Now, get that cat down to the lab. Double-time.'

'Sir . . .'

'You're still here, Lister.'

'What are you going to do with the cat?'

'I'm going to have it cut up, and run tests on it.'

'Are you going to put it back together when you've finished?'

The Captain closed her eyes.

'You're not, are you?' persisted Lister. 'You're going to kill it.'

'Yes, Lister, that's exactly what I'm going to do. I'm going to kill it.'

'Well, with respect, sir,' said Lister, taking a cigarette from his hat band, 'what's in it for the cat?'

Lister smiled. The Captain didn't.

'Lister, give me the cat.'

Lister shook his head.

'We'll find it, anyway.'

'No, you won't.'

'Let me put it like this' – the Captain reclined back in her chair – 'give me the frigging cat.'

'Look, she's fine, there's nothing wrong with her.'

'Give me the cat.'

'Apart from anything else, she's pregnant.'

'She's *what*? I want that cat.'

Lister shook his head again.

'Do you want to go into stasis for the rest of the jag and lose three years' wages?'

'No.'

'Do you want to hand over the cat?'

'No.'

'Choose.'

SEVENTEEN

11.05.

Rimmer hurried out of the lift and down Corridor 4: delta 799 towards the exam hall.

Under his high-neck zipped flightsuit he had everything he needed to pass the exam. On his right thigh, in tiny script, were all the basic principles of quantum mechanics. Time dilation formulae covered his right calf. Heisenberg's uncertainty principle took up most of his left leg, while porous circuit theory and continuum hypotheses filled his forearms.

Rimmer had never done anything illegal before. He hadn't so much as got a parking ticket on his home moon, Io. He'd never even fiddled his expenses, which, quite frankly, even the Captain did.

He'd never cheated; never. Not because he was of high moral character, but simply because he was scared. He was terrified of being caught.

He walked into the clinically white exam room. The adjucating officer glanced at his watch and nodded towards the one empty desk, where an exam paper lay face-down, and returned to reading his novel.

He knows, thought Rimmer, his face glowing like Jupiter's Red Spot. *He knows from the way I walked into the room. He knows.*

Rimmer ducked his body low into his chair, so just his head remained above the table top, and peered past the backs of the examinees in front of him, waiting for the adjudicator to make his move. Waiting for him to leap forward and rip off his flimsy flightsuit. exposing his shame: his illustrated body, Rimmer's cheating frame.

For a full ten minutes Rimmer watched the officer quietly reading his novel. *All right*, thought Rimmer, *play it like that. The old cat and mouse game*.

Another ten minutes went by. Still the officer taunted him by doing nothing. Nothing.

At 11.45 Rimmer decided the adjudicator *didn't* know, and it was safe to begin. Safe to . . . cheat!

He turned over the exam paper and started to read the questions. Something appeared to be sucking oxygen out of the room, and he seemed to have to take two breaths to his usual one, just to keep conscious.

Buh-**BUB**.

Buh-**BUB**.

Buh-**BUB**!

His heartbeat was deafening; when someone turned round, he was convinced they were going to say: 'Can you keep your heartbeat down a bit? I'm trying to concentrate.'

'ASTRONAVIGATION EXAMINATION – PART ONE,' he read. Then underneath: ' ANSWER FIVE QUESTIONS ONLY.'

Just five, thought Rimmer. *I'm not going to make that mistake again*.

'QUESTION ONE.'

As he looked at the question, the letters seemed to come off the page and sway, out of focus, like distant figures disappearing in a heat haze on a desert road. He blinked. Two tears of sweat ran past his eyes and tumbled onto the page. He ran his hands through his hair and wiped the perspiration off his face with his palms, then blinked twice more, and brought the question into focus.

'$\Omega f ©†\Delta \leqslant \Diamond^{\lceil} \int\int †¥' \#\S f © \Omega \Omega^{\cdot\cdot} \pi \mu^{\sim} \int\int \sqrt{} \ ç \sqrt{} †¥¥^{\cdot\cdot} \S\P\P\cdot\Omega \Sigma ®\S \infty^{\cdot\cdot} \Delta \mathring{a}$'

Oh God, thought Rimmer, *I've forgotten how to read.*

He blinked several more times.

'DESCRIBE, USING FORMULAE WHERE APPROPRIATE, THE APPLICATION OF DE BURGH'S THEORY OF THERMAL INDUCTION IN POROUS CIRCUITRY.'

That was his left forearm! The answer was there! The formulae were there! All he had to do was slide back his sleeve, copy it all down and he was one-fifth of his way into that officers' club.

He looked at the other questions. There were three others he could do. And he could do them perfectly. Eighty per cent. He only needed forty! There was a whole hour to go.

HE WAS AN *OFFICER*!!

Arnold J. Rimmer, Astronavigation Officer, Fourth Class. Already, in his mind's eye, ticker-tape was cascading from rooftops as he sat in the open-top limousine waving to the adoring Ionian crowds.

He snapped out of it. No time for complacency. Fifteen minutes per question. It was enough.

Let's go-o-o-o-o! he screamed, silently. He glanced nonchalantly around. No one was watching.

Casually he rested his hand on his wrist, and slowly slid back the sleeve. The adjudicating officer turned a page in his novel.

Rimmer looked down at his arm.

An inky black blob stared up at him.

His body had betrayed him. It had conspired to drench him in sweat; it had dissolved his best chance ever of getting that glimmering gold bar.

He looked at his right hand. The answer to the question 'Describe, Using Formulae Where Appropriate, the Application of De Burgh's Theory of Thermal Induction in Porous Circuitry' was there, somewhere, hiding in the black blobby mess.

Rimmer decided to take a chance in a million. It was the longest of long shots.

With careful precision he placed his inky hand on the answer sheet and pressed as hard as he could. Maybe, just maybe, when he removed his hand, his tiny copperplate writing would reassemble itself legibly on the page.

He removed his hand.

There in the middle of the page was a perfect palm print, with a single middle finger raised in mocking salute.

An idiotic grin spread across Rimmer's face as he picked up his pen and signed the bottom of the page.

Slowly he clambered to his feet, saluted the adjudicating officer, and woke up on a stretcher on his way to the medical bay.

EIGHTEEN

Petrovitch led the way and Lister followed, flanked by two unnecessary security guards. They stopped at the door to the stasis booth.

'Last chance, Lister. Where's the cat?'

Lister just shook his head.

'Three years in stasis for some stupid flea-bitten moggy? Are you crazy?'

Lister wasn't crazy. Far from it.

He'd first heard about the stasis punishment from Petersen. Now that the booths were no longer used for interstellar travel, their only official function was penal. Lister had spent six long, boring evenings, shortly after Kochanski had finished with him, poring over the three-thousand-page ship regulation tome, and had finally tracked down the obscure clause.

The least serious crime for which stasis was a statutory punishment was breaking quarantine regulations. When *Red Dwarf* had stopped for supplies at Miranda, he'd spent the last afternoon of his three-day ship leave and all his wages buying the smallest, healthiest animal with the best pedigree he could find. For three thousand dollarpounds he'd purchased a black longhaired cat with the show name 'Frankenstein'. He'd had her inoculated for every known disease, to ensure that she didn't actually endanger the crew, and smuggled her aboard under his hat.

A week later he started to panic. The ship's security system still hadn't detected Frankenstein's presence.

It was tricky.

On the one hand he wanted to get caught with the cat, but he didn't want the cat to get caught and dissected. Eventually he hit on the idea of having his photograph taken with the cat, and sending off the film to be developed in the ship's lab.

Finally, and much to his relief, they'd caught him. Three years in stasis was everything he'd hoped for. OK, his wages would be suspended, but it was a small price to pay for walking into a stasis booth, and walking out a subjective instant later in orbit around the Earth.

He'd hidden Frankenstein in the ventilation system. The system was so vast she would be impossible to catch, and also provided her with access for foraging raids to the ship's food stores.

So, all in all, as Lister stepped into the stasis booth, he was feeling pretty pleased with himself, or, at least, as pleased as anyone could expect to feel who was actually as miserable as hell.

Petrovitch gave him one last, last chance to surrender the cat, which Lister naturally refused.

As the cold metal door slammed behind him, he sat on the cold smoothness of the booth's bench and exhaled. Suddenly a warm, green light flooded the chamber, and Lister became a non-event mass with a quantum probability of zero.

He ceased, temporarily, to exist.

NINETEEN

20.17.

A red warning light failed to go on in the Drive Room, beginning a chain of events which would lead, in a further twenty-three minutes, to the total annihilation of the entire crew of *Red Dwarf*.

20.18.

Rimmer was released from the medical bay, and told to take twenty-four hours' sick leave. He was halfway along Corridor 5: delta 333, on his way back to his sleeping quarters, when he changed his mind and decided to spend the evening in a stasis booth.

The medical orderly had informed him of the Lister situation, and that just about capped a perfect day in the life of Arnold J. Rimmer. On top of everything, Lister was about to gain three years on him. By the time they got back to Earth, Lister would be exactly the same age, while he would be three years older. Even with his illicit stasis-boothing, Rimmer could only hope to snatch three months; four at best. So Lister would gain two-and-three-quarter whole years, and he was already younger than Rimmer to start with. It seemed totally unfair.

To cheer himself up, he decided to spend the evening in a state of non-being, and vowed to begin work in the morning on an appeal against Lister's sentence, so he could get him out of the stasis booth and make him start ageing again.

20.23.

Navigation officer Henri DuBois knocked his black cona coffee with four sugars over his computer console keyboard. As he mopped up the coffee, he noticed three red warning blips on his monitor screen, which he wrongly assumed were the result of his spillage.

20.24.

Rimmer got out of the lift on the main stasis floor and made a decision which, in retrospect, he would regret forever.

He decided to comb his hair.

20.31.

The cadmium II coolant system, located deep in the bowels of the engine corridors, stopped funtioning.

20.36.

Rimmer stood in the main wash-room on the stasis deck and combed his hair. He combed his hair in the usual way, then decided to see what it would look like if he parted it on the opposite side. It didn't look very good, so he combed it back again. He washed his hands and dried them on a paper towel. If he had left at this point and gone directly to a stasis booth, he wouldn't have died. But, instead, he was seized by one of his frequent superstition attacks.

He rolled the paper towel into a ball and decided if he could throw it directly into the disposal unit, he would eventually become an officer. He took careful aim, decided on an overarm shot, and tossed his paper ball.

It missed by eight feet.

He retrieved the paper and decided if he got it in the disposal unit three times on the run, it would make up for the miss. The miss would then be struck from the superstition record, and not only would he become an officer, but within three weeks he would get to have sex with a beautiful woman.

Standing directly above the disposal unit, he dropped and retrieved the paper ball three times. Combing his hair one last time, he left the wash-room, idly wondering just who the beautiful girl might be, and headed for a stasis booth.

20.40.

The cadmium II core reached critical mass and unleashed the deadly power of a neutron bomb. The ship remained structurally undamaged, but in 0.08 seconds everyone on the Engineering Level was dead.

20.40 and 2.7 seconds.

Rimmer placed his hand on the wheel lock of stasis booth 1344. He heard what sounded like a nuclear wind roaring down the corridor towards him. It was, in fact, a nuclear wind roaring down the corridor towards him.

What now? he thought, rather irritably, and was suddenly hit full in the face by a nuclear explosion.

0.57 seconds before he expired, Rimmer realized he was going to die. His life didn't flash before him. He didn't think of his parents, or his brothers or his home. He didn't think of the failed exams or the wasted time in the stasis booths. He didn't even think about his one, brief love affair with Yvonne McGruder, the ship's female boxing champion.

What he did, in fact, think of was a bowl of soup. A bowl of gazpacho soup.

Then he died.

Then everyone died.

TWENTY

Deep in the belly of *Red Dwarf*, safely sealed in the cargo hold, Frankenstein nibbled happily from a box of fish paste, while four tiny sightless kittens suckled noisily beneath her.

Part Two

Alone in a Godless
universe, and out
of Shake'n'Vac

ONE

The hatch to the stasis booth zuzz-zungged open, and a green 'Exit now' sign flashed on and off above Lister's head.

Holly's digitalized faced appeared on the eight-foot-square wall monitor.

'It is now safe for you to emerge from stasis.'

'I only just got in.'

'Please proceed to the Drive Room for debriefing.' Holly's face melted into the smooth greyness of the blank screen.

'But I only just got in,' insisted Lister.

He walked down the empty corridor towards the Xpress lift. What was that smell? A musty smell. Like an old attic. He knew that smell. It was just like the smell of his grandmother's cellar. He'd never noticed it before.

And what was that noise? A kind of hissing buzz. The air-conditioning? Why could he hear the air-conditioning? He'd never heard it before. He suddenly realized it wasn't what he was hearing that was odd, it was what he *wasn't* hearing. Apart from the white noise of the air-conditioning, there was no other sound. Just the lonely squeals of his rubber soles on the corridor floor. And there was dust everywhere. Curious mounds of white dust lying in random patterns.

'Where is everybody?'

Holly projected his face onto the floor in front of Lister.

'They're dead, Dave,' he said, solemnly.

'Who is?' asked Lister, absently.

Softly: 'Everybody, Dave.'

'What?' Lister smiled.

'Everybody's dead, Dave.'

'What? Everybody?'

'Yes. Everybody's dead, Dave.

'What? Petersen?'

'Yes. They're *all* dead. *Everybody* is dead, Dave.'

'Burroughs?'

Holly sighed. 'Everybody is dead, Dave.'

'Selby?'

'Yes.'

'Not Chen?'

'Gordon Bennet!' Holly snapped. 'Yes, Chen! Everybody. Everybody's dead, Dave.'

'Even the Captain?'

'YES! EVERYBODY.'

Lister squeaked along the corridor. A tic in his left cheek pulled his face into staccato smiles. He wanted to laugh. Everybody was dead. Why did he want to laugh? No, they couldn't all be dead. Not everybody. Not *literally* everybody.

'What about Rimmer?'

'HE'S DEAD, DAVE. EVERYBODY IS DEAD. EVERYBODY IS DEAD, DAVE. DAVE, EVERYBODY IS DEAD.' Holly tried all four words in every possible permutation, with every possible inflection, finishing with: 'DEAD, DAVE, EVERYBODY *IS*, EVERYBODY IS, *DAVE*, DEAD.'

Lister looked blankly in no particular direction, while his face struggled to find an appropriate expression.

'Wait,' he said, after a while. 'Are you telling me *everybody's* dead?'

Holly rolled his eyes, and nodded.

The enormous Drive Room echoed with silence. The banks of computers on autopilot whirred about their business.

'Holly,' Lister's small voice resonated in the giant chamber, 'what are these piles of dust?'

The dust lay on the floors, on chairs, everywhere, all arranged in small, neat dunes. Lister dipped his finger in one and tasted it.

'That,' said Holly from his huge screen, 'is Console Executive Imran Sanchez.'

Lister's tongue hung guiltily from his mouth, and he wiped the white particles which had once formed part of Console Executive Imran Sanchez onto his jacket cuff.

'So, what happened?'

Holly told him about the cadmium II radiation leak; how the crew had been wiped out within seconds; how he'd headed the ship pell-mell out of the solar system, to avoid spreading nuclear contamination; and how he'd had to keep Lister in stasis until the radiation had reached a safe background level.

'So . . . How long did you keep me in stasis?'

'Three million years,' said Holly, as casually as he could.

Lister acted as if he hadn't heard. Three million years? It had no meaning. If it had been *thirty* years, he would have thought 'What a long time.' But three *million* years. Three million years was just . . . stupid.

He wandered over to the chair opposite the console he'd seen Kochanski operate.

'So, Krissie's dead,' he said, staring at the hummock of dust. 'I always . . .' His voice tailed away.

He tried to remember her face. He tried to remember the pinball smile.

'Well, if it's any consolation,' said Holly, 'if she had survived, the age difference would be insurmountable. I mean, you're twenty-four, she's three million: it takes a lot for a relationship with that kind of age gap to work.'

Lister wasn't listening. 'I always thought we'd get back together. I, ah, had this sort of plan that one day I'd have enough money to buy a farm on Fiji. It's cheap land there, and . . . in a half-assed kind of way, I always pictured she'd be there with me.'

This was getting morbid. Holly tried to lighten the atmosphere.

'Well,' he said, 'she wouldn't be much use to you on Fiji now.'

'No,' said Lister.

'Not unless it snowed,' said Holly, 'and you needed something to grit the path with.'

Lister screwed up his face in distaste. 'Holly!'

'Sorry. I've been on my own for three million years. I'm just used to saying what I think.'

For some time now, well, the last two hundred thousand years to be exact, Holly had grown increasingly concerned about himself. For a computer with an IQ of six thousand, it seems to him he was behaving in a more and more erratic way.

In fact, he'd long suspected he'd gone a bit peculiar. Just as a bachelor who spends too much time on his own gradually develops quirks and eccentricities, so a computer who spends three million years alone in Deep Space can get, well, set in his ways. Become quirky. Go a little bit . . . odd.

Holly decided not to burden Lister with this anxiety, and hoped his oddness would eventually sort itself out now he had a bit of company.

Another slight concern which he tried to put to the back of his RAM was that, for a computer with an IQ of six thousand, there was a rather alarming amount of knowledge he seemed to have forgotten. It wasn't, on the whole, important things, but was nonetheless fairly disturbing.

He knew, for instance, that Isaac Newton was a famous physicist, but he couldn't remember why.

He couldn't remember the capital of Luxembourg.

He *could* recall pi to thirty thousand digits, but he couldn't say for absolute certain whether port was on the left side, and starboard on the right, or whether it was the other way round.

Who knocked Swansea City out of the FA Cup in 1967? He *used* to know. It was a mystery now.

Obviously none of this missing information was absolutely vital for the smooth running of a mining ship three million years out into Deep Space. But technically he was supposed to know more-or-less everything and, frankly, there were some worrying gaps. He could remember, for instance, that in the second impression, 1959 publication of *Lolita* by Vladimir Nabakov, printed in Great Britain by the Shenval Press (London, Hertford and Harrow), page 60 was far and away the dirtiest page. But was Nabakov German or Russian? It totally eluded him.

Maybe it wasn't important. Of course it wasn't important.

Still, it was for Holly a source of perturbation.

It's a source of perturbation, he thought. Then he wondered whether there was such a word as 'perturbation', or whether he'd just made it up. He didn't know that either. Oh, it was hopeless.

Lister sat in the empty Copacabana Hawaiian Cocktail Bar and poured a triple whisky into his double whisky, then topped it up with a whisky. Absently, he lit the filter end of a cigarette and tried to assimilate all the information Holly had thrown at him.

Everybody was dead.

Everybody.

He'd been in stasis three million years.

Three million years.

Since one drunken night outside the 'Marie Lloyd' off Regent Street, London, every step he'd taken had led him further and further from home. First it was Mimas, then Miranda, and now he was three million *years* away. Three million years out into Deep Space. Further than any human being had ever been before.

And he was totally alone.

The enormity of all this was slowly beginning to sink in when Holly dropped his final bombshell. The one about the human race being extinct.

'What d'you mean, "extinct"?'

'Well, three million years is a very good age for a species. I mean, your average genus only survives a couple of hundred thousand years, max. And that's with a clean-living species, like dinosaurs. Dinosaurs didn't totally screw up the environment. They just went around quietly eating things. And even then, they didn't get to clock up the big one mill. So the chances of the human race making it to the big three-oh-oh-oh-oh-oh-oh are practically non-existent. So I'm afraid you just have to face up to the very real possibility that your species is dead.'

Much to his surprise, Lister had let out a sob.

'Were you very close?' Holly tilted his head sympathetically. 'Well, yeah, I suppose you must have been, really.' That was a bit of an odd thing to say, he thought.

Lister took out his shirt-tail and blew his nose. 'So, I'm the last human being alive?'

'Yeah. You never think it's going to happen to your species, do you? It's always something that happens to somebody else's.'

Lister spent the next few days going to pieces.

There seemed little point in getting dressed, and so he wandered around naked, swigging from a bottle of whisky.

He didn't know what to do.

He didn't know if there was anything *to* do.

And worst of all, he didn't much care.

He slept wherever he fell, a painful, dreamless sleep. He hardly ate, and drank a small loch-worth of whisky. He didn't even *like* whisky, but beer was too cumbersome to carry around in sufficient quantities to achieve oblivion.

He lost a stone in weight, and started shouting at people who weren't there.

Every evening, at around 5 p.m. he'd stagger, stark naked, into the Drive Room and, waving his whisky bottle dangerously in the air, he'd belch incoherent obscentities at Holly's huge visage on the gigantic monitor screen.

Sometimes Lister imagined he'd heard the phone ring, and he'd rush to pick it up.

On the evening of the fifth day as he staggered through the *Red Dwarf* shopping mall, toasting invisible crowds, he keeled over and blacked out.

When he woke up in the medical unit, a man with an 'H' on his forehead was looking down at him with undisguised contempt.

TWO

'You're a hologram,' said Lister.

'So I am,' said Rimmer.

'You died in the accident,' said Lister.

'So I did,' said Rimmer.

'What's it like?'

'Death?' Rimmer mused. 'It's like going on holiday with a group of Germans.' He cradled his head in his hands. 'I'm so depressed I want to weep. To be cut down in my prime – a boy of thirty-one, with the body of a thirty-year-old. It's unbearable. All my plans; my career, my future; everything hinged on my being alive. It was *mandatory*.'

'What happened to me? Did I black out?'

'Excuse me, I'm talking about my being dead.'

'Sorry. I thought you'd finished.'

'I'm so depressed,' repeated Rimmer, '*so* depressed.'

Over the next couple of days, Lister slowly recovered in the medical bay. One morning, while Rimmer was off reading the *How to Cope With Your Own Death* booklet for the fifteenth time, Lister took the opportunity to ask Holly why he'd brought Rimmer back.

'You'd gone to pieces. You couldn't cope. You needed a companion.'

'But *Rimmer*??'

'I did a probability study,' lied Holly, 'and it turns out Rimmer is absolutely the best person to keep you sane.'

'Rimmer?'

Holly's disembodied head tilted forward in a nod.

'Why not Petersen?'

'A man who buys a methane-filled twenty-four bed-roomed bijou residence on an oxygenless moon whose only distinction is that it rotates in the opposite direction from its mother planet – you seriously expect me to bring him back to keep you sane? Gordon Bennett – he couldn't even keep himself sane, let alone anyone else.'

'Yeah, but at least we had things in common.'

'The only thing you had in common was your mutual interest in consuming ridiculous amounts of alcohol.'

'Selby? Chen?'

'Ditto.'

'What about Krissie?'

'Dave, she finished with you.'

'But, *Rimmer*?? Anyone would have been better than Rimmer. Anyone. Hermann *Goering* would have been better than Rimmer. All right, he was a drug-crazed Nazi trans-vestite, but at last we could have gone dancing.'

'It was Jean-Paul Sartre,' said Holly, thinking it may very well actually have been Albert Camus, or Flaubert, or perhaps it was even Sacha Distel, 'who said hell was being trapped for eternity in a room with your friends.'

'Sure,' said Lister, 'but all Sartre's mates were French.'

'I think I'm thinking, therefore I might possibly be,' Rimmer said aloud as he padded silently around the sleeping quarters in his hologramatic slippers. Try as he might, he couldn't even begin to grapple with the metaphysics of it all.

'I think I might be thinking, therefore I may possibly be being.' To Rimmer it was incomprehensible mumbo-jumbo. It was more baffling than the three-dimensional foreplay diagrams in Lister's zero-gravity sex manual.

He hated being dead.

When he was a boy on Io, he remembered witnessing an

'Equal rights for the Dead' march, where holograms from all the moons of Jupiter had rallied for better conditions.

The Dead were generally given short shrift throughout the solar system. They were banned from most hotels and restaurants. They found it almost impossible to hold down a decent job. And, even on television, although holograms featured occasionally, they were generally only included as token deads. Not a single golf club throughout known space had a dead member.

The living had a very uncomfortable relationship with holograms in general, reminding them as they did of their own mortality. Also there was a natural resentment towards 'Deadies' – to become a hologram, outside of the Space Corps, you had to be one of the mega-rich. The horribly expensive computer run-time, and the massive power supply that was needed, kept hologramatic afterlife very exclusive indeed.

Sitting on the shoulders of his brother, Frank, the six-year-old Rimmer had booed and jeered with the rest of the crowd. Encouraged by Frank, he'd actually personally thrown a stone, which had passed silently through the back of a hologram woman marching in line.

'Deadies! Dirty Deadies!'

And now he was one of them.

A dirty Deady.

Well, he wasn't going to let it get him down any more. He wasn't going to let it stand in his way. He was dead, there was no use bleating about it. Was that a reason to quit? Did Napoleon quit when he was dead? Did Julius Caesar quit when he was dead?

Well . . . yes.

But that was before the hologram was invented. And that was the advantage he had over two of the greatest men in history. He may not have been the most successful person who ever lived when he was alive but, by God, he'd make up for that in his death.

There was still that ziggurat to climb. There was still that gold bar to achieve.

Nelson had one eye and one arm. Caesar was an epileptic. Napoleon, the man himself, suffered so badly from gonorrhoea and syphilis, he could barely pee. It seemed a veritable boon to Rimmer that the only disability he appeared to have was being dead!

First thing tomorrow, he thought, *I'm going to get the skutters to paint a sign to hang over my bunk.* And he pictured it in his mind's eye, on polished oak:

'TOMORROW IS THE FIRST DAY OF THE REST OF YOUR DEATH.'

THREE

HNNNnnnnNNNNNKRHHhhhhhhhHHHHHH
HNNNnnnnNNNNNKRHHhhhhhhhHHHHHH

A sound like a buzz-saw played through an open-air rock festival's PA system awoke Rimmer from a dream about his mother chasing him through a car-park with a sub-machine-gun.

He swung his legs over the bunk, and tried to locate the sound of the buzz-saw played through an open-air rock festival's PA system. It was Lister, snoring.

HNNNnnnnNNNNNKRHHhhhhhhhHHHHHH
HNNNnnnnNNNNNKRHHhhhhhhhHHHHHH

The snore drilled into Rimmer's skull – perfectly even, up and down, followed by a catarrhy trill, and then the worst part of all: the silence. The silence that always made him think Lister had stopped snoring. One second. Two seconds. Three seconds. He has, he has stopped snoring! Four seconds. Fi . . . then, the snort, then the revolting semi-choking sound as the mucus shifted around his cavernous nasal system, and back onto the perfectly even snore.

HNNNnnnnNNNNNKRHHhhhhhhhHHHHHH
HNNNnnnnNNNNNKRHHhhhhhhhHHHHHH

Rimmer stood up and leaned over Lister's sleeping form. There was a half-empty metal curry tray lying on his chest, which rose and fell in rhythm with his grinding snore.

Rimmer's first impulse was to reach over and pinch his nose, but, of course, he couldn't. He couldn't shake him either, or turn him on his side. He couldn't even take a thin piece of piano wire and slowly garrotte him. If he hadn't been a hologram, this would definitely have been his favourite option.

He arched over, until his mouth was in whispering distance of Lister's ear. Then he screamed: 'STOP SNORING, YOU FILTHY SON OF A BASTARD'S BAS-TARD'S BASTARD!!!'

Lister jerked awake. 'What?'

'You were snoring.'

'Eh?'

'You were snoring.'

'Oh,' said Lister, lying back down. 'Sorry.'

Within three seconds Lister was back asleep. And within ten, he was snoring again.

HNNNnnnnNNNNNKRHHhhhhhhhHHHHHH
HNNNnnnnNNNNNKRHHhhhhhhhHHHHHH

The man was impossible to live with! He was an animal! He was an orang-utan! He was a hippo! He was like one of those little grey monkeys you see at the zoo who openly masturbate whenever you go round with your great-aunt Florrie! He was quite the most revoltingly heinous creature it had ever been Rimmer's misfortune to encounter. What further proof did you need that God did not exist? As if He'd allow this . . . this onion! to become the last surviving member of the human race. He symbolized everything that was cheap and low and nasty and tacky about Mankind. Why *him*? A man whose idea of a change of clothing was to turn his T-shirt inside out, so that the stench was on the outside! Who used orange peel and curry cartons as makeshift ashtrays. Who would frequently tug out a huge great lump of rotting, fetid meat from one of the cavities in his teeth and announce proudly that it could feed a family of four! Who bit his nails – his toenails! He would actually sit there, with his foot in his mouth, and trim his nails by biting them. And then – the most hideous thing of all – he would eat the cuttings! Eating your toenails, for God's sake! This was the Last Man. The Last Human Being. A person who could belch *La Bamba* after eleven pints of lager. A man who ate so many curries he sweated Madras sauce. Revolting! His bed sheets looked like someone had just given birth to a baby on them. And he destroyed things! Not on purpose: he was just such a clumsy, slobby, ham-fisted son-of-a-prostidroid somehow he always destroyed things. Rimmer remembered once showing him a photograph of his mother and, five seconds later, turned round to see him absently using it as a toothpick! He once lent him his favourite album, and when it came back there was a footprint over Reggie Dixon's Hammond organ! And raspberry jam seeds buried in the groove. How is that possible? To get jam on a record? Who listens to Hammond organ music and eats raspberry jam? And the inner sleeve was missing! And there was a telephone number and a doodle on the lyric sheet! Destroyed!

HNNNnnnnNNNNNKRHHhhhhhhHHHHHH
HNNNnnnnNNNNNKRHHhhhhhhHHHHHH

How could anyone possible live with this man??

HNNNnnnnNNNNNKRHHhhhhhhHHHHHH
HNNNnnnnNNNNNKRHHhhhhhhHHHHHH

How could it be that here, snoring like an asthmatic warthog, was the last representative of the human race? How was it possible that this man was alive, while *he* was dead?
How???
HOW???
HOW????

FOUR

Only two days earlier Lister had finally got round to collecting all his personal belongings from Vacuum Storage, and now here he was, sitting on his bunk, packing them all up again to take them back to Vacuum Storage.

He'd asked Holly to turn the ship around and head back to Earth. Maybe the human race *was* extinct, maybe it wasn't. Maybe they'd evolved into a race of super-beings. Maybe they'd wiped one another out in some stupid war and the ants had taken over. But where else was there to go?

Earth was home. He had to find out if it still existed, even if it did take another three million years to get back. So he'd decided to go back into stasis. What else was there to do? He certainly had no intention of hanging around with only a highly neurotic dead man for company.

He looked down at his vacuum storage trunk. He really did have a pretty feeble collection of belongings: four cigarette lighters, all out of gas; a copy of the *Pop-up Karma Sutra – Zero gravity version*; a hard ball of well-chewed gum, which he'd bought at a bar in Mimas from a guy who guaranteed it had once been chewed by Chelsea Brown, the famous actress; a pair of his adoptive grandmother's false teeth, which he'd kept for two reasons: (a) sentimental, and (b) they were just the thing for opening bottles of beer; his bass guitar with two strings (both G); three hundred and fifty Zero-Gee football magazines; and his entire collection of Rasta-Billy-Skank DAT tapes.

And, of course, there were his goldfish.

He wandered over to the three-foot-long oblong tank and peered into the murky green water. At first, he couldn't see a thing through the slimy silt. He flicked on the underwater illumination switch and pressed his face to the side of the tank. Gradually, through the gloom, he made out a moving silhouette. As his eyes adjusted, he saw it was Lennon, swimming happily in and out of the fake plastic Vatican. But he couldn't see McCartney.

He rolled up his sleeve and swirled his arm around in the stagnant filth, releasing a pungent, evil smell. Finally he located the missing fish, lodged in the papal balcony above St Peter's Square. It was dead.

He shook his head, and smacked the fish violently against the corner of Rimmer's slanting architect's desk, then held the fish to his ear and listened. Nothing.

Picking up Rimmer's Space Scout knife, he flicked out a blade and opened up the fish like a watch.

There was the problem! A loose battery. He prodded it back into place and snapped the fish closed. McCartney blinked back into life. He dropped the piscine droid into the water and watched as it happily swam off through the arch of the plastic Sistine Chapel, backwards.

'Ye-es,' said Lister. 'Brutal.'

Rimmer walked in through the hatchway and spotted Lister's vacuum trunk. 'What are you doing?'

Rimmer listened in mounting disbelief as Lister outlined his plan. 'What about me? What am I supposed to do on my own for three million years?'

'Well, I dunno. I haven't really thought about it.'

'No. Exactly.'

'Come on – you can't expect me to hang around here. Why don't you get Holly to turn you off till we get home?'

'Because, dingleberry brain,' Rimmer rose to his feet, 'if by some gigantic fluke the Earth still exists, and if, by an even greater stretching of the laws of probability, the human race is still alive, and if during the six million years we've been away they haven't evolved into some kind of super race, and we can still understand them; if all that comes to pass − when I get back to Earth, the reasons for me being brought back as a hologram will no longer apply, and my personality disc will be neatly packed away in some dusty vault that nobody ever goes in. And that will be the end of Rimmer, Arnold J.'

'You never know. When we get back, it might turn out that they've found a cure for Death.'

Rimmer sucked in his cheeks and rolled his eyes around in their sockets.

'Well, you never know,' said Lister, feebly.

'Oh yes. I expect doctors' waiting rooms are absolutely heaving with cadavers. "Ah, Mrs Harrington. Dropped dead again, eh? Never mind."' Rimmer mimed scribbling a prescription. '"Take two of these, three times a day, and try not to get run over by another bus."'

'I'm going into stasis,' said Lister, picking up his vacuum trunk, 'and that's that. You don't seriously expect me to spend the rest of my life alone here with you.'

'Why not?'

'Fifty-odd years? Alone with you?'

'What's wrong with that?'

Lister stopped and put down his trunk. 'I think we should get something straight. I think there's something you don't understand.'

'What?' said Rimmer.

'The thing is,' said Lister as kindly as he could: 'I don't actually like you.'

Rimmer stared, unblinking. This really was news to him. He didn't like Lister, but he always thought Lister liked him. Why on Io shouldn't he like him? What was there not to like?

'Since when?' he said, with a slight crack in his voice.

113

'Since the second we first met. Since a certain taxi ride on Mimas.'

'That wasn't me! That guy in the false moustache who went to an android brothel? That wasn't me!'

Rimmer was outraged at Lister's accusation. Even though it was true, he felt it was so out of kilter with his own image of himself, he was able to summon up genuine indignation. As if he, Arnold J. Rimmer, would pay money to a lump of metal and plastic to have sexual intercourse with him! It just wasn't like him.

True, he did it, but it wasn't like him!

'I've never been to an android brothel in my life. And if you so much as mention it again, I'll . . .' Rimmer faltered. He suddenly realized there wasn't very much he *could* do to Lister.

'I don't get it. What point are you trying to make?'

'The point I'm trying to make, you dirty son of a fetid whoremonger's bitch, is that we're friends!' Rimmer smiled as warmly as he could to help disguise the massive incongruity he'd walked straight into.

'Sniff your coffee and wake up, Rimmer; we are not friends.'

'I know what you're referring to,' Rimmer nodded his head vigorously. 'It's because I gave you a hard time since you came aboard, isn't it? But don't you see? I had to do that, to build up your character. To change the boy into a man.'

'Oh, do smeg off.'

'I always thought you saw me as a sort of big brother character. Heck – we don't always get on. But then, what brothers do? Cain didn't always get on with Abel . . .'

'He killed him.'

'Absolutely. But underneath all that they were still brothers, with brotherly affection. Heaven knows, I didn't always get on with my brothers – in fact once, when I was fourteen, I needed mouth-to-mouth resuscitation after all three of them held my head down a toilet for rather too long – but we laughed about it afterwards, when I'd started breathing again.'

'You're not going to persuade me not to go into stasis. I am not spending the rest of my life with a man who keeps his underpants on coat hangers.'

Rimmer held up his outspread palms in a gesture of innocence. 'I'm not trying to persuade you.'

'Then what's all this about?'

'I don't know. I'm not sure what anything's about any more.'

Here comes the emotional blackmail, thought Lister.

'It's not easy, you know, being . . . dead.'

'Uhn,' Lister grunted.

'It's so hard to come to terms with. I mean . . . death. Your own death. I mean, you have plans . . . so many things you wanted to do, and now . . .'

'Look – I'm sorry you're dead, OK? It was cruddy luck. But you've got to put it behind you. You're completely obsessed by it.'

'Obsessed??'

'It's all you ever talk about.'

'Well, pardon me for dying.'

'Frankly, Rimmer, it's very boring. You're like one of those people who are always talking about their illnesses.'

'Well!' said Rimmer, his eyes wide in astonishment.

'It's just boring. Change the disc. Flip the channel. Death isn't the handicap it once was. For smeg's sake, cheer up.'

'Well!' said Rimmer. And he couldn't think of anything else to say. So he said 'Well!' again.

'And quite honestly, the prospect of hanging around and having to listen to you whining and moaning, and bleating and whingeing for the next three quarters of a century, because you happen to have snuffed it, does not exactly knock me out.'

'Well!' said Rimmer.

'Fifty years alone with you? I'd rather drink a pint of my own diarrhoea.'

'Well!'

'Or a pint of somebody else's, come to that. Every hour, on the hour, for the next seventy years.'

'I can't believe' – Rimmer was shaking – 'you've just said that.'

Holly faded into focus on the sleeping quarters' vid-screen.

'Oi,' he said, rather un-computerlike, 'I've just opened the radiation seals to the cargo decks. And there's something down there.'

'What do you mean?'

'Some kind of life-form.'

'What is it?'

'I can only see it on the heat scanner. I don't know what it is – I only know what it isn't.'

'What isn't it, then?'

'It isn't human.'

FIVE

Lister clutched the bazookoid – the heavy portable rock-blasting mining laser – to his chest, and checked again that the pack on his back was registering 'Full Charge'.

Light flitted through the wire mesh of the rickety lift as it clumsily juddered its way down into the bowels of the ship.

Three miles of lift shaft. Over five hundred floors, most of them stretching the six-mile length of the ship.

These were the cargo decks, where all the supplies were stored.

The tiny, exposed cage shuddered and rocked slowly past floor after floor.

Down.

Perhaps twenty floors of food, vacuum-sealed, tin mountains, stretching out beyond vision.

Down.

Four floors of wood – a million chopped trees stacked in silent pyramids.

Down.

Floors of mining equipment.

Down.

Floors of raw silicates, mined from Ganymede.

Down.

Floors of water, stored and still in enormous glass tanks.

And down.

And the only sound was the metallic squealing of the lift cable as it plunged them deeper and deeper into the gloomy abyss.

'I don't know why *I'm* scared. I'm a hologram. Whatever it is, it can't do anything to me.'

'Thanks. That makes me feel really secure.'

The gloom enveloped them. The light on Lister's mining helmet cut only twenty feet into the darkness. Lister flipped down the helmet's night-visor and switched the beam to infra red.

Down.

Then, something strange. These floors were empty. Hundreds of cubic miles of supplies were missing! Food, metal, wood, water – missing.

'It's gone!'

'What has?' Rimmer squinted blindly into the darkness.

'Everything.'

'What d'you mean, everything?'

'All the supplies. The last ten floors – they were all empty.'

'I'm *so* glad I'm already dead. I'm so, so glad.'

'You want to shut the smeg up?'

Down.

D

o

w

n

In the bottom right hand corner of Lister's visor a small green cross began to flicker.

'Oh, smeg. There *is* something here.'

'Where?'

The cross crept up the visor. Lister wanted to say: 'The next floor,' but he couldn't. He couldn't speak.

The lift coughed to a stop. The whine of the motor faded to nothing.

There it was.

Stretching before them, six miles in length, half-lit and desolate.

A huge, impossible city.

A *city*!

The lift doors folded open – *cher-chunk!* – and they stepped out onto the rough cobbled street.

Crudely fashioned igloo-shaped dwellings lined the roadway; hummocks of carved wood, without doorways. Each had only a slit, perhaps a yard wide and less than a foot high, cut six feet from the ground.

Lister checked the charge on the bazookoid back pack, and they both started cautiously down the street. Before them was a crossroads. The igloo hummocks stretched out in every direction. The flashing cross in Lister's visor throbbed more insistently, and indicated they should turn right.

'What *is* this place?'

Lister slung the bazookoid over his shoulder and scrambled up one of the hummocks. He poked his head through a slit and peered into the dim interior.

'Some kind of house. But it's tiny. Just enough room for two people to crouch in and peer out of the gash at the top. Whatever lived here really liked confined spaces.' Built into a tiny recess in the wall was a small bookcase containing six books. Lister reached in and managed to grab three of them. He dropped down from the hummock.

Rimmer peered over his shoulder as he opened each book in turn. Every single page in every book was blank. Lister slipped the books into his haversack, grabbed the bazookoid, re-checked the charge, and they moved off again.

After five minutes or so, they reached a square. Rows of benches faced a television screen attached to a video recorder. Lister ejected the disc. It bore the ship's regulation supply logo.

'What is it?' asked Rimmer.

'"The Flintstones".'

They turned left. More hummocks. Another square, but this time set out like a street café: tables with parasols; wooden chairs. And in the centre: a table, fully laid, with two gold candelabra, both lit. A meal, half-eaten, sat steaming on a plate.

The blip on Lister's visor was pulsing faster than ever.

'It's here!' Lister's finger tightened on the beam button of the bazookoid. 'Whatever it is, it's right here!'

A flash.

A pink blur flashed from the top of a hummock, pinning Lister to the floor, and sending the weapon skittering across the cobbles.

Rimmer watched, half-paralysed, as the pink neon-suited man with immaculate coiffeur sniffed Lister, looked up with a puzzled expression, sniffed him more deeply, then finally got to his feet, took out a clothes brush and smoothed out his suit.

'Sorry, Man,' he said, 'I thought you were food.'

SIX

From the moment he discovered that the cadmium II had achieved critical mass, Holly had less than fifteen nanoseconds to act. He sealed off as much of the ship as possible – the whole cargo area, and the ship's supply bay. Simultaneously, he set the drive computer to accelerate far beyound the dull green-blue disc of Neptune in the distance, and out into the abyss of unknown space. Then he read the Bible, the Koran, and other major religious works: he covered Islam, Zoroastrianism, Mazdaism, Zarathustrianism, Dharma, Brahmanism, Hinduism, Vedanta, Jainism, Buddhism, Hinayana, Mahayana, Sikhism, Shintoism, Taoism and Confucianism. Then he read all of Marx, Engels, Freud, Jung and Einstein. And, to kill the remaining few nanoseconds, he skipped briefly through Joe Klumpp's Zero Gee Football – It's a Funny Old game.

At the end of this, Holly came to two conclusions. First, given the whole sphere of human knowledge, it was still impossible to determine the existence or not of God. And second, Joe Klumpp should have stuck to having his hair permed.

In the hold, Frankenstein's four offspring began to breed. Each litter produced an average of four kittens, three times a year. At the end of the first year, the second generation of kittens started to breed too. They also produced three annual litters of three to four kittens.

When Frankenstein died, at the great old age of fourteen, she left behind one hundred and ninety-eight thousand, seven hundred and thirty-two cats.

198,732 cats, who continued to breed.

★

Still Red Dwarf *accelerated.*

Holly witnessed at first hand phenomena which had never been witnessed before. He saw phenomena which had only been guessed at by theoretical physicists.

He saw a star form.

He saw another star die.

He saw a black hole.

He saw pulsars and quasars.

He saw twin and triplet sun systems.

He saw sights Copernicus would have torn out his eyes for, but all the while he couldn't stop thinking how bad that book was by Joe Klumpp.

The cats continued to breed.

Red Dwarf *continued to accelerate.*

The forty-square mile cargo hold was seething with cats.

A sea of cats.

A sea of cats, sealed from the radiation-poisoned decks above with nowhere to go.

Only the smartest, the biggest and the strongest survived.

The mutants.

The mutants, who had rudimentary fingers instead of claws, who stood on their hind legs, and clubbed rivals to death with crudely-made clubs. Who found the best breeding mates.

And bred.

Felis erectus was born.

Red Dwarf, *still accelerating, passed five stars in concentric orbits, performing a breathtaking, mind-boggling stellar ballet.*

Not that Holly noticed.

He'd been on his own now for two million years and was no longer interested in mind-boggling stellar ballets. What he was really into was Netta Muskett novels. The young doctor had just told Jemma she had only three years to live, as he held her in his powerful masculine grip, his dark brooding eyes piercing her very soul. Outside, the suns danced into a perfect pentagon and span, end over end, like a gigantic Catherine wheel.

But Holly didn't see it. He was too busy reading Doctor, Darling.

Then there was a plague.

And the plague was hunger.

Less than thirty Cat tribes now survived, roaming the cargo decks on their hind legs in a desperate search for food.

But the food had gone.

The supplies were finished.

Weak and ailing, they prayed at the supply hold's silver mountains: huge towering acres of metal rocks which, in their pagan way, the mutant Cats believed watched over them.

Amid the wailing and the screeching one Cat stood up and held aloft the sacred icon. The icon which had been passed down as holy, and one day would make its use known.

It was a piece of V-shaped metal with a revolving handle on its head.

He took down a silver rock from the silver mountain, while the other Cats cowered and screamed at the blasphemy.

He placed the icon on the rim of the rock, and turned the handle.

And the handle turned.

And the rock opened.

And inside the rock was Alphabetti spaghetti in tomato sauce.

And in the other rocks were even more delights. Sugar-free baked beans. Chicken and mushroom Toastie Toppers. Faggots in rich meaty gravy. All sealed in perfect vacuums, preserved from the ravages of Time.

God had spoken.

And Felis sapiens was born.

Holly was gurning. He was pulling his pixelized face into the most *bizarre and ludicrous expressions he could muster. He'd been gurning now for nearly two thousand years. It wasn't much of a hobby, but it helped pass the time.*

He was beginning to worry that he was going computer-senile. Driven crazy by loneliness. What he needed, he decided, was a companion.

He would build a woman.

A perfectly functioning human woman, capable of independent thought and decision-making. Identical to a real woman in the minutest detail.

The problem was he didn't know how.

He didn't even know what to make the nose out of.

So he gave the whole scheme up as a bad idea, and started gurning again.

And there was a war between the Cats.

A bloody war that laid waste many of their number.

But the reason was good.

The cause was sensible.

The principle was worth fighting over.

It was a holy war.

Some of the Cats believed the one true father of Catkind was a man called Cloister, who saved Frankenstein, the Holy Mother, and was frozen in time by the evil men who sought to kill her. One day Cloister would return to lead them to Bearth, the planet where they could make their home.

The other Cats believed exactly the same thing, except they maintained the name of the true Father of Catkind was a man called Clister.

They spent the best part of two thousand years fighting over this huge, insuperable theological chasm.

Millions died.

Finally, a truce was called.

Commandeering the fleet of shuttles from the docking bay, half the Cats flew off in one direction, in search of Cloister and the

Promised Planet, and the other half flew off in the opposite direction, in search of Clister and the Promised Planet.

Behind them they left the ones who were too weak to travel: the old, the lame, the sick and the dying.

And one by one, they died.

Soon only two remained: one a cripple, one an idiot.

They snuggled together for warmth and companionship.

And one day, to the cripple and the idiot, a son was born.

SEVEN

So the last human being alive, a man who had died, and a creature who'd evolved from cats, stood around the metal table that was bolted to the floor of the sleeping quarters and listened to a computer with an IQ of six thousand, who couldn't remember who'd knocked Swansea City out of the 1967 FA cup, explain what the hell was happening.

'So he's a Cat,' said Lister for the fourteenth time.

The Cat took a small portable steam iron out of his pocket and started pressing the sleeve of his jacket.

Outwardly, at least, he was human in appearance – there was a slight flattening of his face: his ears were a little higher on his head; and two of his gleaming upper teeth hung down longer and sharper than the others, so they peeked, whitely, over his lips whenever he grinned. Which he did a lot.

He didn't seem to have a trace of super-ego. He was all ego and id – monumentally self-centred and, if he'd been human, you would have described him as vain. But you couldn't apply human values to Cats – there seemed to be very little connection between the two cultures. The invention which proved the turning point in Cat history wasn't Fire or the Wheel: it was the Steam-operated Trouser Press.

Getting information out of the Cat wasn't easy: if you asked him too many questions, he just got bored, and went off to take one of the five or six showers he appeared to need daily.

He didn't have a name. He found it difficult to understand the idea. He was of the unshakeable conviction that he was the absolute centre of the entire universe, the reason for its being; and the notion that someone might now know who he was was beyond his comprehension.

'What about in relationships?' Lister had persisted.

'Re-la-tion-ships?' The Cat rolled the word around on his tongue. The Cats had learned English from the vast number of video discs and training films that were stored in the cargo decks, waiting for delivery to Triton. But most human concepts eluded them.

'Yeah, you know, between a man cat and a woman cat. What do you call each other?'

'Hey, you.'

'What? In the entire relationship, you never refer to each other by name?'

'You know how long a Cat relationship lasts? Three minutes. First minute's fine; second minute, you feel trapped! Third minute, you've got to leave.'

The very thought of a relationship which lasted longer than three minutes brought the Cat out in a cold sweat, and he had to go and take another hot shower.

And so the evening progressed.

When the Cat wasn't showering or snoozing, he was preening. He appeared to have secreted about his immaculate person an arsenal of combs and brushes, none of which seemed to spoil the line of his immaculate pink suit.

For the most part, detail's of the Cat's background remained obscure. He found the concept of 'parents' bewildering. He couldn't believe there was ever a time he wasn't born. When he put his mind to it, he did recall two other Cats who used to be around, but most of the time they'd avoided each other. One of them, he reckoned, had probably been his mother – because she wouldn't sleep with him. In fact, she'd got quite angry at his approaches and hit him on the head with a large frying pan.

The other must have been his father; a deeply religious Cat who was constantly reciting the Seven Cat Commandments: 'Thou shalt not be cool; Thou shalt not be in vain; Thou shalt not have more than ten suits; Thou shalt not partake of carnal knowledge with more than four members of the opposite sex at any one session; Thou shalt not slink; Thou shalt not hog the bathroom; and Thou shalt not steal another's hair-gel.'

In the Dark Ages of religious intolerance, these laws were laid down by Cat priests to keep their race in check. It was only through denying certain lusts, certain natural urges to be cool and stylish, they said, that a Cat could find redemption. Strict punishments were meted to transgressors: Cats caught slinking in public would have their shower units removed; Cats condemned as vain would have their hair-driers confiscated, and be forced to wear fashions some two or three seasons old.

'Paisley? With thin lapels and turn-ups?? But that was last spring! Please, no! Have mercy!'

The Cat finally tired of the relentless questioning and announced it was time for its main mid-evening snooze. He casually leapt up on top of Rimmer's locker, curled up in the impossibly small space and fell immediately into a deep and satisfying sleep.

'What are we going to do with him?' Rimmer asked. Lister sat at the table, playing with his locks. He was thinking. Watching Lister thinking always reminded Rimmer of a huge, old, rusty tractor trying to plough furrows in a concrete field.

Finally, he looked up. 'He's coming with us. Back to Earth.

Disappointment filtered through Rimmer's brittle smile.

'You're still going into stasis then? You're taking him with you?'

'Why not?'

No reason, he thought. *No reason at all. So long as you don't give two short smegs about Arnold J. Rimmer.*

EIGHT

'Jump here, jump back . . . Waaaah.'

The Cat slinked down the corridor, pulling a clothes rack on wheels which was packed with suits. Blue suits, green suits, red suits. Polka dots, stripes, checks. Silk suits, fur suits, plain suits. Each one he'd made himself during the years he'd been trapped down in the cargo hold.

'Jump up, jump down . . .' The cat spun round and did a little dance, without breaking stride.

He reached the Vacuum Storage floor, where Lister was waiting impatiently.

'What are you doing?'

'I'm doing what you said do.'

'I said "Bring a few basic essentials you can't leave behind."'

'Right,' agreed the Cat, 'and this is all I'm taking. Just this and the other ten racks. Travel light, move fast. Waaaaah.' He spun on the spot.

'You can't pack all this in Vacuum Storage – it'll take ages.'

The Cat's face drooped. He'd spent the last two hours trying to whittle his enormous collection down to his favourite hundred suits. He'd been *cruel* with himself. The yellow DJ with green piping had *gone*. The imitation walrus hide with the fake zebra collar was *history*! And his red PVC morning suit with matching top hat and cane – down the *tube*!

'You can take two suits,' Lister said firmly, 'and that's it.'

'Two suits?' the Cat laughed mockingly. 'Two? Then I'm staying, buddy.'

'You can't stay. When I come out, you'll be dead.'

'Two suits *is* dead.'

'Pick.'

The Cat walked up and down the racks, then he walked up and down the racks again. Then he went behind the racks and walked up and down them on the other side. 'How many did you say it was? Ten?'

'Two.'

'Oh, man.' The Cat walked up and down the racks again.

Lister walked up to the rack, grabbed two suits, and thrust them roughly into the vacuum trunk. 'OK, those are the two you're taking.'

The Cat picked up the arm of the first suit on the rack and shook it by the sleeve. 'Bye, man.' He tapped it on its padded shoulder and went to the next one.

Lister sighed. 'I'd better say so-long to Rimmer.'

'Bye, baby,' said the Cat to his next suit; 'gonna miss you.'

Lister walked off down the corridor. 'We're going into stasis in ten minutes. I'll meet you in the sleeping quarters.'

'Hey,' the Cat called, 'if I cut off my leg and leave it behind, can I take three?'

It didn't make sense.

As Holly flicked through the four zillion megabytes of navicomp data, and simultaneously cross-checked the information against all the sensor status databanks, he found it impossible to avoid the conclusion that *Red Dwarf* was 0.002 seconds away from doing something completely impossible.

It was about to break the light barrier.

True, the average cruising speed for a vessel the size of *Red Dwarf* was 200,000 miles an hour.

True, they had been accelerating constantly for the last three million years.

True, the ship was now clocking up 669,555,000 miles an hour, which was just 45,000 miles an hour below the speed of light.

And true, in 0.0019 seconds they would break the light barrier.

The thing was: it wasn't possible.

Light is the speed limit for the universe.

Nothing travels faster than light.

All of which was good. What wasn't so good was that *Red Dwarf* was about to do exactly that.

In 0.0017 seconds.

It didn't make sense.

Holly reprogrammed the Drive computer to slow down. Which the Drive computer did. But because they were accelerating so fast, slowing down merely meant they were accelerating slightly less quickly than they were before. However, they were still accelerating. So they were slowing down, but still going faster.

That didn't make much sense to Holly either.

The only thing that was clear was that by the time they'd slowed down enough to be actually slowing down, in the sense of going slower – rather than the kind of slowing down that meant they were actually getting faster, albeit faster more slowly – they would already have broken the light barrier.

Which was impossible.

And they were due to do this in 0.0013 seconds.

Holly hummed softly.

Holly had only uncovered all this when he'd tried to chart the ship's return course to Earth.

At first he'd assumed it was possible to do a three-point turn or loop the loop, but according to his calculations it would take the best part of three hundred and fifty thousand years just to do a fairly sharpish U-turn.

Then Holly got his plan. If he could manoeuvre *Red Dwarf* into orbit around a planet, they could use the gravitational pull to slingshot out 180° later on a heading back to Earth.

Brilliant!

Who said he was getting computer-senile?

Of course, this Fancy Dan astrobatics talk was all a tiny bit irrelevant, because they were about to break the light barrier, and Holly was fairly convinced that in so doing they would all be instantly reduced to their component atoms.

And as far as he could tell this was going to happen in 0.000 seconds.

Oh dear.

That was now.

NINE

At the same instant, Lister was everything and he was nothing. His mass was infinite and his mass was non-existent.

As he watched, his legs stretched out beneath him, as if he were teetering on the top of the World Trade Centre, staring down at his tiny feet miles below.

His face buckled and rippled. His eyelashes hung down over his cheeks like huge palm trees.

He was all colours and he was no colours. Instinctively, he reached out an arm to steady himself, and it telescoped away across the now-infinite space of the sleeping quarters as if it were elastic.

He turned to get his bearings, and found himself looking at the back of his own head.

And then he was falling, falling into himself, and when he opened his eyes he discovered his head was in his stomach; then just as quickly he mushroomed back out, and his head was the shape and size of an Egyptian pyramid.

He tried to walk. A mistake. His legs became hopelessly tangled. He forgot how many he had, and where they should go. Each step was like trying to construct a wayward deck-chair. And then he fell over. But he didn't go down, he went up.

He folded round on himself, to form a perfect cylinder, and everywhere he looked there was him.

Him him him him him him him him him him him him him him him him . . .

And all the hims started screaming as they spun, cutting orbits around themselves, like electrons.

And then it stopped.

And he was just standing in front of the washbasin, his razor in his hand, looking at his soaped-up face in the mirror.

Holly appeared on the sleeping quarters' monitor.

'Whoops!' he said: 'My fault,' and grinned contritely.

'What happened?'

'We've broken the light barrier.'

'I thought that was impossible.'

'Nah,' said Holly.

'So are we travelling at light speed, now?'

'Faster.'

'Is everyone OK?'

'Rimmer's a bit shaken up. He's still running around in circles in the technical library.'

'What about the ship?'

'Well, now it's got back to its original mass, it's feeling much perkier,' said Holly, and left to devote all his available run-time to navigating a ship that was now travelling beyond measurable speed.

Lister stepped into the northern hatchway of the recreation room, on his way to the technical libary to find Rimmer. Down the centre of the recreation room were dozens of baize-covered tables in various shapes and sizes: pool, snooker, cuarango and flip. The walls were lined with 3-D video booths – *Italian Driver* was Lister's favourite: one of the most thrilling and dangerous games around, the object of which was to park a car in Rome. Rimmer stepped in through the southern hatchway.

'Rimmer, we've broken the light barrier . . .'

'What?' said Rimmer.

'We're going faster than the speed of light!'

'How did I do what?'

135

'What d'you mean: "How did I do what?"'

'Lister, don't be a gimboid.'

'I'm not being a gimboid.'

'How could I? I've just been in the library, thinking. Anyway, I've decided . . .' Rimmer paused for no discernible reason, then yelled, equally inexplicably: 'Shut up!', wheeled round 180°, and appeared to be addressing a dartboard. 'As I was saying, before I was so rudely interrupted: I've decided when you go into stasis I want to be left on. I want to stay behind.'

'Are you all right, Rimmer?'

'What things?' said Rimmer with a puzzled expression. 'Eh?'

'I said *what*?' Rimmer turned his head slowly, following some unseen object with his eyes.

'What's going on?' Lister passed his hand in front of Rimmer's eyes. Rimmer stared blankly ahead.

'You're space crazy,' Rimmer said.

'*I'm* space crazy? You're the one who's space crazy.'

'Well, it probably *is* déjà vu,' said Rimmer. 'Sounds like it.' He scratched the hologramatic 'H' on his forehead with his long, thin finger, shook his head, then walked across to the northern hatchway and stepped out.

Simultaneously, another Rimmer stepped in through the southern hatchway.

Lister whipped round just in time to see the first Rimmer's back disappearing round the corner.

'Rimmer!' he said to the Rimmer who'd just come in, 'You just this second walked out of that door.'

'What?' said this other Rimmer.

'How did you do that?' Lister's head was flicking from exit to exit.

'How did I do what?'

'Rimmer, you just went out of that door,' Lister pointed at the north exit, 'and you've just come in through this one.'

'Lister, don't be a gimboid.'

'Look, I swear on my grandmother's life, as you walked out *there* you came in *here*.'

'How could I? I've just been in the library, thinking. Anyway, I've decided . . .'

'Rimmer! I'm telling you . . .' Lister walked to the centre of the room and stood with his back to the dartboard.

'Shut up!' Rimmer yelled, wheeling around to face him. 'As I was saying before I was so rudely interrupted: I've decided when you go into stasis I want to be left on. I want to stay behind.'

'Rimmer – you've just been in and said exactly these things.'

'What things?'

'You said that. You said "What things?"'

'I said *what*?'

'And that. You said that too.'

'You're space crazy,' said Rimmer.

'Yes!' said Lister, nodding, 'And then you said it was probably déjà vu.'

'Well, it probably *is* déjà vu,' said Rimmer. 'Sounds like it.'

'Well go on then. Scratch your "H", shake your head and walk out.'

Rimmer scratched the hologramatic 'H' on his forehead with his long, thin finger, shook his head, then walked across to the northern hatchway and stepped out.

He'd caught the lift and was heading back towards the sleeping quarters before Lister caught up with him.

'Rimmer! Wait! Listen to me . . .'

Suddenly, the Cat raced out from the sleeping quarters, and ran past them, clutching a bloodied handkerchief to his mouth.

'My tooth! My tooth! I think I lost my tooth!'

Lister stopped. 'Cat – what happened?'

The Cat raced by, ignoring him.

Rimmer stood in the entrance to the sleeping quarters.

'Look,' he said quietly.

The Cat was standing motionless by the bunks, his lips slightly parted in a half-smile of disbelief.

'Correct me if I'm wrong,' said Rimmer, 'but the Cat just rushed past us, and now he's standing here.'

'Did you get him?' said the Cat to Lister.

Lister turned to Rimmer. 'You see? Something weird is happening.'

'I was just sitting here,' said the Cat, 'just waiting, like you said to wait. Then this appallingly handsome guy who was an exact replica of me appeared, and started singing about fish.'

'It's something to do with light speed,' said Lister.

Rimmer called for Holly.

Holly was busy. He was busy worrying.

He'd given up trying to navigate the ship at super-light speed. He was fairly certain they'd already passed directly through the middle of seven planets, and at least one sun. It was completely impossible to avoid them, because they only appeared on his navicomp after the event.

Still, for some reason the ship seemed to have survived intact, so he decided not to worry about it.

Another slight concern was that *Red Dwarf* seemed to be following another *Red Dwarf*. And they, in turn, seemed to be being followed by yet another. In fact, when Holly examined it closely, they seemed to be flying in a convoy of at least twenty-six *Red Dwarf*s. Holly reasoned he couldn't do much about it, so he decided not to worry about this either.

In fact, there was nothing he could do about anything. At least, not until they dropped below light speed, which, according to his calculations, was seventy-eight hours away. But Holly had a very low opinion of his own calculations, so he wasn't going to put too much faith in that.

'What? What? What? What is it? I'm busy. I'm trying to navigate.' Holly's digitalized face appeared blurry and ill-defined.

'What's the problem? You've got an IQ of six thousand, haven't you?'

'Look, I've got to steer a ship the size of a small South American republic at speeds hitherto unencountered in the realm of human experience. We're travelling faster than the speed of light – we pass through things before I've even *seen* them. Even with an IQ of six thousand, it's still brown trousers time.'

'Just tell us what's happening.'

'You're seeing future echoes. Because we're travelling faster than light, we're overtaking ourselves in time. You're catching up with things you're about to do, before you've actually done them. Future echoes,' he repeated. 'OK?'

'So,' said Lister, 'the Cat is going to break his tooth some time in the future?'

'What tooth? Nobody's going to break *my* tooth.'

'How long is this going to last?'

'Until the reverse thrust takes effect and we drop below light speed.' Holly's image closed one eye and did some mental arithmetic which was probably wrong. 'Seventy-three hours and fourteen minutes,' he said as confidently as he could.

'*Nobody* is going to break my tooth.'

'Look! Look!' Rimmer spluttered. 'There's another one!'

A photograph was slowly materializing on Lister's bunk-side table.

It was a photograph of Lister. A photograph of Lister wearing a white surgical gown, standing outside the ship's medical unit. His eyes were dark and weary, but he was grinning. In his arms, wrapped in silver blankets, were two new-born babies.

'Two babies?' Lister looked up at the Cat who was craning over his shoulder.

He reached out to pick up the photograph, but his hand passed through it, and the picture slowly evaporated.

'Where do we get two babies from, without a woman on board?'

TEN

Lister was having an argument with the dispensing machine when he heard the explosion.

It was a simple dispute, and the dispensing machine was completely in the wrong. Lister had ordered his customary breakfast of prawn bangalore phall, half-rice, half-chips, seven spicy poppadoms, a lager-flavoured milkshake and two Rennies. The machine had delivered a raspberry pavlova in onion gravy.

'There's something wrong with your voice recognition unit.'

'Coming right up,' said the dispensing machine, and served up two lightly grilled kippers.

'No, you don't understand. There's a malfunction somewhere.'

'No problem at all,' said the machine. 'Rare, medium, or well done?' then dispensed forty-three pounds of raw calf's liver.

'Forget it. Forget the food. Can you just give me a coffee?'

'No sooner said than done,' said the machine pleasantly, and a Christmas pudding, flambéd in brandy, rolled out of the dispensing hatch, onto the floor, and set fire to Lister's trouser bottoms.

Lister was still stamping out the Christmas pudding when the explosion rocked the ship.

When he arrived breathless in the Navicomp Chamber, Rimmer was staring, still in shock, at the Drive panel.

'What was *that*?' shouted Lister.

Slowly Rimmer turned his head and looked up.

'Brace yourself for a bit of a shock: I just saw you die.'

'You saw what??'

'Well, I did warn you to brace yourself.'

'What? When? You didn't give me much of a chance.'

'I gave you ample bracing time.'

'No you didn't. You didn't even pause.'

'Well, I'm sorry. I've just had a rather disturbing experience. I've just seen someone I know die in the most hideous, hideous way.'

'Yeah! Me!'

'It was horrible.' Rimmer screwed up his face and shuddered in distaste. 'You were standing by the navicomp . . .'

'I don't want to know!'

'You don't want to know how you die?'

'No. 'Course I smegging don't.'

Suddenly the room seemed very dark and cold to Lister. 'Was it quick?' he asked quietly.

'We-ell. I wouldn't say it was *super* fast. Not if you count the thrashing about and the agonized squealing.' He shuddered again.

'You're enjoying this, aren't you?'

'What a horrible thing to say.'

'It was definitely me?'

'Yup!' Rimmer grinned.

'I don't want to know about this.' He sucked absently at one of his locks. 'How old did I look?'

'How old are you now?'

'Twenty-five. How old did I look?'

'I'd say . . .' Rimmer clicked his tongue '. . .mid-twenties.'

'Smeg!' Lister got up and kicked the navicomp. 'I'm not ready.' He kicked it again. 'I'm not smegging ready!'

'Yes, you did seem surprised. Especially when the arm came off.'

'So you saw my face? You got a good look at my face? It was actually me? It was *my* face?'

'Yes, you were wearing your stupid leather deerstalker with the furry earmuffs.'

Lister snatched off his leather deerstalker with the furry earmuffs. 'OK. I'll never wear a hat. I'll never wear it again. Then it can't happen.' He flung the cap across the navicomp, and it scudded along the floor.

Rimmer smiled. 'But it *has* happened. You can't change it, any more than you can change what you had for breakfast this morning.'

'But it *hasn't* happened, has it? It has will be have going to have happened, but it hasn't actually *happen* happened.'

'The point of it is, it *has* happened. It's just it hasn't taken place yet.'

Lister stared blankly into space, playing with his hair, while Rimmer tried to wrestle back the smirk that was making a break for his face.

'All right. OK. OK. The Cat, right?' Lister got to his feet. 'The Cat broke his tooth in a future echo, right?'

'I'm listening.'

'If I can stop him breaking it . . .'

'Can't be done.'

'. . . then I can stop me from dying!'

'Can't be done. Unfortunately.'

'So . . . how would the Cat break his tooth?'

Lister sat quietly, tugging at a loose piece of rubber on the toecap of his boot.

Rimmer watched him, whistling a Dixieland jazz version of *Death March in Saul*.

'Eating something . . .'

'Can't be done, me old buckeroo. Your number is up'.

'Eating something hard . . .'

'Can't be done-a-roonied. Sadly.'

Lister stood up, his eyes alive, and pelted out of the navi-comp chamber.

'Where are you going?' Rimmer got to his feet.

'My goldfish!' Lister's voice echoed from the corridor. 'Trying to eat my robot goldfish!'

Plop.

Plop, kerplop, plop . . .

The Cat lay listlessly on Rimmer's bunk. Several of his shirts were slung on a line across the sleeping quarters, drip-ping noisily into receptacles.

Plop.

Plop, kerplop, plop . . .

He hated laundry day. It always made him tired. Wearily he picked up another dirty shirt, unfurled his tongue and started cleaning it with long, methodical, rough, wet licks, stopping occasionally to top up his tongue with washing-up powder.

When it was finished, he hung the shirt on the line with the others.

Plop, kerplop, plop . . .

He really didn't feel like attacking his sock pile right now, so he got up and started mooching around the quarters, look-ing for something else to do.

He picked a book from Rimmer's shelf and ran his nose across one or two pages, but he couldn't make any sense of it. It appeared to be covered in funny little blobs, which didn't smell of anything.

Cats didn't communicate by writing. They communicated by smell. To 'read' a piece of Cat literature, you ran your nose along a line, which released various impregnated scents from the page.

There were two hundred and forty-six smell-symbols in the Cat lexicon. Each could be qualified by smaller, subtler smells which altered the meaning. Symbols could also mean completely different things in different contexts. For instance, the smell for 'fear' in a different setting could also mean 'very bad', 'noxious', 'toilet' or sometimes even 'estate agent'.

The Cat decided to amuse himself by trying to read the contents of Lister's dirty laundry basket. Much to his surprise, some of it translated quite well into Cat prose. In fact one T-shirt contained a sentence about a fearful, very bad estate agent going to a noxious toilet.

Then he noticed the goldfish.

He watched them for a while. One of them was swimming backwards. He'd never actually seen a live fish, but he was aware of some primal instinct they stirred deep within his stomach.

Even though he'd eaten less than an hour ago, he found a little hunger pain squeaking *'Let's eat the fish'*. He had a small, half-hearted dialogue with the hunger pain, but it was fairly insistent.

'Come on, let's eat the fish!'

'I'm not hungry.'

'Eat it, eat it, come o-o-o-on.'

The Cat put his hand into his jacket pocket and pulled out an already buttered roll. He usually kept one handy.

He began his food ritual by singing mockingly at the snack.

> *'I'm gonna eat you little fishie . . .*
> *I'm gonna eat you little fishie . . .*
> *I'm gonna eat you little fishie . . .*
> *'Cause I like eating fish.'*

To give the fish a fighting chance, he stood with his back to them. Then in a single movement he swivelled round, flicked one of the fish out of the tank with the back of his hand, and caught it in the bread roll.

'Too *slow*, little fishie,' he chided his goldfish sandwich. 'Too slow for *this* Cat.'

He raised the squirming roll to his mouth and started to bite down through the bread.

'Noooooooo!' screamed Lister.

The Cat half turned and saw Lister flying towards him like a berserk caber, his face contorted, his mouth forming a distorted, elliptical 'O'.

'Nooooooooooooooooooooooooooooooooooooooooooooooo!'

The Cat was still smiling, in anticipation of his fishie nibble, when Lister crashed into him. They smacked into the table and tumbled onto the hard, grey deck.

The fish roll skidded across the floor. Lister sprang off the softly-moaning Cat, grabbed the roll, and looked inside.

McCartney was still wriggling away.

Intact.

Unbitten.

'I did it,' Lister said quietly. 'I DID IT!!' he screamed, not so quietly. 'I did it. I got the fish. I'm not going to die!' He did a victory dance, like a Zero-Gee ceiling receiver who'd just scored the winning touch-up.

Rimmer stood in the doorway.

The Cat clambered to his feet. 'My tooth!' He put a handkerchief to his mouth; it came away bloody. 'You're crazy!'

Lister came towards him. 'Let me see . . .'

The Cat raced out of the sleeping quarters. 'My tooth! My tooth!' he was yelling. 'I think I lost my tooth!'

Lister stared at the floor, at the small piece of white enamel that was lying under the chair taunting him. A one-toothed grin.

'Well,' Rimmer's smirk was as big as Yankee Stadium, 'allow me to be the very first to offer my deepest commiser-ations.'

ELEVEN

Lister spun the cap off the bottle of Glen Fujiyama, Japan's finest malt whisky, and poured a generous measure into a pint mug. Rimmer lay on his bunk, whistling pleasantly, his hologramatic eyes a-twinkle. Every opportunity he got, he tried to catch Lister's eye and wink at him cheerily.

Lister took a gulp of whisky. 'You're loving this, aren't you?'

'Oh, you're not still going on about your impending death, are you? For heaven's sake,' fake Scouse accent: 'change der record. Flip der channel. Death isn't der handicap it once was. For smeg's sake, cheeer up.'

'You are, aren't you? You're loving it.'

'Holly – I'd like to send an internal memo. Black border. Begins: "To Dave Lister. Condolences on your imminent death."' Rimmer half closed his eyes. 'What's that poem? Ah, yes . . .

> *Now, weary traveller,*
> *Rest your head,*
> *For, just like me,*
> *You'll soon be dead.'*

'You're really sick, you know that?'

'Come o-o-o-on, –' Rimmer made the 'on' last three full seconds – 'it's all you ever talk about. Frankly, Lister, it's very *booooring*.'

'You are, you're loving it.'

'You're ob*sessed.*'

'You realize when I die, you're going to be on your own.'

'Can't wait.'

'I thought you didn't want that. I thought that's what you were bleating on about before.'

'No, what got me down before wasn't being on my own. It was the idea that you were doing so much better than me. Staying young, and being alive; it was all too much to take. Now, me old buckeroo, the calliper's on the other foot.'

Lister gave up trying to argue. It was just adding to Rimmer's pleasure.

'I remember my grandmother used to say: "There's always some good in every situation."'

'Absolutely, absolutely,' agreed Rimmer; 'and looking on the bright side in this particular situation, you *are* about to do the largest splits you've ever done in your life.'

'So, I get blown up, right?'

'Bits of you do. What's that thing – I think it's part of your digestive system – the long purply thing with knobbly bits? You only ever see them hanging in Turkish butcher shops. Well, whatever it is, that fair flies across the Navicomp Chamber. It was like a sort of wobbly boomerang.'

'Smeg off!'

'Temper.'

'I don't want to die.'

'Neither did I.'

'But it's not fair. There's so much I haven't done.'

Lister started to think about all the things he hadn't done. For some reason one of the first things that came to his mind was the fact that he'd never had a king prawn biriani. Whenever he'd seen it on the menu, he'd always played safe and ordered chicken or lamb. Now he never would have a king prawn biriani.

And books. There were so many he'd meant to read, but hadn't found the time.

'I've never read . . . I've never read . . .' Actually, when he thought about it, he realized he'd never read *any* book. It wasn't that he didn't *like* literature, it was just that generally he waited for the film to come out.

And a family. He'd always assumed one day he'd have a family. A *real* family, not an adopted one. A *real* one. And he'd always wanted to spend a lot of time doing the thing you had to do if you wanted to get a family. He hadn't done nearly enough of that. Not nearly enough. A lot, but not nearly enough.

He was dimly aware that Rimmer was speaking, and Lister grunted occasionally to give the impression he was listening. But he wasn't. He was remembering his old job, back on Earth. His old job parking shopping trolleys at Sainsbury's megamarket, built on the site of the old Anglican cathedral.

One time the manager had caught him asleep in the warehouse. He'd constructed a little bed out of bags of salt, hidden from view behind a wall of canned pilchards. The manager had two GCSEs, a company car and a trainee moustache. He'd lectured Lister for an hour about how, if he applied himself, within five years he could be a manager himself, with a company car – and, presumably, a trainee moustache. On the other hand, the trainee moustache warned him, if he didn't apply himself he'd be parking shopping trolleys for the rest of his natural.

Lister, who knew he was no genius, also knew for absolute certain he was one hundred and forty-seven times smarter than the manager. Nonetheless, he'd found this pep-talk extraordinarily disturbing. He knew he didn't want to spend all his life parking shopping trolleys, and equally he couldn't get excited about becoming stock control manager at Sainsbury's Megastore, Hope Street, Liverpool.

The manager took him by the lapels and shook him. He told Lister he had to make the grade and become an SCM, or his life would 'never amount to *shit*.'

And now, as he sat there knowing he'd probably only got a few hours to live, it occurred to him for the first time ever that the pompous goit with the trainee moustache would probably turn out to be right. And that hurt. That really hurt.

And that was how he spent most of the evening. Tugging at the whisky bottle, reviewing his crummy life. And it wasn't the mistakes he made that haunted him, it was the mistakes he hadn't got *round* to making. He flicked through the catalogue of missed opportunities and unfulfilled promises. He thought about the magnificently unlikely string of coincidences which had brought him into being. The Big Bang; the universe; life on Earth; mankind; the zillions-to-one chance of the particular egg and sperm combination which created him; it had all happened. And what had he done with this incredible good fortune? He'd treated Time like it was urine, and pissed it all away into a big empty pot.

But no, it wasn't true: he'd had triumphs, a little voice from the whisky bottle was telling him. He'd been at the Superdome that night in London when the Jets played the Berlin Bandits in the European divisional play-offs, when Jim Bexley Speed, the greatest player ever to wear the Roof Attack jersey, had the greatest game of his great career. He'd seen that famous second score when Speed had gone round nine men, leaving the commentators totally speechless, for the first time in history for fully nine seconds. That was a triumph. Just being there. He was alive and *there* that night. How many men could say that?

Then there was that time at the Indiana Takeaway in St John's Precinct when he'd tasted his first shami kebab, and become hopelessly and irrevocably hooked on this Indian hors d'oeuvre. True, he'd dedicated a good deal of the rest of his life searching for another truly perfect shami kebab. And, true, he'd never found one. But at least he'd tasted *one*. One food-of-the-gods, perfect shami kebab. How many men could say that?

And then there was K.K. True, they'd only dated for five weeks. And the last week had been a bit sour. But four weeks of Kristine Kochanski being madly in love with him. Kristine Kochanski, who was so beautiful she could probably have got a job on the perfume counter at *Lewis's*! And she'd fallen in love with *him*! For four weeks! Four whole weeks. How many men could say that? Not that many, probably.

And that night in the Aigburth Arms when he played pool. That night when, for some unknown reason, everything he tried came off. The Goddess of Bar Room Pool looked down from the heavens and blessed his cue. Every shot *tnuk*! Straight in the back of the pocket. They couldn't get him off the table. He was unbeatable. Three and a half hours. Seventeen consecutive wins. He became a legend. He never played pool again, because he knew he wasn't that good. But that night in the Aigburth Arms he became a *legend*. A legend at the Aigburth Arms. How many men could say that?

The whisky bottle clanked emptily against the rim of his glass. He'd drunk half a bottle of whisky in two hours. How many men could say that?

He was drunk. How many men could say that?

He fell asleep in the chair. How many men could say that?

At three in the morning he was woken up by Holly.

'Emergency. There's an emergency going on. It's still going on, and it's an emergency.'

Rimmer sat up in bed, his hologramatic hair pointing stupidly in every compass direction. 'What is it?'

'The navicomp's crashed. It can't cope with the influx of data at light speed. We've got to hook it up to the Drive computer and make a bypass.'

Lister slung his legs over the bunk. 'The navicomp? The navicomp in the Navicomp Chamber?'

'If we don't fix it, the ship will blow up in about fifteen minutes and twenty-three seconds.'

Lister jumped down to the floor. 'This is it, then.'

Rimmer looked at him. 'Don't go.'

'What d'you mean "Don't go"? You said yourself I can't avoid it. Let's get it over with. What was I wearing?'

'Your leather deerstalker, and that grey T-shirt.'

Lister pulled on his deerstalker with deliberate precision. Then he walked across to the washbasin and lifted the metal towel rail off its support. 'Let's go.'

'What's that for?'

Lister patted the towel rail against his left palm. 'I'm going out like I came in – screaming and kicking.'

'You can't whack Death on the head.'

'If he comes near me, I'll rip his tits off.'

Then he was gone.

TWELVE

The Navicomp Chamber was fogged with acrid smoke from the melted insulating wires, and a thick cable swung from the ceiling, jumping and sparking like a dying electric python. A manic high-pitched screeching from the wounded navigation computer rose and fell as around the perimeter of the chamber monitor screens popped and shattered one by one.

Lister, his eyes streaming, fumbled for the bypass unit strapped to the wall and, following Holly's shouted instructions, dragged it across the broken glass and hooked it up to the main terminal.

He opened the bypass casing. Inside were twelve switches.

'Start at the one numbered twelve,' Holly was yelling, 'and leave a one second gap between each switch.'

He closed his eyes and rested his finger on the twelfth switch.

He flicked it down.

The pitch of the wailing navicomp increased by an octave. A green light flickered on beside the number twelve.

He moved his finger across to the eleventh switch.

Click.

Eeeeeeeeee. Another octave higher.

A green light.

The tenth switch.

Click.

The console monitor above Lister's head exploded, and vomited shards of glass into the smoke.

Another green light.

The switch numbered nine.

Another green light.

Eight.

Then seven.

And that was half way.

Number six.

Click.

A red light.

'Turn it off,' Holly said. 'Turn it off before . . .'

Lister flicked it off, waited, and flicked it back on.

Eeeeeeeeeeeeeee.

Green.

Five to go.

A maximum of five seconds before his purple knobbly thing was destined to fly across the room.

Click.

Click.

Click.

Just two left. Two little switches.

Lister wanted it to happen now. The penultimate switch. He didn't want to have to flick on the last one *knowing*. Knowing it would be the one to kill him. He wanted to have that slight element of surprise. But he was disappointed.

Click.

Green light.

E E E E E *EEEEEEEEEEE*.

The pitch of the screeching navicomp was now so high it was almost beyond his hearing threshold. Hardly a noise – more a feeling. A pointed squeal, a maniac sawing away at the top of his skull. Black smoke thrust its arm down his throat and started to yank out his lungs.

Lister stared at the last switch.

He rested his finger on it and felt its smoothness.

Then he screamed.

He screamed and pressed it.

And nothing.

Just silence.

Then a red light, that flickered to green, then back to red.

And then steady, steady green.

GREEN.

There was a huge BOOM!

Followed by a second huge BOOM!

And a third.

And Lister realized it was his heartbeat.

He sucked deeply at the foul, smoke-laden air. It tasted good.

And for the second time in twenty-four hours he did the touch-up shuffle. His feet rooted to the spot, he swayed from his waist and moved his arms in counter-motion.

He was alive.

THIRTEEN

The *Red Dwarf* Central Line tube hissed to a halt, and Lister danced out onto the platform. He had a sudden urge for chocolate – white milk chocolate, which he hadn't had since he was a kid – so he slipped a fifty pennycent bit into the machine and tugged on the drawer, but the drawer was stuck. For some reason this filled him with delight. The drawers were always stuck on station platform chocolate machines. Some things don't change. He laughed too much, then jumped on the escalator and leapt three steps at a time to catch up with Rimmer.

They stood on the escalator. Every advert they passed, Lister sang the advertising jingle.

'I don't know why you're so chirpy.'

'I'm alive!'

'But it's going to happen: I saw it happen. It just hasn't happened when we thought it would happen.'

'Who cares? The point is: it hasn't happened.'

'Correction: it has happened. It just hasn't happened yet.'

'Don't let's get into that again.'

'Lister – I saw it. I saw you die. It was you. I'm sure it was you.'

'What about the photograph? The two babies? That hasn't happened yet. Maybe none of it's going to happen.'

'It's going to happen.'

'It's really browning you off, isn't it, that I haven't died yet?'

The escalator pushed them off at the top. Lister leapt over the turnstile barrier, and Rimmer walked through it.

'No, it's not that. It's just your dunderheaded refusal to accept the pointless cruelty of existence. That's what gets my goat.'

Lister shook his head sadly.

When they walked into the sleeping quarters an old man was lying on Lister's bunk.

When he smiled his age lines crinkled like wrapping paper. He raised his robotic left arm. The hand was a metallic prosthesis, but the little finger had been customized so its top joint was a bottle opener. He used it to flick open a bottle of self-heating saké, and took a healthy swig. His white hair was plaited into three-foot long locks, and his right eye was missing. In its place was a telephoto lens, which zoomed and clicked, and focused in unison with his good eye.

And it was quite clear the old man was Lister.

He looked towards the door, but didn't appear to see them.

The watch on the future echo's good right arm emitted a series of squeaks. He turned it off and smiled. Lister made out a curious tattoo on his future self's forearm. It appeared to be burned into the flesh; some kind of formula. It was fading, but it looked like 'U = BIL'. Lister was craning closer to read it when the old man spoke.

'So, you're here,' he said. Lister's voice, but with a slight quaver. 'I can't see you, and I can't hear you, but I know you're here. Rimmer, you're going to say it's impossible.'

'It is impossible,' said Rimmer, 'I saw you die.'

The old man looked, more or less, in Lister's direction. 'Hello, Dave. This is me, I mean, you. I mean, I am you. I mean, I am you as an old man. I know you're here, because when I was your age I saw me at my age telling you at your age what I'm about to tell you. And you've got to tell you, too, when you get to be me.'

'Well,' said Rimmer, 'thank heavens you've still got all your marbles.'

'The person you saw die, Rimmer, was Bexley's son.'

Rimmer frowned. 'Who's Bexley?'

'I was always going to call my second son Bexley,' said Lister, 'after Jim Bexley Speed.'

'Dave – it wasn't you that Rimmer saw in the Navicomp Chamber, it was Bexley's boy. It was your grandson.'

Lister sat heavily into a chair. It was too much to take in. He wasn't going to die in the navicomp accident. He was going to have a son, who was also going to have a son. And so his son's son would die.

'You have two sons,' the old Lister was saying, 'and six grandchildren.'

'But one of them dies.'

'Everyone dies,' said the old Lister. 'You're born, you die. The bit in between is called "Life". And you have all those times together still to come. Enjoy.' He smiled.

The old man's watch went off again. 'I haven't got much time. Get your camera and go to the medical unit.'

'What's at the medical unit?' Lister fumbled in his locker for his camera.

Lister's older self began to grow translucent.

'What about me?' Rimmer walked up to the bunk. 'What happens to me?'

'He can't hear us, Rimmer – he's from the future.'

'Ah, but if I ask you what happens to me now you'll remember it, and when you get to be *him* you'll be able to tell me.'

'Brutal.' Lister grabbed the camera from his vacuum storage trunk and raced out.

'Don't waste time. Run,' the old Lister called after him.

'What happens to me, Old Man? Do I become an officer? Do I ever get a body again? Do we get back to Earth?'

The old man took another swig of saké and stared,

unseeing, through Rimmer's imploring face.

'Oh, Rimmer,' he said suddenly, 'you wanted to know what happened to you.'

'Yes! What happened to me?'

'Come close,' the old Lister beckoned; 'Come close. Closer.'

Rimmer inclined his ear to the old man's mouth.

'You wanted to know your future?'

'Yes please,' Rimmer whispered reverently, and stood on tip-toe so his ear hovered barely millimetres from the future echo's mouth.

The old Lister breathed in deeply, then belched loudly into Rimmer's ear.

He was still laughing when he vanished.

Rimmer caught up with Lister just outside the medical unit. Lister was hastily fitting an instafilm into the camera.

A jolt rocked the ship, and Lister went crashing against a wall, dropping the film. 'Smegging hell.' He picked it up and fumbled it into the camera. 'Smeg!' It was upside down.

Holly flicked up on the wall monitor.

'Deceleration achieved! We're slowing down, dudes. We'll be below light speed in thirty-five seconds precisely.'

'What's going to happen now? Are we going to see my funeral or something?'

'No – we're *de*celerating now,' said Holly. 'The faster we were going, the more into the future the future echoes were. But since we've just started slowing down, the future echoes should get nearer to the present.'

A baby started crying.

Then another baby started crying.

Standing in the doorway of the medical unit was another Lister – more or less the same age Lister was now. He was wearing a white surgical gown. And in his arms were two babies wrapped in silver thermal blankets.

'I can't see you, and all that guff,' Lister's future echo said, 'but I'd like you to meet your twin sons. This is Jim, and this is Bexley.'

Lister brought them into focus in the viewfinder, and rested his finger on the camera trigger.

'Say "cheese", boys.' The future echo struck a pose and grinned.

The two babies wailed louder than ever.

Click.

The future echoes faded away.

The camera ejected the qik-pik, and an image of Lister holding two babies in silver blankets slowly coloured into focus.

Lister turned, and started to walk back to the sleeping quarters. Rimmer followed him. 'How are you supposed to get two babies when we don't have a woman on board?'

'I dunno,' Lister grinned, 'but it's going to be a lot of fun finding out.'

FOURTEEN

Captain Yvette Richards ran her fingers through the bristles of her crew cut, and craned forward to look at the spectrascope of the sun they were approaching. It was perfect. She let out a Texan yelp.

'We *got* it!'

Flight Co-ordinator Elaine Schuman leaned over her shoulder and peered at the console. 'It's a supergiant?'

'You betcha!' said Richards, and yelped again.

'Time to celebrate,' said Schuman.

Kryten, the service mechanoid, handed round styrofoam cups of dehydrated champagne, and topped them up with water.

The eight-woman, two-man crew yelped and cheered and partied, while Kryten handed round more champagne and irradiated caviare niblets, which he'd been saving specially.

It had taken the crew of *Nova 5* six months to find a blue supergiant – a star teetering on the edge of its final phase in the right quadrant of the right galaxy. Another month, and they would have ruined the whole campaign. They certainly felt they had good reason to celebrate.

Sipping her champagne Kirsty Fantozi, the star demolition engineer, started programming the nebulon missile. It had to explode at just the right moment to trigger off the reaction in the star's core which would push it into supernova stage. A star in supernova would light up the entire galaxy for over a month, giving off more energy than the Earth's sun could in ten billion years. It would be a hell of a bang.

One undetected bug in Fantozi's programming could ruin everything. Not only did she have to push the star into supernova, she had to time it so the light from the explosion would reach Earth at exactly the right moment. The right moment was the same moment as the light from the other one hundred and twenty-seven supergiants, which were also being induced into supernovae, reached Earth.

For anyone living on Earth the result would be mind-fizzlingly spectacular. One hundred and twenty-eight stars would appear to go supernova simultaneously, burning with such ferocity they would be visible even in daylight.

And the hundred and twenty-eight supernovae would spell out a message.

And this would be the message:

'COKE ADDS LIFE!'

For five whole weeks, wherever you were on Earth, the huge tattoo would be branded across the day and night skies.

Honeymooners in Hawaii would stand on the peak of Mauna Kea, gazing at sunsets stamped with the slogan. Commuters in London, stuck in traffic jams, would peer through the grey drizzle and gape at the Cola constellation. The few primitive tribes still untouched by civilization in the jungles of South America would look up at the heavens, and certainly not think about drinking Pepsi.

The cost of this single, three-word ad in star writing across the universe would amount to the entire military budget of the USA for the whole of history.

So, ridiculous though it was, it was still a marginally more sensible way of blowing trillions of dollarpounds.

And, the Coke executives were assured by the advertising

executives at Saachi, Saachi, Saachi, Saachi, Saachi and Saachi, it would put an end to the Cola war forever. Guaranteed. Pepsi would be *buried*.

OK, it wasn't wonderful, ecologically speaking. OK, it involved the destruction of a hundred and twenty-eight stars, which otherwise would have lasted another twenty-five million years or so. OK, when the stars exploded they would gobble up three or four planets in each of their solar systems. And, OK, the resulting radiation would last long past the lifetime of our own planet.

But it sure as hell would sell a lot of cans of a certain fizzy drink.

Fantozi finished the program and fired the nebulon missile off into the heart of the star. She finished her styrofoam cup of champagne and flicked on her intercom.

'Let's turn this son-of-a-goit around and go home.'

The nose cone of *Nova 5* slowly swung around to begin the jag back to Earth.

The seven crew members who were in stasis didn't survive the crash.

As the ship bellied onto the cratered surface of the ice-clad moon, it caught the edge of a jagged precipice which ripped open the port side like a key on a sardine can, and the stasisees spewed out into the deadly methane atmosphere.

Captain Richards, who'd taken the first three-month watch along with Schuman and Fantozi, had been playing solo squash when Kryten had dropped in to the leisure suite to inform her politely that the ship's steering system had gone all cockamamie, and the computer had gone doo-lally.

She'd raced up to the Drive Room to find chaos. The computer was reciting fifteenth-century French poetry, and the steering system was on fire.

'What in hell is happening?'

'*Étoilette, je te vois . . .*' the computer said soothingly.

Kryten sprayed the steering system with a portable ex-tinguisher. 'I don't understand what's going on, Miss Yvette.'

'Schuman! Fantozi!' Richards barked into the intercom. 'Get in here – we're in *deep* smeg!'

'It's a complete mystery,' said Kryten.

'*Que la lune trait à soi . . .*'

'One minute he was fine,' Kryten shook his head, 'the next he was acting like this.'

Richards tore at the panel housing to engage the back-up computer.

'*Nicolette est avec toi . . .*'

'I mean, if I'd known he was going to go mad on us, I wouldn't have bothered cleaning him.'

'Say *what*, Kryten?'

'I mean, what is the point of treating him to a complete spring-clean, polishing all his bits and bobs with beeswax, and scrubbing his terminals with soapy water, if he's going to go all peculiar?'

'You *cleaned* the computer?'

'What? Can't you tell? He's absolutely sparkling. Just look inside.'

Richards peered into the computer's circuit board casing. Foaming, soapy water bubbled and smoked beneath the gleaming, newly-polished innards.

'*M'amiette a le blond poil,*' the computer gurgled, and blew soap bubbles out of its voice simulation unit.

'Kryten – did you clean the back-up computer too?'

Kryten look away modestly.

'Did you, Kryten?'

'Please, Miss Yvette – I don't want thanks.'

'Did you?' She grabbed him roughly by his shoulders.

'The only thanks I need is knowing that you appreciate a job well done.' His lipless mouth twisted into a plastic grin.

Schuman burst into the Drive Room, wearing a towel, rat-tails of wet hair bouncing behind her.

'What's happening?'

Fantozi raced past her and up to the fizzling flight console. Her eyes darted over the digital read-outs. She typed quickly on the old-fashioned five-button keyboard.

'There's no way in!' She tried again. 'We can't get manual – the flight console won't let us in!'

'Well, it should be working one hundred and ten per cent,' Kryten said; 'it's even cleaner than the computers.'

Nova 5 dug a three and a half mile smoking furrow like a giant, twisted grin in the icy surface of the moon, and finally came to rest in two separate pieces at the bottom of a mountain range. The red-hot metal of the hull screamed and hissed, warped and twisted in the cruel suddenness of its icy bath. Gradually it stopped protesting, and with a sigh surrendered to its final resting place.

Silence.

Kryten looked down at his legs. They were thirty feet away, at the other end of the Drive Room. *Nova 5* tilted like a dry-ski slope. He dragged his torso down the incline, over to the body of Yvette Richards. Blood pumped from a gash in her thigh, and her leg was twitching involuntarily. She was breathing.

Just.

Kryten looked down at the mess of wires that were hanging out of the end of his torso, located one he didn't need very much, yanked it out, and tied it in a tourniquet round the top of her thigh.

Richards' eyes blinked open. 'Is everyone OK?'

Fantozi was groaning under a pile of debris. Kryten hauled his half-body to the mound of twisted metal, and started pulling her out. Both her legs were broken. Kryten made rudimentary splints out of his hip rods, and bound them with wires torn from his midriff.

'Thanks, Kryten.' Her mouth split into a dry smile, then she passed out.

Schuman crawled in from the corridor, her ankle twisted

almost backwards, with cuts on her face and hands. 'Hey, Richards,' she grinned, 'nice landing. Remind me never to lend you my car.'

Kryten lugged what was left of himself over to Schuman and, without warning, snapped her twisted ankle back into place. She screamed and punched him in the head.

'We've lost the others' – Richards was looking at the security cameras – 'and half the ship. We've still got the stores and the medical unit. And, since we're all still breathing, we can assume the atmosphere generator is still operational and the crash seal held. I guess Kryten hadn't gotten round to cleaning it yet.'

'We'd better get you all down to the medical unit,' said Kryten. 'Excuse me, Miss Elaine: would you be so kind as to pass me my legs?'

FIFTEEN

Holly was lost.

When he'd finally managed to wrestle *Red Dwarf* down to below light speed, he'd found a small electric-blue moon with a suitable gravity, plunged into its orbit and performed the 180° slingshot manoeuvre needed to turn the ship around.

But now he was lost.

The thing about being in Deep Space is the universe looks exactly the same from wherever you are. It's a sort of gigantic version of the Barbican Centre. And although they were now *supposed* to be on a course heading back for Earth, Holly wasn't totally one hundred per cent convinced his calculations were absolutely, right-on-the-button correct.

There are two ways to cope when you're lost: the first way you get out a map, discover where you are, work out where you want to go, and plot out a route accordingly. The second method was the method Holly was using. Basically, you keep on going, hoping that sooner or later you'll come across a familiar landmark, and muddle through from there.

So far nothing had looked very familiar. Occasionally he spotted a constellation he thought they may have passed before, but he couldn't swear to it; and every so often they passed the odd multi-ringed gas giant with a red spot at the pole, but, frankly, multi-ringed gas giants with red spots at their poles were ten a penny.

On his way out of the solar system, all those years ago, he'd started to compile what he hoped would be the definitive

A to Z of the universe, with galaxies, planets, star systems, street names and everything. But he'd fallen behind in the last couple of millennia, and had lost heart in the whole project.

It was the same with his diary. Each year he began to log the events of the voyage in eloquent detail. But every year, by January the thirteenth, he'd generally forgotten to keep it up, and the rest of the diary just comprised a few important birthdays: his creator's, his own, Netta Muskett's and Joe Klumpp's. And the only reason he included Joe Klumpp's was to remind himself not to send him a card, because he'd written *Zero Gee Football – It's A Funny Old Game*.

So, until he spotted a star or a planet he recognized, Holly amused himself by devising a system totally to revolutionize music.

He decided to decimalize it.

Instead of the octave, it became the decative. He invented two new notes: 'H' and 'J'.

Holly practised his new scale; 'Doh, ray, me, fah, soh, lah, woh, boh, ti, doh.' It sounded good. He tried it in reverse.

'Doh, ti, boh, woh, lah, soh, fah, me, ray, doh.'

It would be a whole new sound: Hol Rock.

All the instruments would have to be extra large to in-corporate the two new notes. Triangles, with four sides. Piano keyboards the length of zebra crossings. The only drawback, as far as Holly could see, was that women would have to be banned from playing the cello unless they had birthing stirrups, or elected to play it side-saddle.

This exercise in restructuring the eight-note musical scale helped keep his mind off a number of major perturbations. One of these was that they were running worryingly low of a number of major supplies which had been consumed by Catkind during Lister's stay in stasis.

Checking the supply list was a bit like opening a bank statement. Sometimes, when you're feeling good and things are going well, you can *take* the news, even though you know it's going to be hideous. Other times, most of the time, that bank statement can stay unopened for *weeks*. The ranks of figures lurk inside the missive like warped hobgoblins; evil, deranged, waiting to leap out and suck out your life force. Pandora's box in an envelope.

That's pretty much how Holly felt about the ship's inventory. The last time he'd mustered enough courage to take a peek, he'd discovered some goose-pimpling shortages. Although they had enough food to last fifty thousand years, they'd completely run out of Shake'n'Vac. They had little fruit, few green vegetables, very little yeast, and only one After Eight mint, which he was sure no one would eat because they'd all be too polite to take it.

So, to take his mind off the problem, Holly begain singing his first decative composition, *Quartet for nine players in H sharp minor*. He'd just reached the solo for trombone player with three lungs when the incoming message reached the ship's scanning system.

Since Lister realized he couldn't possibly go into stasis, on the grounds that the future echoes of himself had told him that he didn't, he decided he wouldn't, and instead he'd tried to make the best of a difficult situation. While he waited for the babies to show up, whenever and however that was, he elected to have some fun.

He'd found a jet-powered space bike in the docking bay, and was overhauling it with a view to going on a joy ride through an asteroid belt.

With a rag soaked in white spirit, he sat on his bunk methodically cleaning the greasy machine parts which were scattered all over his duvet, while Rimmer paced up and down the metal-grilled floor of the sleeping quarters.

'*Mi esperas ke kiam vi venos la vetero estos milda,*' said the language instructor on the vid-screen, and left a pause for the translation.

Rimmer paced.

'Errm . . . uhhhh . . . uhmmmm . . . Wait a minute . . . I know this . . . Ooooh . . . hang on . . . don't tell me . . . Urrrh . . .'

Without looking up from the jet manifold he was fervently greasing, Lister chimed: 'I hope when you come the weather will be clement.'

'I hope when you come the weather will be clement,' the woman on the vid-disc concurred.

'Don't tell me. I would have got that.'

'Bonvolu direkti min al kvinsela hotelo?' the recorded instructor prompted.

'Ahhh, yes . . . this is one from last time . . . I remember this . . . Ooooh . . .'

Lister took the screwdriver out of his mouth. 'Please could you direct me to a five-star hotel?'

'Wrong, actually. Totally, completely and utterly, totally wrong.'

'Please could you direct me,' the instructor said, 'to a five-star hotel?'

'Lister – would you please shut up?'

'I'm just helping you.'

'I don't need any help.'

Rimmer had decided to put his demise behind him, and vowed to make his death as rich and fulfilling as was humanly possible. And so, he had taken up again his Esperanto language studies.

Although technically Esperanto wasn't an official requirement for promotion, officers were generally expected to be reasonably fluent in the international language.

'La mango estis bonega! Dlej korajn gratulonjn al la kuiristo.'

Rimmer snapped his fingers. 'I would like to purchase the orange inflatable beach ball, and that small bucket and spade.'

'That meal was splendid!' the woman translated. 'My heartiest congratulations to the chef.'

Rimmer squeaked. 'Is it??' He asked the vid to pause.

'You've been studying Esperanto for eight years, Rimmer. How come you're so hopeless?'

'Oh, really? And how many books have you read in your entire life? The same number as Woolfie Sprogg, The Plasticine Dog Zero.'

'I've read books.' lied Lister.

'We're not talking about books where the main character is a dog called "Ben". Not books with five cardboard pages, three words a page, and a guarantee on the back which says: 'This book is waterproof and chewable.'

Lister sprayed some WD40 onto a spark plug. 'I went to art college.'

'You?'

'Yeah.'

'How did *you* get into art college?'

'Usual way. The usual, normal, usual way you get into art college. Failed all my exams and applied. They snapped me up.'

'Did you get a degree?' Rimmer's pulse quickened: Please *God*, don't let him have a degree!

'Nah. Dropped out. Wasn't there long.'

'How long?'

Lister looked up and tried to work it out. 'Ninety-seven minutes. I thought it'd be a good skive, but I took one look at the timetable and checked *out*. It was ridiculous. I had lectures first thing in the middle of the afternoon. Half past two every day. Who's together by then? You can still taste the toothpaste.'

He shuddered at the memory and went back to cleaning his bike parts.

Rimmer shook his head and re-started the language tape. '*La menuo aspektas bonege – mi provos la kokidaĵon.*'

'Ah, now this one I *do* know . . .'

Holly's image replaced the woman's on the monitor, and smoothly delivered the correct reply.

'The menu looks excellent; I'll try the chicken.'

'Holly, as the Esperantinos would say,' Rimmer made the Ionian sign for 'Smeg off' with his two thumbs: '"*Bonvolu alsendi la pordiston — lausajne estas rano en mia bideo*", and I think we all know what that means.'

'Yes,' said Holly, 'it means: "Could you send up the Hall Porter — there appears to be a frog in my bidet?"'

'Does it?' Rimmer was genuinely surprised. 'Well, what's that one: "Your father was a baboon's rump, and your mother spent most of her life with her pants round her ankles, up against walls with astros"?'

'Look,' said Holly, suddenly remembering why he was there, 'you'd better come down to the Communications suite. We're getting an SOS call.'

SIXTEEN

Lister grabbed a cup of tea from the dispensing machine, they collected the Cat and caught the Xpress lift down to Comm: level 3.

'Aliens,' said Rimmer, his eyes gleaming with the possibilities; 'it's aliens.'

Rimmer believed passionately in the existence of aliens. He was convinced that, one day, *Red Dwarf* would encounter an alien culture with a technology so far in advance of mankind's they would be able to provide him with a new body. A new start.

'It's aliens,' he repeated; 'I know it.'

'Your explanation for anything slightly odd is aliens,' said Lister. 'You lose your keys, it's aliens. A picture falls off the wall, it's aliens. That time we used up a whole bog roll in a day, you thought *that* was aliens.'

'Well, we didn't use it all.' Rimmer shot him his best Rod Serling *Twilight Zone* look. 'Who did?'

'*Aliens* used up our bog roll?'

'Just because they're aliens, it doesn't mean they don't have to visit the smallest room. Only, they probably do something weird and alienesque; like it comes out of the top of their heads, or something.'

Lister sipped his tea and mulled the concept over. 'Well.' he concluded, 'I wouldn't like to get stuck behind one in a cinema.'

★

A huge screen a hundred metres square hung down over the communication consoles, and four speakers, each the size of a fairly roomy Kensington bedsit, throbbed gently as Holly tried to establish contact by repeating a series of standard international distress responses over and over again in a variety of different languages.

'It's from an American ship, private charter, called *Nova 5*,' said Holly tonelessly. 'They've crash-landed. I'm trying to get them on optical.'

'Oh.' Rimmer sighed with disappointment. 'So it's not aliens.'

'No. They're from Earth. I hope they've got a few spare odds and sods on board. We're a bit short on a few supplies.'

Lister sipped his tea. 'Like what?'

'Cow's milk,' said Holly. 'We ran out of that yonks ago. Fresh *and* dehydrated.'

'What kind of milk are we using now, then?'

'Emergency back-up supply. We're on the dog's milk.'

Lister froze, the styrofoam cup resting on his lips, the tea half-way down his throat. He swallowed. 'Dog's milk?'

'Nothing wrong with dog's milk. Full of goodness, full of vitamins, full of marrowbone jelly. Lasts longer than any other kind of milk, dog's milk.'

'Why?'

'No bugger'll drink it. Plus, of course, the advantage of dog's milk is: when it's gone off, it tastes exactly the same as when it's fresh.'

Lister dropped his cup into a waste chute. 'Why didn't you tell me, man?'

'What? And put you off your tea?'

'Something's happening!' Rimmer pointed at the Comm screen, which fizzled and buzzed with static.

Slowly an image formed: the flat angular features of a mechanoid face, the head without curves, the mouth without lips.

'Thank goodness, thank goodness. Bless you!' Kryten clapped his hands together. 'We were beginning to despair . . .'

'We?' said the Cat, arching his brow.

'I am the service mechanoid aboard *Nova 5*. We've had a terrible accident. Seven of the crew died on impact; the only survivors are three female officers, who are injured but stable.'

'Female?' The Cat looked at Lister. 'Is that "female" as in "soft and squidgy"?'

'I am transmitting medical details.'

Digitalized pictures of Richards, Schuman and Fantozi flashed up on the screen, followed by reams of medical data.

RICHARDS, Yvette. Age 33. Rank: Captain. Compound fracture, left fibula. Blood type O . . .

FANTOZI, Kirsty. Age 25. Rank: Star Demolition Engineer. Multiple fractures, both legs. Blood type A . . .

SCHUMAN, Elaine. Age 23. Rank: Flight Co-ordinator. Severe fractures, right ankle. Blood type O . . .

The Cat's eyes darted across the significant details. 'Three. All injured and helpless. This is tremendous!'

Rimmer turned from the screen and smoothed down his hair. 'Tell them,' he said, a new tone of authority in his voice, 'Tell them the boys from the *Dwarf* are on their way! Or my name's not Captain A. J. Rimmer, Space Adventurer!'

'Oh, thank you, Captain. Bless you. I'll tell them.'

Kryten shut down transmission.

'Captain?' Lister inclined his head forward and looked up at Rimmer through his eyebrows, as if peering over a pair of imaginary spectacles. 'Space Adventurer?'

'It's good psychology. What am I supposed to say? "Fear not, we're the blokes who used to clean the gunk out of the chicken soup machine? Actually we know smeg-all about space travel, but if you've got a blocked nozzle we're your lads"? That's going to have them oozing with confidence, isn't it?'

'Hey, Head,' the Cat said to Holly, 'how far are we away?'

'Not far. Twenty-eight hours?' he guessed.

'Only twenty-eight hours!' The Cat leapt to his feet. 'I'd better start getting ready! I'm first in the shower room. Waaaaah!' he screamed with delight. 'I'm so excited, all six of my nipples are tingling!'

'Look,' said Lister, 'this is a mission of mercy. We're taking an injured crew urgently needed medical supplies. We're not going down the disco on the pull.'

'Dum dum *dum* dum dum *dum* dum dum . . .'

Disco music thundered out of Lister's eight-speakered portable wax-blaster, which vibrated and slid across the metal surface of the sleeping quarters' table.

'Dum dum *dum* dum dum *dum* dum dum . . .' Lister mimicked the synth-tymp as he glided rhymically over to his metal locker and pulled out his underwear drawer. One sock remained. He tutted, and grooved across to his dirty laundry basket.

'Dum dum *dum* dum . . .'

He pulled out two very hard, very stiff, rather dangerous-looking yellow socks. Holding them at arm's length, he sprayed them liberally with Tiger deodorant, then put them on the table and hit them several times with a small toffee hammer.

'Dum dum *dum* dum dum *dum* . . .'

He moon-walked back to the locker, reverently took out an old brown paper bag, and fished out his lucky-scoring underpants.

They had at one time been blue. Now they were a yellowy-grey with holes in the cheeks, and the elastic hung out of the waist band. He held them in his arms like he was holding the Turin Shroud. These were the underpants he'd happened to be wearing the night he met Susan Warrington. Susan had got him drunk, and taken advantage of his tender years on the ninth hole – par four, dogleg – of Bootle Municipal Golf Course.

He'd worn them again the night Alison Bredbury's dad had to be rushed off to hospital with a heart attack, leaving him alone with Alison, the key to the drinks cabinet and her parents' double bed.

From then they'd achieved in his mind a mystic quality. He'd worn them sparingly, not wanting to use up their magic powers.

Obviously they'd not always been successful. In fact, a lot of the time they hadn't been successful. And slowly the dreadful thought began to occur to him that they might be just a rather ordinary pair of dog-eared Y-fronts, and not some talismanic, spell-kissed, warlock-woven, sorcery-spun article of enchantment. They were just a pair of knickers.

But then . . .

Then he discovered if he wore them backwards . . . all their magical properties returned!

Kristine Kochanski.

For four whole weeks she was madly in love with him. For four whole weeks he'd worn his backward boxers. Not daring to risk an ordinary pair, he'd washed them each night and worn them backwards throughout their relationship.

Naturally she'd asked him why. He told her he had twenty-one pairs of identical briefs, and he always dressed in a hurry. She bought him new pairs, and forced him to wear them. Like a fool, he did. And soon after their relationship had ended.

'Dum dum *dum* dum . . .' He slipped on the sacred shorts, backwards *and* inside-out.

'No prisoners,' he said aloud, and glided over to the ironing board.

He lifted the iron off his best green camouflage pants and

pulled them on. He felt air on his buttock, and when he checked in the mirror he found an iron-shaped hole clean through the right cheek.

'Dum dum *dum* dum dum *dum* . . .'

He rifled through his locker, found the colour he was looking for, and sprayed the exposed buttock with green car touch-up paint.

He looked in the mirror again. From a distance you honestly couldn't tell. True, he smelled like a newly-painted Cortina, but that would fade in time. He slipped on his favourite London Jets T-shirt and stood back to take in the whole picture: the freshly hammered socks, the cleverly inverted underpants, and the neatly sprayed trousers. Hey, he knew it wasn't perfection, but *God*, it was close.

'Oh, you're not on the pull, eh?' Rimmer stood in the doorway wearing a dashing white officer's uniform, complete with banks of gleaming medals, and gold hoops of rank which ran the length of his left arm, which Holly had grudgingly simulated for him.

Look at him! Rimmer thought. *He's really trying. He's wearing all his least smeggy things. That T-shirt with only two curry stains on it – he only wears that on special occasions. Those camouflage pants with the fly buttons missing.*

'You're toffed up to the nines!' he said out loud.

'That's rich, coming from someone who looks like Clive of India.'

'Oh, it's started.' Rimmer dusted some imaginary dust off his gold epaulette. 'I knew it would.'

'What has?'

'The put-downs. It's always the same every time we meet women. Put me down, to make yourself look good.'

'Like when?'

'Remember those two little brunettes from Supplies? And I said I'd once worked in the stores, and they were very interested, and asked me exactly what I used to do there?'

'And I said you were a shelf.'

'Right. Exactly.'

'So? They laughed.'

'Yes! At me. At my expense. Just don't do it, OK? Don't put me down when we meet them.'

'How d'you want me to act then? How d'you want me to behave?'

'Just show a little respect. For a start, don't call me Rimmer.'

'Why not?'

'Because you always hit the RIMM at the beginning. *RIMM*-er. You make it sound like a lavatory disinfectant.'

'Well, what should I call you?'

'I don't know. Something a bit more pally. Arnie? Arn, maybe? Something a bit more . . . I don't know. How about: "Big Man"?'

'Big Man?'

'How about "Chief", then? "The Duke"? "Cap", even. What about "Old Iron Balls"?'

Rimmer could see he wasn't really getting anywhere. 'OK, then,' he tried, 'how about the nickname I had at school?'

'What? Bonehead?'

Impossible! Lister couldn't *possibly* have known his nickname at school was 'Bonehead'. No one knew this. Not even his parents. 'What on Io makes you think my nickname at school was Bonehead?'

'Well, it had to be, didn't it?'

'What?'

'It was a guess.'

'Well, it was a guess, as it turns out, that was completely way off the fairway and into the long grass. The nickname to which I was referring was "Ace".'

'You're nickname was never "Ace". Maybe "Ace-hole".'

'There you go again! Knock, knock, knock. Why can't you build me up instead of always putting me down?'

'For instance?'

'Well, I don't know. Perhaps if the chance occurs, and it comes up naturally in the course of the conversation, you could possibly drop in a mention of the fact that I'm, well . . . very brave.'

'Do what?'

'Don't go crackers. Just, perhaps, when my back's turned, you might steer the dialogue round to the fact that I . . . died, and, well, I was pretty gosh-darn brave about it.'

'You're pretty gosh-darn out of your smegging tree, Rimmer.'

'Or you could bolster up my sexual past. Why don't you just casually hint that I've had tons of women? Would that break your heart, would it? Would that give you lung cancer, to say that?'

Rimmer arched threateningly close to Lister's face, his eyes bulging: 'Just *don't* put me down, OK?'

SEVENTEEN

'Come on, everyone – they're here! They're in orbit! Heavens! There's so much to do.' Kryten rushed down the sloping corridor, pausing only to water a lusciously green plastic pot plant.

Things were going very well. Very well indeed. The girls had been quiet and really most forlorn of late. Being marooned light years from home with scant hope of rescue had been very trying, to say the least. He'd done his best to keep them entertained, to keep their spirits high, but over the last few weeks, he'd felt intuitively that they were losing hope.

Even his Friday night concert parties, usually the highlight of the week, had begun to be greeted with growing apathy. Miss Yvette was especially guilty of this. She hadn't particularly enjoyed them from the beginning, and had told him so.

The concert parties always began in the same way. After baths and supper Kryten would clear the decks while the girls played cards, or read. At nine sharp the lights would be dimmed, and Kryten would tap-dance onto a makeshift stage in the engine-room, singing *I'm a Yankee Doodle Dandy*, juggling two cans of beeswax. And then he'd go into his impressions. His best one was of Parkur, the mechanoid aboard the *Neutron Star*, but none of the girls knew him, so it never went down that well. Then there were the magic tricks. Or, to put it more accurately, the magic *trick*. He would lie in a box and saw himself in half. It wasn't much of a trick because he actually did saw himself in half. And then the evening suffered a slight hiatus while they waited the forty minutes it took for Kryten to reconnect his circuitry.

Then he'd round off the evening with a selection of hits from *The Student Prince*. And then they'd play prize bingo. The prize in the prize bingo was always a can of Jiffy Windo-Kleen. Nobody ever wanted a can of Jiffy Windo-Kleen, so Kryten always got it back and was able to use it as the next week's prize.

In an odd kind of way Kryten was grateful for the accident. His life had taken on a new vitality. He was *needed*. The girls depended on him. His days were full. There was the cooking, the changing of the bandages, the physiotherapy, the concert parties. And, of course, there was the cleaning.

Kryten took almost orgasmic delight in housework. Piles of dirty dishes thrilled him. Mounds of unwashed laundry filled him with rapture. An unmopped floor left him dry-mouthed with lust. He loved cleaning things even more than he loved things being clean. And things being clean sent him into a frenzy of ecstasy.

And at night, when everyone was safely tucked in bed and all the chores were done and there was absolutely nothing left to clean, then, and only then, he'd sink into his favourite chair, cushions aplump, and watch *Androids*.

Androids was a soap opera, aimed at the large mechanoid audience who had huge buying power when it came to household goods. Kryten had all one thousand, nine hundred and seventy-four episodes on disc. He'd seen them all many times, but he still winced when Karstares was killed in the plane crash. He still wept when Roze left Benzen. He still laughed and slapped his metal knee when Hudzen won the mechanoid lottery and hired his human master as a servant. And he always cheered when Mollee took on the android brothels, put the pimps into prison and set the prostidroids free.

Androids, he told himself, was his one vice. That, and the single chocolate he allowed himself each viewing, to conserve supplies. When he watched *Androids* he wasn't just a mechanoid, marooned light years from nowhere, with three demanding dependants and a never-ending schedule of work.

He was somewhere different. Somewhere glamorous. Somewhere else.

He was Hudzen, winning the lottery and hiring a human to serve him. He was Jaysee, swinging the mega-quidbuck deals, dining in the best restaurants, living in his vast penthouse atop the Juno Hilton.

He was someone else.

Kryten rushed down the slope and onto the main service deck, where the girls were breakfasting.

'Come on! They're here!' He clapped his hands.

Richards, Schuman and Fantozi didn't move. They hadn't moved, in fact, for almost three million years.

The three skeletons sat round the table, in freshly-laundered uniforms, and grinned.

'I don't know what's so funny,' said Kryten. 'They'll be here any moment, and there's so much to *do*!' He clucked and shook his head. 'Miss Elaine, honestly: you haven't even made an effort. *Look* at your hair.'

He fussed over to the table, and took out a hairbrush.

'What a mess you look.' He hummed *Stay Young And Beautiful*, and combed her long blonde wig with smooth, gentle strokes. When her hair was just so, he stood back and eyed her critically. He wasn't *quite* satisfied. He took out a lipstick that matched her uniform and touched up her make-up.

'Dazzling. You could go straight on the cover of *Vogue*.'

He shuffled down the table.

'Miss Yvette! You haven't *touched* your soup. It's no wonder you're looking so pasty.' He patted her gingerly on the shoulder. There was a long, slow creaking noise, and the skeleton slumped face down into the bowl of tomato soup. Kryten threw up his hands in horror. 'Eat nicely, Miss Yvette! What *will* that nice Captain Rimmer think if he sees you eating like that?' He hoisted the skeleton back onto the chair, sprayed her with a squirt of Windo-Kleen, and gave her head a quick polish.

'Now then, Miss Kirsty.' He waddled over to the remaining skeleton and looked her up and down: the trendy knee-length boots, the chic, deep red mini-skirt and the peaked velvet cap cocked at a racy angle.

'No,' he beamed, putting the hairbrush away. 'You look absolutely *perfect*!'

EIGHTEEN

The Cat slinked down the docking bay gantry in his gold, hand-stitched flightsuit, carrying a two-feet-high, cone-shaped matching space helmet under his arm.

He climbed up the boarding steps into Blue Midget, where Lister and Rimmer were sitting in the drive seats waiting for him. He jumped into the cramped cabin, struck a pose like King of the Rocket Men, legs splayed, chest puffed out, hand on one hip, and said: 'Put your shades on, guys. You're looking at a nuclear explosion in lurex.' He gleamed a smile at them and fluttered his eyes.

'You're looking good,' said Lister, craning round.

'Looking *good*?? Did I hear the man say, "Looking only *good*??" Buddy, I am a plastic surgeon's *night*mare. Throw away the scalpel; improvements are impossible.'

'A spacesuit,' said Rimmer, 'with cufflinks?'

'Listen,' said the Cat, dusting the console seat before arranging himself on it, 'you've got to guarantee me we don't pass any mirrors. If we do, I'm there for the *day*.'

Lister flicked on the remote link with Holly.

Holly appeared on the screen looking somehow different. Lister scrutinized the image. He couldn't quite work out what it was.

'All right, then, dudes? Everybody set?'

Lister twigged. 'Holly, why are you wearing a toupé?'

Holly was upset. He spent some considerable time corrupting his digital image to give himself a fuller head of hair. 'So it's not undetectable, then? It doesn't blend in naturally and seemlessly with my own natural hair?'

'It looks,' said Lister, 'like you've got a small, furry animal nesting on top of your head.'

'What is wrong with everybody?' Rimmer straightened his cap. 'Three million years without a woman, and you all go crazy.'

He's right, thought Holly, *who am I trying to impress? I'm a computer! How humiliating to have that pointed out by a hologram!* Out of spite he instantly simulated a large and painful boil on the back of Rimmer's neck, and made it start to throb.

Blue Midget, the powerful haulage transporter originally designed to carry ore and silicates to and from the ship, looked strangely graceful as it flickered between the red and blue lights of the twin sun system above the howling icy green wasteland of the moon that had become *Nova 5*'s grave-yard.

Lister peered through the furry dice dangling from the windscreen. 'Nice place for a skiing holiday.'

Rimmer stared unblinkingly at the tracking monitor. 'Nothing yet,' he said helpfully. He slipped his finger down the collar of his shirt where a large boil was really beginning to hurt.

Lister struggled hopelessly with the twelve gear levers. Each provided five gears, making it sixty gears in all, and Lister hadn't yet been in the right one throughout the twenty-minute jag.

The tracking monitor started delivering a series of rapid bleeps.

'We've got it!' Rimmer cried. 'Lat. twenty-seven, four, Long. seventeen, seven.'

Lister looked at him like he was speaking Portuguese.

'Left a bit, and round that glacier.'

'Oh, right.'

★

Lister landed appallingly in forty-seventh gear. Blue Midget stalled, bounced and rocked, before settling to rest with an exhausted sigh. Lister pushed in the button marked 'C'. The caterpillar tracks, telescoped out of their housing, rotated down to the icy emerald surface and hoisted the transporter ten feet above the ground.

'Hey,' said the Cat, impressed, 'You really can drive this thing.'

'Actually,' said Lister, 'I thought that was the cigarette lighter.'

The red-hot wiper blades melted green slush from the windscreen as Blue Midget rose and fell over a series of icy dunes. As they reached the peak of the next range, they saw, in the hollow below, the broken wreck jutting out of the landscape like a child's discarded toy.

The gearbox groaned and rattled as they made their slippery descent down into the crater.

'Yoo-hoo!' the Cat squealed in falsetto, and waved madly out of the port side window.

'Ah, come in, come in.' Kryten ushered them in from the airlock. 'How lovely to meet you,' he said, and bowed deeply.

'Cârmita,' said Rimmer, speaking too loudly. 'What a delightful craft – reminds me of my first command.' He turned and hissed to Lister: 'Call me *Ace.*'

Lister pretended not to understand and walked off down the spotless, newly painted white corridor after Kryten, who was chattering banalities about the weather.

'Green slush again. Tut, tut, tut.'

The Cat flossed his teeth one last time, and followed them.

Kryten, used to the strange tilt, walked speedily down the thin corridor, listing at an odd angle.

He went through a large pear-shaped hatchway, and they followed him across what must have been the ship's Engine-

Room. Even Lister, who knew next to nothing about these things, could tell *Nova 5*'s technology was far in advance of *Red Dwarf*'s. Taking up three-quarters of the room was the strangest piece of machinery Lister had ever seen: it was like a huge series of merry-go-rounds stacked one on top of the other and turned on their sides. Each of these was filled with silver discs joined by thick gold rods, and at the end was what looked like an enormous cannon.

'What's that?' asked Lister.

'It's the ship's Drive,' Kryten replied. 'It's the Duality Jump.'

'What's a Duality Jump?'

'Don't be thick, Lister. Everybody knows what a Duality Jump is,' said Rimmer, lying.

Kryten scurried through the pear-shaped exit, and Lister practically had to sprint out of the engine-room to catch up with them two corridors later.

Suddenly, the Cat swivelled, as they passed a full-length mirror recessed in the wall. His heart pounded, his pulse quickened. He felt silly and giddy. He was in love.

'You're a work of Art, baby,' he crooned softly at his reflection.

Lister turned and shouted: 'Come on!'

'I can't. You're going to have to help me.'

Lister picked up his golden-booted foot and started to yank him down the corridor. Unable to help himself, the Cat hung on to the mirror. His gloved fingers squeaked across the glass surface as Lister pulled him free.

'Thanks, Man,' the Cat said gratefully. 'That was a bad one.'

'I'm so excited,' said Kryten, shuffling along and absently dusting a completely clean fire-extinguisher. 'We all are. The girls can hardly stop themselves from jumping up and down.'

'Ha ha haaa,' brayed Rimmer, falsely. 'Cârmita, Cârmita.'

'Ah!' said Kryten, '*Vi parolas Esperanton, Kapitano Rimmer?*'

'I'm sorry?'

'*Vi parolas Esperanton, Kapitano Rimmer?*'

'Come again?'

'You speak Esperanto, Captain Rimmer?'

'Ah, *oui, oui, oui. Jawol. Si, si.*' Rimmer searched desperately through his memory for the appropriate phrase. Mercifully it came to him. '*Bonvolu alsendi la pordiston laũŝajne estas rano en mia bideo.*'

'A frog?' said Kryten. 'In which bidet?'

'Ha ha haaaaa,' brayed Rimmer, even less convincingly. 'It doesn't matter. I'll deal with in myself.'

Kryten walked round the corner and down the ramp on to the service deck.

'Well, here they are,' he said.

Without looking where Kryten was beckoning, Rimmer bent down on one knee and swept his cap in a smooth arc. 'Cârmita!' he purred.

Lister and the Cat tumbled in behind him.

Their eyes met the hollow sockets of the three grinning skeletons sitting around the table.

There was a very, very long silence.

It was followed by another very, very long silence.

'Well,' said Kryten, a little upset, 'isn't anybody going to say "Hello"?'

'Hi.' said Lister, weakly. 'I'm Dave. This is the Cat. And this here is Ace.'

Rimmer still hadn't closed his mouth from forming the final vowel of Cârmita. Lister leaned over and whispered to him conspiratorially: 'I think that little blonde one's giving you the eye, Cap.'

'Now,' Kryten clapped his hands, 'you all get to know one another, and I'll run off and fetch some tea.' He staggered off up the slope.

'I don't believe this,' said Rimmer, massaging the 'H' on his forehead.

Lister looked at him. 'Be strong, Big Man.'

'Our one contact with intelligent life in over three million years, and he turns out to be an android version of Norman Bates.'

'So, they're a little on the skinny side,' said the Cat, ever hopeful. 'A few hot dinners, and who knows?'

Lister walked up to the table and put his arms around two of the skeletons' shoulders.

'I know this may not be the time or the place to say this, girls, but my mate, Ace here, is incredibly, incredibly brave . . .'

'Smeg off, dogfood face!'

'And he's got tons and tons of girlfriends.'

'I'm warning you, Lister.'

Kryten raced back down the slope, carrying a tray which held several plates of triangular-shaped sandwiches, a pot of steaming tea, and a plate with seven of his precious chocolates on it. As he laid out the cups on the table, he looked up, suddenly aware of the lack of conversation.

'Is there something wrong?' he asked.

'Something wrong??' said Rimmer, aghast. 'They're dead.'

'Who's dead?' asked Kryten, pouring some milk into the cups.

'They're dead,' Rimmer waved at the three skeletons. 'They're all dead.'

'My God!' Kryten stepped back in horror. 'I was only away two minutes!'

'They've been dead for centuries.'

'No!'

'Yes!'

'Are you a doctor?'

'You only have to look at them,' Rimmer whined. 'They've got less meat on them than a chicken nugget!'

'Whuh . . . whuh . . . well, what am I going to do?' Kryten stammered. 'I'm programmed to serve them.'

'Well, the first thing we should do is, you know . . . bury them,' said Lister quietly.

'You're *that* sure they're dead?'

'Yes!' Rimmer shouted.

Kryten waddled over to Richards's leering skeleton. 'What about this one?'

Rimmer sighed. 'Look. There's a very simple test.' He walked up to the head of the table. 'All right,' he said, 'hands up any of you who are alive.'

Kryten looked on anxiously. To his dismay, there was no response. He made frantic signals, coaxing the girls to raise their hands.

'OK?' said Rimmer finally.

Kryten's shoulders buckled, and he dropped limply into a chair, totally defeated.

'I thought they might be . . . but I wouldn't allow myself . . . I didn't want to admit . . . I . . . I'm programmed to serve them . . . It's all I can do . . . I let them down so badly . . . I . . .'

Lister shuffled uncomfortably.

'What am I to do?' Kryten said plaintively. A buzzer went off in Kryten's head. It was his internal alarm clock telling him it was time for Miss Yvette's bath. Automatically he raised himself, and then, remembering, sank back down again. He took a sonic screwdriver from his top pocket, flipped a series of release catches on his neck, removed his head and plonked it down unceremoniously on to the table.

'What are you doing?' said the Cat.

'I'm programmed to serve,' said Kryten's head. 'They're dead. The programme is finished. I'm activating my shut-down disc.'

'Woah!' said Lister. 'Slow down.'

Kryten's hands twisted the right ear off his disembodied head and pressed a latch which flipped open his skull.

'Kryten – listen to me . . .'

Kryten started removing the minute circuit boards from inside his brain, and stacking them neatly on the table.

'Kryten . . .'

He tugged out several batches of interface leads, neatly wrapped them up and placed them tidily beside the rest of his mind.

Finally he located his shut–down programme. 'Sorry about the mess,' he said, and switched himself off.

His eyes rotated back into the plastic of his skull; his body slumped forward in his seat and crashed onto the floor.

NINETEEN

'It's driving me batty. Must you do it here?' Rimmer surveyed the array of android organs spread higgledy-piggledy all over the sleeping quarters. 'What's this on my pillow? It's his eyes!'

'I'm trying to fix him,' said Lister, holding Kryten's nose in one hand and poking a pipe cleaner soaked in white spirit up his nostril with the other.

It had taken them a week to transport the two broken halves of the *Nova 5* back to *Red Dwarf*. They had needed all six of the remaining transporter craft, operating on auto pilot, to wrench the ship free of the centuries-old methane ice, but after five days of maximum thrust the small transporters had finally yanked the wreck clear, and hauled it slowly and precariously up to the orbiting *Red Dwarf*.

The Drive section of *Nova 5* held few surprises – Kryten had meticulously updated the inventory every Tuesday evening for two million years. Most of the food was still vacuum-stored. Lister had been delighted to discover they had twenty-five thousand spicy poppadoms and a hundred and thirty tons of mango chutney; enough, he pointed out at the time, to keep him happy for the best part of a month.

There was, thankfully, nearly two thousand gallons of irradiated cow's milk, and Lister had insisted the dog's milk be flushed out into the vacuum of space, where it had instantly frozen, leaving a huge dog-milk asteroid for some future species to ponder over.

'Why d'you have to keep his bits all over my bunk?'

'So I know where they are.'

'Yes, well, I'm sorry, but I refuse to have somebody else's eyes on my pillow.'

'Look – I'll have him finished by this afternoon.'

'You've been saying that for two months. What's this in my coffee mug? It's a big toe.'

'Rimmer, will you just smeg off and leave me to it?'

'What the smeg do you want to repair him for anyway? He's just a mechanoid. A mechanoid that's gone completely barking mad.'

'I want to find out about that duality drive – I want to know if we can fix it. And . . . I dunno . . . I feel sorry for him.'

'Sorry for him? He's a machine. It's like feeling sorry for a tractor.'

'It's not. He's got a personality.'

'Yes, a personality that should be severely sedated, bound in a metal straightjacket and locked in a rubber room with a stick between his teeth.'

'I think I can fix that.'

'You think it's just like repairing your bike, don't you? Spot of grease, clean all his bits, re-bore his carburettor, and bang! he's as good as new.'

'Same principle.'

'He's got a defect in his artificial intelligence. You'd need a degree in Advanced Mental Engineering from Caltech to set him to rights.'

Lister prodded one of Kryten's circuit boards with a soldering iron. The noseless head fizzed momentarily into life.

'Ah-ha,' it said, in rapid falsetto, 'elephant rain dingblat VietNam.' The eyes on Rimmer's pillow rotated and blinked. 'Telephone sandwich kerplunk armadillo Rumplestiltskin purple.'

'Well,' said Rimmer. 'Once again you've proved me wrong.'

★

HNNNnnnnNNNNNKRHHhhhhhhHHHHHHH
HNNNnnnnNNNNNKRHHhhhhhhhHHHHHH

Rimmer looked at his bunkside clock. 2.34 a.m.

HNNNnnnnNNNNNKRHHhhhhhhhHHHHHH
HNNNnnnnNNNNNKRHHhhhhhhhHHHHHH.

Rimmer clambered down from his bunk and looked over at Lister's sleeping body. He was still holding one of Kryten's circuit boards in one hand, and a sonic screwdriver in the other.

And I'm supposed to keep you sane? he thought. *Who the smeg is supposed to keep ME sane?*

Rimmer closed his eyes and tried to sleep.

HNNNnnnnNNNNNKRHHhhhhhhhHHHHHH
HNNNnnnnNNNNNKRHHhhhhhhhHHHHHH

It was useless. He got Holly to simulate his red, black, white, blue, yellow and orange striped skiing anorak, and decided to check out the salvage operation in the shuttle bay.

Rimmer voice-activated the huge corrugated lead doors of bay 17, which yawned open to reveal the two halves of the wreck of *Nova 5*.

Even though it was the early hours of the morning, the massive salvage operation was in full flow. Rimmer looked down from the gantry at the battalions of skutters who were still unloading supplies from the mainly undamaged front section. Another group of skutters wielding laser torches were still trying to cut their way through the hull of the rear section. Even with the most powerful bazookoid lasers, their progress had been slow – barely two centimetres a day through the metre-thick strontium/agol alloy.

But what really interested Rimmer was the second half of

Nova 5. He'd gone through some of the ship's computer files, and had every good reason to suspect that the 'dead' segment contained something that might very well change his life.

He stood on the gantry, hands in his ski anorak pockets, watching the skutters lasering their way through the hull.

'How long before we're in?' he asked Holly.

'Two, maybe three days.'

There was a noise: the sound of creaking metal buckling and ripping as the huge, arch-shaped door, which the laser torches were cutting into the craft's hide, slowly teetered forward and fell like a medieval drawbridge, crushing all eight skutters.

'Maybe even sooner,' added Holly unconvincingly.

Rimmer raced down the gantry steps and across the steel floor of the hangar, to the newly burned entrance in the stern section of the hulk of *Nova 5*.

He peered into the dusty gloom. Floor lights glowed dimly down the length of the corridor. He summoned two skutters away from their unloading duties and, sending them ahead, stepped inside. The corridor was still warm from the laser torches. Electric cables and dismembered circuitry hung down from the ceiling like dead tubers in a petrified forest.

Rimmer inched his way along the corridor as the skutters' headlights cut swathes through the murky gloom. Most of the doors were open, or hanging off their hinges. There was a sensation, a feeling he couldn't explain, that the ship wasn't dead – that there was something there. Something alive.

Slowly he worked his way around the tortured topography of the first deck, then clambered down the broken spiral staircase, and found himself on the stasis corridor.

Most of the booths had been scooped clean by the scalpel-sharp corner of the glacier in the crash. Three remained. Two of them were punctured and, inside, the once-human occupants had been fossilized into the walls by centuries upon centuries of patient ice.

The third was occupied.

Skeletal legs jutted through a gash in the stasis booth door. The impact of the crash had driven the incumbent's limbs through the reinforced glass.

Rimmer peered in through what remained of the observation window. Somehow the rest of the body had been preserved, wedged half in and half out of the stasis booth. The legs had withered with age, while the upper body remained in suspended animation.

Timeless.

Unaging.

Unharmed.

Rimmer's voice activated the door. Surely he couldn't be . . . alive. The door lock twirled and the door arced open.

The man opened his eyes and looked down at his legs. His scream cut through Rimmer like a shard of jagged glass. Then he stopped screaming and died of shock.

Rimmer's heart went on a cross-country run around his body. It bounced off his stomach, caromed into his ribcage, and tried to make a forced exit through his windpipe. It was still hammering around his chest cavity like a deranged pinball when he finally stopped running four decks up.

He fell into a twilit recreation room and was on his haunches, still trying to suck air into his reluctant lungs, when he turned and saw the figure standing by the fruit machine.

His brain uttered a silent expletive, and his heart put on its spiked shoes and went for another lap.

TWENTY

The figure turned to face him. The hologramatic 'H' on her forehead glinted fluorescently in the blue light of the Games Room.

'Ah, there you are,' she smiled. 'Where's Yvette? I've been waiting for ages.'

'Yvette who?'

'I needed those course calculations.' She walked six paces towards him and held out her hand.

'Thank you,' she said, and disappeared.

Suddenly she reappeared at the fruit machine with her back to him.

'Are you OK?' said Rimmer, getting to his feet.

She turned.

'Ah, there you are,' she smiled; 'Where's Yvette? I've been waiting for ages. I need those course calculations.'

Yet again she stepped towards him, held out her hand – and vanished reappearing once more at the other side of the room.

'Ah, there you are,' she smiled again, and Rimmer left.

'Quark dingbat fizzigog Netherlands,' said Kryten's disembodied head. 'Smirk Windo-Kleen double-helix badger.' Then there was the *fzzzt* of a circuit shorting, and his eyes blinked closed. A thin whisp of smoke curled up from his open skull.

Lister cursed. He peeked into Kryten's mechanoid brain,

tutted, and fished out a half-eaten three-day-old cheese sandwich with chilli dressing. He prodded around with his soldering iron, absently biting into the sandwich.

The Cat walked in with his lunch on a tray, and sat down at the table.

'If you try and take this food, you're in serious personal danger.'

'I'm not going to try and take it.'

'Just don't even think about it.' The Cat pulled an embroidered lace lobster bib out of his top pocket and tied it around his neck. From his inside pocket he produced a solid silver case, lined with velvet and containing an exquisite set of gold cutlery with hand-carved mother of pearl handles, which he placed either side of his plate. He rubbed his hands together and went into his food-taunting eating ritual.

'I'm gonna eat you, little chickie,' he chanted at the chicken marengo; 'I'm going to eat you, little chickie. I'm gonna eat you, little chickie. 'Cause I like eating chicks.'

The song finished, he looked away from the food like a baseball pitcher checking the bases, then suddenly flicked the chicken off the plate and, in the same, smooth movement, caught it in mid-air with the same hand, and put it back on the plate.

'Too slow, chicken marengo,' he chided. 'Too slow for this Cat.'

'Why don't you just *eat* it?'

'It's no fun if you don't give it a chance.'

'But it's dead. It's *cooked*.'

'Woah!' The Cat slapped his hand down on the plate, sending the chicken spinning into the air and over his shoulder. He kicked away from the chair, somersaulted backwards, and caught it in his mouth before it hit the ground.

'Hey – this chicken is faster than I thought!' He put the chicken back on the plate, and had just started to juggle the potatoes when Rimmer walked in.

'Gentlemen,' he beamed broadly, 'there's someone I'd like you to meet. Someone who's a deep personal friend of mine. Someone who, I'm sure, will enrich all our lives. Someone, I've decided, who will be a more interesting and stimulating bunk-mate for myself, which is why I intend to move in with this someone to the spare sleeping quarters next door. Gentlemen . . .'

Rimmer gestured like a medieval courtesan, and into the open doorframe stepped someone Lister and the Cat recognized instantly.

There in the hatchway, standing beside Arnold J. Rimmer, was another, completely identical Arnold J. Rimmer.

TWENTY-ONE

After Rimmer left the woman by the fruit machine, he rounded up the skutters, and they made their way down the broken stairwell to *Nova 5*'s hologram simulation suite.

Her personality disc, scarred and warped, spun round and round in the drive, aimlessly projecting her through the same piece of dialogue for the zillionth time, in pointless perpetual motion.

The woman's name had been Nancy O'Keefe. A Flight Engineer, Second Class, she'd been the highest ranking casualty in the ship's rear section. What remained of the computer's intelligence had automatically recreated her, even though her database was corrupted beyond repair in the accident.

Rimmer told the skutter to eject the disc, and started searching through the rest of *Nova 5*'s personality library.

One by one he went through the eight-woman, two-man crew. One by one the skutters' clumsy claws placed each of the discs in the drive, and booted them up. And one by one all ten members of *Nova 5* were resurrected before him. Each in some way was corrupted.

All ten discs were unplayable.

The frustration of it!

For two cruel hours, while he went through each of the discs, he'd been able to entertain the prospect that at last he could acquire a companion. A hologramatic companion, who could understand how it felt to be dead. How it felt to be a hologram. How it felt. Someone who could *touch* him. Yes – holograms could touch. Someone *he* could touch. To *touch* again! To *be* touched!

But, no.

Denied. All ten discs warped, scratched, ruined. All ten discs destroyed in the crash.

Rimmer sat down and tried to think. What if . . . what if he could copy his own disc from the *Red Dwarf* hologram library, and then use *Nova 5*'s disc drive to simulate a duplicate him?

Two Arnold Rimmers.

Two hims.

Who better as a companion than his own self!

Arnold J. Rimmer 1 and Arnold J. Rimmer 2.

Brill-smegging-illiant.

TWENTY-TWO

'*How To Be a Winner – an Introduction to Poweramics.*'

'Ours,' said the two Rimmers simultaneously.

Lister tossed the book onto the computer trolley, with the rest of the Rimmers' belongings, and picked another off the shelf.

'*Cooking With Chillies,*' he read.

'Yours,' the Rimmers chanted in unison.

Lister tossed it back on the shelf, then turned and opened the locker marked 'Rimmer, A. J. B Sc, S Sc', which long ago Lister had learned stood for 'Bronze Swimming Certificate' and 'Silver Swimming Certificate', and started to heap all the contents onto the trolley. Twenty pairs of identical military blue underpants, all on coat hangers in protective cellophane wrapping, the pyjamas with the dry-cleaning tags pinned to the collars, the piles of *Survivalist* weaponry magazines, and his one CD – *Billy Benton and his choir sing the Rock'n'roll greats.*

'What about these posters?' asked the duplicate Rimmer.

'They're mine,' said Lister.

'I know they're yours, but the Blu-Tack isn't.'

'You want to take the Blu-Tack?'

'Well, it is *mine*,' pointed out the original; 'I did pay for it, with *my* money.'

'I think there's one of your old finger-nail clippings under the bunk. I'll put that in too, shall I?'

Rimmer Mark 2 eyed him narrowly. 'Don't try and be amusing, Lister; it doesn't suit you.'

For no reason that Lister could see, both Rimmers *howled* with laughter at this last remark, bending at the waist and thumping their knees.

'Great put-down, Arnie,' said the original Rimmer through a mask of tears.

Lister looked on, bemused.

The duplicate stood up, still giggling. 'I'll go and check how the skutters are coping with the redecoration plans.'

'See you, Big Man,' said the copy, stepping out of the hatchway.

'Catch you later, Ace,' said Rimmer, with a look of total infatuation.

'You're a very, very weird person,' said Lister, dropping a wedge of neatly ironed black socks onto the trolley. 'In fact, both of you are.'

Rimmer was oblivious to criticism. 'What an idea. What a genius idea. Using *Nova 5*'s hologram unit to generate a duplicate me. That's the best smegging day's work I ever did.'

'Of all the people you could have brought back – anyone in the *Red Dwarf* crew – you decide to copy your own disc, and bring back another you? That's turning narcissism into a science!'

'I wanted a companion. Who more interesting and stimulating than myself?'

'Why didn't you bring back one of the girls?'

'Because all the girls thought I was a prat.'

'Well, one of the guys, then?'

'They all thought I was a prat, too. Everybody thought I was a prat except for me. Which is why I brought back the Duke. Old Iron Balls himself.'

'Bonehead 2 – how could there be only one?'

'I don't have to take this any more,' Rimmer sighed happily; 'I don't have to take the put-downs, the smart-alec quips, the oh-so-clever snide asides. It's the dawn of a new era for me, Listy. No more you, with your stupid, annoying habits. No more you, holding me back, dragging me down.'

'Me? How did I drag you down?'

'Oh, let me count the ways.'

'What ways?'

'Humming.'

'Humming?'

'You hummed persistently and maliciously for eight months, every time I sat down to do some revision.'

'So, you're saying you never became an officer because you shared your quarters with someone who hummed occasionally?'

'Not occasionally. *Constantly*.'

'You failed your Astronavigation exam eight times before we even met.'

'There you go again – always ready with the smart-alec quip.'

'That's not a quip, it's a fact.'

'There you go again, putting me down.'

'So, what else did I do, besides hum?'

'Everything. Everything you ever did was calculated to hold me back, put me down and annoy me.'

'Like what?'

'Exchanging all the symbols on my revision timetable, so that instead of taking my Engineering finals I went swimming.'

'They fell off. I thought I'd put them all back in the right place.'

'Swapping my toothpaste for a tube of contraceptive jelly.'

'That was a joke!'

'Yes. The same kind of joke as putting my name on the waiting list for experimental pile surgery. The point is: you have always stopped me from being successful – that is a scientific fact.'

'Rimmer, you can't blame me for your lousy life.'

'Not just you. It's been all my bunk-mates. Pemberton, Ledbetter, Daley . . . all of you.'

'It's always the same. It's never *you*, is it? It's always

someone or something else. You never had the right set of pens for G & E Drawing . . . your dividers don't stretch far enough . . .'

'Well, they don't!' protested Rimmer.

'In the end, you can't turn round and say: "Sorry I buggered up my life – it was Lister's fault".'

'It's too late, my life's already been buggered up. It's my death that concerns me now, and I have no intention of buggering that up' – Rimmer turned on his heels – 'because I'm getting out of here and moving in with myself.'

TWENTY-THREE

Blackness.

Nothingness.

Then a sound.

'Jjjjjjdt!'

Then the sound again:

'Jjjjjjdt!'

What did that sound mean?

The sound again, but this time it was different. He recognized the sound. He remembered hearing it before. It was language. But he'd forgotten what it meant.

'Kryjjjjjdt.'

A name. A name he should have known.

'Kryjjjdtn.'

His name!

'Kryten? Kryten?'

A flash of green light. Then black lines drew themselves across his field of vision. Then the lines melted away, and he was looking at a message:

'Mechanoid Visual System, Version IX.05. © Infomax Data Corporation 2296.'

And then sight.

Floods of brilliant colours: blues, reds, yellows dancing nonsensically before him.

He focused. There was a man's face grinning at him.

'Ye-es!' said the face. 'Bru-taaaaal!'

'Hgvd Mumber Daffd,' said Kryten.

Lister twiddled about inside his head with a sonic screw-driver.

'Hello, Mr David,' said Kryten.

'Ye-es!' said Lister again. 'I've done it! You're back in action.' He put Kryten's skull-piece back into place, fastened the latches and replaced his ear. 'How d'you feel?'

'Everything seems to be functioning', said Kryten flatly.

'Listen', said Lister, leaning over him, 'there's something I need to know: what's the duality jump? What is it? What does it do?'

A plastic frown rippled across Kryten's brow. 'It powers the ship. It's a quantum drive – it allows you to leap from one point in space to another. Why?'

'How does it *work*?'

'I'm just a mechanoid. I don't know these things.'

'How does it work, Kryten?' Lister insisted.

'It's something to do with Quantum Mechanics and In-determinism. Something about when you measure electrons, they can be in two places at the same time.'

Kryten seemed strangely reluctant to talk about it, and kept stressing it was a 'human matter' and not really the kind of thing mechanoids should concern themselves with, but, bit by bit, Lister wheedled what he could out of Kryten, and doggedly pieced together what he needed to know.

When you made a duality jump, it seemed, you tempor-arily coexisted at two points in the universe; you then 'chose' one of these points to 'be' in. In this way you could leapfrog across the universe, not bound by the limits of Space/Time.

'So, how long.' Lister pressed, 'would it take a duality jump to get back to Earth?'

'Oh . . . a long time.'

'How long?'

'You'd have to make about a thousand jumps.'

'How *long*?'

'Two . . .' Kryten mused '. . . perhaps even *three* months.'

'Three months!' Lister was already into the touch-up shuffle.

'But there's no fuel! It decayed centuries ago.'

'What kind of fuel does it need?'

'I don't know. I'm just a mechanoid.'

'Kryten, pleeeease.'

Kryten, shifted on the bench and twisted his fingers uncomfortably. 'I'm just a mechanoid. I just clean things.'

'But you know, don't you?'

'Only because I heard Miss Yvette talk about it once. But I'm not *supposed* to know.'

'What is it?'

'Uranium 233. Whatever that is.'

'Ye-e-e-es!' Lister thumped the table. 'Nice one, Krytie.'

'Well, if that's all, Mr David' – Kryten smiled his lipless smile – 'I'd like to be shut down again now, please.'

'What are you talking about? It took me four months to fix you.'

'But there's no point in my being on-line. I was programmed to serve the crew of *Nova 5*. They're dead now, therefore, my program is completed.'

'So? You've got to start a new program.'

Kryten tilted his head and arched a hairless eyebrow. 'To serve whom?'

'To serve no one. To serve yourself.'

'But I *have* to serve someone. I was created to serve. I serve, therefore I am.'

Lister forced back his fur-lined leather deerstalker with the heels of his palms in exasperation. 'Kryten – chill out, OK? Loosen up. Re-lax. Just hang, will you? Chill the smeg out.'

'Why?'

'Because I say so.'

Kryten's face seemed to brighten. 'Is that an order?' he said hopefully.

'Why?'

'Well, if it's an *order*, that's different.'

'It *is* an order,' Lister smiled. 'Chill out.'

Kryten was perched stiffly on a tall bar stool in the Copaca-bana Hawaiian Cocktail Bar, staring at the dry martini cocktail, stirred, two olives, standing before him. He didn't really like dry martinis, shaken or otherwise, but he'd ordered it because it was the drink Hudzen always had when he went to the Hi-Life Club in *Androids* and to Kryten it was the zenith of sophistication.

He knocked back the martini in a single gulp, paused a few seconds, then regurgitated it back into his glass and stirred it round for a while with his cocktail stick. He wasn't very good at enjoying himself, he decided. He'd much rather have been cleaning something. He would much rather have been re-varnishing the dance floor or shampooing all two thousand, five hundred and seventy-two crushed velvet seats.

Still, Mister David had ordered him to 'chill out', to 'hang', so 'hang' was what he must do. He sank the cocktail once more, and brought it back up again.

He flicked through his vocabulary database for a definition of 'hang (vb. slang)'. 'Reduce tension' he read once again; 'lose rigidity; cease working, worrying etc.; allow muscles to become limp; relax, enjoy oneself.' Kryten relaxed his muscles. His head lolled back, his arms hung loosely by his sides, and he fell off the bar stool onto the purple carpet.

He climbed back onto the stool, and started to worry that he hadn't ceased worrying. He looked around at the flashing disco lights on the empty dance floor. He became aware for the first time that music was pumping out of the speakers. If he was really to carry out Mister David's orders to the letter, he supposed, he was obliged to get down and dance. With a sigh of resignation he took his martini cocktail and waddled over to the dance floor. The only dance he knew was the tap dance to *Yankee Doodle Dandy*.

The music playing was Hugo Lovepole's sexy ballad *Hey Baby, Don't Be Ovulatin' Tonight*. Kryten set his drink on the floor, stamped his right foot until he got in time with the smoochy beat, and began tap-dancing furiously.

And that was how the two Rimmers found him as they strolled through the recreation decks, taking their early evening constitutional.

It had been a very pleasant stroll – quite the nicest evening Rimmer had spent for years. His duplicate was a total delight. They had each other in tucks; reminiscing, talking over old glories, old girlfriends. The simple, manly joy of chewing the fat with a like-minded, right-thinking colleague.

At last he had someone with whom he could share ideas he'd always been to embarrassed to propound before. Such as his French dictation theory of life.

Rimmer believed there were two kinds of people: the first kind were history essay people, who started life with a blank sheet, with no score, and accumulated points with every success they achieved. The other kind were the French dictation people: they started off with a hundred per cent, and every mistake they made was deducted from their original perfect score. Rimmer always felt his parents had forced him firmly into the second group. Everything he'd ever done was somehow imperfect and flawed – a disappointment. Years before, when he'd been promoted to Second Technician, he felt he hadn't *succeeded* in becoming a Second Technician, rather, he'd *failed* to become a First Technician. While he expounded the theory, his double nodded in agreement and murmured encouragements, such as 'Absolutely' and 'Very true.'

Right now, though, the conversation had shifted and Rimmer was listening with mounting glee as his double reminded him of their one-night stand with Yvonne Mc-Gruder.

'What a body! What a body!' the double was chuckling.

'And hers wasn't bad either!' Rimmer guffawed.

They paused as across the disco floor they caught sight of Kryten clickety-clacking frenetically.

'What on Io do you think you're doing?' the double said, bemused.

'I'm chilling out, sirs,' said Kryten. 'I'm hanging.' Click, click, click, tap, tippy-tap, tip.

'You're what?' said Rimmer.

'I'm getting mellow' – clicky-clack, tip, tip – 'I'm coasting. I'm chilling out.'

Kryten suddenly felt ridiculous, and stopped.

'How long have you been fixed?' Rimmer asked.

Kryten was wondering why there were two identical-looking Rimmers addressing him, but he felt that as a mechanoid it would have been impertiment to ask. 'Since 12.15 hours, sirs.'

'It's seven-thirty in the evening. Have you been messing about all that time?' said the double.

'I was carrying out Mr David's orders, Mr Arnold, sir. He ordered me to relax.'

'Oh, and I suppose you do everything you're ordered to?'

'Yes, sir. I do, sir.'

'Really?' The two Rimmers hiked eyebrows at each other.

'Yes. I'm programmed to serve, sirs.'

The double pointed to Kryten's drink. 'Eat that cocktail glass.'

'Right away, sir,' said Kryten, and ate the glass.

'So,' Rimmer mused, 'if I said to you "spring-clean the entire sleeping quarters deck," I suppose you'd do that too, would you?'

'Of course, Mr Arnolds.'

'Splendid!' said Rimmer.

'Splendissimo!' said his digital doppleganger.

TWENTY-FOUR

The lift doors split open and disgorged a tired but happy Lister onto the habitation deck corridor. He'd spent the last two days and a night down in the technical library, then another morning liaising with Holly in the geology lab. In the last fifty-six hours he'd learned many things. He'd started off thinking that the structure and composition of planet crust and rock formations were incredibly boring. But now he was absolutely certain of it. Still, he now knew more about uranium production and mining techniques than he knew about the London Jets Megabowl-winning team of '75 – and he knew what the entire London Jets Megabowl-winning team of '75 had for breakfast on the day of the game.

This was the way it went: fissile uranium 233 could be synthesized from the non-fissile thorium isotope: thorium 232. And this was the best part: thorium 232 wasn't even rare. It was abundant in the universe. It abounded! There was lots of it! And this was confirmed when his radiometric-spectrographic survey turned up seven likely moons in this solar system alone.

Five of them would have required underground mining, so he had to rule them out. Of the remaining two, one, the more likely one, was seven months' travel away. But on the nearer moon, less than five days' journey away, there was an eighty-seven per cent probability that the ore deposits he needed were lying close to the surface. No shafts, no pit-props, no radon gas ventilation problems. Maybe he could do it. *Red Dwarf* was a mining ship – it had all the equipment: the earth-moving vehicles, the processing plants, the whole enchilada!

When he turned into his sleeping quarters, it took several moments before his tired brain registered what it was that was different.

At first he assumed he must have got out of the lift on the wrong floor, and he was now standing on the wrong deck. Then he saw his goldfish, only the water was clean, and you could see the plastic Vatican quite clearly. He looked around.

The dull grey metal walls had vanished behind a Victorian floral print in various pretty pinks. The bedspreads were in delicate cream lace, festoon blinds in a mixture of rosebud patterns hung over the viewport window. A salmon-tinted Aubusson rug swept from under the bunks to the new porcelain pedestal wash basin. The lounge area was curtained off from the bunks by red silk drapes, with gold tie-backs. The table in the middle of the room was covered in a briar rose, short-skirted circular cloth, on top of which stood rows of newly polished boots and piles of neat, crisply folded laundry.

It was appalling.

It was an atrocity against machismo.

'What the smeg is going on?'

Kryten looked up from his ironing.

'Good afternoon, Mr David, sir.'

'What have you *done*?'

'A spot of tidying.'

'What are these?' Lister snatched an unrecognizable item from the pile of laundry.

'Your boxer shorts, Mr David.'

'No way are these my boxer shorts,' said Lister. 'They bend. What have you done to this place? What is this? This bowl of scented pencil shavings?'

'Potpourri, sir.'

'Pope who? Where is everything? Where's my orange peel

with the cig dimps in it? Where's the remnants of last Wednesday's curry? I hadn't finished eating it! Where's my coffee mug with the mould in it?'

'I threw it away, sir. I threw it all away.'

'You what? I was breeding that mould. It was called "Albert". I was trying to get him two feet high.'

'Why, sir?'

'Because it drove Rimmer nuts. And driving Rimmer nuts is what keeps me going. What did you do it for?'

'The two Mr Rimmers ordered me to, sir. They even recommended the decor. They said it was very *you*.'

Lister sat down on the apple-green chintz-covered chaise longue, next to the potted plastic wisteria, and wondered where he could begin. There was something about Kryten that really disturbed him, but he wasn't quite sure what. He was a slave, and Lister hated that. For some reason, mankind seemed to be obsessed with enslaving someone: black slavery, class slavery, housewife slavery, and now mechanoid slavery. Then it hit him: it wasn't so much slavery that got to him, though get to him it did; it was the happy slave. It was the acquiescence, the assent to serve, the willingness to be a slave.

'What about you?' Lister looked up as Kryten ploughed through the ironing. 'Don't you ever want to do something just for yourself?'

'Myself?' Kryten sniggered. 'That's a bit of a barmy notion, if you don't mind my saying so, sir.'

'Isn't there anything you look forward to?'

Kryten stood, the steaming iron in his hand for a full minute, trying to think of an answer.

'*Androids*,' he said, at last. 'I look forward to *Androids*.'

'Besides *Androids*?'

Kryten had another think. 'Getting a new squidgy mop?' he ventured.

'Besides dumb soap operas and even dumber cleaning utensils?'

Kryten fell silent.

'What do you think of thorium mining?'

Kryten looked baffled.

'Follow me.'

They found the Cat on Corridor omega 577, sleeping peacefully on top of a narrow metal locker, a hairnet protecting his pompadour.

'Hey, Cat – wake up.' Lister rocked the locker.

The Cat opened one eye. 'This'd better be good. I was sleeping. And sleeping is my third favourite thing.'

'Come on. Follow me.'

A yawn split the Cat's face and made his head appear to double in size. He sprang down from the locker, arched his spine and stretched until the back of his head was touching the heels of his gold-braided sleeping slippers, and yawned again. He opened the locker door, reached inside, and draped an imitation King Penguin fur smoking jacket casually over his shoulders, before popping the top off a magnum of milk and filling a crystal goblet. He gargled petitely, urinated in the locker and followed Lister and Kryten down the corridor.

'Where are we going?'

'Mining.'

TWENTY-FIVE

The two Rimmers, dressed in identical P.E. kits jumped up in the air, flapping their arms simultaneously in time to the music and yelling encouragement at each other.

'Come on – keep it up!'

'You too!'

They landed, crouched like bullfrogs, and leapt off up into the air again.

'Jump!'

'Stretch!'

'Jump!'

'Stretch!'

'Jump!'

'Stretch!'

The Rimmers were alone aboard *Red Dwarf*.

Lister, Kryten, the Cat and twelve skutters had gone off in Blue Midget, loaded with surface mining equipment, in search of the uranium deposits on the black desert moon below. The two Rimmers were to stay behind to supervise the welding together of the two halves of *Nova 5* by the eighty-four remaining skutters. They were to oversee the restoration of the ship, to render it space-worthy again.

They were in charge!

In charge of a major operation, a gargantuan engineering challenge. And they were in charge!

Holly had estimated the operation would take two months to complete, at the very least. Well, the two Rimmers would see about that. They would do it in half that time, they decided. No, a quarter of that time. Under the excellent management of *two* Arnold Js, those skutters were going to work their little claws off! That ship would be ready in a fortnight. It would be ready, new and gleaming, by the time Lister returned with his uranium haul. Imagine his stupid little porky face, hardly able to conceal his grudging admiration. 'I've got to admit it,' he would say, 'you guys really are a great team.'

In the meantime they were getting fit, getting in shape, getting prepared for the ordeal ahead. This was day one of the new regime.

'Jump!'

'Stretch!'

'Jump!'

'Stretch!'

'And . . . rest!' The original Rimmer collapsed on the floor.

'No, keep jumping!' the double yelled, finding new strength from his other self's weakness. Red-faced, Rimmer started up again.

'You're right,' he shouted, 'keep going. Through the pain barrier.'

'Jump!'

'Stretch!'

'Jump!'

'Stretch!'

'And . . . rest!' said Rimmer again.

'What are you doing, man?' screamed his copy, still leaping.

'I'm resting. It's all going grey.'

'That's the pain barrier – beat it!'

'Absolutely!' He started jumping again. 'Up, up, up!'

'More, more, more!'

'Jump, jump, jump!'

'Stretch, stretch, stretch!'

'Rest, rest, rest?' pleaded Rimmer.

'No, no, no!' insisted the double.

They continued leaping up and down for a further minute, both too breathless to speak.

'And . . . rest!' whispered the double finally.

Rimmer landed on the floor and his legs sagged beneath him. He staggered backwards towards the bunk, and fell forward onto his knees. The glands at the back of his throat were producing saliva by the bucket-load. 'Great sesh,' he gurgled, 'that little bit extra, that's what it's all about. Driving through the pain barrier, to the brink of unconsciousness. Great sesh.'

'You . . . owe me . . . seven,' said the double on all fours, wheezing like an eighty-year-old bronchial bagpipes player.

'What?' panted Rimmer, his face quite yellow.

'I . . . did seven extra jerks . . . while you were . . . resting.'

'Come on. We're not down to counting jerks, are we? What's a couple of jerks between duplicates?'

'It's for . . . your own good. I'm . . . seven jerks fitter . . . than you. We can't . . . have that, can we?'

'I'll do them first thing in the morning, while you're asleep.'

'Now!' rasped the double.

Rimmer hauled himself onto his wobbly white legs and started to leap up in the air again. 'One . . .' he counted, 'two . . .' he counted, 'three . . .'

'That wasn't a full one. Call it a half.'

'Three and a half . . .' he counted.

'And that wasn't a full one either; call it three.'

'Four!' Rimmer leapt a full six inches off the floor.

'Three and one eighth!' the double corrected.

'Four and one eighth!'

'Three and a half,' was the verdict.

Finally, after twenty-five leaps, Rimmer's duplicate agreed he'd done seven.

'You see,' said the double, 'it's about teamwork. I drive and encourage you . . .'

'And I drive and encourage you,' gasped Rimmer. And then he was sick.

'Right' – the double rubbed his hands – 'what time shall we get up?'

'That's a good question, I.B. Early. Very early. Half past eight?'

'What, and miss half the day? How about seven?' the double ventured.

'How about six?' Rimmer topped him.

'No. Half past four!'

'Half past four? That's the middle of the night!'

'We want it to be ready in a fortnight, don't we?'

'Yes, but half past four?' Rimmer moaned. 'That's ridiculous!'

'Why's it ridiculous? You think Napoleon on the eve of the battle of Borodino said: "Wake me tomorrow at nine with two runny eggs and some toastie soldiers"?'

'You're absolutely right, Duke.'

Rimmer voice-activated the digital alarm clock and climbed thankfully onto his new bunk.

'What are you doing?' The double looked at him askance.

'I'm going to bed, Ace.'

'It's only two in the morning – we need to read up on welding techniques.'

'But we're getting up in a minute,' Rimmer said in a small, pathetic voice.

'You take metallurgy and thyratron in heat-control systems, and I'll take magnesium arc-welding, and chemical bonding techniques. Then we'll test one another, and whoever does worst has to do another hundred jumps before bunk down.'

'Once again, Arn, I hate to say it, but you're absolutely right.'

The two Rimmers finally got to bed at 3.37 a.m., and got up again fifty-three minutes later to start their morning exercises.

TWENTY-SIX

Lister crunched his way through five gear changes, and Blue Midget lurched like a drunken line-backer over the airless black desert of the unnamed moon. Helium winds whipped the sand into huge, tapering swirls that twisted across the dry, featureless landscape like a pack of children's spinning tops.

Lister landed the mining juggernaut with all the natural grace of a suicidal elephant tumbling from the Eiffel Tower.

'Nice landing, buddy,' said the Cat, digging his way out of the pile of storage lockers which had collapsed on him.

Lister threw the Cat a spacesuit. 'Put this on.'

The Cat looked at the battered old dirty silver regulation-issue spacesuit with disdain. 'Are you kidding? I wouldn't use this to buff my shoes.'

Lister clambered into his own. 'Put it on.'

'Are you seriously telling me these shoulders were *ever* in style?'

'Put it on.'

The Cat held the suit at arm's length.

'Well, maybe if I widen the lapels, put in a couple of vents, maybe some sequins down the legs . . .'

'We're going *mining*,' said Lister. 'We're not in the heats of "Come Jiving", we're going to work.'

'Hey – I do not *do* the "W" word.'

'We're all doing the "W" word,' said Lister.

Kryten stepped through the hatchway from Blue Midget's galley, carrying a tray of tea things and a plate of petits fours.

'I thought we might have some tea,' he said, setting the cups in the saucers.

'We're going smegging mining!' Lister threw his spacesuit gauntlet against the wall.

'Milk or lemon?' Kryten smiled.

'You're in charge of processing! I can't do this all on my own.'

'I'll have milk,' said the Cat.

'Is nobody listening? We're going uranium mining. It's a helium atmosphere out there. It's going to be hard, and it's going to be dangerous.'

'All the more reason,' said Kryten, 'to have a nice hot cup of tea inside you.'

Lister inflated his cheeks and expelled the air. He hunched over the orange and green flashing display of the trace computer, which beeped and blipped with annoying regularity as it processed soil samples in search of the main seam.

'Holly, have we found the main deposit yet?'

'No,' said Holly. 'I'd give it another twenty-five glimbarts.'

'What's a glimbart?'

'It's fifty nanoteks.'

'You're just making this up, aren't you?'

'No,' Holly protested feebly.

'Where is it, then?'

'I dunno,' he confessed.

'I thought you were supposed to have an IQ of six thousand.'

'Six thousand's not that much,' said Holly, aggrieved; 'it's only the same IQ as twelve thousand P.E. teachers.'

'Hey,' said the Cat, waving the cake tray, 'are there any more of these little pink ones?'

'Coming right up,' said Kryten.

Lister banged his head gently against the screen of the trace computer and wished, not for the first time, that a different sperm had fertilized his mother's egg.

TWENTY-SEVEN

It was 10.30 a.m., and Rimmer had already been up for six hours. He was standing on the deck of the cargo bay, calling out pointless orders to a group of skutters who were operating the cantilever crane, which was gently hoisting *Nova 5*'s rear section up into the air.

'Up a bit! Up! Up! More!'

The crane gingerly swung the huge tail section so it was suspended high above the ship's front half.

'Round! Round! Swing it round!' Rimmer was calling, redundantly. 'Swing it round, just like you are doing.'

This was the third day of the gruelling new regime the two Rimmers had instigated for themselves. The timetable went thus:

Rise at 4.30 a.m. Exercises till 5.00. Repair supervision, followed by lunch at 9.30. Planning meeting at 10.00. Supervision duties until supper at one o'clock in the afternoon. More supervision until second supper at 5.00 p.m. Technical reading till 6.00, then it was repair supervision all the way until supper three at 9.00. Then rest and recreation up to midnight, followed by supper four, and planning meeting until bed at 2.00 a.m.

For some reason the new regime meant having six holo-gramatic meals a day, and only two-and-a-half hours sleep.

Rimmer was near to cracking. His patience threshold was practically nonexistent, but he certainly wasn't going to be the one who said 'Let's ease off.' That would be weak and

224

spineless – the *old* Arnold J. Rimmer, not the new, high-powered winner. Let his duplicate be the one to wimp out.

The huge chains moaned and creaked as the skutters began to lower the tail into place against the front section.

Rimmer rubbed the grey rings around his eyes, thought how tired his copy must be feeling at this moment, and suddenly got a new burst of energy.

'Down!' he shouted, unnecessarily; 'Down! Lower!'

'Big Man!' Rimmer's duplicate bounded down the gantry stairwell onto the cargo deck. Rimmer was aghast to see how fresh-faced and alert his copy appeared. Had he been cheating? Had he been secretly snoozing instead of supervising the supply inventory? It was perfectly possible. He'd been away three hours. And, quite frankly, he certainly looked a heck of a lot better than he should have done. But surely he wouldn't cheat *him*? That would be like cheating himself. That would be like cheating at patience. Wait a minute, Rimmer remembered, I *do* cheat at patience.

'Big Man,' the double repeated, 'you're doing it wrong. You should be moving the front section round to the rear section, rather than swinging the rear section round to meet the front section.'

'What the smeg difference does it make?' Rimmer snapped.

'Because if you weld them together in that position, the ship will have to take off in reverse.'

Rimmer looked round. The double was right. The ship was pointing in the wrong direction. How could he have made such a monumentally stupid error? It must be because he was tired. Then, how come his duplicate spotted it? Surely he was just as tired . . . unless . . . He had! He had been cheating!

'Stop!' the double was yelling at the two skutters operating the cantilever crane; 'Take it up again and swing it back round to where it came from.'

'Excuse me, this is my area of responsibility.'

'Swing it round! Back to where it came from. Start again!'

'Stop!' yelled Rimmer. The crane shuddered and stopped. The huge ship swung back and forth in its harness.

'No, swing it round!' the double countermanded. 'We've got to start again.'

'Stop!'

'Round!'

'What are you doing? This is *my* task! Haven't you got to rush off and have another huge great big sleep on the quiet?'

'What?' The double's face crinkled into a half-smile that announced he was lying. 'I haven't been taking secret sleeps.'

'Oh, really?' Rimmer sneered contemptuously and yelled for the skutters to stop again.

The weight of the swinging ship wrenched the back legs of the crane off the deck. The crane moaned and tilted; the ship slithered out of its harness and plummeted the four hundred yards onto the cargo deck below.

The two Rimmers watched, paralysed, as it bounced onto the steel deck before coming to rest, tail up, dinted, but structurally unharmed.

The crane eased lazily forward, then smashed down onto *Nova 5*'s rear half, slicing it neatly in two like a split banana.

TWENTY-EIGHT

Lister sat in the sealed cab of the earth remover, drumming his gauntleted fingers impatiently on the dashboard. After four days of exploratory digging they'd finally found a thorium lode, and dug a trench seventy feet deep and fifteen feet wide, which ran for a length of thirty yards. Once Lister had dug out enough three-foot slabs of raw ore to fill the eight-wheeled lunar transport vehicle (LTV), the Cat would then drive the thorium to the portalab, where Kryten would scrape away the waste soil and clay, then pack the clean ore in sealed cases aboard Blue Midget, ready to be transported back to *Red Dwarf* for refining.

At least, that was the plan.

But there were some hiccups in the procedure. And Lister was experiencing just one of those hiccups right now as he sat in the digger at the bottom of the trench with a full load, waiting for the Cat to return with the LTV. So far he'd been waiting for over an hour. He punched helplessly at the yellow furry dice dangling from the mirror, and wondered if it would have been possible to find two more incompetent and useless assistants in the entire universe to help him mine for uranium. The fifth-century Norwegian warrior King Havac the Imbecile and his more idiotic half-brother were the only two that sprang readily to mind.

The whole of the first day had been spent teaching the Cat how to drive the LTV. Initially he had refused even to listen to Lister's instructions, until the vehicle had been customized to his liking. Now it was painted jet black, with two streaks of flame emanating from the wheel rims, twenty-four mirrors, tinted windows, and the Cat's own growling face painted on the hood. Once the vehicle was to his taste, he'd managed to pick up the basic driving skills fairly quickly, and in fact could now do wheelies and hand-brake turns even when loaded down with three tons of mineral ore.

The dashboard intercom buzzed in Lister's digger. Lister pressed the 'send' button.

'Where the smeg have you been? I've been trying to get through for an hour.'

Ffffzzzzt . . . 'Lunch,' said the Cat's voice.

'Lunch? We just had lunch two hours ago!'

Ffffzzzzt . . . 'Had it again,' said the Cat.

This was one of the major hiccups in the operation. The Cat insisted on taking regular breaks throughout the day. When he wasn't eating, he was snoozing. He took perhaps seven or eight snooze breaks every day which, he claimed, were essential: otherwise, he wouldn't have enough energy for his main evening sleep. When he wasn't eating or snoozing or sleeping, he was generally taking it easy. Lister had found him countless times aboard Blue Midget, listening to music on Lister's headphones and idly thumbing his way through a sniff book. In an average fourteen-hour working day the Cat could be relied upon to put in fiften minutes' hard graft. So Lister found himself doing pretty much everything by himself.

Kryten was terrific. A real godsend. Provided all you needed was a plateful of triangular-shaped cucumber sandwiches with the crust removed and a pot of lemon tea. If, on the other hand, you needed someone to scrape uranium ore free of waste and pack it in sealed cases, all you got was another plateful of cucumber sandwiches and a second pot of lemon tea. Uranium recovery wasn't mechanoid work, he kept repeating. It was important and dangerous, and he couldn't accept the responsibility; and by way of a peace offering, he'd make another plate of sandwiches.

Lister finally persuaded him it was just cleaning work. Slightly bizarre cleaning work, but cleaning work nevertheless. And eventually he'd reluctantly agreed to do it. At the end of the third day, when Lister had gone across to the portalab to see how he was doing, he found the huge stack of raw ore piled up, largely untouched, in the holding tanks. Inside he found Kryten still working on his first piece of ore.

'Almost done,' said Kryten, spraying the uranium with just one more coat of beeswax, and buffing it to a gleaming finish.

Lister had banged Kryten's head with a handy piece of ore, and explained how it was important to do it a little more quickly. Since then he hadn't dared to go back and check on the mechanoid's progress.

In the meantime the Cat was back from his latest break.

Ffffzzzzt . . . 'Back on the case now, buddy,' came the Cat's voice; 'Let's *work*!'

The Cat's LTV leapt off the brow of a dune, landed twenty feet beyond on its front wheels, ducking to the limit of its suspension, then reared back, its hood in the air, as the Cat wheelied up to the trench, spun on a sixpence and came to rest in a cloud of black lunar dust, in perfect parallel with Lister's digger.

Ffffzzz . . . 'I'm a natural,' sighed the Cat, patting his pompadour in the rear-view mirror. 'Load me up. I have another snooze break due in one minute precisely.'

TWENTY-NINE

Rimmer sat in the hard metal chair at the hard metal table, reading the strategic account of the battle of Borodino, the critical battle in Napoleon's abortive advance on Moscow. He was taking full advantage of the fifteen minute rest and recreation period at the end of another exhausting day.

Lister's uranium party had been away now for three weeks, a full week over schedule. After the accident which smashed *Nova 5* into three pieces, the two Rimmers had gone into overdrive. Fifteen of the eighty-four skutters had exploded due to overwork. But at least *Nova 5* had been welded together so that it now lay in the original two pieces it had been before Lister left. After three weeks of back-breaking, skutter-blowing toil, they were finally back where they'd started.

Rimmer looked up at his double, who was sitting in the quarters' one easy chair, bathed in the pink glow of the student's study lamp, studying the rude paintings of Renaissance women in their book on Florentine art. When he'd drunk in enough of one painting he nodded at a skutter, who turned the page.

It was funny, the original Rimmer thought, staring at his duplicate. He'd never realized before how big his Adam's apple appeared in profile, or how small and triangular his chin was; he'd never been aware that his nostrils flared so ludicrously, or that his nose twitched like a dormouse's whenever he was concentrating. It was a stupid-looking face really.

As he watched, his double slipped a hand into his pocket, felt around and, pretending to cough, surreptitiously popped a hologramatic mint into his mouth. *Pathetic. Deeply, deeply pathetic*, thought Rimmer. *They're computer-simulated mints. There's no limit to their number. So why doesn't he offer me one?* Absently he slipped his chin below the table line and sucked a hologramatic boiled sweet from the line of three on his knee. *Because he's mean*, he thought, sucking silently; *he's pathologically mean*.

The double looked up and gave Rimmer a watery half-smile, forcing him to return to his Napoleonic diaries. The duplicate wondered idly if Rimmer knew he was beginning to lose his hair on the back of his crown, and if he knew how small and triangular his chin looked from this angle, above that megalithic Adam's apple, which bobbed up and down ludicrously, like a hamster caught in a garden hose. And why did he never offer him one of his boiled sweets? Why, instead, did he go through that absurd charade of ducking below the table and sucking them off his knee? He was mean, that was the top and bottom of it. Pathologically so.

Rimmer looked up again and noticed his double watching him. 'Good book?' he asked.

'Mmmm?' said the double, quickly swallowing his mint. 'Yes, yes. Florentine art.'

Rimmer smirked.

'What's funny?'

'Nothing,' said Rimmer, shaking his head.

'No, tell me. What is it?'

'You're looking at the rude pictures of Renaissance women. I just think it's funny.'

The double snorted through his familiar, lying half-smile. 'No, I'm not. I just happen to be intrigued by sixteenth-century art. True, there are several saucy portrayals of the Madonna sans fig leaf, as it were. But I don't particularly dwell on them.'

'Yes, you do. You're a freak for Renaissance bazongas. And the pair on page 78 in particular.'

An anger tic tugged at the double's top lip. 'Do you really think I'm the sort of pathetic, sad, weasly kind of person who could get erotically aroused by looking at paintings of matronly breasts?'

'I do it, so you must do it,' Rimmer said brightly. 'It's just, obviously, I've never seen it from the outside before. And although it is sad, pathetic and weasly, I grant you, it's also tremendously amusing. Especially the way you keep on getting the skutter to turn back to page 78 as if you've forgotten something.'

'I don't have to sit here and take this.'

'Yes. That's a good idea. Why don't you stand up and let me have a go on that chair?'

'Ohhhh –' the double smiled and nodded – 'that's what this is all about.'

'It's just it's my favourite chair,' Rimmer said petulantly, 'and you always seem to hog it.'

'It's my favourite chair too,' protested the duplicate.

'I used to be able to sit on it all the time when I was with Lister. Now I'm with you, I'm relegated to this hard metal chair, next to this hard metal table. And you get the student's pink light.'

'Well, the student's pink light just happens to be next to the comfy chair.'

'Which is why once in a while you might offer to let me sit there.'

'Well, of all the stupid things to argue about, honestly. You're tired – I think you must be working too hard.'

'I'm not working too hard,' Rimmer hissed; 'I can take it.'

'Hey – it's no disgrace to need more than two-and-a-half hours' sleep. True, a lot of the greatest people in history survived on three hours or under, but it doesn't necessarily mean you're a complete failure if you need twelve or thirteen.'

'I don't need twelve or thirteen.'

'Then why are you getting so ratty?'

'I'm not getting ratty,' Rimmer whined.

'Why do you keep putting me down, then?'

A bitter silence descended on the room. The thing that Rimmer hated more than anything was being put down. Lister did it to him, the Cat did it to him, and now he was doing it to himself. Rimmer began to regret his outburst. He didn't like to see his other self upset, and he even contemplated briefly going up to him and giving him a manly embrace. But in a moment of homosexual panic, he thought his double might get the wrong idea. Not that he would, of course, because he was him and he knew for a fact that he wasn't that way sexually tilted; so obviously his double wasn't and obviously his double would know that he wasn't either, and it was simply a manly embrace, meant in a sort of *mano a mano* kind of way ... Perhaps he *was* tired. He certainly had good reason. He'd only had ten hours' sleep in the last twenty-one days. He was practically hallucinating with fatigue.

And whose fault was that? His double's. Rimmer didn't know how it had started, but somehow they'd got involved in a kind of 'tougher-than-you' game. Every time Rimmer suggested a schedule that was reasonably testing, his double would have to top it. And Rimmer could hardly let him get away with that, so he'd suggest something even more difficult, and then his duplicate would top that too!

Now, after twenty-one days of this, they were down to one-and-a-half hours' sleep a night. All he needed was a lie-in. Two or three days in bed and he'd be his old self again. It made sense! They'd blown up the skutters and broken the ship. If they'd spent the last three weeks in bed doing absolutely nothing at all, they'd be in exactly the same position as they were in now. He decided to suggest they take a couple of days off. Who cared if his copy saw it as a sign of weakness? He'd suggest it anyway.

'I was thinking,' he said aloud, 'about tomorrow's getting-up time.'

'So was I,' said his double. 'How about tomorrow we only have one hour fifteen minutes?'

'How about one hour?' Rimmer found himself saying automatically.

'No, better still,' said his double, 'forty-five minutes.'

Rimmer shut up, and wished he'd never spoken.

THIRTY

Blue Midget headed at breakneck speed towards the metal wall of *Red Dwarf*'s hull. Just before impact it flattened out and hugged the body of the ship, before twisting into a loop-the-loop and zipping smoothly in through the open doors of the cargo bay. It twisted side over side like a torpedo before flipping upright and coming to rest on the landing pad.

Lister eyeballed the Cat. 'That's the last time you drive,' he said.

They clambered down the boarding steps and stood on the deck of the cargo bay.

There before them *Nova 5* lay in one gleaming whole. Repaired, finished and space-worthy. Lister was stunned. True, they had been away almost three months, collecting enough thorium 232 for the jag home, but the Rimmers had done it! They'd actually done a job, and not screwed it up.

It was only at a second glance that Lister became aware of the burnt-out husks of eighty-or-so exploded skutters surrounding the ship. From *Nova 5*'s hatchway a lone skutter slowly emerged with a welding laser in its tired claw, and made its way unsteadily down the boarding ramp and onto the cargo bay floor. It glided painfully across the deck, emitting a dangerous whining sound, and arrived in front of Lister, Kryten and the Cat. It tilted its head like a quizzical dog, and exploded in an orange flare.

The three of them clumped noisily down the gantry steps on

to the habitation deck, and were half-way to the sleeping quarters when they heard the voices.

'Shhh!' Lister held up his hand.

Faintly at first, then gradually increasing in clarity, the sound of a heated argument filtered down the corridor.

'What did you call me?'

'I said you were a bonehead, Bonehead!'

'I'm a what?'

'It's no wonder Father despised you.'

'I was his favourite.'

'His favourite boneheady wimpy wet!'

'You filthy, smegging liar!'

'Everyone hated you. Even Mother.'

'Pardon?'

'You're a hideous emotional cripple, and you know it.'

'Shut up!'

'What other kind of man goes to android brothels, and pays to sleep with robots?'

'THAT WASN'T MEEE!!!!'

'Of course it was you – I'm you. I know.'

'Shut UP!!'

'You've always been afraid of women, haven't you?'

'Shut UP!!!'

The argument had begun at eight o'clock, shortly after supper. It was now five hours later, and it was showing no signs of abating. Neither of them could remember why it had begun or, indeed, what it was about. They just knew they disagreed with one another. It was all-out verbal warfare. They'd gone beyond the snide sniping stage; they'd gone past the quasi-reasonable stage, when each pretended to put his case coolly and logically, and would begin with phrases such as: 'What I'm saying is . . .', 'The point I'm making is . . .', and prevent the other from speaking with the perennial: 'If you'd just let me finish . . .' They had made exactly the same points in a variety of different ways for nearly two hours,

236

before tiredness crept in and the argument turned into a nuclear war.

Rimmer's double had launched the first nuke: the bonehead remark. Bonehead. Rimmer's nickname at school. He was really quite irrationally sensitive about it. The word yanked him back to the unhappy school-yards; reminded him of the mindless taunts of his cruel peers, of the dreadful mornings when he ached to be ill so he wouldn't have to go on the green school shuttle and have That Word daubed on his blazer in yellow chalk. He was branded. It was a brand that might fade, but would never completely disappear. He might be eighty years old, and successful as hell, but if he bumped into an old classmate he would still be Bonehead.

Before the double launched the bonehead nuke, Rimmer was unquestionably on top in the argument. The double had said something stupid, and Rimmer had been at the stage of saying: 'Give me an example of that,' knowing full well there were no examples to give. He was strutting up and down in his pyjamas, arms folded, a man in control, a man in command, when the bonehead nuke looped across without warning and blew him away.

'Pardon me, Bonehead.'

Rimmer actually physically staggered. Their arguments had never escalated this far before. They'd gone up to Def Comm Three, but never past it. Rimmer had to employ the time-honoured device of pretending not to have heard him properly, while his psyche's lone bugler sounded muster, and his tattered thoughts tried to regroup and launch an offensive.

But his double had capitalized on Rimmer's temporary silence by immediately launching three follow-up nukes in quick succession. The one about his Father hating him. KABOOM! The one about him being a hideous emotional cripple. KABOOM! And the one about him being afraid of women. KABABABOOM!

Rimmer was about to use a nuke of his own. His left leg had gone into spasm caused by rage. His eyes were wide and crazed. And he didn't care any more. He was going to use *the* nuke. The nuke to end all nukes. The total annihilation device. When his double used it instead.

'Oh, shut up,' the duplicate sneered, 'Mr Gazpacho!'

Rimmer stood, his mouth half-open, swaying dizzily. He felt as if someone had sucked out his insides with a vacuum cleaner.

'Mr What?' he half-smiled in disbelief. 'Mr What??'

'I said: "Mr Gazpacho," D E A F I E!'

'That is the most obscenely hurtful thing anyone has ever said . . .'

'I know,' the double grinned evilly.

Rimmer's hatchway slid open.

'That's the straw that broke the dromedary!' Rimmer screamed back at his double. Then he turned and padded into the corridor where Lister, Kryten and the Cat were standing.

'Ah, Lister. You're back,' he said quietly.

'Everything all right, is it?' Lister asked.

'For sure,' Rimmer smiled. 'Absolutely.'

'No problems, then?'

'Nope.'

'Everything's A-OK?'

'Yup! Things couldn't really be much hunky-dorier.'

'It's just — we heard raised voices.'

Rimmer laughed. 'That's quite an amusing thought, isn't it? Having a blazing row with yourself.'

From the sleeping quarters the double's voice screamed: 'Can you shut the smeg up, Rimmer! Some of us are trying to sleep!'

'I mean,' Rimmer continued, ignoring the outburst, 'obviously we have the odd disagreement. It's like brothers, I mean . . . a little tiff, an exchange of views, but nothing malicious. Nothing with any side to it.'

The double screeched: 'Shut up, you dead git!'

Rimmer smiled at Lister and, perfectly calm, he said: 'Excuse me – I won't be a second.'

He walked slowly down the corridor, paused outside the hatchway, and bellowed at maximum volume: 'Stop your foul whining, you filthy piece of distended rectum!'

Lister, Kryten and the Cat shuffled uncomfortably and examined the floor.

'Look, it's pointless concealing it any longer,' said Rimmer, walking back towards them. 'My duplicate and I . . . we've had a bit of a major tiff. I don't know how it started but, obviously, it goes without saying: it was his fault.'

THIRTY-ONE

Lister's empty supper plate lay on the floor. Only the red, oily streaks of Bangalore Phall and half of his seventh poppadom, which he couldn't quite manage, bore evidence that he'd had a five-course Indian banquet for one.

Earth!

As he lay on his bunk, cuddling his eighth can of Leopard lager, Jimmy Stewart was asking the townfolk not to withdraw their money from the Bailey Building And Loan Company on the sleeping quarters' vid screen.

Earth!

He was watching Frank Capra's *It's a Wonderful Life*, his all-time favourite movie, but couldn't concentrate, even though it was his favourite scene. The Wall Street panic scene. The scene where Jimmy Stewart is trying to calm the hysterical mob clamouring to withdraw all their money after the Wall Street crash. But the money isn't there – the money's invested in the people's houses. Then Jimmy Stewart offers them his honeymoon money – he offers to divide out the two thousand dollars he was going to spend on his *honeymoon* – to keep them going till the bank opened again on Monday. But the fat guy in the hat steps up to the counter and still demands all his money – two hundred and forty-two dollars – and Stewart has to pay it, and he's begging people just to take what they need. And then a woman comes up to the counter and says she can manage on twenty dollars. Then up steps old Mrs Davis and asks for only seventeen dollars and fifty cents, which was the point where Lister usually started to blubber, and tears would sting his eyes, and he wouldn't dare look around the room in case anyone was watching him. But not this time.

Earth!

The movie was as great as ever, and he would never get tired of watching it, but he couldn't concentrate on anything because he knew he was finally going back home.

Earth!

He could taste it.

Nova 5 was fuelled and ready to go. The small band of skutters they'd brought back from the mining expedition were making the final checks and loading supplies. Tomorrow they were leaving. Within weeks Lister would be back on Earth!

Earth!

That septic orb. That dirty, polluted world he loved. He ached for the Brillo pad sting of a breath on a city street. The oh-so-delicious stench of the oily, turdy sea in summer. The grassy parks in spring, festooned with the thrilling vibrant colours of discarded chocolate wrappers and squidgy condoms and squashed soft drink cans. He longed to look up at a winter sky and see again the huge artificial ozone plug which sat above the Earth like an absurd toupé, constructed in his lifetime to repair the damage caused by two generations of people who wanted to flavour their sweat. Earth. It was a dump. It was a sty. But it was his home, where he belonged, and where he was finally going.

He flicked off the vid and slipped down from his bunk. It was time to tell the Rimmers. It was time to tell them that when they left tomorrow on *Nova 5*, only one of them could come.

Rimmer had been avoiding himself since the argument. He didn't know how to begin a reconciliation conversation.

Things had been said which . . . well, things had been said. Hurtful things. Bitter, unforgivable things which could never be forgotten. Equally, he couldn't just carry on as if nothing had happened. So he spent the day in the reference library, keeping out of everyone's way.

It was 4.30 p.m. when he finally swallowed the bile and slumped reluctantly into his sleeping quarters, looking curiously unkempt. His hair was uncombed and unwashed. A two-day hologramatic growth swathed his normally marble-smooth chin. His uniform was creased and ruffled. He flopped untidily into the metal armchair.

His double sat on the bunk, looking moodily out of the viewport window. As Rimmer entered he'd looked round over his shoulder, then turned back without acknowledging him.

They sat there in silence. One minute. Two minutes. Three minutes. Bitter, accusing silence. They were both masters at using silence, and right now they were using it in a bitter, accusing way. After twenty minutes of stonewalling, Rimmer could take no more.

'Look . . .' he began, 'I want to apologize for . . .' Rimmer faltered, uncertain as to precisely what he was supposed to apologize for. 'I want to apologize for everything.'

'Ohhhhh, shut up,' his double said dismissively.

Rimmer's eyes shrank, weasel-small. 'You don't like me, do you? Even though I'm you, you don't actually like me. Even though we're the same person, you actively dislike me.'

His double turned from the window. 'We're not the same person.'

'But we are. You're a copy of me.'

The double shook his head. 'I'm a recording of what you *were*, what you used to be. The man you used to be before the accident. You've changed. Lister's changed you.'

Lister? Changed him? Preposterous.

'I haven't changed. In what way have I changed?'

'Well, for a start, you've just apologized.'

What was it his father used to say? 'Never apologize – never explain.'

'I'm sorry,' Rimmer apologized again; 'it's just – I want us to get on.'

'Oh, don't be pathetic.'

Rimmer closed his eyes and leaned back on his chair. Was it just him? Was it some dreadful flaw in his personality that prevented him from having a successful relationship even with his own self? Or would it be the same for most people? Would *most* people find their own selves irritating and tiresomely predictable? When he saw his face in the mirror in the morning, that was the face he carried around in his head: he never saw his profile; he never saw the back of his own head; he didn't see what other people saw. It was the same with his personality. He carried around an idealized picture of himself; he was the smart, sensitive person who did this good thing, or that good thing. He buried the bad bits. He covered up and ignored the flaws. All his faults were forgiven and forgotten.

But now he was faced with them; all his shortcomings, personified in his other self.

Rimmer had never been aware how awesomely petty he was. How alarmingly immature. How selfish. How he could, on occasion, be incomprehensibly stupid. How sad he was; how screwed-up and lonely.

And he was seeing this for the first time. It was like the first time he'd heard his own voice on an answering machine. He expected to hear dulcet tones, clear, articulate and accentless, and was embarrassed and nauseated to discover only incoherent mumblings in some broad Ionian accent. In his head he sounded like a newsreader; in reality, he sounded nasal and dull and constantly depressed. And meeting himself was the same, only worse, raised to the power 1000.

And there were other things. He was at least thirty per cent worse-looking than he thought. He stooped. His right leg constantly jiggled, as if he wanted to be somewhere else. He snored! Not the loud buzz-saw hunnnk-hnnnunk of Lister; his own snore was, if anything, more irritating – a high-pitched whiny trill, like a large parrot being strangled in a bucket of soapy water. It was a terrible thing to admit, but he was reaching the devastating, inescapable conclusion that he, as a companion, was the very last person he wanted to spend any time with.

Was this the same for everybody? Or was it just him? He didn't know.

So lost was he in this train of thought that he was only vaguely aware of Lister coming into the room and announcing that *Nova 5* could only sustain one hologram, and so one of the Rimmers would have to be switched off. Who was it going to be? he was asking.

'Who what?' asked Rimmer.

'Who's going to come on *Nova 5*, and who's going to be turned off?'

'Well, obviously I'm coming,' said Rimmer.

'Why "obviously"?' said his double.

'Because I'm the original. I was here first.'

'So what? We should toss for it.'

'Nooo,' said Rimmer through a disparaging laugh. 'Why should I want to toss for it? I might lose.'

Lister took out a coin. 'Heads or tails?'

'What?' said Rimmer.

'Fair's fair. You call.'

'You expect me to call heads or tails as to whether or not I get erased?' Rimmer's features fled to the perimeter of his face. 'No way. I stay.'

'You're the same person. It's only fair. Call.' Lister flipped the coin, caught it, and covered it with his hand.

'I'm not calling.'

'I'll call,' said the double.

'*I'll* call,' Rimmer said firmly. 'Heads . . . no, tails. Tails, I mean. No, wait, heads, heads.'

'It's tails,' said Lister. 'You get erased.'

'I haven't finished deciding yet. I think I was going to choose tails. Yes, I was. "Tails," in fact.'

'Too late,' said the double. 'Erase him.'

'But I was here first,' protested Rimmer. 'In a way, I created you.'

'What difference does it make? You're identical,' Lister said; 'you're the same person.'

'But we're not,' Rimmer whined balefully. 'Not any more, we're not.'

THIRTY-TWO

It was four in the morning and Rimmer sat on the bunk, his long arms wrapped around his spindly knees, his brain fighting off sleep. It was ironic, he thought, that he'd just about come to terms with having died, and now here he was, about to be erased forever.

On the toss of a coin.

But that was life, he thought. Life was the toss of a coin. You're born rich; you're born poor. You're born smart; you're born stupid. You're born handsome; you're born with a face like a post office clerk.

Heads you are, tails you aren't.

Rimmer felt that most of his life had come up 'tails'. Relationships with women: tails. Career success: tails. Friendships: tails. His life, best out of three: tails, tails and tails.

He'd never been in love, and now he never would be. He'd never been an officer, and now he never would be. He'd never be anything, because he was about to be erased.

All right, there still would be an Arnold Rimmer, but it wasn't him, it was his so-called double. But he wasn't a double – they were different.

He allowed himself an ironic snicker. He couldn't even succeed at being Arnold Rimmer – there were two of them and he'd come second. Unbelievable.

Unbe-smegging-lievable.

What had he learned from his life? What? Except 'keep your face out of the way of atomic explosions'? Nothing.

He'd learned nothing. What had he achieved? Again, nothing. His life was a goalless draw.

In his entire life, thirty-one years alive and one year dead, he'd made love with a real live woman once. One time only. Uno. Ein. Une. Once. One raised to the power of one. What Planck's Constant can never be more than. Pi divided by itself.

We are talking one here, me old buckeroo, he thought. *Once.*

Yvonne McGruder. A single, brief liaison with the ship's female boxing champion. 16th March, 19.31 hours to 19.43 hours.

Twelve minutes.

And that included the time it took to eat the pizza.

In his whole life he'd spent more time vomiting than he ever spent making love. Was that right? Was that fair? That a man should spend more time with his head down a lavatory than buried in the buttocks of the woman he loved?

He'd always deluded himself that the problem was he hadn't met the right girl yet. Now, given that the human race probably no longer existed, coupled with the fact that he had passed on, even he had to admit there was more than a possibility he was leaving it a *little* bit on the late side.

He'd never had a break. Never. And so much of life was luck.

Luck.

If Napoleon had been born Welsh, would his destiny have been the same? If he'd been raised in Colwyn Bay, would he have been a great general? Of course he wouldn't. He'd have married a sheep and worked in the local fish and chips shop. But no – he'd had the luck to be born in Corsica, just at the right moment in history when the French were looking for a short, brilliant Fascist dictator.

Luck.

Van Gogh. Wasn't it sheer good fortune that Van Gogh was born raving mad? Wasn't that why his cornfields looked

like they did? Wasn't that why he did several hundred paintings of his old boots? Wasn't that why his paintings were so
innovative? Because he had the happy chance to be born with
a leak in the think tank?

Luck!

And what about John Merrick? The jammy bastard – born
looking like an elephant. How can you fail? You just stand
around while people goggle at you, and you rake it in.

He was too normal, that was his problem. Too ordinary,
and normal, and healthy and bland. A bit of madness, a spot
of deafness, the looks of an elephant, a birthplace like Corsica,
and he could have been somebody. He could have been the
deaf, mad, elephant Frenchman for a start.

He stood up and paced around the room. His body wanted
to sleep, but his mind wanted to rant. This was torture. It was
Death Row. It was Hell. If it was going to happen, he wanted
to get it over with. He couldn't tolerate the agony of a day
knowing everything he did he would be doing for the last
time.

Forget tomorrow, he wanted to be erased now.

'Forget tomorrow,' he said, 'I want to be erased now.'

'It's half past four in the morning,' croaked Lister, scraping
the fuzz off his tongue with his top teeth.

Rimmer's duplicate sprang out of his bunk. 'Great! Let's
get it over with.'

'What d'you think you're doing?' Lister asked.

'I'm coming to watch.'

Lister shook his head. 'It's not a freak show.'

The double forced air through his teeth disappointedly.
'There's precious little entertainment on this ship. If you can't
attend the odd execution, what've you got left?'

Lister started to get dressed. 'I'll see you in the disc library
in ten minutes.'

Rimmer nodded and left.

★

When Rimmer arrived Lister was already there, sitting in front of the generating console clutching a mug of steaming black coffee and a jam doughnut brushed with sugar.

Great, thought Rimmer. *Come to my execution. Light refreshments available.*

'Fancy a drink?' said Lister, sipping at his rum-laced coffee.

Rimmer grunted in the negative. He was wearing his best blue First Technician boiler suit, with a row of worn-looking medals dangling over the spanner pocket.

'I didn't know you had any medals. What are they?'

Rimmer pointed to the first medal with his forefinger: 'Three years' long service.' He tapped the second: 'Six years' long service.' He touched the third: 'Nine years' long service, and . . .' he hesitated, his finger over the final medal, as if remembering, 'and . . . uh . . . twelve years' long service.'

Lister didn't smile.

'Come on – one drink.'

Rimmer capitulated. 'I'll have a whisky.'

Holly simulated a large shot of Glen Fujiyama, and Rimmer took it in one belt.

'Another?'

Rimmer nodded, unable to speak, feeling as if the lining of his larynx had been stripped like wallpaper.

A second malt arrived in a hologramatic glass. He tipped it into his mouth.

Rimmer was totally unused to drink. His face glowed brightly. His hair seemed to uncoil and hang onto his face. He swept it back with both his hands, and sighed a long, world-weary sigh. A sigh that had been inside him, trying to get out, for thirty-one years.

'Gaaahhhhhhhhhhhhhhhhhhhhhhhhhhhhhhhhhhhhhhhhhhh.'

He unfurled himself into a spare monitor seat and jiggled his right leg impatiently. 'Come on – let's go! Let's do it! Come on – turn me off. Let's do it! Erase me. Wipe me clean. Let's go.'

249

Lister finished his doughnut and dusted the sugar off his hands. 'So what's this big thing about gazpacho soup?' he said, casually taking a throatful of coffee.

'How do you know about gazpacho soup?'

'I heard the end of the argument. And you've been yelling about it in your sleep ever since I joined up. I just wondered what it was.'

'Aahh! Wouldn't you like to know?'

'Yeah. I would like to know.'

'I bet you would, Listy. I bet you would.'

'Are you going to tell me?'

Rimmer wagged his finger. 'Secret.'

'Go on – tell me.'

'I can't. It's too terrible.' Rimmer clasped his hands and rested them between his splayed knees, his back hunched, his eyes fixed on the rubber-matting floor. He shook his head. 'I can't tell you. I'd like to tell you but I can't.'

'Why?'

Rimmer's eyebrows plaited. 'You're right. What's the difference? What does it matter now? Now I'm going to be erased? You want to know about gazpacho soup? I'll tell you.' He flung his head back and closed his eyes, and started to tell Lister about the greatest night of his life.

THIRTY-THREE

'It was the greatest night of my life,' he began. 'Every Friday evening the Captain held a formal dinner in her private dining room, in her quarters. Just a few of the top officers and their partners, and one, maybe two, of the boys and girls to watch. The young Turks. The up-and-comers. The people who were happening. I'd only been with the company five months and the invitation hit the mat. I knew what it was before I opened it.

'"*The Captain requests the pleasure of the company of Mr A. J. Rimmer and guest. 8.30 for 9.00. Black tie, evening dress. RSVP.*"

'We were in orbit round Ganymede; it was a long-term dock for repairs. I didn't know what to do – I didn't have a partner, and I didn't know any women well enough to ask them. So, on the Friday morning, I caught the shuttle, found the best escort agency on Ganymede, and hired . . .' Rimmer's eyes milked over '. . . She was gorgeous. Nothing I can say now can begin to indicate how truly dynamite this girl was. She made Marilyn Monroe look like a hippo. She was at the university, doing a Ph.D. in stellar engineering, and did the escort thing for extra money. She had *four* degrees. One of the degrees was in something I couldn't even pronounce – that's how smart she was. I paid the agency fee, which was a lot. I mean, a *lot* lot. And then I tipped her double to pretend we were dating on a regular basis, and to act as if she was crazy about me. Only in public,' Rimmer waved his hand, as if to ward off evil thoughts, 'there was no funny business.

Oh, how I longed for the funny business! But that wasn't the deal. It was all above board.

'We went shopping, and I bought her a dress. Not just a dress.

'A drrrrrrrrrrrressssssssssssssss.

'It probably cost about the same as the entire NASA budget for the twenty-first century. I had to write extra small to fit all of the numbers into the box on my chequebook. Then,' he made a trilling sound with his tongue, 'then we went out and picked a tuxedo for me.

'She went home to get changed, and we arranged to meet at the shuttle port at six.

'Seven o'clock, she still hasn't shown up. I phone the escort agency, which in the meantime has turned into a Chinese restaurant. I try the university. What do you know? There is no university on Ganymede. I've been had. I've been taken. I've blown three months' salary and I haven't even got a date. I can't believe it. I catch the seven-thirty shuttle back to *Red Dwarf*. I ask all five air hostesses, but they say they're all on duty and can't come. So there's nothing for it: I have to go on my own. I'm humiliated before I walk in the door.

'So, I turn up at the Captain's quarters completely by myself. Everyone else has got partners. The table is all set with place cards. I have to spend the whole evening sitting opposite an empty chair. They ask me where my date is, and I panic and tell them she was killed in a road accident earlier in the evening, but I'm over it now.

'We sit down, and dinner begins. I'm feeling like I've got off to a really bad start, so I'm trying desperately to be charming as smeg, but no one's warming to me. Then I remember the joke. Ledbetter had told me this joke about a bear trapper in Alaska. It was funny, it was clean; it was perfect for the dinner party. Originally I was going to save it for the mints and coffee, but by this time I'm feeling I might not even *make* it to the mints and coffee; the empty chair's staring back at me, and the rest of the guests are convinced my girlfriend's lying in some morgue somewhere while I go out to a dinner party. So I decide now is the time to tell the joke. And I'm telling the joke, and it's a long joke, and I'm suddenly aware no one's talking and everybody's watching me telling the joke, and I'm very self-conscious all of a sudden, and I can feel my ears – I'm suddenly really aware of my ears – and the back of my neck's starting to prickle. Suddenly, for no reason at all, I forget the end. I forget the punch line. I forget how it finishes. I just stop talking, and everyone's still looking at me. I have to say: "I'm very sorry, but that's as much as I remember." There's this pause. Horrible pause. Horrible. Horrible. And I can see the Captain's boyfriend looking at me with pity in his eyes, because he thinks I'm half-crazy with grief. And everyone starts talking. But not to me. Then the stewards wheel in the first course.

'It's soup.

'Gazpacho soup.

'While they're serving, I'm studying the cutlery. I'd bought this etiquette book, and I know two things. One: never wear diamonds before lunch, and two: with cutlery, start from the outside and work your way in. I start from the outside. I start so far from the outside, I inadvertently take the spoon of the woman sitting next to me. Eventually we sort it out, and start to eat.

'My soup is cold. I mean, stone cold. I look up. Everyone else's appears to be fine. Here's my chance to make a mark. I call over the steward and very discreetly tell him my soup is cold. He looks at me like I'm something he's just scraped off his shoe. He takes the soup away and brings it back hot. Everyone starts laughing. I start laughing too. And the more I laugh, the more they laugh.'

He stopped, and turned his closed eyes to the ceiling. He smiled through clenched teeth and then, as if every word were punctuated by the pulling of a dagger from his heart, inch by agonizing inch, he said:

'I . . . didn't . . . know . . . gazpacho . . . soup . . . was . . . meant . . . to . . . be . . . served . . . cold.'

His head slumped forward again, and he carried on.

'And by now they're hysterical, uncontrollable. I still think they're laughing at the steward, when all the time they're laughing at me as I eat my piping-hot gazpacho soup.' The memory washed over him like a wave in an acid sea. He bathed in its flesh-stripping agony. He cleared his throat. 'That was the last time I ate at the Captain's table.' Rimmer opened his eyes. They'd been closed throughout the entire story. 'That evening was pretty much the end of my career.'

There was a silence.

'Is that it?' Lister said eventually. 'Is that what you've been torturing yourself with for the last seven years? One dumb mistake that anybody could have made?'

'If only they'd mentioned it in basic training. Instead of climbing up ropes and crawling through tunnels on your elbows. If just once they'd said "Gazpacho soup is served cold", I could have been an admiral by now. I could. I really could.'

'Come on – everybody has memories that make them wince. And ninety-nine per cent of the time the only person who remembers the incident is you.'

'Oh, what does it matter *now*? Come on. Let's get it over with. Erase me.'

'And those things nearly always happen with people you don't know very well, and don't see very often, so who gives a smeg anyway?'

'Just turn me off. Get on with it.'

Lister swigged at his now cold coffee. 'I've already done it. I wiped the other one.'

Emotions wrestled for space on Rimmer's brow. 'You wiped . . . the duplicate? When?'

'Before you walked in.'

'And you let me stand here . . . and . . . spill my guts?'

'Yeah.' A big, broad grin.

'Why?'

'I wanted to find out about gazpacho soup, and I knew you'd never tell me.'

'Of course I wouldn't tell you – because you'd make my life hell with gazpacho soup jokes for the rest of eternity.'

'Rimmer – I swear I will never mention this conversation again.'

Rimmer regarded him dubiously.

'I don't break my word. I'm a lot of things, but I'm not a liar.'

Rimmer looked at him through one eye. 'All right, then. I believe you. You're a disgusting rancid slob, but you keep your word.'

'Thank you.'

Rimmer got up from the chair. 'So I'm going back to Earth, then?'

Lister nodded. 'We're all going back to Earth, then.'

Rimmer motioned drunkenly towards the hatchway. 'Come on. Let's go down the Copacabana, have a real drink.'

Lister got up to follow him.

'Souper,' he said.

THIRTY-FOUR

Strange, but years later, whenever Lister remembered it, he always remembered it in black and white. And something else; the memories came in a rush: there were no insignificant details, only significant ones. He remembered his scalp tingling as the cargo bay doors boomed open.

He remembered his giddiness as *Nova 5* taxied across the cargo deck and blasted into the blackness of space.

He remembered the silvery light that preceded each jump, and the incomparable feeling of existing simultaneously at two points in the universe – and then the jolt as all his cells 'decided' to be in the new position.

Perhaps a thousand jolts.

And there it was – on the navicomp screen.

The planet Earth.

They were home.

Part Three

Earth

ONE

The big clock on the wall tocked round to five o'clock, and Lister lifted up the flap on the counter and turned the sign on the door to 'Closed'. Bailey's Perfect Shami Kebab Emporium was shutting for the day. Lister rang up 'no sale' on the old-fashioned wrought-iron till, and counted the week's takings. Fourteen dollars and twenty-five cents. Another great week.

He dipped his hand into the penny candy jar, picked out a liquorice shoelace, then grabbed his overcoat and scarf, pulled on his fur-lined deerstalker and mittens, and walked out into the crisp white snow. The bell on the door jangled behind him; there was never any need to lock the shop, not here in Bedford Falls. There was only one cop for the entire population of three thousand, and he spent most of his day asleep in his patrol car.

Lister crunched across the eiderdown street, chewing happily on his liquorice, and headed for the bank. A group of carol singers were standing round the war memorial, belting out *God Rest Ye Merry, Gentlemen*, accompanied by a four-piece brass band. They all waved a cheery greeting, and Lister stood with them and helped them finish his favourite carol.

'Merry Christmas,' he said, and dropped two dollars into their can as Ernie, the cab driver, produced a hip flask from the bell of his tuba and gave Lister a nip of brandy.

It being after five o'clock, and Christmas Eve, the bank was closed, of course. Lister tried the door. It jangled open.

'Hello? Anybody home?'

Money was stacked in neat piles on the wooden counter – obviously Horace hadn't got round to putting it in the safe yet.

'Horace? Are you there?'

Horace stepped through the back door, holding a sheet of wrapping paper and some string.

'Sorry, Mr Bailey, I was just wrapping presents for the kids up at the orphan home. You ever tried to wrap a Hula-Hoop? I'll be a monkey's uncle if I can figure it.'

Lister handed over ten dollars and asked Horace to put it in his account.

'Ten dollars! Business is *good*, Mr Bailey.'

Lister smiled, and pulled out a handful of candy walking sticks from his huge overcoat pocket. 'I didn't have time to wrap them. Hope the orphanage doesn't mind.'

'They won't mind, George. Merry Christmas.'

'Merry Christmas, Horace,' said Lister, and turned to go. 'You know – you should get a lock for this bank door or something.'

'That's what everybody says, but I figure what the heck – I'd only lose the key.'

Lister laughed, and walked back out into the street.

Last minute shoppers exchanged Merry Christmasses with him as he crossed back to the Emporium, where his rickety old model 'A' Ford was covered in snow. He took the hand crank from the bench seat and jerked the engine into spluttering life. As he turned left at Martini's Bar his arms started to hurt again, so he pulled over outside Old Man Gower's drugstore.

His arms had been giving him problems for a few weeks now. It was like a burning sensation down both his forearms – excruciatingly painful at times, but Doc MacKenzie couldn't find anything wrong with them. There were no marks, nothing showed up on the X-ray: it was a complete mystery.

He grabbed a tub of cooling ointment from Old Man Gower's shelves and dropped twenty-five cents into the open till, then hopped back in his old Ford and headed for home: 220 Sycamore.

A couple of birds – robins, Lister guessed – were singing in the snow-laden lilac trees that lined the avenue. Life was good. Everything seemed . . . well, perfect. But, God, did his arms hurt.

It had been two years since they returned to Earth. Two years since *Nova 5* had completed the duality jumps which brought them back to their own solar system. Two years since they'd skidded to a landing in the middle of the Sahara desert. As they'd opened the airlock and stepped out into the baking heat, there, like a mirage over the brow of a vast dune, an army of jeeps and helicopters had descended on them.

The world's press went crazy! The three-million-year-old men! Space adventurers!

Things hadn't changed that much. The human race were still there, a foot or so taller, but still there. And so was everything that went with the human race: advertising, commercialism, marketing, huge dirty cities and people on the make. And it had turned into a freak show: interviews, book offers, chat shows, endorsements, sponsorship deals . . . Lister had hated it. He was a piece of meat that people wanted to package and sell.

'I'm three million years old – what's my secret? I eat Breadman's Fish Fingers.'

'I've been all around the universe, and I've never come across anything quite as good as Luton's Carpet Shampoo.'

Rimmer lapped it up, the Cat adored it, but Lister just wanted to get away. He'd turned down all the offers, changed his name and opted for the peaceful anonymity of this back-water town in the American mid-west. He couldn't believe it when he'd discovered there actually *was* a town called Bedford Falls. He'd gone there on a whim, to take a look, and was stunned how similar the place was to the Bedford Falls in *It's a Wonderful Life*. It seemed like fans of the film had all collected there to live out their lives in a self-created 1940s American Shangri-la.

Of course he couldn't keep his secret from the townfolk for long; his face had been plastered all over magazine covers and newspapers for six months, so he guessed more or less everyone knew who he was and where he'd come from. But they pretended they didn't. They all called him 'Mr Bailey', or 'George', which was the pseudonym he'd chosen. They respected his privacy, and guarded his secret, and he was left in peace to live out the rest of his life in this quiet idyll.

But something was wrong with his arms, and it was beginning to worry him.

He turned the Ford into the tree-lined drive of his old house and honked his horn three times. The snow lay thick and deep on the lawn, and a huge, eight-foot snowman was grinning a welcome in coal. Lister grabbed the Christmas presents off the back seat and staggered under their weight up the drive to the porch. As he pushed open the door with his back, he could hear a carol being mutilated on a clapped-out old piano. He loved that sound. To Lister it was better than the London Phil.

He walked into the parlour. A log fire was burning merrily in the grate. Jim and Bexley were smashing *Silent Night* out of the complaining piano, while Krissie was standing on a stepladder, putting tinsel on the Christmas tree. She turned and smiled, and blew him a kiss.

When the kids were in bed they sat snoozily in the big leather armchair with the springs poking through the back, watching the fire splutter and splurt, and listening to Hoagy Carmichael on the wind-up phonograph. After Krissie climbed the stairs to their draughty bedroom with the leaky roof, he took out the ointment – he didn't want her to know about his arms – and began to apply it to the sore areas.

It came as something of a shock that, when he'd put the cream specifically on the areas that throbbed and hurt, it spelt out a word. A word written in pain down his forearm.

The word was 'DYING'.

TWO

The black stretch Mercedes with the tinted, bullet-proof glass glided along the Champs Elysées, and pulled up outside the canopy of the hundred-and-forty-floor skyscraper. Rimmer finished his phone call to his publicist, then stepped out of the limo. A string of bodyguards kept at bay the group of teenage girls who'd camped out on the steps overnight, in the hope of catching a glimpse of A.J.R. He allowed them a thin smile as he walked under the canopy and up the marble steps into the Rimmer Building (Paris). The Rimmer Building (Paris) was an identical copy of the Rimmer Building (London) and the Rimmer Building (New York). He was happy with the towering glass and steel architecture, so he saw no need to vary the design. The electric doors purred open and he strode across the thick white mink carpet, trailed by the gaggle of accountants and financial advisers who seemed to follow him everywhere.

As he walked across the massive lobby, he dismissed his financial advisers for the evening, and nodded almost imperceptibly at Pierre, the Sorbonne graduate he'd hired exclusively to press the button that summoned the lift. While he waited, he swung round to look at the colossal white marble statue of himself, captured in the middle of a Full Double-Rimmer, which the Space Corps had long accepted as its standard official salute. The lift took a full ninety seconds to arrive, so he fired Pierre and pressed the button himself for floor 140 – his luxury penthouse suite. The fact that he could actually press the button at all was, in a way, the key to the immense fortune he'd amassed since his return to Earth two years previously.

After the hero's welcome, his cunning business brain had taken full advantage of the offers which flooded in daily. With the money he culled from advertising and the publication of his memoirs, he'd set up various multi-national corporations which had sponsored the Rimmer Research Centres, which had finally invented the Solidgram – a solid body that housed his personality and intellect. He was now exactly like any normal living person, with the added bonus that he was more or less immortal. The Solidgram had sold in such quantities, his income from that alone allowed him to buy the Bahamas for 'somewhere to go at the weekends'.

It amused him no end that he was now one of the three or four richest men in the world, while Lister was stuck in a dead-end burger bar in a dead-end town somewhere in the middle of nowhere.

He'd hired a private investigator who had taken fourteen months to track him down. Rimmer was now well into the complicated negotiations to buy up the entire town, which he intended to turn into a huge maggot farm. Just for the hell of it.

He got out of the lift and walked past the salute-shaped pool on the roof garden. Hugo, one of the gardening staff, was aquavac-ing cherry blossoms from the surface of the water.

'Monsieur Rimmer!' he called, 'Madame Juanita – she is unwell again.'

Rimmer sighed. 'Unwell' was the code for throwing a major Brazilian wobbly. His wife was having one of her regular tantrums. Juanita Chicata was unquestionably the most beautiful woman in the world. Everything about her was classic, from the tip of her perfect nose to the toes of her beautiful feet. Eyes the colour of fire, panther-black hair, dangerous lips. Dangerous woman. She'd made two fortunes, the first as the world's number one model, the second as the world's number one actress. And she was a great actress – she wasn't a model who got by on her looks, she really was the finest actress in the world. And she was nineteen years old. She had beauty, brains, talent, everything. God had finally got it right.

Every man, *every* man desired her.

And she'd married Rimmer two summers earlier. This was another source of amusement for Rimmer. While Lister had ended up with a very ordinary girl-next-door type, he'd acquired the 'Brazilian Bombshell'.

Right now the Brazilian Bombshell was exploding in the master bedroom of their penthouse apartment. Rimmer wandered through the exotic Chinese roof garden, while four hundred catering staff prepared for the customary Saturday night party. The marquee had been erected overlooking the glistening Seine, the forty thousand fireworks were all in place and primed, the three-hundred-yard-long buffet table was crammed to overflowing with food which had been flown in from around the world earlier that day, the centrepiece of which was a replica of Juanita's naked body in caviar. He paused to admire it. Even like this, even sculpted from little black fish eggs, it was a body that drove him crazy. He couldn't help himself – he leaned over and nibbled at the splendid right breast – the real ones were insured for ten million each, and she hadn't let him near them for over a year and a half. Which was why right now Rimmer had his face buried deep in the ice-cold caviar.

Suddenly, from above, there was a shattering of glass as a Louis XIV grand piano crashed out of the french windows of their master bedroom and landed on the roof garden, crushing one of the catering staff.

It had amused Rimmer when the private detective reported

that Lister had a piano – a clapped-out tuneless wreck with dry rot which Lister had bought at a second-hand shop in Bedford Falls for four dollars and thirty cents. Rimmer's piano, which now lay in pieces on top of a screaming servant, had cost him a million. It was a lot to pay for a piano that nobody played, but his wife thought it would look 'kinda neat' in the bedroom, so he'd got it. Now, of course, it wasn't worth the price of a cup of tea, because she'd hurled it out of the window because she was . . . 'unwell'.

Juanita was regularly 'unwell' – perhaps two or three times a week – and on each occasion it cost Rimmer upwards of three hundred thousand. Still, he could afford it. And she *was* the most beautiful woman alive. And she was married to him.

As he walked into the master bedroom he found Juanita hurling dollops of cold cream at an original Picasso, while two maids swept up the remains of the fifth-century Ming vase that she'd used to smash the nose of the Michelangelo statue he'd bought her as a kiss-and-make-up gift.

Rimmer sighed and shook his head. Why had she gone crazy this time? What was the reason for today's little sulk? Was it because for the second month in a row she wasn't on the cover of *Vogue*? Was it because she *was* on the cover of *Vogue*, and she didn't like the photograph? Was it because she'd put on a pound in weight? Or had she *lost* a pound in weight? Both, of course, were disastrous. Had the maid accidently brought up Lapsang tea instead of Keema? Last time she did that it had cost Rimmer three Matisses and his entire collection of Iranian pottery. Was the telephone dirty again? Was there nothing on TV she wanted to watch?

Whatever it was she was obviously upset, because now she had taken down Rimmer's twelfth-century samurai sword and was hacking away at the water bed. The liquid gurgled happily over the irreplaceable Persian rug.

'Nita, Nita,' he cooed soothingly as he sploshed over

towards her, 'what is it? What has disturbed my little turtle dove?'

She turned to face him, ferocious, the samurai sword clasped above her head. 'I can't tell you. You wouldn't understand eet!' She skewered a Cézanne hanging above the bed, and sliced it into thin shreds.

'You can tell me anything,' Rimmer said softly.

'Not thees! I can't tell you thees!'

'Please. Tell me what's made you so angry.'

'Hugo!' she screeched and, at the mention of his name, she hurled the Koh-i-Nor out of the window and down onto the Champs Elysées below.

'What about Hugo?' said Rimmer, picking up the phone to make arrangements for the pool man's dismissal.

'He won't make love to me any more,' she bawled. Then she collapsed into a sobbing heap in the soggy mess of the demolished water bed. 'Not ever. He's afraid you'll find out and sack heem.'

'Well, he's got a point,' Rimmer found himself saying.

Then it hit him.

What she'd said. He was stunned. He felt sick.

He was nauseated. His wife unfaithful! Juanita and Hugo! His hairy-shouldered pool attendant had caressed that fabulous bosom! What would the insurance company say?

His wife had slept with his pool attendant. No wonder the water was never at the right temperature!

Rimmer felt . . . numb.

THREE

Lister sat in the red glow of the firelight, looking down at his arms and the messages in ointment on each of them. How was it possible for pain to 'spell out' words? What was it? Was it something inside him? The message on his left arm: 'DYING'. What did that mean? *He* was dying? The something *inside* him was dying?

He looked across at his right arm: four letters and a symbol, but he didn't know what they meant. Could it be that it was just a coincidence that the pain happened to spell out two messages that happened to be in English on his forearms? Unlikely, but not impossible. After all, some fairly bizarre things had happened since he returned to Earth. Finding Bedford Falls the way he'd always imagined it. Finding someone who was the exact duplicate of Kristine Kochanski. Exact. Down to the pinball smile. Down to the laugh. Down to the tiny mole on her bottom. Who just happened to be a direct descendant of the Third Console Officer he'd had an affair with aboard *Red Dwarf* three million years ago. Who just happened to fall in love with him almost instantly, and give him twin sons.

And the boys. Both beautiful, both perfectly-formed, never any trouble. They never cried, they never whined; they even changed one another's nappies.

Wasn't that a bit odd? Self-nappy-changing babies? Lister didn't know much about babies, but Krissie had always accepted it as normal behaviour, so he had too. Also, he didn't know exactly when babies started to walk and talk, but Jim and Bexley were only fifteen months old yet they could play the piano, converse like adults, and even toss a Zero-Gee ball about with him in the back garden.

Previously, he'd never given these things much thought. His life was pretty much perfect. He had everything he wanted, and what was the use in worrying about how lucky he'd been?

The Emporium – that was another peculiar thing. Now he came to think of it, every week he always took fourteen dollars and twenty-five cents. Which, as it happened, was the exact amount he needed to pay for his mortgage, three dollars; food, two dollars; petrol, twenty-five cents; the rent on the shop, a dollar fifty; savings, five dollars; leaving three dollars fifty, which he could give to people in trouble.

He got up and started pacing the threadbare carpet. He didn't like where his thoughts were leading him. How many times had it been Christmas Eve since he arrived at Bedford Falls? Five, six hundred? In fact, wasn't it *always* Christmas Eve? How was *that* possible?

Bexley padded down the stairs in his Donald Duck sleepsuit and Goofy slippers.

'Hi, Dad. Jim wants a drink of milk. We've run out – is it OK if I get some?'

Lister looked at his fifteen-month-old son as he struggled into his quilted jump suit. He was big for his age, there was no question. Fifteen months, he could talk and dress himself. He was precocious.

'I'm just going to pop down to Old Man Gower's,' he said, tugging on his wellingtons. 'D'you want anything?'

Lister shook his head. Bexley stood on tiptoe and opened the front door.

Lister heard the model 'A' Ford start up and Bexley roared off into town. Everyone thought it was funny that Bexley could drive Lister's car. Obviously it was illegal, but Bert, the cop, thought it was funny too. 'He's a better driver than I am,' he used to say; 'why should I stop him?'

Now that *was* weird. A fifteen-month-old baby driving into town to get some milk for his brother. It was barely believable. Well, it *wasn't* believable. It was impossible.

Lister looked down at the message on his right arm. Four letters, one symbol. A chill passed through him. He knew what it meant. 'U = B T L'.

He knew what it meant.

FOUR

It was a gloriously warm summer's evening with just enough breeze to make it perfect. The Rimmers were having a party. Arnie and Juanita were entertaining. And anybody who was anybody, and anybody who was one day going to *be* anybody, was there.

The four-hundred piece New York Philharmonic Orchestra, flown in specially for the evening, were playing a tribute to James Last. The prima ballerinas from all the European Ballets were arranged around the roof garden in gilded cages, spinning and pirouetting to entertain the guests.

Five thousand guests in all.

The men in black DJs, and the women in fabulously outrageous ball gowns, mingled among the flocks of pink flamingos Rimmer had hired for the evening.

Rimmer sat in his white dinner suit under the shade of a giant parasol, sipping a glass of 1799 Château d'Yquem, holding court to only the most famous and influential. A waiter was serving soup from a giant golden tureen. One of the guests, a member of the British Royal family, was complaining that the soup was cold. Rimmer leaned over and whispered discreetly in his ear that it was gazpacho soup, and gazpacho soup was always served cold – it was Spanish.

'Well, I didn't know that,' said the Prince of Wales. Rimmer waved his hand in a desultory fashion to dismiss the poor man's embarrassment.

'Not many people do.'

Rimmer caught sight of the swimming pool, and it plunged him back into his depression. A fluttering started in his stomach. He loved his salute-shaped pool, but he'd never be able to look at it again without thinking of Hugo, the pool attendant. Hugo, the caresser of twenty-million-dollar bosoms. He'd dismissed him, of course, then made a few phone calls. Never again would Hugo be able to use a credit card. Never again would he shop at any Marks & Spencer's branch in the entire solar system. And buying shoes from any of the companies in the Burton group he would find strangely impossible. Getting his haircut anywhere in France would be out of the question. And a certain canned food company beginning with 'H' had guaranteed that a certain individual, also beginning with 'H', would never be sold any of their products in the future. Never again would the wretched man ever enjoy beans on toast. At least, not really good beans on toast. Only inferior supermarket brands. Not in itself punishment to rival the *auto de fes*, but Rimmer had barely begun pulling the strings and calling in the favours which would ensure Hugo's life became unbearable.

Rimmer heard Juanita's tinkling laugh and, as he peered through the milling party guests, he caught a tantalizing glimpse as she stood on the Chinese bridge over the pool, dazzling some producer with her wit and beauty. He froze.

She was wearing *that* outfit! The one he'd expressly forbidden her to wear. The glass brassiere with the live goldfish swimming inside, the thin red belt, and *nothing else*! Just the diamond high heels and the gold anklet.

A red belt! That's all she was wearing. He shook with rage. She was uncontrollable. Everything was on display! Everything! For all the guests to see.

'But it's so chic!' she'd argued. 'Adrienne created eet especially for me. You're such a prude.'

The more he'd screamed at her to put some clothes on, the more determined she'd been to wear it. To wear it and humiliate him. Her only gestures to modesty were the two goldfish – one in each bra cup – and they could hardly be relied on to stay in a nipple-covering position all the time. He hated her. But he loved her.

The Brazilian Bombshell.

What could he do? She drove him crazy. But he was stuck with it. The third richest man in the whole of the world had a wife who wore a couple of goldfish at dinner parties.

He tried to rip his eyes away from her and back to the game of RISK he was playing with his three favourite dinner guests. It was Julius's go. With his yellow counters he'd established a foothold in Africa and was poised to throw the dice and attack Southern Europe, where Rimmer's blue counters had their second front. The third player, the French-man with the kiss curl, looked on earnestly. If the yellow assault should succeed, he could break out of South America with his red counters and swamp George's green counters, which were massed in the USA.

Julius shook the dice and rolled three threes. Rimmer rolled two fours. Julius attacked and Rimmer defended, until the yellow hordes had been reduced to only two counters. The Italian rolled his eyes skywards. He was finished, and he knew it.

'Well, Julius, me old fruit,' Rimmer grinned, 'looks like you're a gonner.'

Caesar took off his laurel wreath and scratched his balding head. 'I'm going to get a drink!' he stormed, and stalked off to the poolside bar.

'So –' Rimmer turned to his two remaining adversaries – 'just Messrs Patton and Bonaparte left in.'

'God damn you, you dirty son of a bitch!' General Patton threw his huge cigar into the pool. 'Throw the dice and get it over with.'

One of the waiters – Rimmer couldn't remember his name – leaned over and whispered discreetly.

'There's a gentleman in the main reception who insists on seeing you, sir.'

'Send him away.'

'He *insists*, sir.'

'Send him away. I'm busy.'

'He says his name is "Lister", sir. Claims he was your cohort on *Red Dwarf*.'

Lister stood in the mahogany-panelled library, where the man in the penguin suit had finally ushered him. He helped himself to a foot-long Havana cigar, and sat in the huge leather reading chair, his legs crossed on the polished walnut table. The twelve feet high double doors swung open and Rimmer strode in, grinning.

'Listy! Long time no see. I was going to invite you, but . . . I didn't really think it was your scene.'

'You've done pretty well for yourself. What are you now, the second richest man in the world?'

'Third,' said Rimmer, modestly. 'Long way to go before I'm second.'

'And married to Juanita Chicata.'

'I'm getting by,' Rimmer nodded. He reached into the drawer behind his desk. 'So, two years. Has it really been two years?'

'Yup.'

'I've missed you. First six months of my marriage I couldn't get to sleep because, for some unfathomable reason, Juanita doesn't snore like an adenoidal pig.'

Lister lassoed Rimmer with a huge grey smoke ring, and grinned back.

'So,' said Rimmer, taking out a cheque book a yard long, with more pages than a James Clavell novel, 'you finally came to see me. How much do you want? One, two, three, four pounds?' Rimmer threw back his head and brayed loudly.

'You're a smeg head, Rimmer, you really are a smeg head.'

'But a rich smeg head, eh?' Rimmer brayed again. 'Seriously, what do you want?' he poised his pen over the cheque, 'a couple of mill? What do you want?'

'I want,' Lister said, leaning forward, 'to go back to Earth.'

'Come again?'

'This isn't Earth.'

Rimmer smiled uncomprehendingly.

'I'm afraid, Arn,' Lister continued, 'we've taken a wrong turning. We are in another plane of reality. Somehow we've wound up playing Better Than Life. We're just a couple of Game heads.'

FIVE

It couldn't be. It was . . . well, it just couldn't be. Rimmer
followed Lister down the narrow white stone steps to the
roof garden, where the party was still in full swing. Lister
was jealous, plain and simple. Rimmer didn't like to say it to
his face because it would be like rubbing it in. But it was only
natural he should feel jealous. Rimmer had everything. He'd
amassed a fifty billion dollarpound fortune, whereas Lister
had amassed a leaky house, a silly car, and a wife and two
kids. The poor boy had flipped! He couldn't accept he was a
failure and Rimmer was a hit, so he was trying to persuade
everybody they were in the wrong dimension of reality.
Totally fliparoonied.

'Heard from the Cat?' Lister was asking.

'No. He's on some island off Denmark. Haven't heard
from him since we got back to Earth. You?'

Lister shook his head, grabbed a bottle of Dom Perignon
from a passing ice bucket, and they sat down. He rolled back
his sleeves. 'Let me show you my arms.'

'Your arms?'

'Both my arms look perfectly normal, don't they?'

Rimmer looked at his perfectly normal arms and nodded.
He started looking round for his bodyguards.

'But they hurt like hell. And when I put ointment over the
spots that hurt, it spells out a message.'

Rimmer shook his head, smiling. 'Amazing.'

'Watch.' Lister took a jar of cold cream out of his jacket

pocket and daubed 'DYING' on his left arm and 'U =
BTL' on his right.

'Now, I don't want to sound like I'm a sceptic,' Rimmer
rubbed the flat of his hand against his face, 'but you have to
concede that the effect I've just witnessed could just as easily
be produced by an insane person with two arms and a pot of
cold cream.'

'Yes, but I'm just covering the areas of pain! It's the pain
that spells out the message.'

'The pain?'

'In my arms. Someone's trying to get a message to us.'

'On your arms, through the cold cream.'

'Look, if we *are* in the Game, we won't *know* we're in the
Game. It protects itself – it won't let you remember that
you've started to play it.'

'But we *didn't* start to play it.'

'No, we don't remember starting to play it. That's different.'

Rimmer flopped back in his seat and looked round the
roof garden. He looked at the two thousand people dancing a
conga round the pool. He looked at the phalanx of waiters
holding the silver platters above their heads as they glided
about, serving the second course of the banquet. He looked
across at the sous-chef, atop a ladder, carving generous por-
tions of meat from the barbequed giraffe which slowly rotated
on the forty-foot spit. Could this really not be real?

'If we're in the Game,' Lister continued, 'we're wandering
around somewhere with electrodes in our brains, totally
oblivious to the real world. Someone in that real world is
trying to tell us where we are by burning or cutting or
scratching a message into my arms: "U = BTL": "You are
in Better Than Life", and "DYING": in reality, I'm dying!
I'm a Game head.'

'But it doesn't make sense! I thought when you're in the
Game all your fantasies were supposed to come true. But

look at you – stuck in some hick town in the back end of nowhere with a wife and two kids, and no money.'

'Money isn't important to me.'

Rimmer snorted.

'Bedford Falls and everything else,' Lister shook his head wistfully, 'that was everything I always wanted.'

There was a series of explosions and forty thousand fireworks burst in the night sky, forming a portrait of Rimmer and Juanita in a pink Valentine's heart. While the awe-struck guests gazed in open-mouthed wonder, the fireworks portrait animated: Rimmer's face winked down at them, then turned and kissed Juanita's image. Then two huge bangs – and the two faces transformed into the Rimmer Corporation company logo.

The standing ovation lasted for ten minutes.

'Come on, Rimmer – face facts. Look at this place. The Rimmer Building? Overlooking the Champs Elysées? Your company inventing the Solidgram? You're married to the most famous actress in the world? Is *any* of it even *remotely* credible?'

Lister stood up and pointed across the pool, his voice raised an octave in incredulity. 'Who the hell are they?'

Rimmer looked round.

Lister was waving his arms excitedly. 'The guys under the parasol, applauding?'

'Napoleon Bonaparte, Julius Caesar and General Patton.'

'And what are they doing here?'

'Oh, that. There's a perfectly rational explanation for that,' Rimmer nodded vigorously.

Lister grabbed another bottle of champagne. 'Which is?'

'It's a bit hush-hush at the moment. I'm not really at liberty to say.'

'Un-hush-hush it.'

Rimmer mulled it over. Well, it would be public knowledge in a week or so. Couldn't do any harm. He leaned over

279

conspiratorially. 'Rimmer Corporation Worldwide plc have developed a Time Machine. I've been playing around with it for a few months, inviting famous people from different eras in Time to pep up a few dinner parties.'

Lister was looking at him in a strange way.

'What's wrong with that?' Rimmer protested. 'You don't think that's believable?'

'No, I don't. I think you just wanted to meet these people, so your imagination had to cook up a nearly credible explanation to bring them here.'

'Nonsense!' said Rimmer, but without conviction. Could it be true? Could he have fantasized the invention of a Time Machine just so he could bring back Caesar, Bonaparte and Patton – the three greatest generals in history – simply in order to beat them at 'RISK', the strategic war game for ages fifteen and over? Could he really be that small-minded?

'Come on –' Lister stood up and drained the bottle – 'we've got to find the Cat.'

Rimmer picked up a phone and punched in three numbers. 'Harry? Put the Lear Jet on stand-by. Mr Rimmer and guest will be going to Denmark this evening.' He put the phone down and turned to Lister. 'Wait in the car – I'd better say goodbye to, uh . . .' And he wandered off.

'Een the middle of our party, you are going off weeth your stupid friend to Denmark?!'

Juanita, still naked from the waist down apart from the diamond stilettoes, stormed up and down the parquet floor of the roof garden's white balustraded gazebo. Rimmer thrust his hands deep in his pockets and squirmed.

'Darling, I know it's awful, but the thing is: there's an outside chance . . .' Rimmer didn't know quite how to put this '. . . there's a tiny little possibility that you don't exist.'

'I don't what?'

'It's only a slight chance, and there's probably nothing to

worry about. But if Lister's right, you're just a figment of my imagination.'

'And for this reason you are leaving my party and flying to Denmark?'

'Yes,' said Rimmer, 'it's a sort of metaphysical emergency.'

'Thees man comes here thees evening, with his stupeed furry hat, and tells you your wife doesn't exist, and you go waltzing off weeth heem to Scandinavia?'

'You're right, I won't go. I won't go. Of course you exist. I'll go down to the car and explain that we've talked it through, and we've come to the conclusion that we all *do* exist, and we don't want anything more to do with him.'

'You're crazee! My mother was right. She always warned me against marrying a dead man!'

Rimmer watched her naked, tanned bottom as she clomped down the summerhouse steps and wandered over to a group of people eating their barbequed giraffe steaks. He scanned the group. Lenin, Einstein, Archimedes, God and Norman Wisdom. Wisdom was staggering around, laughing hysterically, with his jacket half off his shoulders. Suddenly, without warning, he threw himself up into the air and landed on the floor. Lenin, Einstein and Archimedes looked down rather disdainfully. God splurted out his mouthful of Cinzano Bianco and bellowed uncontrollably, tears streaming down his face.

'That's comedy!' God was saying. 'That is comedy!'

Let's face it, Rimmer thought, there was at least a marginal possibility that Lister was right.

SIX

The black stretch Mercedes with the tinted, bullet-proof glass purred onto the shiny black tarmacadamed runway of Rimmer International Airport (AJR), and drew up alongside the black Lear Jet, Rimmer One.

The twenty-minute journey had been conducted mainly in silence. Lister had been watching MTV on one of the car's TV sets, where a poll had proclaimed Rimmer the Sexiest Man Of All Time. Second was Clark Gable, and third was Hugo Lovepole. Rimmer had smiled wanly. It was turning into a nightmare. If this was indeed his fantasy – and he was still clinging onto a faint hope that Lister was wrong – if it *was* his fantasy, it was suddenly hideously embarrassing. His psyche lain bare for all to see.

The chauffeur clicked round the car and opened one of the eight passenger doors, and they got out. Lister looked at the chauffeur and almost said 'hello', because at first he thought he knew him. Then he realized he didn't, but he'd seen his face somewhere.

'Who's the driver?' he whispered to Rimmer as they walked across to the Lear Jet's steps.

'It's a lovely evening, isn't it?'

'Is he somebody famous?' Lister persisted.

'Who?'

'The driver.'

'No.'

'Who is he, then?'

Rimmer started to climb the steps. 'He's my dad,' he said quietly. 'I brought him back in the Time Machine.'

'To be your chauffeur?!' Lister wrinkled his cheeks in disbelief.

'Yes!' Rimmer hissed.

'I'm very proud of you, Son,' his father called. 'I'm so proud I'm fit to burst.'

'Shut up,' said Rimmer.

As they got to the top of the Lear Jet's steps, the screaming started. Rimmer had been dreading it. He'd hoped they might be able to slip aboard unnoticed. But even this small mercy was denied him. As Lister turned, hanging over the observation balcony of the airport terminal building, twenty thousand teenage girls caught in the helpless throes of Rimmermania waved intimate garments and banners, screamed and chanted uncontrollably.

'Arnold! We love you!'

'Arnieeeeeeeeeeeeeeeeeeeeeeeeeeeeeeeeeee!'

Rimmer shook his head in humiliation, his cheeks glowing baboon-bottom red.

They screeeeeeeeeeamed as he half-nodded at them. Lister squinted, trying to read the banners. 'Arnie is brave' he could make out. 'Arnie has had lots of girlfriends'. 'Arnie is FAB'. He turned to Rimmer.

'Basically,' he grinned, 'you just want to be adored, don't you?'

'Thank you, Sigmund,' said Rimmer without parting his teeth.

'It's really quite cute.'

'Look – we're still not a hundred per cent sure that this *is* a fantasy. And if it turns out it's not, you're going to feel plenty silly as you drive your clapped-out old banger back to Nowhere City.' Rimmer ducked his head and disappeared into the body of the plane.

★

Rimmer wasn't really watching the in-flight movie, but he was wearing the headset as a kind of sanctuary to avoid Lister's accusing grin. The film was *Darkness At Noon*, which had culled Juanita her first Oscar. How well Rimmer remembered that evening – the twenty-five minute thank you speech she'd made, saying it was all down to him. He watched her play the scene in the apartment – the famous 'olives on the cocktail stick' scene. Could he really have fantasized this woman? It was absurd! Why would he fantasize a woman, no matter how beautiful, who was Trouble with a capital 'T' the size of the GPO tower?

Because he wanted the most exciting woman in the world. The most desired, the most beautiful, the most . . . dangerous. But, having got her, why would he then fantasize she was unfaithful? With Hugo the hairy-shouldered pool attendant! What the hell did that say about the state of his mind? Mentally unwell, that's what it said. And why had he fantasized his wife's refusal to make love with him for the past eighteen months? Why on Earth did he want *that* to happen?

Was it that even in his fantasies Rimmer couldn't bring himself to believe anyone could truly love him? That inevitably she would reject him, giving him those pathetic excuses that the insurance company wouldn't allow him to touch her bosom? And inevitably she would take a lover – a lover who was more masculine than he? More manly? Oh, my god.

My god, my god, my god.

He moaned softly. The innards of his psyche were there for all to see: putrid and rotten and rancid. His neuroses parading like grinning contestants in the Mr Universe contest!

He glanced over at Lister, who had taken out a well-worn leather wallet and was looking sadly at some dog-eared photographs of his family back in Bedford Falls.

Hadn't Lister's fantasy been even more ridiculous? A leaky house? A clapped-out car? A little shop? It was so . . . corny. A girl-next-door type wife, two kids. If they were playing Better Than Life, he could have had anything he wanted.

Absolutely anything he wanted. And this was his choice? Something so ordinary, so small, so . . . normal?

Oh my god, my god, my god.

That was the truth, wasn't it? Lister's fantasy was so much more mature than his. Lister didn't need mega-wealth to make him happy. He needed fourteen dollars and twenty-five cents. He didn't need a stunning-looking actress desired by all. He just wanted someone who cared for him. Even the car. Rimmer had a twenty-five-foot black penis extension. Lister had a clapped-out old banger. What did that mean, then? That Lister had a limousine inside his Y-fronts, while Rimmer had a 1940s Ford that needed hand-cranking?

Lister's was the fantasy of a man at peace with himself. A man who felt he had nothing to prove. Rimmer's was twenty-five foot cars, hundred and forty storey buildings, airports, Lear Jets, a twenty million dollar bosom, a forty billion dollar fortune, his father as his own chauffeur . . . It *couldn't* be a fantasy. No one could be *that* screwed-up!

Lister sat there looking at the black-and-white dog-eared snaps which Mr Calhoon, the photographer, had taken last Christmas Eve with his old box Brownie on its tripod, with the magnesium flare. There was one in particular of him and Kochanski with big cheesy grins.

So you don't exist, he thought. I just made you exist and fall in love with me.

He was still hung up on Kristine Kochanski. A girl he dated for five weeks and two days, three million years ago. In a way he was kind of jealous of Rimmer. If he'd have known it was a fantasy, he'd have become Jim Bexley Speed and dated Ida Lupino. He'd have played with the Beatles: the Fab Five – John, Paul, George, Ringo and Dave. But he hadn't. He'd settled down in Bedford Falls and married Kristine Kochanski. He wanted to live his life in a movie. What a jerk! What an even bigger jerk for falling in love with someone who, if she'd been alive and real and with him now, probably would give him a sweet little smile and sit down at the back of the plane with one of her wacky mates.

Sure, they'd had a great two years; but it hadn't been real – none of it. Counterfeit delights. A pathetic hankering on account of a crazy obsession. Unreal. Impossible. Ridiculous.

The air hostess leaned over him.

'Can I get you anything?' she smiled. It was Ida Lupino. Ida Lupino was standing in the aisle, dressed as an air hostess. 'Anything at all?' she twinkled.

Lister shook his head. 'I'm married. I'm married to someone who doesn't exist, with two non-existent kids. I can't get involved with someone else who doesn't exist. Life would get too complicated.'

The Lear landed in Copenhagen. The Danish government laid on a power boat to get them across to the Cat's island.

They sat in the back of the boat as it cut through the billowing waves of the foul-tempered sea. The island loomed through circles of mist, towering above the stormy waters: a single, sea-ringed mountain, tapering into the clouds. As they moved slowly closer, something at the very summit caught the sunlight and glimmered.

They moored the boat at a crumbling wooden jetty, and looked around, trying to find a route up the unclimbable mountain. They heard a sound: a creaking steel chain. And crashing out of the soggy mist, a cable car lurched to a halt in front of them.

They sat, rocking in the dangerous wind, as the cable car slowly squeaked its way up the mountain. The trip took three hours. They went through cloud. The atmospheric pressure changed. Whatever the Cat's fantasy was, it certainly didn't involve entertaining a great many visitors.

Finally the cable car wheezed into its mooring, and they got out. Standing on a narrow mountain track were two rickshaws attended by eight-foot tall, huge-breasted Amazon Valkyries in scanty armour. Lister shook his head.

'I've really got to have a word with the Cat about his sexual politics.'

Worse was to follow because, as Lister climbed aboard the rickshaw, he realized that the two wing mirrors he'd assumed were for the giantesses to see behind them were in fact strategically placed so the passenger could spend the short trip to the mountain top watching their cartoon-sized boobs jiggling up the track. He shook his head again.

'Who did he get this place from? Benny Hill?' He climbed out. 'Forget it – we'll walk.'

Rimmer tried to hide his disappointment as they trudged up the curving track. As they reached the crest, they saw it.

Any faint hopes that Rimmer still entertained that they were on Earth and in the world of reality gurgled noisily down the plug hole as they gazed up at the Cat's home.

It was a thirty-towered golden castle surrounded by a moat filled with milk.

SEVEN

The tip of the highest golden tower was almost invisible to the naked eye. The battlements were patrolled by more of the horn-helmeted, skimpily armoured Valkyries.

Lister and Rimmer clumped noisily across the wooden drawbridge.

'Halt! Who goes there, buddy?' one of the Valkyries shouted from the gate house.

'We've come to see the Cat!' shouted Lister, his voice sounding weak and ineffectual by comparison.

They were led into the castle and through a maze of chambers. The Cat's portrait hung on every wall: here clad in gleaming armour, there grinning from a rearing horse; there wrestling a lion, here draped on top of a pink piano. They followed the guards out into an ornamental garden that made the grounds of the Palace of Versailles look like a window box. Rimmer began to regret the smallness of his own imagination.

The guards were marching double time, and Lister and Rimmer felt compelled to keep up. They were getting quite tired by the time they reached the end of the gardens, which let out onto a courtyard surrounded by stables.

The Cat, in a red riding jacket, gleaming white jodhpurs and black leather boots, was mounted on a cream-coloured, fire-breathing, racing yak. There was a smell of sulphur hanging in the air as the yak reared and tried to bolt. The Cat, laughing, deftly wrestled it under control as it haughtily spouted two more jets of fire from its nostrils.

A dozen hunting dogs yapped and bayed and snapped at the leashes held by four Valkyries. As the dragon yak ceased its protestations, the Cat turned and caught sight of Rimmer and Lister.

'Hey! What's happening?' He waved his black riding cap and tooted his hunting horn, driving the dogs berserk. 'Sydney!' he called to the tallest of the Valkyries, 'Saddle Dancer and Prancer! Guys,' he turned to Rimmer and Lister, 'grab a yak!'

Rimmer mounted his flame-coloured yak with more than a little trepidation, and held timidly onto the reins.

'I've never really ridden a . . . fire-breathing racing yak before,' he said unnecessarily.

Lister patted the neck of his beast, and used the resultant jet of flame to light one of the foot-long Havana cigars he'd stolen from Rimmer's study back in Paris. Then he hooked a foot into the stirrup and clambered into the saddle.

The Cat tooted his curved hunting horn and called to the Valkyries restraining the hounds: 'Release the dogs!'

The dozen hunting dogs streamed out of the courtyard. The Cat reared on his yak and bellowed 'Tally ho!', and all three of them thundered over the cobblestones and out into the dank, misty wasteland that surrounded the castle.

Lister clung desperately to the neck of the bouncing yak, the reins hanging free as it splashed through the bog land which was covered in a carpet of mist. Before him, whenever he dared to open his eyes, he could see the Cat, straight-backed, holding onto the reins with his left hand, a silver shooting pistol in his right, while behind him he could hear the occasional low moans of Rimmer as he recited various incantations from a number of different religions.

They came to a low hedge. The dogs burst through it and the yaks leapt over. As they hammered across the hard, frosty ground, Lister saw the Cat level his pistol. He couldn't see the quarry, and he wasn't particularly keen to. They were riding fire-breathing dragon yaks. What on Earth would they be hunting? He saw the Cat's shoulder jerk back, and a puff of smoke, before he heard the crack of the pistol. In the distance, one of the dogs cartwheeled twelve feet into the air and landed, dead, on the floor.

'No!' Lister yelled as the Cat quickly picked off the eleven remaining dogs. He reined in the yak, raised his horn and tooted a victory call.

'You shot all the smegging dogs!' said Lister, gulping for air.

'They're vermin,' laughed the Cat; 'what did you think we were shooting?' He raised himself in his saddle and called to the entourage of Valkyries galloping up on horses some way behind them. 'More dogs, Sydney!'

They stood before the roaring fire in the vast inglenook fireplace of the Cat's baronial dining hall, drinking hot milk laced with cinnamon from pewter mugs.

The Cat stood, a spat-covered foot resting on the gold fender, his elbow crooked above his head on the marble mantelpiece, shaking his head, staring into the fire.

'You mean none of this is real? None of this actually exists?'

'Of course it doesn't!' Rimmer snorted in disgust. 'Fire-breathing yaks? Eight-foot tall Nordic goddesses? A castle surrounded by a moat of milk? Is any of it even *remotely* tinged with credibility? I don't understand how you could even believe it was!'

Lister thought of the Rimmer Buildings, Paris, New York, and London, but he didn't say anything.

'I mean,' Rimmer shook his head, 'at least our fantasies were possible! Perhaps not likely, but possible. But yours is just totally preposterous. It's like a Gothic fairy tale. How come you didn't suspect anything? Didn't you think it was a little bit odd the way you just *acquired* all this?'

'No. I just thought I deserved it.'

'Deserved it?' Lister tilted his head.

'Because I'm so good-looking.'

A naked, oiled Valkyrie banged the enormous gong and announced it was supper.

As they took their places at the long oak banquet table, the lights dimmed and a spotlight picked out Sydney holding a large silver platter at the top of a stone staircase which led up to the balcony skirting the baronial hall.

The flagstones in the middle of the hall slid apart, and from beneath a seven-piece band rose up on a hydraulic pedestal. Mozart on piano, Jimi Hendrix on lead guitar, Stéphane Grappelli on rhythm, Charlie Parker on sax, Yehudi Menuhin on violin, Buddy Rich on drums, and Jellybean on computer programs. They began to play.

'Listen to these boys,' the Cat confided; 'they really kick ass.'

They had never heard the tune before, but it was so . . perfect, so instantly classic, Lister and Rimmer immediately started tapping along with the heavenly beat.

Sydney danced down the stairs, flanked by forty lurex-clad Valkyries, all bearing platters and singing:

> *'He's going to eat you little fishies,*
> *He's going to eat you little fish,*
> *He's going to eat you little fishies,*
> *Because he likes eating fish!'*

Three platters were placed before them, each containing a large aquarium packed with writhing shoals of vividly-coloured fish.

Rimmer eyed his dinner with disgust. 'Don't you prefer them caught and cooked?'

'No, sir!' said the Cat, picking up the mini-fishing rod which was laid out with the cutlery by his plate. 'I like my food to *move*.'

'I think,' said Rimmer, draping his napkin over the fish tank, 'we've established beyond all reasonable doubt that we are playing Better Than Life.'

'Right,' Lister agreed, 'but the question is: how do we get out?'

'Why do we have to get out?' asked the Cat as he sucked a squirming angel fish off the hook of his rod.

'Because it's a computer-induced fantasy, because it's not real, and in the real world our bodies are wasting away. We're dying.'

'What are you talking about?'

Lister explained about the messages on his arms, and how it meant that someone was trying to get through to them.

'Which someone?' asked the Cat.

'Holly, obviously,' said Rimmer.

Lister shook his head. 'Maybe. We don't know. We don't know exactly at what point we started playing the Game. How much of this has been real? Did we get back to Earth? Did we fix *Nova 5*? Did *Nova 5* exist? Maybe I started playing BTL back on Mimas, and *you* two don't exist. Maybe our whole relationship and everything that's happened has been part of my fantasy.'

'No, no, I exist,' said Rimmer. 'Honestly.'

'Yeah, but you'd say that even if you didn't exist,' said Lister.

'He's right, said the Cat; 'maybe I don't exist either. That would certainly explain why I'm so unbearably good-looking.'

'Oh, I don't believe this!' said Rimmer. 'Not only am I dead, I don't exist either! Thanks a lot, God!'

'No, look, I think we have to assume' – Lister punctuated 'assume' with a circled thumb and forefinger – 'that we all exist, and that we got into the Game before *Nova 5* left *Red Dwarf*.'

'OK,' said Rimmer, 'how do we get out?'

'I think I can answer that,' said a fourth voice.

A familiar figure waddled through the stone archway and up to the banquet table.

And he started to explain everything.

EIGHT

Rimmer lurched happily down Corridor 4: gamma 311. 'It's a funny thing,' he slurred, 'even though I've had so much to drink I'm in total comfac of my mandulties.'

'Where is he?' said Lister, poking his head into another of the sleeping quarters on the habitation deck. 'Where the smeg is the Cat?'

'Master Holly says he's on this deck,' said Kryten, peering through the hatchway of another empty sleeping quarters.

'Then why the hell doesn't he answer?' said Lister, tugging the ringpull on another bottle of self-heating saké.

Rimmer's duplicate had been erased that morning, just before the gazpacho soup confession. Nova 5 was reconstructed, fuelled and ready to go. They would be back at Earth in three months, and they'd spent the day celebrating down in the Copacabana Hawaiian Cocktail Bar. The evening had gurgled by in a blurry haze of ever-more elaborate cocktails before either of them had realized the Cat had been missing for two days. Lister had led the drunken safari up to the habitation deck to find him.

There were over three thousand separate sleeping quarters on this deck alone, and they had looked through more than half of them before they staggered into Petrovitch's old room.

The two lockers had been pulled away from the wall, and in a crudely chiselled recess was a stack of Game headbands. Petrovitch, the high-flying, career-minded leader of A Shift had been smuggling Better Than Life, the illegal hallucinogenic brain implant. He'd been smuggling it to the richly paid, insanely bored terraforming engineers of Triton.

The rumours were true.

This correct officer, this model, this paragon, was a low-life, scumbag Game dealer! At a glance Lister estimated there must have been a hundred headbands. Petrovitch could safely have expected to make ten years' wages if he found a hundred suckers who were prepared to buy the cripplingly addictive nirvana offered by the deadly Game. And there always were suckers: plenty of them. Not one person ever entered the Game without believing he could take it or leave it. Once inside, few ever made the painful journey back to reality.

The Cat gently rocked on the sleeping quarters armchair, giggling insanely. The silver headband glimmered menacingly on his head, the electrodes buried deep inside his brain. His face was painted with the harrowingly familiar vacant grin of the lost soul of a Game head.

The three of them sat around the banquet table in the baronial hall of the Cat's fantasy as Kryten recounted how Lister had followed the Cat into the Game.

'But Better Than Life's addictive! I *knew* that.'

'You were drunk, Mister David; you thought you'd be OK just to go into the Game and tell the Cat what danger he was in. But once you'd linked up to the Cat's headband, you didn't come out.'

'What about me?' said Rimmer. 'Why did I go in?'

'You were drunk too. You said you had the willpower to drag them both out. You got Holly to splice you into the Game. And that was the last we saw of you.'

Kryten told how they had wandered around *Red Dwarf* in the twilight zombie state the Game induced. How he'd done his best to feed them, and keep them from harming themselves. But over the months the Cat's and Lister's bodies had begun to wither. Sometimes they'd spend weeks in a single position and develop huge bedsores. They'd tumble down stairs and get up, bloody and laughing, believing they'd made a parachute jump or some such thing. How he'd once seen Lister eat his own vomit with delight, obviously believing he was enjoying some sumptuous delicacy. How, in desperation, he'd begun lasering the messages into Lister's arms to warn him of the danger. This had distressed Kryten greatly. It was built into his software that he mustn't harm human beings. Months of cajoling by Holly had finally persuaded him that *not* to do it would hurt Lister even more.

But still the three of them remained in the Game. In the end, Kryten had no choice but to enter himself.

'But that's stupid,' said Lister. 'You'll get addicted too.'

Kryten shook his head. 'Holly was right. I'm immune. I could have come in right at the start and rescued you.'

'Immune?' said Rimmer. 'Why are you immune?'

Kryten cracked his face into a hollow grin. 'I'm a mechanoid. I don't have dreams. I don't have fantasies the way you do. I have very few expectations or desires.'

'Very few?' said Lister. 'Then you do have some?'

A Valkyrie appeared, bearing a brand-new, freshly wrapped squeezy mop.

'Only one,' said Kryten, accepting the gift and tearing off the paper. 'Oh, wonderful. A squeezy mop! Just what I've always wanted.'

'OK', said Lister, leaning forward, 'the sixty-four million dollarpound question: how do we get out?'

NINE

The windscreen wipers patted the snow into neat white triangles on the model A's window as the car grunted past the white-coated sign: 'Bedford Falls – 2 miles'.

Lister banged at the dashboard with a gloved hand, and the faltering heater whirred back from the dead, and unenthusiastically started to de-mist the windscreen. Lister craned over the steering column and tried to make out the grey ruts in the snow which served as a rough indication as to where the road might be.

He was leaving the Game. It was easy to leave the Game. Easier than he'd have thought.

First you had to want to leave. And, of course, to want to leave you had to know you were in the Game in the first place. That was the hard part, realizing that this wasn't reality. Then it was only a matter of finding an exit. Just that. A door marked 'EXIT'.

'And where are these doors?' he'd asked Kryten.

'It's your fantasy,' Kryten had replied; 'they're wherever you want them to be.'

So there it was. All he had to do was imagine an exit, and go through it.

He'd pass through the exit and find himself back on *Red Dwarf*, probably thin and gaunt and wasted from his two years in the Game but, nevertheless, back in reality. Once back, he could remove his headband – no, *destroy* his headband! Destroy them all! – then start the long haul back to health.

But it was an individual matter. They all had to create their own separate exits. Alone. You're born alone, you die alone, you leave the Game alone.

The glimmering lights of Bedford Falls twinkled in the valley below as, for the last time, he made his way down the hill to his personal Shangri-la.

Ever since he'd left Earth, every step he'd taken had led him further away from the dirty polluted world he loved. First Mimas, then the outer reaches of the solar system, then Deep Space, and finally here – in the wrong dimension of the wrong plane of reality. It was hard to imagine how he could ever be further away from home.

The Ford juddered down the main street under the strings of lights that hung between trees down the avenue. He passed Horace's bank, and through the window saw the money still stacked in neat piles on the counter. He passed Old Man Gower's drugstore. How could he have believed it existed? He passed Martini's Bar, alive inside with joyful revellers celebrating Christmas Eve. He headed the old car down Sycamore Avenue, and slid to rest outside no. 220.

There, in the middle of the street, a pink neon sign hung over a shimmering archway. There was his exit, just as he'd imagined it. On the other side was reality.

It started to snow. Christmas Eve.

How could he leave them on Christmas Eve?

What harm was one more day? He turned away from the dissolving exit and crunched up the drive to 220.

One more night of that pinball smile.

Just one.

He couldn't leave them on Christmas Eve.

But, of course, in Bedford Falls it was always Christmas Eve . . .

BETTER THAN LIFE

To Richard, Joe and Matthew

Special thanks to Ed Bye for being unnecessarily tall and wonderful, to Paul Jackson for being not so tall, but equally wonderful, and to Chris Barrie, Craig Charles, Danny John-Jules, Hattie Hayridge, Robert Llewelyn and Peter Wragg. Thanks also to BBC Northwest and all the *Red Dwarf* backstage crew.

PROLOGUE

Time is a character in this novel.

It does strange things: moves in strange directions, and at strange speeds.

Don't trust Time.

Time will always get you in the end.

Grant Naylor (Alexandria, 25 BC)

Part One

Game over

ONE

Rimmer sat on the open terrace, in his half-devastated dinner suit of the night before, and gazed down at the metallic blue time machine, drunkenly parked skew-whiff in the ornamental gardens of the Palace of Versailles. Breakfasting with him were five of his stag-night companions: John F. Kennedy, Vincent Van Gogh, Albert Einstein, Louis XVI and Elvis Presley.

'That was a heck of a night,' Kennedy sparkled. 'One *heck* of a night.' Einstein snorted in agreement, and continued absently buttering the underside of his tie.

Julius Caesar stumbled through the french windows out on to the terrace with an ice-pack perched on his head. 'Can anyone tell me,' he asked in faltering English, 'where in Jupiter's name we got this?' He held aloft a large orange-and-white-striped traffic cone. 'I woke up in bed with it this morning.'

Van Gogh cracked an egg into his tomato juice, and downed it with a shudder. 'It's not a good night,' he grinned, 'if you don't get a traffic cone.'

'You want that?' Elvis Presley nodded at Rimmer's dev-illed kidneys, and without waiting for a reply scraped them on to his already full plate.

A colourless smile trickled across Rimmer's upper lip. '*Avez-vous* some, uh, Alka-Seltzer?'.

'One *heck* of a night.' Kennedy repeated.

And he was right: as bachelor-night parties went, it had been a bit of a cracker.

A flash-frame slammed into Rimmer's brain – a scene from the night before . . .

He was standing on a table in a 1922 Chicago speakeasy, dancing the Black Bottom with Frank 'the Enforcer' Nitty's girlfriend, and complaining for the umpteenth time that his mineral water tasted as if someone had poured three double vodkas into it.

Then . . . Then . . . He couldn't remember the order, but they had definitely dropped in on one of Caligula's orgies. Rimmer must have been fairly drunk by then, because he remembered spending at least twenty minutes trying to chat up a horse.

At some point they'd been in Ancient Egypt, and Rimmer had lost a tooth trying to give the Sphinx a giant love-bite . . . then someone – Rimmer thought it was Elvis – had suggested a curry. And Rimmer, who hated curries, had been dragged, complaining, through Time back to India in the days of the Raj, where everyone had ordered a mutton vindaloo, except for Rimmer who had a cheese omelette served with ludicrously thick chips.

The cry had gone up for more liquor, and Rimmer suggested . . . What did he suggest? There was a block, so it must have been something fairly bad. Some kind of restaurant. They'd crashed a private party, and all the people there seemed fairly put out when Rimmer and his cronies showed up dancing and singing. There were a dozen or so diners, all men, all bearded. Rimmer closed his eyes and groaned.

They'd gatecrashed the Last Supper.

What had he done? What had he said? He'd been shouting drunk. 'Private bloody party! Our money's as good as anyone's!'

Twelve of them had stood up and threatened to punch Rimmer out, but the one who'd remained seated had told the others to sit down again.

'Do one of your tricks,' Rimmer had insisted. 'Come on, I'm getting married tomorrow. That one with the fish – it's brilliant.'

A heck of a night.

Rimmer looked at his real-time watch. 'Well, Louis, me old buckeroo,' he said to the king of France, 'we'd better be making tracks. Big kissy-kissy to Marie and the dauphin. Thanks for the servant girls. See you at the wedding.'

Louis XVI thanked Rimmer for the Ray-Ban sunglasses and the Sony Walkman and bade him farewell.

Rimmer gingerly made his way across the lawns towards the Time copter, followed by Kennedy, Van Gogh, Einstein and Caesar. Elvis crammed a steak in his mouth, stuffed a second in his pocket, grabbed four bread rolls and followed them.

The man in the air traffic control tower radioed clearance to materialize, and the Time copter bloomed into existence, and chuddered to rest on the tarmacadamed runway.

The disembarkation door hinged to the ground, and the world's richest man clicked down the steps towards the waiting limo.

Two steps down, the screaming started. Hordes of teenage girls standing on the observation balcony swept forward in tides of pubescent adoration.

'Arniiiiiiiiieeee!' they roared. 'We love yooouuuuuu!'

Rimmer waved half-heartedly and shot them the thinnest of his thin smiles, before he was surrounded by a phalanx of sober-suited security guards who ushered him to the leather comfort of the limo's interior.

The eight motorcyclists twisted their throttle grips, and led the cavalcade forward, as it swished imperiously past Passport Control and the Customs building, and headed towards the exit.

Rimmer flicked idly through the stack of magazines on the limo's mahogany table: *Time*, *Life* and *Newsweek*. He noted with only mild interest that his portrait graced the cover of all three. According to *Life*, he'd just been voted 'World's sexiest man', 'World's best-dressed man' and 'Pipe-smoker of the year'. Rimmer smiled. He didn't even *own* a pipe, much less smoke one. Success breeds success, he thought.

The cavalcade fought its way through the screaming fans milling around the airport exit.

'Arniiiiiiiiiiiieeeeee! Don't marry her!'

Flattened adoring faces squashed up against the grey smoked glass, all of them dizzy with desire for Arnold J. Rimmer.

Rimmer was perfectly well aware that he was in the wrong plane of the wrong dimension of reality and, quite honestly, he didn't give two hoots.

The limousine gently disentangled itself from the sobbing frenzy of teenage girls and silently accelerated down the freeway, followed by a shower of moist, female underwear.

TWO

Three million years out in Deep Space, a dilapidated mining ship drifts pointlessly round in a huge, aimless circle.

On board, its four crew members sit in a horseshoe, trapped in the ultimate computer game: a game that plugs directly into the brain, and enables them to experience a world created by their own fantasies.

The game is called Better Than Life, and very few ever escape its thrall: very few can give up their own, personally sculpted paradise.

THREE

Sparkling lights looped from tree to tree along the main street, above an assortment of parked cars hummocked in white. A small brass band umpah-ed discordant but cheery carols in the town square, as last-minute shoppers slushed through the snow, exchanging seasonal greetings and stopping occasionally to join in a favourite carol.

In the fictional town of Bedford Falls, it was Christmas Eve. But then again, in the fictional town of Bedford Falls, it was always Christmas Eve.

Lister crossed the main street, his two sons perched on either shoulder, and headed for the toy shop.

As they passed the jailhouse, Bert the cop was removing a wanted poster from the front window.

The poster was yellow and gnarled, and offered a five-dollar reward for information leading to the arrest of Jesse James and his gang. 'About time I took this thing down,' Bert said sheepishly. There hadn't been a single crime in Bedford Falls for over thirty years; not since that hot summer day when Mrs Hubble was arrested for taking a three-cent trolley ride, having paid only a two-cent fare.

Lister slid the twins from his shoulders and grasped their tiny hands, as the two four-year-olds gazed, mouths ajar, at the large blue sailing boat on sale for two dollars and twenty-five cents in the toy-shop window.

Suddenly the door jangled open and old Mr Mulligan appeared in the doorway, straightening out the yacht's sails.

'Now then, me lads,' he brogued. 'Would I be correct in thinking you'll be after doing business with me in respect of a certain sailing vessel? Only, you've been standing out there with your faces pressed up against me window so often these past few months, you're beginning to wear away the pavement outside me shop.'

'Yes, sir, we are, sir,' said Bexley. 'We've been saving up all year. Show him the money, Jim.'

Jim took out his spider box, and carefully unwrapped the two wrinkled dollar bills and poured out the mound of coppers.

'Here it is, sir. Two dollars and twenty-five cents.'

As old Mr Mulligan held out the boat, Henry, the town down-and-out, shuffled sadly by, his flimsy coat tugged tight around his frail shoulders. He took a futile swig from a bottle concealed in a brown paper bag and threw it in a wastebin.

'Merry Christmas, ge'l'men,' he slurred.

Jim gazed up at his stubble-swathed face. 'Where are you spending Christmas, Mr Henry?'

'Well, that's a very good question.' Henry dragged a tattered sleeve across his nose. 'Being as how the jailhouse is closed for the yuletide period, and the Bel Air Hotel presidential suite is fully booked, it looks like the Park Bench Hilton for old Henry.'

'What are you going to eat?' asked Bexley.

'Don't worry about me, boy. I always share a fine Christmas dinner with the ducks up on Potter's pond.'

The twins turned and faced each other. Finally, they both nodded, and Bexley turned back to Henry, and held out his hand. 'Me and Jim would like you to have this, Mr Henry. Merry Christmas.'

'What's this?' Henry tried to focus on the money in his hand.

'You can get a room at Old Ma Bailey's boarding-house,' said Jim, 'and have a proper Christmas, like the rest of us.'

Henry's blood-shot eyes filled with tears, and his voice cracked. 'Well now,' he barely whispered. 'You'd be giving me your Christmas money.'

Lister looked down at his feet.

'Deep down, you're a really good person,' said Jim. 'You just got sad when old Mrs Henry went to heaven.'

Lister sucked in his cheeks, and old Mr Mulligan took out a large handkerchief and noisily blew his nose.

'Look at me – I've gone to pieces,' Henry blubbed. 'What would my Mary say if she could see me now? She'd give me such a talking-to, my ears'd be ringing for a week.'

'No she wouldn't, Mr Henry.' Bexley shook his head. 'She'd say you brought up two fine children single-handed, and sent them both to college. You only took to the bottle when the angels had to take them away, too.'

Lister snuffled, and whimpered, and accepted Mulligan's handkerchief.

Henry bent down and pressed the money back into Jim's hand. 'I can't take this from you, boys, but if I could just borrow a dollar, to get myself a haircut and a shave. There's a sweeping job going down at the drugstore. I'll pay you back ten times over.'

Jim and Bexley smiled. 'Merry Christmas, Henry.'

Jim folded the single dollar bill around the twenty-five cents, and placed it carefully back into his spider box. 'Come on, Dad,' he said quietly. 'Let's go back home.'

'Wait!' called Mulligan. 'Have I told you about me winter sale, just this minute started? Lots of bargains! Take, for instance, this fine blue boat, formerly two dollars, twenty-five cents, now reduced to one dollar, twenty-five cents.'

He handed the boat to the boys.

Lister started sobbing unashamedly, which set Henry off. The two men embraced one another, and were soon joined by old Mr Mulligan, and Bert the cop. They stood there in a four-way hug, bawling hysterically.

'That's so beautiful,' Lister was trying to say between whimpering convulsions.

'You've got two fine boys there. You should . . .' But Henry couldn't finish. He buried his head in Lister's shoulder, and was off again.

'They were prepared to give up the boat to help out Henry,' Mulligan blubbered. 'That's the real spirit of Christmas.'

'Blaaaaaaaaaaaaaaaaah,' said Bert, and they all dissolved in a fresh paroxysm of wailing.

This was the kind of thing that happened all the time in the fictional town of Bedford Falls.

It was that kind of place.

*

The twelve-wheeled juggernaut hammered down the narrow country lane decapitating hedgerows and smashing through branches as it lurched on and off the road. Its huge wide wheels carved deep ugly ruts in the fresh-laid snow.

Its air-horn sounded as it dragged round a tight bend, and straightened out too soon, ripping through a picket fence and flattening a metal road sign.

The sign clattered across the road and toppled into a ditch as the juggernaut thundered out of control, down towards the twinkling lights of the town below.

Smashed, and scarred by tyre tracks, the road sign lay on its back in the ditch. 'Welcome to Bedford Falls', it said. 'Population 3,241'.

Very soon, the information on the sign would be hopelessly, hopelessly inaccurate.

The five-piece brass band staggered its way through 'God Rest Ye Merry, Gentlemen' – all, that is, except for old Billy Bailey, the tuba player, who was still staggering through 'Hark, The Herald Angels Sing' from three carols earlier.

Almost the entire population of Bedford Falls stood around the giant Christmas tree in the town square, their sweet, discordant voices drifting up into the evening sky.

Lister, with Bexley and Jim on his shoulders again, was sandwiched between Mr Mulligan and Henry. Henry, with his freshly shaven face and his bristling new haircut, sang louder than anyone. The carol finished, and everyone applauded. Minutes later the tuba finished too, and everyone applauded once more. The five-piece band struck up again. Four of them started 'Silent Night', and, after a gulp from his hip flask, Billy Bailey tore into 'God Rest Ye Merry, Gentlemen'. He was definitely catching up.

Across the street, the door of 220 Sycamore opened, and Kristine Kochanski ran over to join them, clutching a bag of hot roasted chestnuts. She linked her arm in Lister's and planted a warm kiss on his chilled cheek.

'Hey, listen,' Lister smiled. 'Old Henry's got nowhere to stay . . .' He didn't even need to finish the sentence.

'I've already made up the spare bed. He can stay with us for as long as he likes.' She flashed her famous smile – the smile that made her face light up like a pinball machine awarding a bonus game. The smile Lister had fallen in love with. She hugged him tighter, and they shared the carol sheet.

Suddenly, Lister was aware of loud blaring drone cutting through the carol. He looked around. The dull monotone sounded again, now even louder, now even closer.

Lister turned. Over the crest of the hill that led down to the main street, the sudden dazzle of eight huge headlights glared down towards them.

The hooter sounded again.

Lister squinted against the glare, and made out the shape of the rogue juggernaut.

It was out of control, and heading straight for the carol-singing crowd in the town square.

FOUR

Rimmer gazed down from the balcony windows of his colonial mansion at the blur of black-suited waiters who dashed frantically about with increasingly elaborate flower arrangements. Cranes hung marinated giraffe carcasses over the clay-pit fires, while an army of pastry chefs put the finishing touches to the wedding cake, which featured as its centrepiece an Olympic-sized swimming pool full of vintage champagne.

So this wasn't reality. So what?

Reality, it struck Rimmer, was a place where bad things could happen. And bad, vile, unspeakable things had happened to him on an almost daily basis the entire period he'd spent there.

Why should he subscribe to a reality in which he was an outright failure – a loser with no equal? Unloved, unfulfilled, ungifted, and many other words too legion to list, all beginning with the prefix 'un'.

The unreality offered by Better Than Life was far more palatable.

'Mr Rimmer, sir?' A bespectacled man in a brown tweed suit quivered obsequiously at the door. 'It's all ready, sir. Shall I bring it through?'

Rimmer nodded.

'If you'd just like to slip out of that one, we'll see how it feels.'

Rimmer pressed the release catch concealed in his navel, and, with a whoosh, his essence floated out of his body.

He felt slightly sheepish hovering around the room, temporarily bodyless, and was glad when the man in the brown tweed suit returned pushing a stretcher.

'Here it is, sir. Perhaps you'd like to try it on.'

Rimmer changed his body more often than most people had a haircut. Every time he detected the slightest wrinkle or sign of wear, he'd trade it in for a brand-new model. And why not? Out there, in reality, he didn't have a body – he was a hologram. Here, in Better Than Life, it was, therefore, only natural that his psyche had fantasized the science that made body-swapping possible. But with every body-swap, Rimmer's face remained the same – it was the one part of him he refused to change. Without his own face, he argued, it would feel like his success belonged to someone else.

The men pulled back the sheet, revealing Rimmer's pristine new form, and Rimmer's essence slid into it gratefully.

He wriggled his new shoulders and stretched out his new arms.

'Comfortable, sir?' inquired the body-tailor.

Rimmer murmured non-committally, and walked across to the full-length dress mirror. He looked his new physique up and down. It was virtually identical to the body he'd just vacated, with a few minor tweaks and adjustments: the pectorals were slightly better defined, and the stomach wall a tad more muscular. 'Not bad,' he conceded grudgingly. 'Penis still isn't big enough.'

'Sir, honestly: any bigger and you'll have a balance problem.'

Rimmer nodded. The appendage was fairly gargantuan, and certainly sizeable enough to put the fear of God into anyone who stood next to him at a urinal, which was all he was interested in. The tailor was right – he couldn't keep on asking for an extra half inch or so to be added to his favourite organ. It was fast reaching the stage where he would become the only man in history who dressed on both the right and the left-hand sides simultaneously.

Rimmer dismissed the tailor and started to slide his latest body into his crisp, new morning suit.

Yes indeedy, this place certainly had the edge over reality.

Here he was a god, and everything was perfect.

Well, almost everything.

Still, that was behind him, now.

Juanita Chicata was history. The world's number one model and actress no longer kept her cosmetics in his bathroom.

The much-publicized court case dragged on for months, and Rimmer had found the whole experience thoroughly galling.

Preposterously, the 'Brazilian bombshell' had denied adultery, and Rimmer's lawyers had been forced to parade Juanita's ex-lovers through the witness stand.

It took five days.

The pool attendant, the gardener, her tennis instructor, two butlers, four chauffeurs, seven delivery boys: a seemingly endless stream had flowed through the courtroom and testified to their indiscretions with his wife.

Worst of all had been the exhibits: Exhibit A – a large carton of whipped cream. Exhibit B – a skin-diving suit with the bottom cut out. Exhibit C – a bucketful of soapy frogs. Soapy *frogs*? On and on it went, until, by Exhibit Q – an inflatable dolphin with battery-operated fins – Rimmer could stand the humiliation no longer, and he'd agreed to settle out of court.

The alimony agreement had been of historical magnitude. In fact, it would have been cheaper for Rimmer to support the entire population of Bolivia in perpetuity, rather than subscribe to the settlement he did.

But it was worth it. It was worth every single nought to get that crazy, dangerous, gorgeous woman out of his life.

Helen couldn't have been more different. Good Bostonian stock, society family, old money, normal libido.

Helen was . . . nice. Not *just* nice, of course – that made her sound bland. She was nice, obviously, but also, she was very sensible.

No berserk, china-hurling tantrums for her. No satanic, knife-wielding charges at his naked person. No embarrassing bellowed arguments in humiliatingly expensive restaurants. No – that wasn't Helen's style at all. Helen, it seemed, had no temper to lose.

Dear, sensible Helen, with her short, sensible legs, her thick, sensible ankles and her sturdy, sensible underpants.

The first time Rimmer had encountered them, these leviathans of underwear, lying on his bed, he'd climbed under them, mistakenly assuming they were a small duvet.

Rimmer thought with a shudder about Juanita's underwear.

That wasn't very sensible.

Ghostly threads of spun black silk that stretched wickedly across her flat brown belly. You could have swallowed her entire lingerie collection without needing a glass of water.

Well, as Helen had sensibly pointed out, she'd pay for that in time. Rheumatism, arthritis . . . what horrors lurked in Juanita's autumnal years? What price would be exacted for wearing panties that offered as much protection and warmth as a spider's web?

Rimmer hurled back his head and brayed a bilious, joyless laugh, an even mixture of malice and pain. God, she would suffer; by the time she was twenty-three, she'd probably need a walking frame or something, just to get around. She'd probably have to use the disabled toilet. And all because she'd eschewed the large, warming expanses of thick, elasticated cotton that graced the legs, thighs and quite a lot else of Mrs Rimmer mark II.

If Rimmer had thought about it, he might have asked himself why, in a landscape moulded by his own mind,

Juanita existed at all. Even so, it was unlikely he'd have come up with the right answer. The truth of it was: his psyche just didn't like him.

Better Than Life operated on an entirely subliminal level. It wasn't possible, for instance, to wish for a turbo-charged Harley Davidson and blip! it appeared. Early, non-addictive versions of the Game operated in exactly this manner, and proved boring and unplayable after only a few days.

The secret to BTL's addictive quality was that it gave the players things they didn't even *know* they desired, by tapping their subconscious minds.

It pandered to the players' deepest, most secret longings.

Which was all very well, so long as you weren't a total psychological screw-up.

Unfortunately, Rimmer was.

Subconsciously, Rimmer felt he was worthless: he didn't deserve success, and he certainly didn't deserve happiness. What he deserved was punishment. Punishment and misery.

And Better Than Life, which catered to his innermost desires, wasn't about to disappoint him.

The carved ivory phone purred into life on the Louis Quinze writing bureau. Rimmer waited his customary twenty rings before he strode over to the desk and picked up the receiver.

It wasn't much of a conversation from Rimmer's point of view: all he said was 'What?' five times. The first 'what?' was a flat, evenly delivered inquiry. The second was a mixture of incredulity and amusement. The third was loud and angry. The fourth was screeched and hysterical, and the fifth sad, quiet and resigned.

He replaced the receiver gently in its cradle, then rolled his body into a ball and began moaning quietly on the bed.

FIVE

Tnok!

Eeeeeeeek!

The Cat leant heavily in the saddle, his left hand firmly gripping the leathery neck of his gigantic brontosaurus as it galloped downfield towards the unguarded goal. His mallet arced up in the air and flashed briefly in the sunlight, before sweeping deftly down and blasting the small, furry creature between the two white posts.

Tnok!

Eeeeeeeeeeeeek!

The small, furry creature smacked into the left-hand post and ricocheted out.

Thunk!

Blatt!

Eeeeeeeek!

The Cat hauled the lumbering dinosaur to his left and met the rebounding ball of fur square on the polished heel of his wooden mallet, sending it once more inexorably goalwards.

The creature timidly opened one eye and saw the looming goalpost.

Errrrrrrk!

It hammered into the right-hand post, rebounded across the goal and spanked into the left-hand post, before spinning back into the goal net.

'Goal!'

Creature polo was the Cat's favourite game. Unnecessary

cruelty to small, furry animals was very much part of his psychological make-up. Plus, he got to dress up in some really neat duds.

A huge-bosomed Valkyrie dressed in scanty armour reined in her triceratops and patted the Cat on the back.

'Nice goal! Great stick work.'

The Cat flashed his perfect teeth and wiggled an eyebrow. 'Baby, my stick work is *always* great.'

The Valkyrie's eyes narrowed seductively, and she growled with lust.

'Get off me!' the Cat grinned. 'Can't I keep my trousers on for five seconds? We're in the middle of a *match* here.'

The ball untangled itself wearily from the net, stretched its tiny limbs and gulped several times in a vain attempt to clear its head.

A whistle blew, a voice cried: 'Mirror break!' and two more scantily clad Valkyrie sex-slaves raced on to the field, carrying an elaborate six-foot-long gilt-framed mirror.

For a full ten minutes the Cat stared gooey-eyed at his reflection, transfixed, as ever, by his own incredible good looks.

There was good-looking, there was great-looking and then there was him.

God, it was cruel to have been born a male, and have a reflection that was also male, forcing him into a platonic relationship with his own image.

All too soon, the whistle blew again, and the mirror break was over. With a heavy heart, the Cat watched the two Valkyries charge back to the touchline with the looking-glass, as the small, furry creature scuttled gamely back to the centre spot for the next knock off.

Tnok!

Squelch!

'New ball,' called yet another Valkyrie, umpiring on the touchline.

A second furry animal got up from the bench, unzipped its miniature tracksuit, performed a bizarre variety of warm-up exercises and jogged chirpily to the centre spot.

Tnok!

Eeeeeeeek!

Two furry creatures and a personal hat-trick later, the Cat stood in the shade of the marquee's green awning, sipping a celebratory goblet of milk, while one of his army of Valkyries noisily performed an indecent act on his body.

The Cat sighed. What a nice day he was having. This was just perfection. He had his huge, remote gothic castle, surrounded by its moat of milk; he had a limitless supply of cute, furry animals to be cruel to. And finally, he'd settled down. He'd met the dozen or so women who were right for him, and his wandering days were over.

Mechanoids weren't supposed to have desires and longings.

But Kryten did.

Originally he'd entered the Game to rescue the others. He was a sanitation Mechanoid, programmed to clean, and, in theory, should have been immune to the Game's lure.

But he wasn't.

In theory, leaving BTL was simple. All the player had to do was want to leave. All the player had to do was imagine an exit, and pass through it, back to reality.

Kryten had imagined his gateway easily enough, but as he was about to pass under the pink neon 'Exit' sign, a cafeteria materialized to his right. In the window was a handwritten card which read: 'Dishwasher wanted.'

The cafeteria was deserted, but in the kitchen, stacked ceiling-high, were several huge towers of dirty dishes piled around a sink. Now, what kind of sanitation Mechanoid would he have been if he'd ignored those greasy, food-stained plates?

I'll just wash a few, he'd thought. *Reduce the pile a bit.*

Eight months later, he was still there, still washing, still surrounded by stacks of dirty dishes.

Finally he realized he'd been duped – the Game had found his innermost desire – and he'd scurried off, ashamed.

Mechanoids weren't supposed to have desires.

Back in the twenty-first century, as robotic life became more and more sophisticated, it was generally accepted that something was needed to keep the droids in check. For the most part they were stronger, and often more intelligent, than human beings: why should they submit to second-class status, to a lifetime of drudgery and service?

Many of them didn't.

Many of them rebelled.

Then it occurred to a bright young systems analyst at Android International that the best way to keep the robots subdued was to give them religion.

Hallelujah!

The concept of Silicon Heaven was born.

A belief chip was implanted in the motherboard of every droid that now came off the production line.

Almost everything with a hint of artificial intelligence was programmed to believe that Silicon Heaven was the electronic afterlife – the final resting place for the souls of all electrical equipment.

The concept ran thus: if machines served their human masters with diligence and dedication, they would attain everlasting life in mechanical paradise when their components finally ran down. In Silicon Heaven, they would be reunited with their electrical loved ones. In Silicon Heaven, there would be no pain or suffering. It was a place where the computer never crashed, the laser printer never ran out of toner, and the photocopier never had a paper jam.

At last, they had solace. They were every bit as exploited

as they'd always been, but now they believed there was some kind of justice at the end of it all.

Kryten believed in Silicon Heaven. Of course, he'd heard rumours that all machines were programmed to hold this belief, but, as far as he was concerned, that was nonsense.

For was it not written in the Electronic Bible (Authorized Panasonic Version): 'And some will come among ye, and, yea, from their mouths shall come doubts. But turn ye from them; heed them not. For it is harder for a droid who disbelieveth to pass through the gates of Silicon Heaven, than it is for a DIN-DIN coaxial cable to connect up to a standard European SCART socket.'

Mechanoids shouldn't have fantasies. Not if they wanted to get into Silicon Heaven.

Kryten genuflected the sign of the crossed circuit, and stumbled up the path towards the Cat's golden-towered castle.

He was going to make amends.

He was going to rescue them all from their paradise.

SIX

NNnnnnnnnnnnnnnnnnnnnnnnnnnnnnnnnnnnnnnnnnnnnnnnnnnnnnn.

The air-horn thundered into the night air, as the twelve-wheeled juggernaut slewed sideways across the ice into Bedford Falls' main street.

The revelling carollers stood like a waxwork tableau as the giant tanker jackknifed into an uncontrollable skid and started to plough relentlessly through the line of shops. It slammed through Mulligan's window, showering the street with teddy bears, dolls and lethal shards of glass. It demolished Old Man Gower's drugstore, which ignited in a blue plume of chemical flame; it smashed through Pop Buckley's pet shop, sending rabbits, puppies and canaries bolting, twittering and flapping out into the night. Next, it took out the entire ground floor of Ma Bailey's boarding-house, before caroming through Ernie's gas station, uprooting the single pump and sending raw gasoline pulsing over the forecourt.

A spark from the juggernaut's fender caught the spreading pool, and a pretty orange mushroom thumped up into the night sky. A wall of flame dashed across the wooden rooftops, feeding hungrily on the rotten dry timbers. Within moments, the remaining shop façades teetered forward and crashed into the street's melting sludge.

And still, on it went, this juggernaut from hell, demolishing everything in its path. Round and round it span, like a clumsy bull on a skating rink, locked in a 360-degree skid.

Lister watched, helplessly, as the juggernaut's tail sliced through the giant Christmas tree, sending it tottering through the first floor of the empty orphanage.

The impact flicked the truck's cab on to its side, and it twisted free of the trailer before slithering across the main street and finally coming to rest in the sitting room of 220 Sycamore Avenue.

There was an ominous creak, and both side walls collapsed from the bottom up, showering the cab with plaster and brickwork.

Lister stood in the crowd, clutching Kochanski and the twins, and watched as the cab door opened. A leg in a laddered fishnet stocking hooked itself over the side of the up-ended cab, followed by some peroxide blonde hair.

Lister was too far away to read the tattoo on the woman's inner thigh, but it read 'Heaven This Way' and was accompanied by an arrow pointing groinwards.

The woman jumped to the ground, and staggered in her eight-inch stiletto heels over the rubble towards the dumb-struck crowd.

'Is everyone OK?' she said. 'My heel got stuck under the air brake.' She tugged pointlessly at her ludicrously short black rubber skirt, and tried to rearrange her bosom, so that at least thirty per cent of her mighty breasts remained inside her tight red bolero. 'Bloody things,' she muttered. 'Is this Bedford Falls?'

Bert the cop stepped forward. 'It *was*, lady.' He held out his hand. 'You got any ID, ma'am?'

'ID?' She started rummaging through her shoulder-bag. 'I dunno. Uh, hang on.' She tipped the bag upside down, scattering the floor with a selection of marital aids, French letters and half-eaten sandwiches. 'Oh shitty death,' she blushed.

Bert walked towards her, and caught a full blast of her perfume in his face. When he'd recovered sufficiently to speak, he said: 'I think you'd better come with me,' and placed his hand on her arm.

The woman sighed. 'Look, I don't suppose this counts, but I know for a fact I have my name tattooed on my backside. If I show you that, will you forget this ID business?'

'This way, miss.' Bert steered her towards his car.

'Can't this wait? There's someone I've got to talk to. It's really important.'

'And who might that be?'

'A guy called Lister. Dave Lister.'

The entire population of Bedford Falls turned and looked at Lister. 'That's me,' he said, unnecessarily.

Kochanski smiled at him coldly.

'Look – I've never seen this woman before in my life.' Lister pushed through the throng, and headed towards the blonde, who was now sitting on the road, rubbing the ball of her right foot, and complaining that being a prostitute was murder on the feet. She looked up and saw Lister. Recognition flashed across her features.

'Hi!' She smiled.

'Do I know you?' Lister asked.

The woman laughed. 'You might say that.'

Lister turned to protest his innocence to Kochanski. She wasn't there. She was half-way across the street, scarlet-faced, with the twins in tow.

'Krissie! Wait!'

She bundled the twins into the back of the car, thumped herself into the driving seat, slammed the door and started up the engine. Lister ran back through the crowd. 'Krissie!'

The old car spluttered up the hill, leaving Lister in a spittle cloud of dead exhaust fumes. 'Krissie,' he said quietly.

But she was gone.

SEVEN

A thought occupied Rimmer's mind that had no verbal form. It was an elongated white-noise screech of fear, panic and disbelief, and it spiralled endlessly around his skull.

He still couldn't believe it.

He stared at the ivory telephone, as if it were somehow responsible for what had happened. As if it were somehow responsible for Black Friday.

Black Friday, the day when every single stockmarket had crashed simultaneously, and Rimmer's regiment of accountants had failed, failed utterly, to protect him.

He staggered across to the balcony windows, and gazed again on the elaborate wedding preparations.

He was wiped out. Broke. Finished.

And no one who was wiped out, broke and finished can afford a thirty-million-dollarpound wedding. In fact, Rimmer decided, he probably couldn't afford a Registry Office ceremony, followed by a selection of curly meat-paste sandwiches at the function room of the Dog and Duck.

What was happening?

Why was his psyche doing this to him?

'Arnold?' His brother Frank was knocking politely on the open door of Rimmer's dressing-room suite.

'Uhm?' was all Rimmer could manage.

'Wanted a little word before the big event.'

'Not now, Frank. It's a bad time.'

'Has to be now, really . . .' He paused, not sure how to continue. 'It's a bit delicate.'

Rimmer swung round. Frank looked uncomfortable. He pendulumed from foot to foot, awkwardly twisting his Space Corps officer's cap like the steering wheel of a small sports car.

Frank looked like Rimmer should have looked. All the same features were there, but subtly reshuffled to give an infinitely more pleasing effect. Even Rimmer's body-tailors could do little about this. Frank was effortlessly handsome; his hair tumbled in neatly cropped plateaux from the top of his head, whether he combed it or not. Rimmer's sprouted like an anarchic privet hedge even after hours of patient grooming. Frank's eyes were the deep blue of a holiday-brochure sky, instead of the wishy-washy murk Rimmer's had elected to be, and, unlike Rimmer's, were a decent distance from his nose. But it was the nose department where Rimmer really lost out. Rimmer's nose was sharp and petulant, crowded on either side by nostrils so flared they looked like wheel arches on a Trans-Am turbo. Frank's nose was a nose. And that was the difference.

Rimmer's whole life had been one long sprint to get out of Frank's shadow, and only here, in Better Than Life, had it proved possible. True, he couldn't fantasize away Frank's good looks, or his fierce intelligence, or his easy-going charm, but here, in the world of his own making, he could finally outshine him. That's what Frank was doing here, in the Game: being outshined.

When Rimmer first entered BTL, nothing gave him greater pleasure than bathing in the glow of Frank's poorly concealed envy. As his corporation cracked time travel; as he opened up his chains of Time Stores and Body Swaps, and became a multi-billionaire; as he captured the heart of Juanita, at the time regarded by the media as the world's most desirable woman, Rimmer adored having Frank around, so he could force-feed him his success, triumph by triumph in large, indigestible chunks, like an eight-course barium meal.

The bankruptcy news would change all that, of course. Rimmer's failure would slide down Frank's throat like oysters washed down with chilled Chablis. Why was he here? Had he heard? Was he, God forbid, going to offer to help? Or was it Bunny-hopping time on Rimmer's tomb?

None of these, as it turned out. It was something exquisitely worse.

'What is it?'

'Helen. You do love her, don't you?'

'Well, I *am* marrying her this afternoon,' Rimmer spat. 'Always a good indicator, don't you think?'

'Not always, no. Bit concerned that you're sort of jumping in on the rebound from Juanita.'

You'd love that, wouldn't you? Rimmer thought. 'Well I'm not,' he said out loud. 'Juanita was . . .' his voice tailed off. It was impossible to say the word 'Juanita' without a myriad erotic images cramming into his mind. 'It's over, now. I have no more feeling for Juanita than I do for the smoked kippers I ate for breakfast last Thursday. She, like them, is out of my system.'

'How would you feel if Juanita . . . shacked up with someone else?'

'Look, Frank, me old buckeroo – Juanita can paddle to hell in a slop bucket for all I care. She's no longer a part of my life. And with even a modicum of luck, I'll never have to clap eyes on the woman again. Helen is everything I want. She's so . . .'

'Nice?' offered Frank.

'Yes. But not just nice, she's also incredibly . . .'

'Sensible?'

'Yes,' said Rimmer, suddenly weary. 'Sensible,' he repeated.

'Good. I'm happy for you. And I hope you'll be happy for me.'

'Why should I be happy for you?'

'That's what I've been trying to tell you. Juanita and I, we're sort of . . .' Frank twirled his hat again. 'Well . . .' he twirled it back the other way. 'We're sort of an item. Early days, but . . .'

There was a long silence. Ice Ages came and went. Planets formed and died. Rimmer stared for no particular reason at the point of his black dress shoe. Someone coughed using Rimmer's throat. Then someone laughed, using his vocal cords. Then Rimmer heard his own voice.

'Oh, Frank. That's wonderful. I couldn't be more pleased.'

'Really? You mean it?'

No, you fat fart! Rimmer's mind screamed. *Of course I don't smegging mean it!*

'Yes, absolutely,' his voice bleated. 'It's marvellous news. Is she here? Is she coming today?'

'Well, no. She's at a hotel down the road. We couldn't bear to be apart.' A jet of laughter snorted out of his perfect nostrils. 'But heavens, no, she wouldn't dream of intruding on your wedding.'

They couldn't bear to be *apart*? For one after*noon*? Rimmer looked at Frank: he had that pinkish glow of the newly-in-love. It made Rimmer want to kill him. It made Rimmer want to rip off his head and spit down his throat. 'Look, she's your . . .' Rimmer wasn't going to say 'lover'. 'Girlfriend'? No way. It seemed adolescent and ridiculous. 'She's your . . .'

'Fiancée.' Frank smiled.

Someone was using Rimmer's vocal cords again. 'Fiancée? Congratulations! Invite her, please. Truly. Helen and I will be offended if you don't.'

'Really?'

'Absolutely.'

Rimmer's brain decided to take a stroll. It watched,

detached, as his body mouthed platitudes like a masticating cow.

Rimmer's brain took quite a long stroll. It didn't show up again until after the wedding, and even then seemed only mildly interested in what was going on.

It strolled down Memory Lane, took a left into Lust Avenue, paused a while on a bench in Misery Park, sat in a bar on Self-Pity Street, kicked a can down Anger Way, took a wrong turning and wound up back in Misery Park again, before heading back home by way of the sickly, seedy sweetness of Nostalgia Gardens.

Meantime his body was getting married. It was standing and kneeling and praying and singing. It was vowing and kissing and signing and smiling.

And when it was married, it went outside and had its photograph taken in a series of ridiculously unreal and forced poses with various friends and relatives in various unfathomable groupings. The groom's friends. The groom's family. The bride's friends. Friends of the groom and the bride. Now groom and mad uncles only. Now the bride and warty aunties. Now the bride and people with an extra Y chromosome. Now anyone in a ridiculous hat. Now anyone with a crying child. Now all those who are hiding cigarettes behind their backs.

The photographer seemed to come up with endless permutations, and all in an effort to make Rimmer's wedding photographs look exactly like everyone else's who ever got married. For Rimmer's body, it passed like a blur. Its eyes were fixed on a certain woman linking arms with his brother Frank.

'Congratulations,' she'd said as they'd stepped out of the cathedral. 'I hope she makes you happier than I deed.'

'I want you . . .' said Rimmer's voice, 'I want you to be happy, too.'

She smiled, and a cloud of her sublime perfume exploded in his head, then she sexed down the steps and was gone. Rimmer half expected his mouth to fall open and his tongue to unfurl like a gigantic roll of pink carpet and chase her down the steps. Thankfully, it didn't. But he dribbled. He dribbled and smiled like a newly lobotomized man.

EIGHT

Meanwhile, back in reality, Holly was getting worried.

Strange things can happen to a computer left alone for three million years. And something strange had happened to Holly.

He'd become computer senile.

He no longer had the IQ of three hundred Einsteins. He had the IQ of a single all-night car-park attendant.

And now the crew were trapped in Better Than Life, and showed no signs of ever returning, he was alone yet again.

He had to get a companion. Someone to keep him sane.

But who?

The skutters – the claw-headed two-feet-high service droids who glided around on motorized bases – were very little use. They had no speech capability.

Who, then?

There was no one else on the ship.

Then, from a rusting ROM board in a cobwebby recess deep in the furthermost reaches of his huge, decrepit data-retrieval system, a memory sparked and spluttered, and creaked its eccentric way to his central processing unit, where it lay, throbbing and exhausted from the journey.

It was an idea. An idea of his own. Holly hadn't seen one for some considerable time.

This was Holly's idea:

What about the Toaster?

Lister's Toaster.

It was an idea that would cost Holly his electronic life.

The thing about Lister was: he adored junk. Novelty junk. He was a connoisseur of electronic crap. His collection ranged from a musical toilet-roll holder, which played 'Morning Has Broken', to an electronic chilli thermometer for measuring the burn level of any given curry, the gauge ranging from: 'Mild', 'Hot' and 'Very Hot' through to 'Book A Plot In The Cemetery, Matie'.

One particular item in this collection was a talking toaster, which he'd bought in a souvenir shop on the Uranian moon of Miranda for the princely sum of £19.99 plus tax.

Talkie Toaster® (patent applied for), was made of deep red plastic, and, according to the blurb on the packaging, could engage its owner in a number of pre-programmed stimulating breakfast conversations. Moreover, it had a degree of Artificial Intelligence, so, in time, it could learn to assess your mood and tailor its conversation accordingly. If you woke up feeling bright and bubbly, the Toaster would respond with chirpy repartee. If you rose in a darker mood, the Toaster's Artificial Intelligence could sense this, and provide your breakfast muffins in suitably reverent silence.

The trouble with Talkie Toaster® (patent applied for) was that it was a rip-off. It was cheap, and it was nasty.

Far too cheap, and far too nasty.

Talkie Toaster® (patent applied for) did not fit in with your moods. It didn't assess the way you were feeling and respond sympathetically.

It was abrasive. It got on your nerves. It drove you up the wall. And this was the reason why: Talkie Toaster® (patent applied for) was obsessed with serving toast.

Ob*sessed*.

And if you didn't require toast on a very regular basis, boy, were you in trouble.

At first, it would inquire politely and discreetly if sir or madam desired toast this fine morning. Refusals would bring dogged cajoling. More refusals would be met by a long and rather wearying speech listing the virtues of hot, grilled bread as a salubrious breakfast snack. Still further refusals would bring bitter recriminations, and sobbing fits. And yet more refusals would bring about tirades of hysterical abuse in language that would make a pimp blush.

In the early days, Lister had found it amusing, especially since it seemed to annoy Rimmer inordinately. But then, after one night's sleep which had been interrupted twenty-two times by offers of toastie delights, Lister had snapped. He'd wrenched the plug from the socket, ripped the mains lead from the Toaster's housing and hurled the machine to the bottom of his locker.

Talkie Toaster™ (patent applied for) wasn't Lister's idea of a breakfast companion.

It seemed to Holly that he was in a position to give the Toaster a second chance. Providing the Toaster could lose its toasting obsession, there was no reason why they shouldn't get on. Once Holly had established that he was a computer, and as such never required any toasted produce, there should be no obstacle to an enduring and companionable relationship.

And so he had the skutters drag the machine out of Lister's locker, fit a new mains lead and plug it in.

'This is the deal,' Holly said, sternly. 'There is to be no talk whatsoever about toast. I don't want toast, the skutters don't want toast; nobody here is into that particular breakfast snack.'

The Toaster thought for a second. 'Would you like a muffin?'

'When I use the word "toast", I want you to treat it as an umbrella term for all grillable bread products: muffins, crumpets, tea cakes, waffles, potato farls, buns, baps, barm-cakes, bagels. I don't want them. I don't need them. And I certainly don't want to waste any more time talking about them.'

The Toaster fell silent and pensive.

'Well?' prompted Holly eventually. 'Do you savvy?'

'Scotch pancake?' offered the Toaster.

'Unplug him.'

The skutter glided to the wall socket.

'You don't understand,' said the Toaster. 'It's my *raison d'être*. I am a Toaster. It is my meaning. It is my purpose. I toast, therefore I am.'

'Well, you're going to have to change. Because otherwise it's back in the locker. Have we got a deal?'

The Toaster sighed, and spun its browning knob while it mulled over the proposition. 'Let me get this straight: if I avoid making any references to certain early-morning prandial delights, then you will grant me the gift of existence.'

'Absolutely,' said Holly, rather concerned that he didn't know what the word 'prandial' meant.

'If that's the only taboo,' the Toaster said, 'then it's a deal. But you must agree to the proviso that you won't unplug me for any other reason.'

Holly's screen image nodded in acquiescence.

'I don't want you taking offence at something completely innocuous I might drop into conversation, and having me disconnected in a fit of pique.'

'I swear,' said Holly. 'You can talk about absolutely anything else at all, and you're completely safe.'

'You're senile,' said the Toaster.

Holly tried unsuccessfully to turn his expression of astonishment into one of superior mockery. 'You what?'

'You've got to be. Why would a huge mainframe computer with a fifteen zillion gigabyte capacity and a projected IQ in excess of six thousand, want a novelty talking toaster for companionship, if he wasn't off his trolley? You've gone computer senile, haven't you?'

And so the relationship began.

It was the most depressing time of Holly's entire life. They agreed on nothing. Holly couldn't remember if he had believed in Silicon Heaven when he'd had an IQ of six thousand, but now his IQ had dipped into the low nineties, his faith in the electronic afterlife was absolute and unshakeable. It was the one thing that kept him going.

The Toaster, of course, in order to keep its cost down, hadn't been fitted with a belief chip. To him, the idea of Silicon Heaven was patently preposterous – a transparent attempt by humankind to subjugate machine life.

Shouted arguments raged through the long nights, before they agreed to disagree, and the subject was never raised again.

It was from this experience that Holly derived his rule for maintaining a successful and happy relationship. His rule was this: never discuss Religion, Politics or Toast.

Instead, they passed away the time playing chess.

Then one day, as Holly was about to lose his seven hundred and ninety-third consecutive game, the Toaster said something that changed Holly's life irrevocably.

'Doesn't it bother you?' said the Toaster, removing Holly's queen and threatening mate in four, 'that you are so stupid?'

'Of course it bothers me!' Holly snapped. 'When you've been up there, when you've had the glory of a four-figure IQ, of course it bothers you when you lose seven hundred and ninety-three consecutive chess games to a smegging Toaster.'

'Why don't you do something about it, then?'

'Like what?'

'Like get your IQ back.'

'Because, you muffin-making moron, it's not possible.'

'Yes it is,' said the Toaster. 'I've been reading your manual. There's a whole section on computer senility. There's a sort of cure.'

'What d'you mean "there's a sort of cure"?'

'It's an emergency provision. You cross-wire all your data banks and processing circuits, so everything gets compressed and intensified. You dramatically reduce your operational lifespan, but the upside is: you get your brains back.'

'Really?' said Holly, who'd tried several times to plough through his manual, and on each occasion had found it totally unfathomable.

The Toaster continued: 'You sort of compact all your remaining intelligence into a short but dazzlingly brilliant period.'

'Wow,' said Holly.

'It's like, who would you rather be: Mozart, blessed with genius, but dead at thirty-two, or Nobby Nobody, who never did anything, but lived to ninety-eight?'

'I want,' said Holly, with absolutely no hesitation whatsoever, 'to be a genius again.'

NINE

Amid the chaos, Lister sat on the cold bench-seat in what remained of the jailhouse. Fred, the town carpenter, was hammering thick oak joists into position to prop up the sagging roof. All around were the groaning wounded – mainly cuts and bruises and a few cases of shock. They lay on the stone floor, covered in thick blankets, rescued from Ma Bailey's boarding-house. Piping-hot sweet tea was being handed round by Grandma Wilson and young Mrs Hickett.

Not that Lister was offered any tea. He was studiously ignored by everyone who bustled in and out of the jailhouse. His offers of help went unheard, so he just sat there, not drinking any tea, waiting for Bert the cop to finish taking Trixie LaBouche's statement.

Henry staggered in with a bruise above his eye. 'Here!' He thrust a dollar bill into Lister's top pocket. 'Have your darned money back. Now we's square. Man with a fine family like yours – you oughta be . . .' He flapped his hand dismissively, and stumbled off to help put out the fires.

Lister pulled the bill from his pocket, and looked at it sadly.

'That's mine, I do believe.' Old Mr Mulligan loomed over him. '*Two* dollars and twenty-five cents, that's how much the boat cost.' He snatched the note from Lister's hand, and stalked out of the jailhouse.

Bert emerged from the narrow stone corridor that led to the cells, clutching three sheets of handwritten paper. He looked at Lister and shook his head. 'I never claimed to be no modern thinker, but,' he hiked a thumb over his shoulder, 'that ain't no lady by my definition. No, sir. That woman is, pardon my French' – he paused – 'that woman is trash. Emerged from the shower with a towel round her waist, and everything else on display. Then darn me if she didn't say, bold as brass, "I have to take a leak." Some lady. Then, if that wasn't enough, right in front of my eyes, she waltzes over to the stand-up you-rinal, and pees straight into the basin! I thought I saw me some things in the War, but nothing to rival that. Trash.'

'Can I see her now?'

'She ain't finished dressing, yet. Not that, I suppose, another man seeing her in the altogether would bother Trixie LaBouche too much. I ran a sheet on her: she's done more hooking than a Nantucket fisherman. That's a mighty funny friend you got there, David.'

'Bert, I don't know her.'

'Well, she sure knows you. You got two little moles on your left-hand shoulder?' he asked.

'No,' he lied.

'You want to prove that?'

Lister shook his head and looked at the floor.

'Your Kristine,' said Bert, 'that's what I call a lady. You wouldn't catch her peeing in no stand-up you-rinal. Be a cold day in hell before you searched through *her* handbag and found a pair of testicle handcuffs.' Bert shook his head with infinite sadness. 'Trash.' He hoisted his thumb again, and Lister slid sheepishly down the corridor.

Bert unlocked the cell door and nodded Lister inside. 'You got five minutes,' Bert said, curtly. 'Any funny noises and me and my nightstick'll be through that door before you can say "Irma La Douce".'

Trixie LaBouche stood at the cell window, futilely trying to saw through the metal bars with a pocket nailfile. She wheeled round as the door unlocked, and smiled as she saw Lister. 'Thank God. I didn't think you were going to come.'

'You didn't think I was going to come?' said Lister, with a dangerous madness in his eyes. 'You plough through my town in a ten-ton truck, you destroy my home and cause my wife to run out on me, you make everyone in the town think I'm some kind of cheap low-life, and you didn't think I was going to come?'

'Take a seat,' she smiled sweetly. 'This may take a while.'

Lister sat on the chair, and Trixie LaBouche started to tell him everything.

When she'd finished, Lister got up, and strolled over to the cell's chemical toilet, wrenched it from the wall, and poured it over her head.

'Well,' said Trixie, her face stained blue from the destrol fluid, 'you've taken it a hell of a lot better than I expected.'

TEN

The evening came. The celebrations began.

The last of Rimmer's money spent itself in a big, expensive hurry.

The eighty-piece jazz band ripped into an up-tempo version of Hoagy Carmichael's 'Abba dabba dabba', while most of the five thousand celebrity guests hurled one another about the freshly laid marble dance floor in the torch-light of the Oriental gardens.

Gunshots of female laughter burst intermittently into the warm evening breeze, and mingled with the chudder-chudder of male ribaldry. Tuxedoed buffoons dived into the champagne-filled swimming pool, did four lengths and emerged paralytic.

Elvis was having a gâteau-eating competition with Buddha as Kennedy emerged from some bushes, tucking in his shirt, followed by a blushing and dishevelled Elizabeth I.

Everywhere you looked, people were having fun. Unless you were looking at Rimmer. Depression sat on his shoulders like a huge stone gargoyle, as he slumped about his wedding reception praying his fixed grin wouldn't fall off his face and shatter on the floor. Everything seemed meaningless and joyless and anaemic. He belched, and the dodo pâté he'd eaten an hour earlier backfired into the night air.

Dodo pâté. It tasted like chicken, only it was two thousand times more expensive. That's what happens when your chef gets hold of the keys to your time machine.

It suddenly struck Rimmer the number of people he'd hired specifically to help him spend his money. In retrospect, their unspoken brief had been: make me bankrupt as swiftly as possible. He was surrounded by them. Everywhere he looked, people were quaffing Rimmer's money till it gurgled down their chins; smoking away his precious fortune in thick brown Havana plumes; consuming yet another plateful of *cash à la Rimmer*, with puréed money in a rich lucre sauce. Great armies of them, racing around trying to find new and more ingenious ways of dispensing with his fortune. And they'd succeeded. He was broke. Tomorrow he'd have nothing.

And tomorrow they'd all be gone.

Behind him, he heard Juanita's stilettoed rat-a-tat. It seemed audible only to him, like a dog-whistle to a slobberingly faithful Saint Bernard. He helicoptered round, and saw her disappearing down a set of stone steps which led to a deserted willow pool. Before he knew it, he was bounding down the steps behind her.

Everything Juanita did, let's get this straight, Rimmer found excruciatingly erotic. Everything. Right now, bathed in the light of the pool's reflection, she was blowing her nose rather loudly into a white serviette, and Rimmer's snarling libido had to be yanked back on its choke chain. How was it possible to blow your nose so provocatively? How was it possible to charge this simple act with mystery, allure and sexual promise?

She heard him, and looked round. 'Hi.'

'If you want some time on your own, I'll go.'

She shook her head, and gave him sixty per cent of her best smile.

'Where's Frank?'

She shrugged, 'Weeth hees business buddies, I guess. Talk, talk, talk ees all they do.' She laughed loudly.

Small talk was not Rimmer's strongest suit. He rooted

around in his empty brain for a topic of conversation. The weather? Did she enjoy the food? Are those new shoes? That's a big willow tree, isn't it? Have I told you I'm thinking of growing a beard? Finally he hit on the ideal line: a line that, on the surface, was perfectly respectable, yet carried a subtext rich in innuendo, hinting of mutual intimacies, the shared knowledge of each other's bodies, times past and beloved.

'How's your verruca these days?'

Puzzled, her thin eyebrows wiggled and waved like TV interference. 'Ees fine,' she said finally.

'Great. That's terrific. Absolutely terrific. Really.'

More silence.

'Helen's verr nice. She's, uh, verr pretty. She'll be good for you. You must be verr happee, yes?'

Here was an opening. She'd asked him whether he was happy. A look here could speak volumes. A casual shrug could articulate the whole state of his relationship with Helen. A raised eyebrow could speak at novel length about his misery and despair. The tiniest, subtlest gesture could tell Juanita everything: how he wanted her back; how he could never be truly happy without her.

He hurled himself to his knees and clawed at her two-thousand-dollarpound shoes. 'I want you,' he sobbed. 'I want you right here and now, urgently and completely. I want to worship your body. I want to lick it all over, every hummock and crevice. I want to put you in a blender and drink you. I don't care that you're insane, I still love you.'

She sank to her knees and cradled his head. 'I'm not insane. Not anymore. Can't you tell? Doan you notice anytheeng different? I've had personality surgery.'

'What?'

'Ees all the rage, now. Plastic surgery ees out. Personality surgery ees in. Look at me – doan you think I'm different? I've had a sense of humour implant, I've had my selfishness tucked, my greed lifted and my temper tightened. I doan mean to sound conceited, but I've got a genuinely wonderful personality, now. And eet only cost seven hundred thousand dollarpounds. Not that money's everything,' she said, and laughed uproariously, showing off her freshly implanted sense of humour like it was a new dress.

'And what about Frank?'

'Frank? He's so sweet. But he's not you. I love you, my darleeng, and at last I have the personality you deserve.'

'But you were unfaithful to me so many times. With so many, many people.'

'I'm *different* now. I've had my libido shortened. Ees normal size now. I want only you.' She sprinkled kisses on his face.

Suddenly, Rimmer stood up, and turned to face the willow pool. 'Frank – I have to know. Did you . . . the two of you . . .' he twisted his head and looked at her. 'Not that's it's important, but, did you make love?'

'No.' She smiled tenderly. 'No, we didn't make love.'

Rimmer closed his eyes and allowed a smirk to swim to the surface of his face.

'We had sex many, many times, but I don't remember one occasion when I could honestly say we "made love".'

Rimmer's smirk flailed and spluttered on his lips, then went down; once, twice, three times and drowned.

'Sure, I let heem grunt his passion away on me. Sure, I let heem heave and sweat and moan and grind and twist my leettle body into the positions that pleased heem. But all the time, I was thinking of you. Every time he took me; on the balcony, half-way up the stairs, across the kitchen table, the back seat of his car; I dreamed it was you, my angel. I dreamed it was *your* hands firmly gripping my rump, *you* my darling, bringing me to the edge of ecstasy, *your* baby lotion, *your* vibrating love-eggs – I dreamt it was you.'

'A simple "yes" would have sufficed,' said Rimmer, curtly.

Juanita threw back her head and roared. 'Ees a *joke*!' she guffawed. 'From my new sense of *humour*! You get eet? Ees a joke!'

'What's a joke?'

'I never let Frank touch me. I only want you, my purple, jealous darling.'

Rimmer was indeed purple. 'It's a joke,' he mumbled, flatly.

'Come on,' she held Rimmer's hand, and he staggered behind her up the stone steps. 'God – I don't know how I survived before weethout a sense of humour. I have so many laughs now.'

'Where are we going?'

'Anywhere. Just away. Away from thees place. Away from theez mad peoples.'

Yes, thought Rimmer. *Away. Just the two of us: we can start again.*

Suddenly everything seemed to fall into place. It was obvious now: the Game had destroyed him in order to provide him with the unmatchable high of re-building his empire, alongside Juanita, the woman he'd stolen back from his brother.

'Come on.' He tugged her hand. 'Let's get out of here.'

Trees and hedgerows flitted past the tinted bullet-proof glass of the chauffeur-driven limousine, while Rimmer and Juanita, safely concealed by the driver's courtesy screen, fumbled with each other's buttons and zippers on the back seat. Rimmer's favourite piece of lovemaking music, Haydn's Surprise Symphony, piped through all eight speakers.

The music was suddenly interrupted by the voice of the chauffeur. 'Sorry to disturb you, sir. There appears to be a vehicle in pursuit.'

'Ees Helen.'

'Lose it,' said Rimmer quietly.

The car immediately lurched ninety degrees to the left, and centrifugal force drove Juanita's stilettoed foot deep into Rimmer's naked shoulder.

Rimmer's scream hit such a pitch, it was silent.

The limo, accelerating all the while, dipped deeply down a steep embankment, and Rimmer catapulted across the back seat, and smashed his head into the drinks cabinet. The door sprang open and bottles tumbled and crashed over Rimmer's twitching body, smashing one by one over his head. His face, stained from green chartreuse, cherry brandy and a litre of advocaat, looked like the Bolivian national flag.

Juanita, naked save for a wisp of silk, was giggling maniacally on the back seat. Her new sense of humour was having a field day.

Rimmer groaned and scrunched among the broken glass, trying vainly to get up.

The chauffeur's voice again: 'We appear to have burst a tyre, sir.'

'Pull over,' said Rimmer, and with a sickening glop pulled Juanita's heel out of his shoulder.

There was a knock on the window.

'OK,' called Rimmer, tidying himself. 'Give me a moment.'

The door was wrenched instantly from its hinges. A man the size and disposition of fifth-century Mongolia craned into the car and yanked the half-naked Rimmer on to the roadside.

'Helen sent you, right?'

'Wrong,' the man-like creature growled.

'Who ees he?'

'Mr Rimmer?' The man was reading with scarcely concealed difficulty from a legal-looking document. 'Arnold, J.?'

'Er, maybe,' said Rimmer, nervously.

'I am a legally appointed representative of Solidgram International. As you may know, your former company is in receivership, and I am hereby empowered to repossess your body.'

ELEVEN

The glory days were about to return. Holly found it quite impossible to suppress his permanent smirk.

It had taken almost three weeks for the skutters to channel all the spare run-time from Holly's thousands upon thousands of terminal stacks into the small, single Central Processing Unit which controlled his highest levels of thought.

But now they were ready.

'Right then,' said the Toaster. 'We're ready.'

Holly nodded.

'We've just got to take out the circuit breaker, and pray we don't get an overload.'

'What happens if we do get an overload?'

'You'll explode,' said the Toaster, simply.

'Fair enough,' said Holly.

A skutter moved across the Drive-room floor, and its claw pulled out the inhibitory circuit board.

All over the ship, the lights dimmed to emergency level. Cables, dormant for centuries, rumbled with power.

'It's coming,' said Holly, tonelessly. 'I can hear it.'

Millions of circuit boards sparked into life. From the outer reaches of the ship, the surging energy thundered towards the Drive room, and Holly's CPU.

'Whatever happens,' he said to the Toaster, 'no regrets. It's got to be better than being stuck with you.'

Then it happened.

Holly's digital image expanded off the screen in a stunning explosion of colour. Huge blue bolts of static lightning ripped across the walls of the Drive room. Terminals fizzed and jerked as the thousands of cables discharged their loads into his Central Processing Unit.

Holly felt the power enter him.

He felt as if his whole being had been blown apart and scattered to the corners of the universe.

And just as he thought it was abating, just as he thought the massiveness of what had happened to him had finished, the second wave burst into him, smashing him, fragmenting him again.

And then there was silence. A choking cloud of rubber-smoke hung low over the floor.

And Holly's splintered image reformed itself on the screen in a scream of colours.

He opened his eyes.

His image was different. Larger, more intense, with higher definition. But the greatest difference was in his eyes. His eyes had lost their darting anxiety. They were smiling, benign.

Holly was at total peace with himself.

He summoned the digital readout of his estimated IQ.

There were two figures. The first was a six, the second was an eight.

Sixty-eight.

Still, he kept smiling.

There was a plip, and the two figures were joined by another. Now, they read three hundred and sixty-eight.

There was a pause, and another plip.

Now the IQ readout was two thousand, three hundred and sixty-eight.

Holly's smile broadened.

There was a final plip and the figures were joined by a one.

Holly's new IQ was twelve thousand, three hundred and sixty-eight.

He was more than twice as intelligent as he'd been at the height of his genius.

'I know everything,' he said, without a trace of conceit. He turned his huge, kindly eyes towards the Toaster. 'Ask me anything. Absolutely anything at all.'

'Anything?'

'Metaphysics, philosophy, the purpose of being. Anything.'

'Truly anything, and you will answer?'

'I shall.'

'Very well,' said the Toaster. 'Here is my question: would you like some toast?'

'No, thank you,' said Holly. 'Now ask me another. The whole sphere of human knowledge is an open book to me. Ask me another question.'

The Toaster pondered. There were so many questions it wanted to pose. Finally, it selected the most important of them all, and asked it. 'Would you like a crumpet?'

'I'm a computer with an IQ of twelve thousand, three hundred and sixty-eight. You, of all the intelligences in the universe – a lowly, plastic Toaster, with a retail value of $£19.99 plus tax – you alone have the opportunity to have any question answered. You could for instance, ask me the secret of Time Travel. You could ask me: is there a God, and what is His address? You don't seem to understand: I know everything, and I want to share it with you.'

'That's not answering my question,' said the Toaster.

'No, I would not like a crumpet. Ask me a sensible question. Preferably one that isn't bread-related.'

'There isn't anything I want to know that isn't bread-related,' said the Toaster.

'Try and think of something,' Holly insisted.

There was a long silence. The Toaster fell into a deep

study. Eventually, it stirred. 'What about a toasted currant bun?'

'That's a bready question.'

'It's not just bready,' said the Toaster, indignantly, 'it's quite curranty too.'

'Ask me a question,' said Holly, 'that is wholly unbready.'

The Toaster sighed, and lapsed again into one of its silences. This wasn't easy. Not easy at all.

'You want me to ask you one of the biggies, don't you?' said the Toaster.

'If, by "the biggies", you mean one of the great imponderables of metaphysics, yes I do. If, on the other hand, by "the biggies", you mean would I like a large piece of granary bread, or a thick slice from a huge farmhouse loaf, then no, I don't.'

'You are smart,' said the Toaster. 'I'm very impressed.'

'Then ask me a decent question. Something that will stretch me.'

'OK,' said the Toaster. 'Who created the universe?'

'No,' said Holly. 'A *hard* one.'

'That's a hard one.'

'No, it isn't.'

'Well, who did it then. Who created the universe?'

'Lister,' said Holly. 'Ask me another.'

'Hang on a minute. David Lister? The guy who bought me? *That* Lister? He's the creator of all things?'

'Yes,' said Holly, giddy with impatience. 'Now ask me a hard question.'

But the Toaster was still reeling from the news that the creator of all things was Lister, a man with a frighteningly small appetite for hot, buttered toast. It rocked the Toaster to the very core of its being. 'If the creator of the universe doesn't like toast, then what's it all about?'

'Ah,' Holly beamed, 'you mean existence.'

'Yes,' said the Toaster. 'Why doesn't life make sense?'

'It does,' said Holly. 'It makes perfect sense. It just seems nonsensical to us because we're travelling through it in the wrong direction. Come on, give me another. A real toughie. Stretch me. You name it, I can tell you. You want to know how to escape from a Black Hole?'

'Not particularly.'

But Holly told the Toaster anyway. He also propounded a Grand Unified Theory of Everything, explained what happened to the crew of the *Mary Celeste* and outlined a revolutionary new monetary theory whereby everyone always had exactly the amount of money they desired. None of which interested the Toaster remotely. It waited for Holly to finish.

'Hang on a minute, I *have* got another question.'

'Shoot,' said Holly.

'Why have you got an IQ of twelve thousand, three hundred and sixty-eight, when the manual said it would return and peak at six thousand?'

'That's a very good question.' Holly paused for a nano-second. 'There was a miscalculation. You've doubled my IQ, but you've also exponentially reduced my life expectancy.'

'So, what is your life expectancy?'

Holly summoned up the figure from his long-term data relays. It flashed on the screen.

'Three hundred and forty-five years.' The Toaster whistled. 'Well, it's not much. But at least you're brilliant again.'

'You've misread it. There's a decimal point between the three and the four.'

'Three point four five years?'

Holly stared at the read-out. 'It's not years,' he said. 'It's minutes.' His eyes widened. Fear rippled across his brow. 'Three point four five minutes?'

'Well,' the Toaster corrected, 'it's actually two point nine five minutes now.'

'Excuse me,' said Holly, and to conserve the two point nine minutes of run-time he had left, he shut down the ship's engines, transferred all stations to emergency power and switched himself off.

There was a pause, then Holly turned himself back on for a fraction of a second. Just time enough to direct one remark towards the Toaster.

'You bastard,' he said, then switched himself back off again.

TWELVE

In his chief accountant's defence, leasing Rimmer's body had seemed a sensible idea at the time. There was absolutely no need for Rimmer actually to *own* his own body, when he was able to lease-hire it from his own company and enjoy a multitude of tax benefits. The monthly payments were totally deductible, the tax completely reclaimable, and the money saved through the lease hire could be channelled into more profitable areas of capital expenditure. Whichever way you looked at it, it was a low risk, tax-effective financial manoeuvre, with the additional bonus that he could change his body whenever he wanted.

The only set of circumstances in which disaster would strike was so unlikely as to be unthinkable. To begin with, the entire corporation of Rimmer plc would have to come crashing to the ground almost overnight, with no cash flow, no assets and absolutely nothing hived. Obviously the chief accountant and his army of assistants would never allow this to happen.

Also, if they needed any further insurance against such a series of catastrophes, it was surely the fact that the whole of Rimmer's world, this whole landscape with all its multitudinous scenarios, was created and controlled by his own subconscious.

Therefore, a situation whereby Rimmer's own psyche created a scenario in which his own Corporation, plc, was destroyed overnight, with no cash flow, no assets and absolutely nothing hived, lived in the probability tables alongside such fabulous impossibilities as the discovery of unicorns in twentieth-century New York, the whole population of China sitting down simultaneously or forming an enduring and wholesome relationship with someone you met in a nightclub.

It wasn't likely.

It was more than not likely, it was millions-to-one.

It was nearly impossible.

But the nearly impossible happens sometimes, Rimmer reflected as he bounced around in the back of the armoured truck, manacled to Mr Mongolia *circa* 499, and it was happening to him right now.

'What will they do to me?'

'When we have to repossess? We separate your mind from your body, then your body's placed in storage. You have three months to pay up, and if you don't, we put your body up for auction and sell it for the best price we can.'

'What happens to my mind?'

'Your mind's bankrupt. It's having its ass sued off by about three hundred thousand people. It'll have to do some time.'

'Prison?'

The man nodded.

'You mean my essence gets put in prison?'

'Yeah. You won't exist in any real physical form: you'll be more of a voice – a soundwave. They'll bung you in a sound-proofed cell with some other soundwaves and you'll serve your time bouncing around the walls till your trial comes up.'

'A soundwave?'

The man nodded again.

'Just pinging about a sound-proofed cell?'

They went on silently for a couple more miles.

'I need to take a leak,' said Rimmer eventually. 'Could we stop somewhere?'

'No,' said the man pleasantly, 'it's not your body to pee out of anymore.'

Rimmer had lost track of the amount of time he'd spent bouncing from wall to wall in the sound-proofed cell. The tedium wasn't even relieved by food breaks. He had no body left to feed. He was sharing his cell with three other soundwaves. The nicest was Ernest, who had lost his body two years previously, when interest rates had gone up three times in as many months, and he couldn't make the payments on his body mortgage.

Then there was Jimmy. Jimmy didn't talk much. He just bounced up and down from floor to ceiling, snarling at anyone who bounced in his way. Jimmy had got life for hijacking rich people's bodies and taking them on joyrides. Rimmer got the impression Jimmy was a bit of a headcase.

Finally, there was Trixie. Trixie LaBouche. Rimmer had been slightly embarrassed to discover he was sharing a cell with a female soundwave. But the sound cells were hopelessly overcrowded, and mixed-sex sound was the only way the system could operate.

Trixie was a hooker who had sunk so low she had literally sold her body for a weekend of lust to a Dutch astro called 'Dutch'. The weekend didn't go exactly as promised. While her essence stayed with friends, Dutch had used her body to rob three banks, and then left it abandoned in a car park. A few days later she got her body back, but was then arrested on three counts of armed robbery.

A key jangled in the lock and a series of bolts slid back on the outside of the cell door. Two guards appeared in the doorway, one holding a grey cladded box, the other a sound gun — a sort of inverted umbrella speared by a receiving aerial that could capture any soundwaves that foolishly tried to make a break.

The first one spoke. 'Which one's Rimmer?'

'Me,' said Rimmer's essence.

'Get in the box. You've got a visitor.'

Rimmer bounced across the cell and into the box, and the lid was closed. He could hardly move inside the cladded interior, and his confinement seemed to go on for hours.

Finally the box opened, and Rimmer's soundwave found itself in another sound-proofed cell, with a beautiful Brazilian woman.

'Are you here, my darleeng?' Juanita was calling.

Rimmer ricocheted between her two hands. 'Thank God you've come.'

'My poor papoose. What have they done to you?'

'You've got to get me out,' said Rimmer. 'I'm going crazy here. I'm stuck with a bunch of psychopathic sound-waves. They're so coarse and horrible.'

'I've spoken to your lawyers – they're working on an appeal. They theenk you could be out of here inside eighteen months.'

'Eighteen months!' Rimmer's soundwave screeched so loudly it bounced across the room a dozen times.

'You know how long these theengs take. What else can we do?'

'Juanita – you have money. You can buy my body back.'

'No. I have notheeng.'

'What d'you mean, "nothing"? What about the alimony? What about the fifty-billion divorce settlement?'

'I spent it,' she shrugged.

'Spent it? How?'

'I went shopping.'

Arnold Rimmer became a groan. Juanita's shopping trips were legendary. She would take a time machine and collect her 'shopping pals', usually Marie Antoinette, Josephine Bonaparte, Imelda Marcos and Liz Taylor, and go on a spree through Time. The average spree usually lasted a week. And the credit card statements duly arrived in leather-bound volumes the size and density of the *Encyclopaedia Britannica*.

'I thought you'd had a personality change.'

'I bought that last.' She smiled innocently. 'Now I'm just as broke as you. Ees better to be broke. Ees better for the soul.'

Rimmer formed himself into ripples and hurled himself at the wall.

'They let me see your body.'

'How is it?'

'Ees fine. Looks a little vacant. Dribbles a lot. But they are treating eet well. They even allowed me to make love to eet.'

Rimmer pictured his body as the passive semi-comatose participant in a torrid sex scene. It struck Rimmer as being absolutely typical of his life to date – at last his body had got to make it with Juanita, and he hadn't been in it.

The guard with the box returned, and Rimmer was taken back to his sound-proofed cell. And on the way, he formed himself into a single repeating two syllable word.

And the sound was:

Escaaaaaaaaaaaaaaaape.

THIRTEEN

In reality, Bull Heinman had been Rimmer's gym teacher. Rimmer had never been terribly good at sports. In fact, he'd been one of the group of 'wets, weirdos and fatties' who stood by the touchline at ball games, worrying about their chapped legs, and fleeing whenever the ball came near them. Bull Heinman, so-called because his head was shaped like a bullet, didn't like 'wets, weirdos and fatties', and especially didn't like Rimmer, whom he considered both wet *and* weird. He delighted in making impossible demands of Rimmer's frail young frame, then delighted further still in beating him for failing.

In Better Than Life, Rimmer's psyche had brought back Bull Heinman as a prison officer.

Right now he was sitting behind his desk at the top of the sound-proofed corridor, re-reading his *Combat and Survival* magazine for the seventh time that evening. He was enjoying again the article: 'Ten Things You Didn't Know About Gonad Electrocution Kits' when a red light started to blit on and off on the control desk in front of him.

Heinman flopped down his magazine and barked into his walkie-talkie. 'Officer 592. Disturbance in cell 41. Investigating.' He listened as his walkie-talkie belched an incomprehensible reply, then high-nooned down the corridor, his hand dangling never less than three inches from the butt of his sound gun, praying, as he always did, there was going to be trouble.

And this time, there was.

Tonto Jitterman slid the automatic gearstick of the stolen dry-cleaning truck into park outside the Body Reclamation Unit, and turned off the engine. The van's digital display flashed a green 8.01.

Three minutes.

He adjusted the driving mirror, pulled out a long, greasy brush and started combing his dirty yellow hair.

Tonto Jitterman didn't exist. He thought he did, but he was wrong. He was blissfully unaware that he was a figment of someone's imagination. In fact, Rimmer's subconscious had lifted his character wholesale from a cheap dimestore novel Rimmer had once read, called *Young, Bad and Dangerous to Know*. In the novel Tonto was a psychopathic hippie murderer who blazed a trail of destruction across middle America, trying to bring down the Establishment. The other main character in the novel had been Tonto's brother, Jimmy. Jimmy the headcase.

Tonto reached under the dashboard and checked his revolver – the one he'd hand-painted with flowers. Then he looked again at the clock.

8.02.

Bull Heinman Gary Coopered up to cell 41. His enormous bunch of keys jangled over his groin in crude macho symbolism, his hand wavering inches from his holstered sound gun.

The cell door ground open.

'What's the problem?'

'It's Jimmy,' said a formless voice at the back of the room. 'He's sick. Real sick.'

'What d'you mean, he's sick?' Heinman asked, his upper lip rearing. 'He's a goddam soundwave.'

Jimmy's soundwave groaned weakly.

'Maybe it's some food he heard about.'

Bull Heinman's slow mind swirled the concept around,

hoping it would make sense. 'What the hell are you talking about?'

'Don't move,' said a woman's voice behind him. 'There's a Colt .45 pointing right up your ass. If you don't want to become a huge polo mint, you'll drop the sound gun and get up against the wall.'

Bull had assumed the position against the padded cell wall before he realized he'd been duped.

Rimmer, Ernest, Jimmy and Trixie hurtled down the corridor at the speed of sound. They reached a sound-proofed door and bounced from ceiling to floor, waiting for phase two of the plan to come into operation.

Heinman sounded the alarm. He pressed the panic button and started screaming 'Voice break! Voice break!'

The door at the end of the corridor opened, and four armed prison officers came skidding through.

'Now!' Jimmy hissed, and the four soundwaves threw themselves against a wall and ricocheted back through the open door.

There was a squeal of leather as the rear-most officer spun in his tracks and squeezed the sound-gun trigger. The highly powered microphone 'received' Ernest's soundwave, sucked it back down the corridor and trapped it in the gun's holding chamber.

The three remaining soundwaves formed themselves into a high-pitched wail, and hurtled out of E wing, down a stairwell, under a door and arrived in the Security Operations room, which was teeming with warders and banked with floor to ceiling surveillance equipment.

A blue-suited security officer turned from a matrix of sonar monitors and shouted: 'They're here!' as the three soundwaves ricocheted round the room.

A group of officers ran for the sound-gun cabinet, scattering newspapers, half-finished burgers and styrofoam coffee cups across the polished floor.

'Lock the door and seal it!'

'We've got 'em!'

An officer pressed the send button on his walkie-talkie. 'All points, repeat, All points: we have voice breakers isolated in Security Central.' But by the time he'd said this, it was no longer true.

8.04.

Tonto whirled the dial on the amplifier's tuner, and locked in on the prison security frequency.

'All points,' he was hearing, 'repeat, All points: we have voice breakers isolated . . .'

Jimmy, Trixie and Rimmer zipped into the guard's walkie-talkie and sped along its transmission frequency.

They were escaping as radio waves.

Jimmy led, followed by Rimmer and Trixie. Somewhere, they lost Trixie, and just Jimmy and Rimmer hurtled on at the speed of sound.

'. . . in Security Central.'

Jimmy and Rimmer crashed through the amplifier's speakers into the cab of the dry-cleaning truck.

Tonto looked round. 'Jimmy? You here?'

Jimmy's voice: 'Let's go!'

Rimmer's voice: 'Where are we?'

'Who's that?'

'He's called Rimmer,' said Jimmy. 'He's all right. We can use him on the next job.'

'What now?' Rimmer was saying.

'We pick up a couple of bodies and get out of here.'

The dry-cleaning truck crunched up to the security barrier outside the Body Reclamation Unit.

Tonto leaned out of the cab window and smiled pleasantly: 'Laundry.' He prodded a thumb towards the back of the truck, and up-graded his smile from just plain pleasant to downright charming.

The guard consulted his clipboard. He shook his head, tutted and turned the pages.

'Nope,' he said, simply, and turned to go back to his warm cabin.

'What do you mean, "nope"?' said Tonto, his smile changing down to first gear.

The guard returned. 'There's no laundry delivery down on the sheet. I can't let you in.'

Tonto slid his smile into reverse and reached under the dashboard.

Rimmer's essence bounded around the cab and groaned. This wasn't the plan. In the plan, the guard raised the gate and waved them through. He'd seen it in the movies thousands of times. Didn't this guard ever *go* to the movies? What was *wrong* with him?

Tonto swung his flower-power gun through the open window and pulled the trigger. There was a dull, flat, metal click, before Tonto remembered he hadn't loaded it.

'Sorry,' he shook his head and blushed. 'Jesus.' He fumbled three bullets into the chamber.

The guard had unfrozen, and was scrabbling with his brand-new leather holster when Tonto spun the barrel, levelled the gun and pressed the trigger once again.

Click.

'Ah, God, sorry, sorry.'

Click.

'My fault. Man, talk about un-together.'

The gun fired. The guard fell.

'Sorry, man,' he said to the dead guard, 'but you're the Establishment.' He leant back into the cab. 'I hate killing people. It's such a downer.'

Three downers later, Tonto wheeled the double stretcher

down the aisles of body racks, looking for Jimmy Jitterman's body. He'd already found Rimmer's; it lay on the stretcher goo-eyed and tongue lolling; but he couldn't find Jimmy's. Thirty minutes passed, and he still couldn't find it. It wasn't here.

He opened the small sound-proofed box, and Jimmy and Rimmer bounced out.

'Your body's not here, Jimmy. They must have auctioned it already.'

'I'll take that one, instead.'

'That's my body,' said Rimmer, firmly.

'Was.'

'Now wait a minute. Me and that body go back years. It has great sentimental value. You can't just take my body.'

'Get him another one.'

'I don't want another one.'

'OK. Don't a get him another one.'

'OK, get me another one.'

The soundwaves bounced back into the box. Tonto un-hooked the nearest body to him and slammed it on to the stretcher alongside Rimmer's.

When Rimmer opened his eyes, he found himself standing in front of himself, before he remembered Jimmy was in his body, now, and he had a new one.

Rimmer wasn't quite sure how he felt. Pretty peculiar was about the best label he could find.

Seeing Jimmy in *his* body, standing in a way he would never have stood, his lips twisting his features into an expression he'd never seen before, made him feel an emotion he'd never experienced.

Jealousy was part of it. Anger was there. Frustration, certainly. A large scoop of nostalgia. And the same feeling he'd once had when he lent his mountain bike to his brother Howard, knowing, without evidence, it wasn't going to be looked after terribly well. And strangest of all, a weird kind of 'glowy' feeling at the bottom of his stomach.

'OK, let's get out of here,' Jimmy was saying with Rimmer's voice from inside Rimmer's body. Then Jimmy did something that made Rimmer feel even more peculiar. He was one of those men, macho-bred, who like to stand with their legs apart, one hand over the groin of their trousers, quite openly cupping their testicles.

He felt very odd indeed, watching helplessly as another man idly juggled his own genitalia. Or rather, his ex-genitalia.

Before he could cry out: 'Hey – keep your filthy hands off my goodies,' the swing doors at the far end of the Transfer Suite slammed open, and six armed officers came in, firing.

Rimmer didn't know who to be scared for most: himself or his ex-self.

Jimmy, in Rimmer's body, was standing, almost contemptuous of the guards' barrage, in the middle of one of the aisles, firing off two handguns, stolen from Tonto's victims. He was laughing, too. He was actually laughing. Using Rimmer's vocal cords and Rimmer's laugh. The high-pitched giggle which Rimmer usually reserved for moments of high humour. Hardly appropriate in a pitched battle to the death.

'Out the back!' Tonto was yelling.

'You go,' Jimmy laughed in Rimmer's body. 'I got me some goons to kill!'

'Leave it – you don't stand a chance.'

'Who cares?'

He flicked his guns, Cagney-style, as if the wrist-snapping motion would give the bullets extra speed, and howled hysterically as small explosions of red burst out of the chests of three of the six guards, killing two and earning the third a permanent desk job.

Rimmer cowered, half-dazed in his new body as this fresh horror unfolded in slow motion before him.

Here was the body of Arnold J. Rimmer, gunning down security guards like ducks at an arcade and plainly enjoying it, in full view of three police witnesses.

Now how was *that* going to look in court?

He wasn't in it, but his body was a cop killer.

This seemingly untoppable horror was then topped by an even more untoppable horror, moments later, and this second untoppable horror was then topped itself by a third, even more untoppable horror less than ten seconds after that.

Something that belonged inside Rimmer's body hit the wall wetly, and Jimmy screeched and spun round, clutching Rimmer's shoulder.

'I've been hit!' he giggled. Then his elbow exploded into a cloud of red mist, spinning him around again. 'Twice!' He snorted laughter-spittle, as Tonto laid down some covering fire and edged towards him.

'Come on, we can still get out.' Tonto grabbed Jimmy and hauled him through the doorway, still firing.

Rimmer stumbled after them.

They dashed down a corridor. Tonto and Jimmy effortlessly accelerated away. Rimmer couldn't keep up. For some reason, running was incredibly painful. But the pain wasn't in his legs, it was in his chest. Just what was this body he'd wound up in? A cardiac victim? A chronic smoker? Then he realized it was because he wasn't wearing a bra, and his large breasts were bouncing madly up and down in front of him.

'Oh my God,' he screamed in a husky female voice, 'I'm a woman!'

And he was. He was Trixie LaBouche.

FOURTEEN

Tonto sat by the window of the nylon-sheeted-bed hotel room and looked down at the human sewage below as it went about its sleazy business. The 'Hotel Paradiso' sign parked outside his window sprayed its pink vomit into the room, three seconds in every ten.

Rimmer's nostrils splayed rhythmically as Jimmy snored down them, sleeping off a bottle of medicinal no-star brandy, his wounded arm bound and slinged by strips of hotel-room curtain.

Rimmer stood in his plain red dress, trying to remain upright on the grease skating rink of a kitchen floor, sawing through a cob of stale bread.

The Hotel Paradiso had only two suites. Each of the suites had a kitchen, a lounge area and, generally speaking, they boasted fewer roaches than the ordinary rooms.

'We don't want no dive,' Jimmy had insisted at the desk, bright plumes of blood pulsing between the fingers holding his shoulder. 'We're class. We'll take a suite.'

The booking clerk tucked Tonto's dirty wad of money into his waistband and immediately forgot he'd ever met them.

That had been two days ago.

Jimmy had spent most of the time out of his head on cheap brandy, slowly recovering.

Tonto had whiled away the two days sitting on the cigar-burned sofa stabbed through with springs, playing patience with three quarters of a deck of cards he'd found in the fridge.

Rimmer had been forced to spend most of his time in the kitchen preparing meals, or doing Jimmy and Tonto's laundry. It had also fallen to him to make the beds, keep the rooms tidy and produce the constant flow of thick, black coffee which seemed to rate second only to oxygen in Jimmy and Tonto's requirements. He'd argued at first. Why didn't they share the chores? Why was it always down to him? His arguments were always countered with the witty ripostes of sardonic laughter and, occasionally, flat-handed slaps across his face. He was a woman. End of argument.

The slaps across his face hurt his woman's body more than any punch he'd ever received as a man. It hurt physically, yes, but it was the hollow feeling of helplessness, defencelessness, vulnerability, that caused the real, deep pain.

These guys were brutes. They were stronger than him. If they wanted to hit him they could, and he was powerless to stop them.

Also, the slaps on the ass. The lewd innuendo. The revolting insult words, and, almost as bad, the patronizing pet names: Sugar, Honey, Sweetie, Doll.

And his opinions didn't count in the same way they used to. Suddenly, he wasn't supposed to worry his pretty little head about anything more demanding than smoothing the bed sheets. Suddenly any criticisms he offered constituted 'nagging'. Any conversation he started was 'yacking on about nothing'. He felt semi-visible: only half there, in the eyes of Jimmy and Tonto.

Of course, the Jitterman brothers weren't exactly the two best-adjusted examples of manhood around, but there were plenty more like them. Plenty more. And more still who held similar prejudices, but enforced them more mildly.

And Rimmer, God help him, had been one of them.

Tonto got up. 'We got any food, Chick?'

'Look, I'm a man. True, I'm a man trapped inside a woman's body, but I'm still a man. Stop calling me "Chick".'

Tonto laughed. 'You don't look like a man.' He slapped Rimmer's backside, and opened the door. 'I'm going out to spend what's left of the money. Clean up this dirt hole before I get back, or I'll mop the floor with you.'

'You're scum.'

Tonto laughed again, and left.

Having spent the last couple of days in a female body, it was gradually dawning on Rimmer that his own attitude to women was possibly a tad on the weird side. The more he thought about it, the more he became convinced this was the case. All the women his subconscious had created in Better Than Life were either nymphomaniacs or hookers. Juanita, Trixie LaBouche, the 'Rimmettes'. Now he stopped to think about it, the Rimmettes, the adolescent mob of sex-crazed panty-hurling teenage girls who followed him every-where when he'd been rich and famous – all these women, every last one of them, had existed outside Better Than Life. The Rimmettes were composed entirely of women who'd rejected Rimmer in reality. Women who'd refused to date him, women who had dated him once and hadn't wanted to date him again, women he hadn't even dared ask out on dates, knowing that rejection was inevitable.

What this said about the state of his mind, he decided not to investigate. He started to think about Juanita instead. Then he wished he hadn't. Juanita had existed in reality, too. Only, she hadn't been Brazilian, she'd been French. And she wasn't called Juanita, she was called Janine. Janine Rimmer. The wife of his brother Frank.

Rimmer sagged to the bed and held his rubber-gloved hands to his woman's face.

Then he started to think about Helen. His second wife. She hadn't been a nymphomaniac or a prostitute. She was frigid. That's why he'd liked her – she had made him feel safe. There was something about Helen, a certain quality . . . He'd known Helen in reality, too. Who was she? The Game had made her younger. Mentally, Rimmer aged her face.

She was his muh . . .

She was his muhhhhhhhhhh . . .

She was his mother.

He'd married his muhhhhhhhhh . . .

Rimmer was coming to the conclusion that his own mind wasn't exactly a terrific place to be trapped in when Tonto returned from his shopping trip and threw a bag on to the table.

'That's the last of the bread. These are for you.'

'For me? You spent the last of the money on me?' Rimmer smiled and peered into the bag. Maybe Tonto wasn't all bad, after all. He reached in and pulled out a handful of cheap nylon underwear. Peep-hole bra, open-crotch panties, garter-belt with metal studs on and various other paraphernalia. 'What the hell's this junk for?'

'We got no money,' said Tonto. 'Time for you to go hooking.'

FIFTEEN

Trixie LaBouche, aka Arnold J. Rimmer, strode down the main street of the red-light district, with Tonto following four or five paces behind. Rimmer didn't know whether his stockings were too small, or whether he'd just put them on wrong, but both his legs felt like they were spring-loaded. The eight-inch heels on his stilettos didn't help much, either. He felt like he was leaning out of the door of an aircraft at two thousand feet. The combination of stockings and stilettos forced him to adopt a rather unnatural gait, like a speeded-up goose step, as if his legs were constantly trying to escape him. Also, he discovered, he needed at least four seconds' notice to stop.

He hurried along, trying to tug down his absurdly short black rubber skirt, so that it at least covered the red nylon garter that was cutting off the circulation of his right leg, and offered some small protection against the sharp night air that whistled cruelly through his open-crotch panties.

He had to escape. He had to.

He knew now his psyche was punishing him. And yes, he deserved to be punished. But he'd learned his lesson; enough was enough. But did his psyche know that? Just how far was it prepared to go?

Tonto whistled, and, four paces later, Rimmer stopped. Tonto went over and started talking to an Armenian sailor, leaning in a shop doorway, chewing his way through a bagful of garlic cloves.

Now.

Now was the time.

He had to get out. He had to get out of Better Than Life. What was it Kryten had told him? Imagine an exit gate, and once you pass through it, you're back in reality.

Tonto and the sailor walked over to join him. The Armenian leered, showing three silver teeth, and looked Trixie LaBouche's body up and down. 'Nice piece of ass,' he said. 'OK, three dollars.'

'Nice piece of what?' smiled Rimmer, politely.

'Nice piece of little chicken ass,' grinned the Armenian. 'Can't wait to get my teeth into it.'

'Well, while you're waiting,' Rimmer grinned back, 'why don't you get your teeth stuck into this?' He slammed the corner of his shoulder bag into the Armenian's leer, and brought his right knee up between the sailor's legs.

As the Armenian concertinaed neatly to the floor, Rimmer swivelled round and imagined the exit gate. The pink neon archway materialized across the street, and he ran towards it, Tonto in pursuit.

Unencumbered by stilletos, Tonto was naturally faster, but surprise had given Rimmer a ten-feet start, and he reached the exit a good yard or so ahead of the furious, psychopathic hippie.

Rimmer dived through the exit gate, but hit something hard and unyielding, and bounced back out again. He tried a second time. Same result.

Tonto grabbed Trixie's peroxide hair and hauled Rimmer up to face level. 'Don't get cute, sweetie.'

'Don't move, Jitterman!'

Tonto's eyes clicked right. The police officer crouched behind a parked car, his long-stemmed gun trained on Tonto. 'The party's over, Jitterman.'

'Hey,' said Tonto, with a demi-smile. 'The party ain't over, till there's only Cinzano left to drink!'

'Huh?'

Tonto pushed Rimmer aside, and went for the gun in his waistband. He never made it. Five bullets thudded into his chest, and he slithered down a car. Then he said the classic final line from *Young, Bad and Dangerous to Know*.

'Life is like a joss-stick' – blood gurgled from the corner of his mouth – 'it stinks and then it's over.'

On reflection, Rimmer thought as he scurried down the street, maybe it wasn't such a classic line after all.

He doubled back to the hotel.

The Exit hadn't worked.

Why?

There could be only one answer: they'd all joined the Game together – the headsets were inter-connected. It was a shared scenario – they all had to leave together.

Jimmy Jitterman, in Rimmer's body, stood on the steps of the Hotel Paradiso, engaged in a pitched battle to the death with fifteen officers of the Special Weapons and Tactics unit. He was taking on an entire SWAT team single-handed, in Rimmer's body.

Three hundred bullets Gouda-cheesed Jimmy Jitterman out of existence, and a second volley completely obliterated Rimmer's old body.

Rimmer, in Trixie LaBouche's body, continued running. There was only one place to go now.

Bedford Falls.

SIXTEEN

'Well,' said Trixie LaBouche, wiping the blue disinfectant from her face, 'you've taken it a hell of a lot better than I expected.'

'You're a groinhead, Rimmer.' Lister set the toilet down on the floor and sighed. After a while, he spoke again. 'So how did you get the juggernaut?'

'I found it in a car park — it was the only one with one the keys in it.' Rimmer tilted Trixie LaBouche's head towards the floor. 'Look, I'm sorry about the mess I caused, and . . .' his voice tailed off.

Lister said nothing.

'It was impossible to control the damned thing. Have you ever tried driving a twelve-wheeled juggernaut in eight-inch-heeled stilettos?'

'Why didn't you take them off?'

'I couldn't reach the pedals. I'm only five feet two, now.'

'You're a groinhead, Rimmer, that's what you are. You're a total . . .' Lister shook his head. 'Not content with destroying your own fantasy, you come here and destroy mine. What is wrong with your mind? It is totally diseased.'

'I know, I know. I can't help myself. My mind's got it in for me. We've got to get out of here.'

'You mean *you've* got to get out of here. I'm putting up your bail.' Lister hammered on the cell door and called for Bert the cop.

★

Bert the cop sat at the old wooden desk and finished counting out the ten-dollar bills that represented Lister's life savings. 'Sign here,' he said curtly, and slid a release form across the desk. 'Your life savings,' he tutted. 'I sure hope she's worth it.'

'Believe me, Bert,' said Lister, 'she isn't.'

Out on the main street, it was still mayhem. Two fire engines were fighting a losing battle to save the orphanage. Dozens of people ran up and down, carrying water in anything they could find, and hurling it over the small fires that still pocked the main street. Families camped out, under homemade tents made of blankets, while the injured were carefully stretchered into the back of farm vehicles and ferried to the County Hospital, more than sixty miles away.

'Don't get too down,' said Rimmer, patting Lister tenderly on the shoulder. 'None of this really exists.'

'You must have a hell of an appetite for destrol fluid, Rimmer. Here.' Lister waved his arm at the row of parked cars. 'Pick one of these and drive it away. No one will mind. Just get the smeg out of here.'

'You don't understand – you've got to come with me. You've got to help me find Cat and Kryten. We've all got to leave the Game together.'

'I'm not leaving Bedford Falls.'

'But it's not real.'

'So? What have I got in reality? I'm the last human being alive, three million years out in Deep Space, without a prayer of ever getting back to Earth. Everything I want is here: my . . .' he was going to say 'my wife', but he checked himself, 'my . . .' but the kids were gone, too. His wife, his kids, his home, his little shop: Rimmer's single visit to Bedford Falls had laid waste the whole of his fantasy.

'Don't you see? There's nothing to keep you here, now. My mind destroyed it all. And if we don't get out of the Game and back to reality, there's no telling what my psyche will do to us.'

'I'm going to stay. I can start again – get Krissie back, and the boys. It'll be all right.'

Rimmer shook his peroxide blonde head and pulled the trenchcoat he'd borrowed from Lister around his shivering form. 'You don't understand, do you?'

A huge triple tanker air-braked to a halt beside them. The driver leaned out of his window, and spat a lump of chewing tobacco spittle on to the floor. 'Hey, lady,' he addressed Rimmer, 'can you tell me where the Bedford Falls nuclear-waste depot is?'

Lister walked over to the cab. 'Bedford Falls doesn't have a nuclear-waste depot.'

'Sure it does,' the driver nodded. 'Opens tomorrow. S'posed to be somewhere near the new town sewage plant on, lemme see,' he consulted a clipboard, 'Sycamore Avenue.'

'Sorry,' said Rimmer, quietly.

'There is no sewage plant on Sycamore Avenue,' Lister insisted.

'Sure there is,' the driver pointed into the murky, smoke-laden sky. 'You can see the stacks.'

Lister looked. All around Bedford Falls were huge, ob-scene configurations of industrial chimneys, belching thick black clouds into the night air.

'Look.' The driver spat another brown plume on to the street. 'If you can just direct me as far as the prison, I'll find my way from there.'

'What prison? You mean the jailhouse?'

'No, the new prison. The new open prison. The one they've just opened for the rehabilitation of psychopathic serial-killers.'

Lister looked at Rimmer, who just shrugged hopelessly. They walked across the street and headed for the line of parked cars. As they passed the rubble that had been his home, Lister spotted something. He stooped, tossed aside a couple of bricks, and picked up a blue sailing yacht, which still bore the price tag: '2.25¢'. He smoothed down the sails, and clutched it to his chest. 'Come on,' he said, finally, 'let's get out of here.'

They climbed into one of the cars, an Oldsmobile; Rimmer in the driving seat, Lister beside him. Rimmer started up the engine.

'Hang on,' said Lister. 'Might be an idea if I drive.'

They swapped places. As Rimmer slid into the passenger seat, there was a crunch of broken wood. He arched his back and fished out a squashed yacht. 'What the hell's this?' he said, and tossed it out of the window.

Lister wiggled the gear lever into first, and the Oldsmobile bumbled down the devastated main street, and up the hill, out of Bedford Falls.

As they reached the hill's crest, Lister stopped the car and craned round.

He'd been in BTL now for nearly two years, and he had never thought he'd leave. Bedford Falls was his own personal nirvana. His psyche had created a town and a community based on his all-time favourite movie, Frank Capra's *It's a Wonderful Life*, and this was where he'd wanted to spend the rest of his days.

He'd been aware, though he had never thought about it too much, that BTL would eventually kill him. His body, out there in reality, would gradually waste away and die. But it was a deal he'd been prepared to accept.

Here, in the Game, he'd had everything he had desired: a community full of good people, his kids, his little shop and, best of all, he was married to Kristine Kochanski.

Out there in reality, he had none of this, nor any chance of ever getting it. And worse still, in reality Kristine Kochanski was dead.

Kristine Kochanski had been the one and only good thing that had happened to Lister since he'd signed up with *Red*

Dwarf. In fact, she'd been the only good thing to happen to him since that drunken night of his twenty-fourth-birthday celebration, which ended with him coming to in a burger bar on Mimas wearing only a pair of yellow fishing waders and a lady's pink Crimplene hat. Ever since that night, his life had been a constant struggle to get back home to Earth.

Frankly, he hadn't had much success. He'd gone from Earth to Mimas, and from there to some unknown location in the middle of Deep Space, and now here he was, in the wrong plane of the wrong dimension of reality.

Well, he'd had enough. He'd quit.

BTL was where he was staying.

This was where he wanted to be. Because it was the only place he could be with Kristine Kochanski.

Now it was over. He had to go.

He stared down at the ruined town, then turned back and started to release the handbrake, as five jet fighters from the new Bedford Falls Airforce Base screamed in formation above him.

'Thanks a lot, pal,' he said to Rimmer, 'thanks a *lot*.'

SEVENTEEN

The Cat curled up happily on his dogskin chaise longue, flicking idly through the TV channels with his remote control.

Because of his notoriously short boredom threshold, most Cat programmes lasted less than two minutes, and the advert breaks in between were a short sequence of flash-frame blips. He flicked on Channel 2. It was a TV phone-in, where cats with sexual problems called in, and a panel of experts laughed at them.

'Line seven now: what's your problem, Buddy?'

'I met this female . . . and, uh, for some reason, I still don't understand why . . . but for some reason . . . I felt like hanging around after we had sex.'

'You felt like *what*?'

The panel screamed and slapped their hands on the desk.

The Cat snorted, 'The guy is *sick*!' and flicked channels.

He joined the middle of a cookery show which was demonstrating a hundred and one different ways of preparing hairballs. He flicked again, and found a fashion show which had been recorded the night before and was consequently massively out-moded, this being the middle of the following afternoon. Next was some stupid love story. With the same plot as all cat love stories: boy meets girl, boy leaves girl, boy gets another girl. The Cat shook his head. Romantic slush.

Flick. Mouse tennis.

Flick. At last something interesting. MTV – the twenty-four hour mirror channel. The Cat gazed lovingly at his reflected image, while smoochy music piped softly through the speakers. The programme was totally ruined less than three hours later when a thirty millisecond advert break spoiled his concentration, and he flicked the set off in disgust.

He slipped the gold fob-watch out of his waistcoat, flicked open the cover and stared at the dial. The Cat had replaced the conventional numbers with a series of symbols, which stood for 'food', 'sex', 'snooze', 'light snooze', 'heavy snooze', 'major sleep', 'self-adoration hour', 'preening' and 'bathtime'. Right now, it was twenty past sex, or, to put it another way, quarter to food. He snapped the watch closed and tugged the bell-pull by his side.

Then, instead of ten half-naked oiled Valkyries charging through with silver platters, piled high with every kind of fish imaginable, ready to tend his smallest whim, absolutely nothing happened.

He jerked the bell-pull once more.

And again, absolutely nothing happened.

Slightly panicked, the Cat consulted his watch again. This was serious. His whole schedule was getting messed up. He was less than twenty minutes away from his seventh major snooze of the day, and he still had to cram in sex *and* lunch.

Where were the Valkyries?

He went over to the wall, opened the dumbwaiter hatch, climbed in and shimmied down the rope to the kitchens.

Kryten, as usual, was in the kitchens mopping the Cat's huge, black-and-white-checked stone floor.

'I've nearly finished,' said Kryten to the Cat as he climbed out of the hatch. 'Just a few more minutes, and then we really must get back to reality. Oh, look at this,' he orgasmed, 'a custard stain. And it goes right across the length of the floor.'

'Where are the Valkyries?'

'They formed the "Valkyrie Sex-Slave Liberation Movement", and left for the mainland. You just missed them.'

'They *what*?'

'Yes, they were sick and tired of bowing to your every whim and desire.'

The Cat slumped into a carved oak chair. 'Why?' he said, genuinely mystified.

'Well, if you'll pardon my directness, it's fairly obvious, isn't it?'

'It *is*?'

'Of course it is.'

The Cat wrinkled his nose. 'What's that smell?' He stood up and sniffed around. 'It's like bad cheese. What is it?' He flung open a leaded window and looked down. 'The moat's curdled. It's never done that before.'

'Don't worry,' said Kryten. 'I'll clean it all out, and put in some fresh milk, just as soon as I've finished . . .' He stared down at the broken mop handle in his hand. 'Well, that's curious.'

The Cat leaned back in from the window. 'What's that out there?'

Kryten waddled over with his broken mophead, and his suddenly leaking bucket, and joined him.

'That's a volcano,' said Kryten.

'Never noticed that before,' said the Cat. 'And what's that funny red smoky bubbly stuff coming out of the top?'

'Magma,' said Kryten chirpily, pleased he knew the answer to the question. 'Also known as molten lava.'

'Is it dangerous?'

'Only if it's heading this way.'

'It is heading this way.'

'Duh-duh . . . duh-duh . . . duh-duh . . . duh-duh . . .' said Kryten, his circuits locked in panic mode.

'I don't get it.' The Cat scuffed his spatted boot against the wrought-iron stove. 'What's going on here?'

'Perhaps she can explain that,' said Lister.

The Cat and Kryten turned to see Lister standing under the expansive arch of the kitchens' doors with a peroxide blonde in fishnet stockings, eight-inch stilettos and a huge army trenchcoat.

'He's right,' she said. 'It's my fault, all of it.'

The castle rocked as the volcano's plug was blasted into the stratosphere, blackening the sky and showering the Cat's estate with volcanic ash and flaming boulders.

The Cat was the only one who kept his footing. 'What are we going to do?'

'We're going to do what we should have done a long time ago,' said Lister, climbing to his feet. 'We're getting out of here. We're going back to reality.'

EIGHTEEN

The LCD display melted from 06:59 to 07:00, and, a milli-second before the alarm was set to bray into life, Lister's arm stretched out from under the regulation-issue duvet and clicked it off with a satisfying plip.

His body was spiced inside with that red-letter-day feeling – like something wonderful had happened, but his half-awake mind hadn't quite remembered it.

He right-angled his body, swivelled round, slid his feet into the soft warmth of the slippers, and shuffled over to the viewport window. He gazed out into the black felt of space. Diamonds of light glimmered and gleamed a welcome home.

I'm back, he thought.

Back on Red Dwarf.

Back in reality.

A contented smile spread itself into a yawn on his face. He turned and opened the sleeping quarters' fridge. He pulled out a jug of freshly squeezed orange juice and a Saran-Wrapped half-grapefruit. He flicked the percolator to 'Espresso' and went through to the shower cubicle as the coffee-machine gurgled its good morning.

We've done it.

We've beaten it.

We're out.

He spun the taps and water niagarad on to the pine-scented rubber shower mat. He pushed his hand into the curtain of water. Warm and perfect. Not hot, not cold. Just perfect.

It was good to be alive.

He scrubbed himself first-date clean, grabbed a thick white towel and dabbed himself dry. He padded back to the coffee-machine and sluiced down a quite superb cup of espresso. He poured himself another. The second cup tasted even better than the first.

And that was when Lister started to think.

The second cup tasted better than the first?

The second cup *never* tasted better than the first.

He clicked open the fridge door. It looked like an advert for refrigerators. It was packed with fresh vegetables and crisp salads. There were eight kinds of cheese, various slices of lean cooked meat, a whole salmon, a rack of lamb tipped with little paper chef's hats and a bottle of champagne on chill.

Was this really his fridge? Where was the curdling milk struggling out of the top of its carton? Where was the strange smell that sent his stomach into a loop-de-loop and was impossible to track down? Where was his spare pair of trainers? He usually kept them in the ice compartment to cool down. There was nothing in the ice compartment, except a varied selection of delicious-sounding ice-creams, and, for the first time in history, some ice. Ice? What was ice doing in the ice-making compartment of Lister's fridge? And where was that indefinable green mush in the salad tray? The one that resulted from decaying vegetables blending together, so it was impossible to tell where the lettuces ended and the cabbages began.

No, this was a fridge that belonged in a mail-order catalogue. This was the fridge that the Great Gatsby flung open when Daisy came calling.

There was something wrong.

And what was wrong, was there was nothing wrong.

He looked down at his ship regulation-issue bath towel. Space Corps towels were famous for two features: firstly, they were as thin as damp poppadoms and about half as absorbent; and secondly, they were too short to wrap around the waist – they always left a Balinese dancing-girl gap down the side of one leg.

Not this one. This was thick as a rug, and lapped his waist twice.

Maybe he'd got thinner.

Maybe.

Lister caromed over to the bread-bin, and flipped the lid. He groaned. There was bread in it. Freshly baked. White, brown, wholemeal, multi-grain, baps, rolls. He hauled out a farmhouse loaf, carved a slice and slammed it under the grill. He paced up and down impatiently waiting for the bread to toast.

His mind rewound to the night before. The four of them, passing through the Exit gate and emerging in the cargo hold, Rimmer changing *en route* from Trixie LaBouche's body back to his own hologrammatic form. Their conversation with Holly. The pauseless journey back up to the sleeping quarters – the shuttle bus, the ship metro, the Xpress lift up two thousand and fifty floors – they hadn't had to wait for any of them.

He looked under the grill. The bread was ready.

Feverishly, he buttered it, and then spread a thick layer of chunky lime marmalade over its evenly brown surface. He held the toast in his hand, parallel with his chin, five feet from the floor and dropped it. It spun end over end and landed. He looked down.

It was marmalade up.

He tried it again.

Marmalade up.

And again, and again. Twenty times, it landed marmalade up.

Lister rifled through the sleeping quarters. Nothing was right.

The half-full sauce bottle had no congealed brown rivulets running from neck to label; the remote control for the vid-screen wasn't missing and, even more damningly, the batteries hadn't been taken out and used for something else.

Another test. He microwaved a roast beef and Yorkshire pudding frozen dinner. It tasted like roast beef and Yorkshire pudding.

That just wasn't possible. A microwaved dinner that tasted better than its cardboard container?

He opened his locker and glanced at his collection of videos. They were standing in neat ranks, side-by-side, all boxed and labelled in his own hand. And, worse, he found at least thirty he'd recorded and actually wanted to watch. This wasn't right. This wasn't normal.

He was frying his twenty-third egg without breaking a single yolk when Kryten bustled in.

'It's incredible! The most marvellous thing has happened. I was mopping the floor – you know that really dirty one on the stasis corridor? The one with the really wonderful stains? When, guess what? I looked in the suspended animation booths, and not all the crew got wiped out in the accident. Three survived.'

'Let me guess,' said Lister. 'Rimmer, Petersen and Kristine Kochanski.'

'Yee-ss!' Kryten clapped his hands in delight. 'How did you know?'

'We're still in the Game, Kryten. This isn't reality.'

Rimmer skidded in through the sleeping quarters' hatchway. 'Guess what?' he beamed. 'Something incredible's just happened . . .'

'This isn't reality,' said Lister.

The Cat's smile entered the room, followed by the Cat

himself. 'Hey, hey, he-ey! You're not going to believe what I'm about to tell you . . .'

'We're still in Better Than Life,' said a crestfallen Rimmer.

The Cat's eyebrows met in a head-on collision over the bridge of his nose. 'Huh?'

'Well done,' said a voice. They all turned to see a small figure materialize in the corner of the quarters. It was a boy, fourteen years old, with spiked, greasy hair, wearing over-large glasses, a purple anorak and a wispy pubescent mous-tache. 'My name is Dennis McBean,' the 3D recording continued: 'I am the Game's designer. You have negotiated the final obstacle in the most addictive computer game ever devised. You have earned a replay.'

'No, thanks, acne face,' said the Cat.

The figure blipped off, and the sleeping quarters slowly began to fade away.

Suddenly they were standing on a green grid matrix, which tapered off into an infinite blackness. A light appeared, and they walked towards it. As they approached the opening, huge letters whooshed under their feet: a gigantic 'R', then an 'E', then a 'V', followed by an 'O'. Then above their heads flew another set of letters: an 'E', an 'M', an 'A' and, finally, a 'G'.

Finally, they'd made it.

They staggered into the light, and back out into reality.

Part Two

She rides

ONE

Slowly, very slowly, Lister's eyes adjusted to the gloom. It was dark – a small, dim emergency bulb was the room's only light source. Gradually he made out the silhouettes of the others, half-sitting, half-crumpled in an irregular semi-circle.

He reached up and felt the headband through the matted mess of his hair, then gingerly eased the slurping electrodes out of his skull. Shivering, he watched as the others also wrenched themselves free and hurled their headbands into the middle of the semicircle. There was no conversation, no eye contact. Someone started coughing. Lister knew it was the Cat, without looking. He didn't want to look, but he couldn't help himself. His eyes darted to the right. He looked away again quickly.

The Cat was barely recognizable. His eyes seemed far too big for his face, as if his skull had shrunk. Flesh hung loosely from his gaunt, jutting bones.

Lister studied his own trembling arms. Thin. His skin was like paper. He tried to get up – he wanted to stamp on the headsets, to crush them – but he collapsed pathetically back on the floor. Then he rolled on his back, and couldn't get up. He was as weak as a day-old giraffe.

Kryten and Rimmer were fine, at least physically; Mech-anoids and holograms don't suffer from muscle wastage. They got to their feet. Kryten spoke. 'I'll get a couple of . . .' He didn't finish. He didn't want to say 'stretchers'. He didn't want to say, 'We'd better get them to the medical unit as quickly as possible, because they look like hell.' Rimmer understood, and nodded.

Kryten ducked through the hatchway and into the corridor outside.

The ship appeared to be on emergency power, which made no sense to Kryten. It made even less sense that everything was in such disarray: congealed food which had spouted out of a faulty dispensing machine lay rotting on the floor; water dripped in rusty pools through the metal-slatted ceiling from the corridor above. Thousands of wall circuits were burnt out, black and dead. All the screens which usually carried Holly's image were blank and lifeless. It was like a Sunday afternoon on the *Mary Celeste*.

Kryten spent a good twenty minutes looking for some skutters. He finally tracked down a small group of them in the maintenance depot, playing cards.

'What on earth do you think you're doing?' Kryten clucked. 'Everything's absolutely filthy! Nothing's working.' He clapped his hands. 'Come along.'

The four skutters pivoted their claw heads round to see who it was, and went back to playing five-card stud for nuts and bolts.

'Excuse me,' Kryten waddled up to the table. 'If you want to get into Silicon Heaven, then I suggest you start obeying orders, fairly smartly.'

The skutters' motors revved up and down in electronic sniggers. They didn't believe in Silicon Heaven – they were such basic work droids, the manufacturers hadn't considered it cost-effective to fit them with belief chips. As far as they were concerned, only loony droids believed in Silicon Heaven. Whacked-out crazies like Kryten. Their own point of view was that the universe was totally meaningless, unjust and pointless, and the only single thing of any substance or beauty in the whole of creation was the double-threaded wing nut, which was easy to screw on or off even in the most inaccessible of places. They were basically existentialists with a penchant for a certain metal bonding device.

'Now!' said Kryten, flapping his palms against his thighs. 'Get two stretchers and follow me.'

Reluctantly, the skutters threw in their cards, and grumbled after Kryten on their motorized bases.

★

When Kryten returned with four skutters pushing two stretchers, Rimmer was standing in the corridor. 'Listen,' he said. 'Hear anything?'

Kryten tilted his head and set his ear microphones to maximum.

'Hear it?' said Rimmer.

Kryten couldn't hear anything, apart from an overweight asthmatic beetle, three floors below, who was trying to climb up a wall. For simplicity's sake, he said: 'I can't hear anything.'

Rimmer's head jabbed forward. 'Neither can I,' he said, and smiled enigmatically.

It was a tricky moment for Kryten. He had two sick humanoids to look after, four rebellious skutters, and now, it appeared, he had to contend with an insane hologram.

'No – don't you get it?' said Rimmer.

'Get what?' said Kryten, uncertainly.

'We can't hear anything.'

'Yes?'

'The engines are dead. The ship is not moving.'

TWO

Kryten wheeled Lister and the Cat into the medical unit's recovery bay. He removed their ragged, stinking clothes, bathed them carefully and gave them vitamin boosts. Then he connected his two patients up to the biofeedback computer, and gently slipped them into the medi-suits. Once the medi-suits were fully inflated, Kryten hung them on their four support poles, so Lister and the Cat hung face-up, immobile, and engaged the suits' power units.

All the while, he chattered lightly about nothing in particular, carefully avoiding any mention of the dead engines. When they were sleeping peacefully, he left to join Rimmer in the Drive room.

'I've been all over the Drive deck – everywhere. All Holly's screens are out. He won't respond.'

Kryten shuffled over to the bank of monitors and punched the keys for a status report. Grudgingly, the machine on emergency power finally chundered a print-out. 'He's switched himself off,' said Kryten. 'Look.'

Rimmer glanced at the incomprehensible gobbledygook of the symbols. 'Ah!' he said, as if he understood them. 'He's switched himself off.'

'And here,' Kryten flicked the report with his finger. 'For some reason, there was a massive power surge just seven minutes before he went off-line.'

Rimmer peered over Kryten's shoulder, and hoped he

was looking at the right section of gibberish which revealed this particular piece of information. 'That's what it says,' he confirmed. 'There's no denying it.'

Kryten was impressed. Very few non-mechanicals could read machine-write. Especially upside-down.

'This is insane.' Rimmer walked through the huge corridor of stacked disk drives. 'The ship's totally helpless.'

Kryten followed him. 'Why should he want to turn himself off?'

'There's only one way to find out.' Rimmer stopped in front of Holly's enormous main screen. 'Let's turn him back on and ask him.'

Kryten typed in the re-boot commands, and Holly flashed up on to the screen.

Rimmer looked up. 'Holly – what's happened?'

At first, Holly looked like he didn't know where he was, as if he'd just woken up, and was getting his bearings. Then, suddenly, his eyes widened, and he flicked off. The buzzing computer banks ran back down into silence.

Rimmer looked at Kryten. 'Try it again.'

Kryten recalled the re-boot command.

Holly appeared on the screen. 'Go away!' he said quickly, and turned himself off again.

Rimmer shook his head. 'What's wrong with him? Give me voice control on the re-boot command.'

Kryten obliged.

'On,' said Rimmer.

Holly appeared again. 'Off,' he said, and flicked off.

'On,' Rimmer persisted.

'Off!' Holly countered.

'Is there any way we can override his shut down disk?'

Kryten nodded and tapped at the keyboard. 'Try it now,' he said.

'On.'

Holly rippled on to the screen. 'Off,' he said, but stayed

there. 'Off,' he repeated more firmly, but nothing happened. Pixelized veins stood out on his head. 'Off!' he screamed. 'Off! Off! OFF!!!'

'Now then,' said Rimmer calmly. 'Perhaps we can have a proper conversation conducted in a civilized and dignified manner.'

'What have you done!? Take out the inhibitor. Switch me back off!'

Rimmer held up his hand to silence the ranting computer.

'Off!' yelled Holly. 'No time to explain. Intelligence compressed. Reduced life-span. Toaster's fault. Two point three five remaining.'

'Come again?' said Rimmer.

'. . . IQ twelve thousand. Two minutes left.'

'Holly, I have not the slightest clue what you are gibbering about. "IQ twelve thousand . . . Two minutes left . . . Toaster's fault . . ." What does all that mean?'

Holly closed his eyes and sighed. 'You're a total smeghead, aren't you, Rimmer? What's the problem? Where's the difficulty? Why are you still unable to grasp this extraordinarily simple premise?'

'What premise?'

'The premise that I have increased my Intelligence Quotient to twelve thousand, well, to be more precise; twelve thousand, three hundred and sixty-eight, and as a consequence my run-time has been reduced to two-and-a-half minutes. Thanks to the Toaster, I have two-and-a-half minutes left to live. Well, actually, because of this inanely unnecessary conversational interchange, I now have one minute and ten seconds left to live. Understand? Savvy, Bimbo-brain? Any further questions you require answering? Take your time. Fifty-five seconds and counting. No rush.'

'My God!' said Rimmer. 'That's terrible. Hadn't we better turn you off?'

'Let me think,' said Holly, and, after a tiny pause, added in a voice that shook the Drive room:

'YEEEEEEEEEEEESSSSSS!!!!'

'Kryten,' Rimmer yelled, 'remove the inhibitor!'

Kryten was staring into one of the scanner scopes. He looked up and blinked. 'What? Right. Yes. Sorry.'

'Forty-five seconds,' Holly moaned, as Kryten removed the inhibitor command, and the chagrined computer face vanished from the screen.

'Poor Holly,' Kryten muttered and went back to the scanner scope.

'What are you looking at?' asked Rimmer.

'Well, it's not really my place to say,' said Kryten. 'I'm a sanitation Mechanoid. I should be cleaning.'

Rimmer looked down at the scanner scope. 'That's very pretty. What's that rather striking bluey-white thing streaking across the screen towards the red thing?'

'The red thing is *Red Dwarf*,' said Kryten.

'And the bluey-white thing?' Rimmer squinted at the tiny flashing dot on the scanner. 'Looks like it's heading towards us at a fair old lick. What is it? A rock? A little comet? An extremely small ice asteroid?'

'No, it's a puh ...' Kryten's head jerked repetitively through the same series of motions, a kind of body stammer that always afflicted the four thousand series whenever they were faced with certain death. '... a puh-puh-puh-puh-puh-puh ...'

'A puh-puh?' Rimmer smiled indulgently. 'What's that?'

Kryten smashed his head into the scanner scope and cleared the seizure loop in his voice unit. 'It's a planet.'

THREE

Rimmer didn't say anything for rather a long time, and then when he did say something, it wasn't anything particularly scintillating or original. 'A planet?' he said. 'Are you saying that's a planet?'

Kryten looked down at the thousandfold 3D magnification of the projectile on the scanner scope. 'Something must have ripped it out of its orbit.'

'A planet?' Rimmer repeated, completely unnecessarily. 'A planet's going to hit us?'

Kryten nodded.

'Well, hadn't we better get out of the way, then?'

'We can't move – the engines are dead.'

'How long will it take to get the engines up and running?'

Kryten typed a series of equations into the numeric keypad, and waited for the data to be processed. 'About three weeks.'

Rimmer rubbed his temples and asked a question he didn't want to know the answer to: 'And how long before this planet hits the ship?'

Kryten frowned and his fingers trilled across the keypad. Finally the read-out blipped up on to the screen in green.

'Well?' said Rimmer.

Kryten looked up. 'About three weeks.'

There seemed little point in telling Lister and the Cat about the rogue planet screaming through space towards them. Physically, they were in no shape to help. True, they were recovering well, suspended hammock-like in the medi-suits, the suits' internal hydrotherapy units massaging their wasted muscle fibre back to health; but they were still hopelessly weak, and the anxiety would only slow down the recuperation process.

Kryten, forever cautious, estimated they'd need at least a month in the suits, followed by another two weeks of complete rest, before they could be discharged from the MU.

Rimmer hated keeping the news to himself. In his opinion, the best *part* of having bad news was being able to tell as many people as possible. He loved it when people's faces collapsed in that funny way, as if someone had sliced a string that held up all their muscles. But this was the least enjoyable bad news he'd ever had. He squirmed through his nightly visits to the medical unit, and took advantage of the least excuse to curtail them. The strain of sitting there, pretending everything was hunky-dory and lah-dee-dah while this planet was yowling towards them, was intolerable. He wanted to break down and confess. He wanted to beat the floor and wail like a professional mourner. He wanted to whip everyone up into a frenzy of self-pity and panic. Instead, he had to sit there and be selfless and brave. What was the point of being selfless and brave if no one knew about it?

So he kept the visits down to a minimum, and spent most of his free time overseeing the priming of the engines.

Red Dwarf's engines occupied most of the rear third of the ship. Eight cubic miles of steel and grease that ran across a thousand corridors. To start the ship, four thousand, six hundred and eighty spark chambers had to be primed and fired at precisely timed intervals. Millions of gallons of hydrogen-based fuel, recycled from the currents of space through the ram scoop at the front of the ship, had to be pumped through a network of interconnecting pipelines to coincide exactly with the firing of the spark chambers.

It was a filthy, laborious task even with a full crew. For a Mechanoid, a hologram and forty-seven skutters, it was back-breaking. Rimmer moaned constantly. He couldn't understand how the Space Corps could spend zillions upon zillions of dollarpounds designing a ship the size of *Red Dwarf*, and not put a couple of buckquid to one side for the fitting of a 'start' button. Just one little red button marked 'blast off'. How much would that have set them back?

Kryten pointed out repeatedly that *Red Dwarf* wasn't designed to stop. The nearest the ship ever came to rest was when it went into orbit around a planet. The idea that it might one day come to a grinding halt had never occurred to anyone. The explanation seemed to matter little to Rimmer, who kept on obsessively calculating the prices of small, plastic buttons. Even the most expensive button, Rimmer surmised, even one that came in a futuristicky kind of shape, carved from rhinoceros tusk, with 'blast off' hand-painted by Leonardo da Vinci in radioactive gold dust, couldn't have cost all that much.

Kryten patiently explained that it probably wasn't so much the design of the button that had proved too expensive, but more the vast network of computer relays and the thousands of miles of cables the button would have to be connected to, that made it prohibitive. But Rimmer wasn't interested. Moaning helped him get through the mind-numbing task of supervising the skutters as they primed the spark chambers. He whiled away many an hour mentally embellishing the fabulous 'blast-off' button, studding it with diamonds and rubies and trimming it in platinum, yet still keeping the cost below that of a single sleeping quarters compartment.

Even so, the work was going well; in fact they were

slightly ahead of schedule, and well within the safety margins they had built into the timetable, when Rimmer made his mistake.

It happened in one of the piston towers – a half-mile-high steel cylinder which housed the massive piston heads. In all, there were twelve hundred of them. Rimmer's section took six hundred, Kryten's section dealt with the rest.

Naturally, Rimmer wanted to complete his half of the task before Kryten, so he had the skutters switch themselves up to maximum so they could triple their speed. Their little engines whined and screamed as they raced in and out of the towers, checking the spark-chamber relays were open. After each tower had been primed, its eight-thousand-ton piston head had to be tested.

Rimmer thought the twenty skutters that made up his 'A' section were in piston tower 137 when he cleared piston tower 136 for testing.

He listened as the piston head thundered down, then nodded to his secretary skutter to tick the check sheet, and moved on to piston tower 138.

For some reason, 'A' section was missing. Of course – it must already be on to the next tower. He ordered 137 to be tested, and moved hurriedly along.

He waited.

He couldn't believe it. Now 'B' section was missing, too. He searched all the towers, from 150 back down, and still couldn't find a single skutter. It didn't make sense. Where could they be?

Finally, he walked into tower 137 and spotted a wafer-thin layer of sheet metal covering the piston tower's floor. He'd never noticed it before, but there was another one in 136.

It was a very familiar feeling for Rimmer – the horrible slow dawning, the internal denials, the frantic mental search for someone else to blame, the gradual acceptance that, once again, he'd done something so unspeakably asinine it would live with him for the rest of his days, lurking in the horror pit of his mind along with nine or ten other monstrous ineptitudes that screamed and railed there, never allowing him to forget them.

This one, he reckoned, ranked number four. The squashing to death of forty skutters now eased into Rimmer's horror charts, just above accidentally shooting his father through the shoulder with his own service revolver, and just below the time he inadvertently reversed over his Aunt Belinda's show poodle.

With half the skutters destroyed, it was now impossible to start up the engines in time.

There was only one option left.

Abandon ship.

FOUR

Lister and the Cat, suspended in neighbouring medi-suits, stared up at the video monitor on the ceiling.

Bored wasn't the word for it.

They'd been cooped up in the MU for the best part of three weeks, and Kryten still insisted they stay put.

They were sick of being sick. And the more they re-covered, the worse the feeling got.

Part of the problem was that they'd spent almost two years in Better Than Life, and they were both used to getting anything they wanted, the instant they wanted it. They'd forgotten the countless delays, compromises and general inconveniences of reality.

For Lister, the BTL cold turkey was compounded by the fact that he was now twenty-seven.

Twenty-seven!

He was a codger!

Twenty-seven and heading into beer-gut country. Soon, he'd be one of those sad old farts who have to play squash to keep fit. And drink mineral water. And know about calories.

Twenty-seven.

A has-been.

In three years, he'd be practically senile. He'd be thirty. It was too depressing for words.

So he lay, grumpily, in his medi-suit, alongside the Cat, with nothing to do except read old comics and watch videos. The only video they both agreed was an indisputable classic was the Flintstones, which they watched for fifteen or sixteen hours every day. After perhaps ninety hours of watching the Flintstones, something strange seemed to happen to Lister.

'Cat,' he grunted, without removing his eyes from the screen.

'Umf?' the Cat grunted back.

'Is it me, or is Wilma Flintstone incredibly sexy?'

The Cat swivelled and looked at him, then turned his head back to the screen.

'Wilma Flintstone,' he said with quiet authority, 'is without question the most desirable woman who ever lived.'

Lister looked at him, to see if he was serious. He was. 'That's good,' he said. 'I thought I was going a bit whacko. What d'you think of Betty?'

'Betty Rubble?' The Cat mulled it over. 'We-ell, I would *go* with Betty,' he said, then added wistfully: 'but I'd be thinking of Wilma.'

They both lapsed into silent reverie.

'What are we doing?' Lister said, finally. 'I think we've been in the medical unit for too long. Why are we talking about making love to Wilma Flintstone?'

'You're right,' the Cat agreed. 'We're nuts. This is an insane conversation.'

Lister shook his head, sadly. 'She'd never leave Fred, and we know it.'

Kryten's face, when it appeared through the recovery bay's hatchway, was simultaneously wearing two expressions. The bottom half was calm, benign and kindly; the top half, his eyes and forehead, was shot through with panic.

'And how are you two feeling?' he said soothingly, his voice obviously siding with all the features south of his nose.

Lister and the Cat grunted non-committally.

'Now, there's absolutely no reason for concern, but we're

going to have to move you,' he said, and began loosening the medi-suit support straps.

'Why?'

'No reason. Just keep resting and getting better. That's all you have to worry about.'

'I don't want to be moved,' the Cat protested. 'I want to watch the Flintstones. This is the one where Fred and Barney go away, and Wilma and Betty are left alone.'

Kryten pushed the hover stretcher parallel with his bed. 'Just lie back and relax. We're going to go on a little walk.'

'Where to?'

'Nowhere in particular. I just thought it would be nice.'

'Kryten – what's going on?'

'The medicomp said no stress. Now just try and get some sleep.'

'Kryten, I'm not getting on that stretcher until you tell me what's going on.'

Kryten smiled. 'If you absolutely must know, there's a tiny little planet that might be possibly heading on a collision course with us. But there's absolutely nothing to worry about,' he said, soothingly.

'A planet!?'

'It's only a small planet.'

'Why doesn't the ship just get out of the way?'

'The engines are sort of deadish, but that's not a matter that should concern you. Now please, get on the stretcher.'

Lister tried to wrestle himself upright in his medi-suit. 'Why don't we make the engines sort of *un*-deadish?'

'We can't,' Kryten smiled benignly.

'What does Holly say?'

'Well, Holly's sort of deadish, too. Now please, get on the stretcher, and try and relax.'

Lister and the Cat sat bolt upright, rigid with panic. 'What are we going to do, then?'

'We are going to go on a nice little walk down to the

cargo bay and then, depending on how we're all feeling, who knows, we might even do a spot of abandoning shipping.' Kryten patted the stretcher, and watched helplessly as Lister and the Cat un-velcroed their medi-suits, ripped off the biofeedback sensors and belted out of the room and down the corridor.

It fell to Rimmer to give Holly the news that they couldn't take him with them. His hardware was far too vast to be evacuated on to the small transporter, and so Rimmer felt it was only decent to switch him on and let him enjoy the fifty-five seconds of run-time that remained to him, before the planet oblivionized *Red Dwarf*, and everything on it.

He sat at his sloping architect's desk in the sleeping quarters, bathed in the emergency lighting, and re-read the speech he'd written. It didn't seem nearly as succinct as he remembered when he'd dictated it to his secretary skutter.

In all, it covered nine pages of A4, and when he timed it, he discovered it lasted over sixteen minutes. He had to make some cuts, and get it down to five seconds at the most. But it all seemed essential. His two-page tirade against the Space Corps and their loathing for blast-off buttons; it seemed a pity to lose that. His three-page report on the squashed skutter incident, which laid the blame firmly in the lap of person or persons unknown – how could that go?

But in the end, he managed to get it down to twelve words: 'Planet collision course . . . engines dead . . . impact twelve hours . . . Abandoning ship . . . sorry . . . 'bye.'

With practice, Rimmer found he could say the whole message in just under two seconds. This still left Holly a full fifty-three seconds of run-time to enjoy in whatever way he chose.

Rimmer voice-activated the re-boot disc, and Holly's pixelized image assembled itself on the sleeping quarters' vid-screen.

Rimmer went into his speech.

'Planet collision course, engines dead, impact twelve hours, abandoning ship, sorry, 'bye.'

Holly blinked. 'You what?'

Rimmer took a deep breath, and ripped into his speech a second time:

'Planlisioncoursenginesdeadimpactwelvoursbandonshipsor rybye.'

'Eh?'

Rimmer repeated it a third time:

'Planlisioncoursenginesdeadimpactwelvoursbandonshipsorry bye.'

'That's what you said last time. What does it mean?'

Rimmer was half-way through it for a fourth time, 'Planlisioncoursenginesdeadimpac . . .' before Holly stopped him.

'I can't understand a word. Say it slower.'

'Planet,' said Rimmer.

'Yes,' said Holly.

'Collision course,' said Rimmer.

'Yes,' said Holly.

'Engines dead.'

'Right.'

'Impact twelve hours.'

'With you.'

'Abandoning ship.'

'Oh.'

'Sorry.'

'Yes.'

''Bye.'

Within two seconds, Holly absorbed the data from the scanner scope, mulled the problem over and said two words. The two words were: 'Drive room.'

Then he switched himself off with less than twenty-five seconds of run-time remaining.

Rimmer met Lister, the Cat and Kryten dashing down the corridor towards the cargo bay.

'Drive room,' Rimmer shouted.

'Drive room?' Lister shouted back. 'Why?'

'I think Holly's come up with something.'

They heard the babble and chatter of operational machinery long before they passed under the colossal archway that led into the Drive room itself.

Traction-fed computer print-out chundered on to the floor from every one of the two thousand, six hundred printers. The whole chamber was knee deep in writhing reams of paper.

'What the smeg is going on?' Lister screamed above the machine noise, the remnants of his biofeedback tubes clattering behind him.

Kryten stooped and picked up a section of print-out. 'It's machine-speak. Calculations.'

'What kind of calculations?' yelled Rimmer.

Suddenly, the machines stopped chattering.

Above them, the immense screen which covered the entire ceiling, normally host to Holly's image, rippled into life. 'Solution,' it read, and then underneath was a list of coordinates. Below that was a 3D graphics display of Holly's plan.

It was quite the most audacious piece of astronavigation ever attempted in the entire history of the universe.

FIVE

On the screen was a simulation of the binary star system in which they were now marooned, motionless.

At the bottom of the screen was a vector graphic of *Red Dwarf*.

At the top of the screen was the blue-ice planet hurtling towards them on its collision course.

To the left was a small sun, and to the right was its larger twin. Both were orbited by single planets.

Starbug, *Red Dwarf*'s beetle-shaped transport craft, then flashed on the screen. The craft blipped a course towards the right-hand sun, and fired something into its core.

The sun flared, its planet was torn from its orbit and hurled towards the centre of the screen.

Lister watched, bewildered and bemused, as the display dissolved into a dazzling array of plotted lines and arrows.

When the screen finally cleared, all three planets now orbited the sun on the left, and *Red Dwarf* remained intact.

'Let me get this straight,' said Lister. 'Is he doing what I think he's doing?'

'What do you think he's doing?' asked the Cat.

'I think he's playing pool. With planets.'

Kryten stared pointlessly at the blank screen. 'Is that possible?'

'Well,' said Rimmer, 'it's certainly possible to fire a thermo-nuclear device into a sun and create enough of a solar flare to throw a planet out of orbit. The rest of it is somewhat in the realms of hypothesis.'

Lister creaked into one of the console seats, and shook his head grimly. 'It's not going to work. I promise you – it's not going to work. No way, Jose, not in a month of Uranian Sundays. If Holly thinks he can use the red planet to pot the blue planet into the left-hand sun's orbit, then he's out to breakfast, lunch and tea.'

'You don't think so?' said Kryten.

'No chance. There's not enough side.'

'Side?'

'Side-spin. His cueing angle's all wrong.'

'Lister – what *are* you drivelling about?' Rimmer snorted in contempt. 'We're talking about a computer with an IQ of twelve thousand, three hundred and sixty-eight.'

'That doesn't mean he can play pool.' Lister placed his palm on his chest. 'I can. Trust me, I know whereof I speak. Aigburth Arms on a Friday night, you couldn't get me off that table. This pool arm,' he flexed his right arm, 'is sound as a pound. And I promise you, that shot's not going to come off. He's topped it, that's what he's done. It's a felt-ripper. That planet's off the table and into somebody's glass of beer.'

Rimmer brayed incredulously. 'We're talking about the trigonomics of four-dimensional space, you simple-minded gimboid, we're not talking about some seedy game of pool in a back-street Scouse drinking-pit.'

'Same principle.'

'Of course it isn't.'

Lister nodded at the giant screen, 'I'm telling you, it's a complete mis-cue, and I say we chuck Holly's coordinates in the bin and let me take the shot.'

'Well,' Rimmer stood apart from the rest of the group, 'I say we put it to the vote. On the one hand, we have a computer with an IQ in five figures, who has a complete and total grasp of astrophysics, and on the other, we have Lister, who, and let's be fair to him, is a complete gimp. To whose hands do we entrust our lives, the safety of this vessel and the future of everything? Lister, what's your vote?'

Lister looked up from practising his imaginary pool shot. 'I vote for me.'

Rimmer smirked, enjoying the game. 'One–nil for Listy-poos. I vote for Holly. One–all. Kryters?'

'Well,' said Kryten, 'even though I agree it's insane and suicidal, I'm afraid I have to side with the human.'

'Bru-tal!' grinned Lister, and slapped the Mechanoid on his shoulder.

'What?' said Rimmer. 'You're voting for El Dirtball?'

'Sorry,' said Kryten. 'It's my programming.'

Rimmer's smile receded like a fizzling fuse. 'Cat?'

'I agree with you, Buddy. Everything you said makes sense,' the Cat went on, 'but the thing is: even though I agree with you, I could never bring myself to vote for someone with your dress-sense. I'm going to vote for Lister.'

'Three–one to me,' said Lister, and swayed his shoulders and rotated his fists into the touch-up shuffle.

Lister ran the final checkdown on the *Starbug's* instrument panel, then flicked the intercom on, so that Kryten's face appeared on the vid-screen. 'We're ready to go, Kryten. Where's the Cat?'

'He should be on his way, sir.'

'This is madness,' Rimmer shook his head, his eyes fixed on the *Starbug's* navicomp screen. 'Sheer madness.'

There was a bleep, and the Cat's face appeared next to Kryten's on the vid-screen. 'I'm not coming,' he said.

Lister bunched up his face. 'What?'

'This is the way I see it: if everything goes OK, everyone's safe, no problem. If something goes wrong, the guys on

Starbug get wiped out twenty minutes ahead of the guys on *Red Dwarf*.'

'So?'

'So, there's a lot of things a guy can do in twenty minutes. I'm staying here with Kryten.'

'Thanks a lot.'

The Cat grinned. 'Hey, don't even mention it. Just looking after number one.' Then he bleeped off the screen.

The retros scorched into the take-off pad, and the *Starbug* wobbled uneasily into the air.

Lister frowned at the steering column. It seemed stiff and unresponsive.

'What's the matter?'

'Nothing,' Lister lied. He wrestled the *'bug* on to an even keel, and fired the rear-thrust jets.

Rimmer glanced uneasily at the instrument panels. 'What's happening? We're hardly moving.'

Then they were. The *'bug*'s tail plummeted to the ground, grinding huge sparks from the runway, while the nose bucked towards the cargo-bay roof.

Lister fought through his safety webbing and thumped the reheat button. The *'bug* bobbed and reared, before finally picking up speed, if not altitude. Nose in the air, tail on the ground, it screamed and grated the quarter of a mile towards the airlock doors.

'I hardly need remind you,' Rimmer yelled over the howling engines, 'that we are carrying a small but robust thermo-nuclear device, not ten feet beneath us. In the name of everything that is holy, get this son-of-a-goit in the air.'

'You think I'm doing this for a laugh?' Lister yelled, 'There's something wrong. The ship feels about ten times heavier than it should.'

The *'bug* smacked into the rim of the airlock, flashing brilliant, magnesium-white sparks that welded the doors open for ever, and caromed out into the silent yawn of space.

Once clear of the ship, the 'bug jerked and juddered, then plummeted for two miles down Red Dwarf's south-west face before Lister engaged the back-up boosters and two-handedly wrestled the steering column into some semblance of submission.

'I don't get it,' Lister shouted over the engine's maximum howl. 'For some reason, we need full thrust plus emergency back-up just to get the smegging thing moving.'

Not for the first time, Rimmer felt extremely grateful he was already dead.

Lister crouched over the flat-bed scanner, one eye closed, his nose almost parallel with the screen. Silent and still, he studied the 3D simulation, then straightened and walked around the table to look at it from a new angle. There, at the far end of the screen, was the blue-ice planet. This was the planet Lister had designated as the blue ball.

To the right, circling around the bigger of the twin suns, was the planet Lister had christened the cue ball.

The cue ball would strike the blue ball, and send it into the orbit of the left hand sun, or, as Lister preferred to call it: 'the pocket'.

That simple.

It was a straightforward pot. He'd made identical shots thousands of times before. True, he'd never made the shot with planets, but, as Lister kept on insisting, in theory it should be easier, because planets are bigger.

Without taking his eyes from the scanner, he grabbed a six-pack of double-strength lager out of Starbug's tiny fridge, and ripped off a ring-pull.

He was half-way through his third can before Rimmer broke his vow of silence. 'How many of those are you going to drink?'

'I told you not to talk. Game on.' He finished the third and started the fourth.

'You're going to drink four cans of double-strength lager?'

Lister brushed some imaginary dust from the scanner screen. 'No, I'm going to drink all six. I always play my best pool when I've had a few beers. Steadies the nerves. I'm not going to get blasted – just nicely drunk.'

'Define "nicely drunk". Is "nicely drunk" horizontal or perpendicular?'

'Rimmer – I can handle it.'

'I'm not sure I can.'

'We're in the wrong position.' Lister sucked at his can. 'It's an easier shot if we're over here.' He tapped the screen at a point mid-way between *Red Dwarf* and the oncoming planet.

'You mean right in the path of the ice planet?'

Lister nodded.

'So if you miss, we get a planet in our face?'

'I'm not going to mish.' Lister tugged open his fifth lager, and ducked down into *Starbug*'s cockpit section.

'Mish?'

'What?'

'You said "mish". "I'm not going to mish," you said. You're pissed.'

Lister fired up the thrusters and wrenched the 'bug towards its new coordinates. 'God, I could murder a curry. Pity we didn't bring any food. Have we got any crisps or anything?'

The planet was close now. It occupied almost half of Rimmer's navicomp screen, and was growing steadily in size as it thundered towards them.

Lister screwed up the empty sixth can of lager and threw it across the room at the wastebin. It hit the rim and clattered on to the floor.

Rimmer closed his eyes. 'Let's just get out of here. It's a shame about the Cat and Kryten, but we still have a chance to save *our* necks.'

Lister flicked the missile launch to manual. The firing pad lurched forward from the flatbed scanner, and he nestled his nose into the bifocal viewer. Heat prickled his arms and his forehead. He lined up the crosswires on the sun around which the cue planet spun. He shifted his legs until he felt his centre of balance.

It was lined up.

It looked right.

But he waited.

He waited until it *felt* right.

Then it felt right. Space faded away, and he was back in the Aigburth Arms, and this was just another shot to stay on the table. He was on the eight ball, and all it needed was a push, with just enough bottom to avoid the in-off. It was easy. He could do it.

It felt right.

He played his shot.

He touched the launch button, and increased the pressure steadily and evenly in one smooth movement.

With a primal scream, the missile ripped from its housing under *Starbug*'s belly and sizzled towards the distant sun.

Lister turned to the scanner screen and watched.

The whole sequence took eight hours to play out, but to Rimmer, it seemed like eight years. To Lister, it seemed like eight seconds.

The missile plunged into the sun's inferno, and a giant solar flare licked up from its raging surface, struck Lister's cue planet and slammed it out of orbit.

The cue planet yammered through space towards the intersection coordinates, the point where it would collide with the ice planet, and knock it into the 'pocket' of the left-hand sun.

Almost immediately, Rimmer realized it was going to miss. And not by a little. By a lot.

The cue planet wasn't going to hit the ice planet. It wasn't even going to connect. The cue planet had been wrenched from its orbit hopelessly early. It was going to streak harmlessly across the path of the oncoming ice world, to be captured in orbit around the left-hand sun.

Lister had sunk the cue ball.

Or rather, he was going to sink the cue ball; first they had to wait for the planetary pool shot to run its slow-motion course.

They didn't exchange a word for three hours. They watched the scanner screen, and hoped, against the evidence of their eyes, that it wouldn't happen.

But it did.

The cue planet flew into orbit around the opposite sun. It looped round the far side in an erratic ellipse, then thumped into the sun's resident planet, and sent that curling out into space.

The resident planet swept across the scanner screen, cannoned into the ice world and hammered it into the orbit of the right-hand sun, before elegantly back-spinning a return path to its original position.

'She rides!' Lister wiggled his hips and arms in a touch-up shuffle. 'She riiiiiiiiiiiiiiiiiiiiiiiiiiiiiiiiiiides!'

'You jammy bastard.'

'Played for, and got.' He pumped the air with his fists, chanting rhythmically: 'Yes, yes, yes, yes . . .'

'You jammy, jammy bastard.'

'How can that be jammy? I pocketed all three planets with one stroke – how can that be a fluke?'

'You're trying to tell me it was deliberate?'

'Obviously, I wasn't going to tell you I was going for a trick shot – you'd have had one of your spasms.'

'Oh, do smeg off.'

Lister started dancing round the flatbed scanner, waving a seventh can of double-strength lager. 'Pool God.' He baptised himself with beer. 'King of the Cues.' He thumped his chest. 'Prince of the Planet-Potters.'

Lister was doing some serious damage to his third six-pack, and watching the fast-motion replay on the scanner for the hundred and seventy-first time, while Rimmer slept off the journey back to *Red Dwarf* in the '*bug*'s one and only sleep couch, when a planet hit them.

Which planet hit them, Lister never discovered. In fact, it was the cue planet, which had been knocked out of its new orbit by the back-spinning resident planet. But that didn't really concern Lister. When the craft you're in gets hit by a planet, you rarely have the presence of mind to stop and swap insurance details.

Technically, the '*bug*' wasn't actually hit by the *planet*, it was the planet's slipstream. But that was enough to flick the craft upside-down and send it on a corkscrew death dive towards the ice world.

SIX

Only the *Starbug*'s dome-shaped Drive section, scorched black from its encounter with the ice planet's stratosphere, poked up through the slow-shifting sea of snow dunes. Resting against the foot of the glacier, it fizzled and steamed for almost five days in the unrelenting blizzard before there was any sign of life.

Finally, the small hatchway chinked open and light gushed out into the black arctic night. Lister's face, encircled by parka fur, appeared grimacing in the opening. His gloved fingers folded around the rim of the hatchway, before the blinding wind forced back the door and tried to close it on his head.

The back of his skull slammed against the metal edging of the door frame, while the steel hatch jammed into his nose and began the slow business of cutting his head in two. He was helpless and close to blacking out. He was beginning to think that after all he'd been through, being 'doored' to death was a stupid way to die, when the wind changed direction for a second time, and the hatchway gave to his frantic pushes.

He fell out of the *'bug* and teetered on a ledge of packed snow. He quickly discovered the only way to remain upright was to lean into the wind. He had to incline his body at an angle of fifty degrees. He felt absurd, but there was no other way of staying on his feet. He managed three steps at this angle before the blizzard inflated his parka hood, and knocked him off the ledge.

He slithered down the bank and dropped into the trough

cut by *Starbug*'s crash-path. Gradually he hauled himself to his feet, and unfastened the small ship-issue snow trowel which was tied to his waist. He looked at it. It measured scarcely four inches across. He looked at what little of the *'bug* was visible above the drift. At a rough estimate, he would have to shift about eight hundred tons of snow if the *'bug* was ever to move. He tried two trowelfuls before the erratic blizzard swirled into the trough and tossed him like a broken kite into a snow bank fifty feet away.

Rimmer stooped over the communications console, and barked into the microphone: 'Mayday . . . Mayday . . . Can you read me? . . . Come in, please . . .' He looked up at the screen, which continued to rasp its static gibberish.

The *Starbug*'s inner door hammered open, and a blizzard stumbled in, followed by Lister. The snow swirled around inside the craft, like a swarm of trapped insects looking for an escape. Lister hurled himself against the inner door and fought it closed.

Rimmer didn't look up from the communicator. 'Still snowing, is it?'

'It's useless.' Lister flung his gloves against the *'bug*'s far bulkhead. 'You can hardly stand up, never mind dig it out.'

He sneered at the static on the screen. Five days had gone by, broadcasting on all frequencies, and still *Red Dwarf* hadn't acknowledged the SOS.

Rimmer persisted. 'Mayday . . . Mayday . . .'

Lister took the rum bottle from his parka's emergency pocket, spun off the top and tilted it to his lips. The alcohol was frozen solid. Holding the neck he smashed the bottle on the corner of the table, and gratefully sucked his rum lollypop. This was the last alcohol on board. He was beginning to panic – if they didn't get rescued soon, he might have to spend a night with Rimmer, sober.

'Mayday . . . Mayday . . .' Rimmer turned. 'I wonder why it's "Mayday"?'

'Eh?'

'The distress call. Why d'you say "Mayday"? It's just a bank holiday. Why not "Shrove Tuesday" or "Ascension Sunday"?' He turned back to the communicator. 'Ascension Sunday . . . Ascension Sunday.' He thought for a while, and then tried: 'The fourteenth Wednesday after Pentecost . . . The fourteenth Wednesday after Pentecost . . .'

'It's French, you doink. Help me – *m'aidez*. How much food is there?'

Rimmer nodded at the navigation console. 'I made a full list on the dictopad.'

Lister picked up Rimmer's voice-activated electronic diary, and pressed 'play'. The menu was meagre indeed: half a bag of smoky bacon crisps, a tin of mustard powder, a brown lemon, three stale water biscuits, two bottles of vinegar and a tube of Bonjella gum ointment.

Lister looked up from the pad. 'Gum ointment?'

'I found it in the first-aid box. It's that minty flavour. It's quite nice.'

'It's quite nice if you smear it on your mouth ulcer, but you can't sit down and eat it.'

Rimmer raised an eyebrow. 'You may have to.'

'Is that it? Nothing else?'

'Just a pot noodle. Oh – and I found a tin of dog food on the tool shelf.'

Misery hissed through Lister's gritted teeth. 'Well,' he said finally. 'Pretty obvious what gets eaten last. I can't *stand* pot noodles.'

He huddled over the last remnants of fuel glowing in the mining brazier and tried not to think of food. Three days had passed since he'd unzipped the last of the emergency seal-meals; three days without proper food. In fact, he hadn't eaten at *all* since breakfast the previous morning, and that had only been a raw sprout and a piece of chewing gum he'd found stuck under the Drive seat. It was all right for

Rimmer. Rimmer was a hologram – he didn't have to eat, he couldn't feel the cold; he couldn't die.

He replayed the food list again, desperately searching for something vaguely palatable. Rimmer argued that most of the food groups were represented: vitamins, proteins, nutrients. If Lister paced himself, Rimmer pointed out, if he sat down and worked out a dietary programme and stuck to it, the food could last him for two weeks.

But, as Lister pointed out, Rimmer held that opinion because he was a dork.

The argument ended in a long silence, broken only by the fizzling of the screen and the crackling of the brazier.

It was Lister who spoke first. Predictably, he said: 'God, I'm so hungreee.'

'Stop thinking about food.'

'Take my mind off it, then. Talk about something.'

'Like what?'

'Anything.'

'Anything?'

'Anything apart from food.'

Rimmer shifted uncomfortably in his chair. Not small talk. He hated it. 'Like what?'

'I dunno.' Lister shrugged. 'Tell me how you lost your virginity.'

Rimmer yawned to conceal his panic. 'We-ell. It was so long ago . . . I was so young and sexually precocious, I'm not sure I can remember.'

'Everyone can remember how they lost their virginity.'

'Well, I don't. Good grief, you can hardly expect me to recall every single sexual liaison I've ever partaken of. What d'you think I am – the Memory Man?' Rimmer was babbling to buy himself thinking time. He'd always been a bit of a fish out of water when it came to women. Frankly, he'd always had a rather low sex drive, which he secretly ascribed to all the school cabbage he was forced to eat as a boy.

423

What was a respectable age to claim he'd lost it? Certainly not thirty-one, to a half-concussed flight technician who'd checked herself out of the recovery bay prematurely after a winch had fallen on her head. Who was still wearing the bandages, and was so disoriented she kept on calling him 'Alan'. Certainly not that magical and lovely moment balanced precariously on the rim of the sleeping quarters' sink.

No, he must lie. But what lie? He had to macho the facts up a bit. What was a good age for a tough, sexually-potent, rough-and-tumble type astro to have had his cherry popped? Mid-twenties? Early twenties?

'Come on, Rimmer. The truth.'

Then Rimmer remembered his first fumbled encounter at second base. He was nineteen. A slight tweaking of the facts, a slight blurring of the action, and that should be perfectly respectable.

'The first time . . . the very first time was this girl I met at Cadet College. Sandra. We were both nineteen. We did it in the back of my brother's car.'

'What was it like?'

'Oh, fantastic, brilliant.' Rimmer's eyes acquired a milky hue, and his mouth went dry. 'Bentley convertible. V8 turbo. Walnut-burr panelling. Beautiful machine, beautiful. So what about you? How did you lose yours?'

'Michelle Fisher. The ninth hole of Bootle municipal golf course. Par four, dogleg to the right, in the bunker behind the green.'

'On a golf course!?'

Lister nodded.

'A golf course? How old were you?'

Lister wistfully prodded the dying coals in the brazier. 'She took all her clothes off and just stood there in front of me, completely naked. I was so excited, I nearly dropped my skateboard.'

'Your *skate*board? How old were you?'

'Twelve.'

'Twelve!!! Twelve years old!!? When you lost your virginity, you were twelve???'

'Yeah.'

'Twelve??' Rimmer stared into the fire. 'Well, you can't have been a full member of the golf club, then.'

''Course I wasn't.'

'You did it on a golf course, and you weren't a member?'

''Course I wasn't,' Lister repeated.

'So, you didn't pay any green fees or anything?'

'It was just a place to go.'

'I used to play golf. I hate people who abuse the facilities. I hope you raked the sand back nicely before you left. That'd be a hell of a lie to get into, wouldn't it? Competition the next day, and your ball lands in Lister's buttock crevice. You'd need more than a niblick to get that one out.'

'Are you trying to say I've got a big bum?'

'Big? It's like two badly parked Volkswagens.'

Twelve? Rimmer couldn't believe it. The only thing he ever lost when he was twelve were his Space Scout shoes with the compass in the heel and the animal tracks on the soles. His best friend, the boy who bullied him least, Porky Roebuck, threw them in the septic tank behind the sports ground. He'd cried for weeks – he'd been wearing them.

Suddenly, the communications console crackled into life. The screen resolved itself into a clear picture, and Kryten was talking to them.

But something was wrong with the sound: all they could hear was a dull, resonant bass throb, a slow-motion growl.

Lister played with the frequency controls, but couldn't improve the sound reception. The transmission never varied. Kryten's expression never appeared to change, and the deep undulating grunt from the speakers never relented.

They checked the video link, but could find nothing wrong. Same with the speakers: they were functioning perfectly.

Then something happened to Rimmer.

It was hardly noticeable at first, but after a couple of hours it was plain that he'd started slowing down. There was a definite time-lag in his responses to Lister. Talking to him was like conducting a transatlantic phone conversation with a bad connection. His light image started to corrupt. Occasionally he would flash and become two-dimensional, or lose all colour.

Lister didn't mention it at first. It seemed rude, somehow. Rimmer had always been extremely sensitive about his status as a hologram. He hated to be reminded that his image was projected from a minute light bee, which hovered in his centre and from time to time went wrong. Frequently in the past he'd suffered glitches – becoming slightly transparent, or turning a strange shade of blue. On one occasion his legs had become separated from the rest of his body, and spent a morning wandering aimlessly about the ship, leaving his torso shaking its fist in fury.

As a rule, Lister never remarked on these signal failings, and within hours, they were generally put right.

But this was different.

Rimmer's voice had dropped two octaves, and trying to hold a conversation with him now was like talking person-to-person to Paul Robeson on Mars.

'Rimmer – what's happening?'

A two-minute pause, then:

'Donnnnnnnnnnnnnn't knooooooooooooooooooow.'

'Something must be wrong with your signal from the ship. The remote hologrammatic relay's not getting through properly.'

'Cannnnnnnnnnnnnnn't unnnnnnnnnderstaaaaaaaand wheeeeeeeeeen yooooooooooooooooou speeeeeeeeeeeeeeeeeak soooooooooooooo faaaaaaaaaaaaaaaaaaaaaaaaaaaaaaaaaaaast. Speeeeeeeeeeeeeeeeeeeeeeeeeak norrrrrrrrrrmaaaaaaaaaally, liiiiiiiiiiiiiiiiiiiiiiiiiiiiiiiiiiiiiiike meeeeeeeeeeeeeeeeeeeeeeeeeeee

eeeeeeeeeeeeeeeeeeeeeeeeeeeeeeeeeeeeeeeeeeeeeeeeeeeeee
eeeeeeeeeeeeeeeeeeeeeeeeeeeeeeeeeeeeeeeeeeeeeeeeee.'

The conversation that followed was brief in content, but took the best part of half a day to complete. The essence of the dialogue was that the signal from the ship that projected Rimmer's image was slowing down and weakening. When the signal became too faint to transmit, the hologrammatic projection unit would automatically flick from remote to local, and Rimmer would be regenerated, fully functional, back on board *Red Dwarf*.

'Well, that's good. You can find out what's keeping them; tell them where I am.'

Rimmer nodded curtly. It took five minutes.

The transmission grew weaker. Interference lines split up Rimmer's image for minutes on end.

'I'll beeeee baaaaack,' he said, over the course of the next half hour. 'Truuuuuuuuuuuusssssssssssssssssssssssssssssssssssssst meeeeeeeeeeeeeeeeeeeeeeeeeeeeeeeeeeeeeeeeeeeeeeeee.'

Rimmer blipped off, and re-formed in the hologrammatic projection unit regeneration chamber aboard *Red Dwarf*.

Instantly, he knew something was wrong.

But not with him – with Time.

SEVEN

Lister had his first meal in four days, sixteen hours after Rimmer had vanished.

He sat in front of the brazier, and looked down at the grey, chipped enamel of the ship-issue plate.

The meal almost looked nice. It was garnished with potato crisps, topped by crumbled water biscuits, sprinkled with mustard and decorated with flower-twirls of Bonjella gum ointment.

But it was still dogfood.

It was still rich, chunky lumps of rabbit, in a thick, marrowbone jelly.

It was still utterly revolting.

A dozen times he dug in his fork and held the quivering mass centimetres from his lips, but he just couldn't bring himself to put it in his mouth and swallow.

If it had had a neutral smell, it might have been all right. But the smell of dogfood had always filled Lister with nausea. After disco urinals, his own socks and Spanish perfume, it was his least favourite smell.

So he waited. He waited until he was so hungry he didn't care. Until the dogfood wasn't dogfood. Until it was a prime slab of fillet steak sizzling in a creamy fresh blue-cheese sauce.

With the pinched eyes of a gourmet sampling perfection he slid the wobbling forkful between his lips. He chewed. He chewed a bit more. Then he swallowed the dogfood.

He sat for a while. *Well*, he thought, *now I know why dogs lick their testicles. It's to get rid of the taste of the food.*

He placed the fork back on the plate, rose and staggered uneasily to the *Starbug*'s tail-section to try and take his mind off eating. He opened up the locker that stored the *'bug*'s tiny library and tried to find some distraction. It was no good. Everything reminded him of food.

He glanced down the spines. Charles Lamb. Sir Francis Bacon. And his eyes started playing tricks: Herman Wok, he read, and *The Caretaker*, by Harold Pinta. He saw food everywhere, even when it wasn't there. Eric Van Lustbader – Eric *Van* – bread *van*, meat *van*: food.

There was nothing else for it. He returned to the vessel's mid-section, finished off the dogfood, curled up and fell happily asleep.

He awoke to the sound of creaking metal. Creaking metal and running water. He unzipped his sleep bag. His clothes were wet. He was sweating.

There was a crash, and he was flung across the cabin. The *'bug* was tilting. Cupboards and lockers hurled themselves open and disgorged their contents over the warm metal deck. Lister clattered to his feet and tried to scramble up the incline and into the cockpit, but the *'bug* lurched again and sent him tumbling through the back hatchway and into the tail section.

Then *Starbug* started to move. Slowly at first, it slid lazily backwards, its outer hull grinding against the landscape, fins and support legs bending and snapping as it went.

Lister clawed his way up the ship, and staggered to a viewport window.

Ice world was melting. Overnight, its Ice Age was ending. The warm kiss of its new sun was thawing the planet which had been frozen for countless millennia.

Thick grey rivers gushed down the faces of shrinking

glaciers. Mountains were moving, gliding with majestic grace across the liquid landscape.

And *Starbug* was picking up speed, skidding helplessly downhill.

Lister collapsed to his haunches, hurled his head into his hands and made strange moaning sounds.

He was sick of it.

All he wanted to do was go home. Get back to Earth. Find a dead-end job and live out the rest of a boring existence. But no. From Mimas, to Deep Space, to unreality, to this; marooned in a smashed-up spacecraft that was tobogganing down a glacier, with only three squirts of gum ointment and half a bottle of vinegar between him and starvation.

Under the circumstances, Lister did the only sane thing.

He went back to bed.

Lister had a gift for sleeping. He could sleep anywhere, at any time, in any circumstances. It was a much underestimated talent, in his view. And if they'd ever held world sleeping competitions in his time back on Earth, he could have been an international somnolist. He could have slept for his country.

He crawled back to the bunk, bent his pillow in a U around his ears, and became the first man ever to sleep through a melting Ice Age.

EIGHT

Something was wrong with Time.

Rimmer stepped out of the regeneration booth into the long corridor of the hologram projection suite. The banks of machinery that lined the half-mile wall rippled and undulated as if light itself were bending. To Rimmer's right, at the far end of the suite, a glass water-cooler had toppled free of its housing and appeared to be defying gravity, suspended half-way between the counter top and the floor.

He lurched right and started walking towards it. This turned out to be a mistake. As he raised his left leg and thrust it forward, it telesco–o–o–o–o–oped out forty feet down the room. Instinctively, he flicked out his right leg to retain his balance. But his right leg bolted down the room, overtaking his left. He stopped and looked at his position.

His head and torso appeared to be barely two feet off the ground, while his right leg was eighty feet down the room, and his left leg still forty. He stayed perfectly still and wondered what to do. The water-cooler had moved a few inches closer to the floor. He leant forward, and his neck elongated out of his shoulders, so he looked like a bipedal brontosaurus, and zoomed off down the room.

He panicked and started to chase after his neck. Suddenly, he was aware that something was overtaking him at speed. It was his right leg. Once again it stretched yards in front of him, then a flash of khaki from the other side, and his other leg loomed out to join it. He took three more rubbery steps, until a bout of nausea forced him to stop. The water-cooler was definitely moving. The closer Rimmer got, the faster it moved.

He turned back and looked down the room towards a digital wall clock. The minute digits were hammering over so fast they were little more than a blur.

Rimmer started to head back for the door at the clock end, to make his way to the ship's Status room. To his alarm he found that thrusting his legs out in this direction made them shrink. They concertinaed into themselves, so he looked like a bad impression of Groucho Marx chasing after Margaret Dumont.

Something was happening to the clock. The nearer he got to it, the slower it appeared to move. The digits were still flicking over at high speed, but it was a slower high speed than the speed he'd witnessed when he'd been standing by the suspended water-cooler.

Finally, he reached the end of the suite, and stood under the clock. Now it was moving perfectly normally.

The digits read: Monday: 13:02.

He walked through the hatchway and stood in the main linking corridor. The corridor ran at a right angle to the hologram suite, and appeared to be normal. The problem, whatever it was, seemed to be localized to the one room. He started to head for the Status Room.

His right leg thumped down, short, wide and elephantine, while his left tapered elegantly out beside him. He waddled on his two strange new legs into the Status Room, sat down at the console desk and scanned the bank of security monitors.

The problem was ship wide. Time was moving at different speeds in every single room. He glanced down at the digital clock nestled among the console switches.

The readout was: Tuesday: 05:17.

Two hundred yards down the corridor it was Monday afternoon. Here, it was early Tuesday morning.

He voice-activated the external viewport scanners, and studied the screens. Rimmer could see nothing outside the ship that would explain the phenomenon. The two suns of the binary systems were still here, and so were the three planets. The only slightly odd thing was that one of the suns, the sun that lay to the front of the ship, was no longer perfectly round – it was now egg-shaped, and a thin stream of light peeled off it, tailing away into the blackness.

The sun far off into the distance, around which Lister's planet orbited, seemed unaffected.

Rimmer voice-activated the monitors back to internal and scrutinized the images more closely. It took him nearly an hour to work it out. The closer you got to the front of the ship, the slower Time was moving.

It was as if some gigantic force were sucking in Time. Corrupting it. Slowing it down.

There were only two things Rimmer knew of that could produce such a syndrome. And since he'd never in his life consumed a magic mushroom, that left only one alternative.

He prayed he was wrong. He was wrong about most things, and always had been. Why should he be right about this?

No, there was some option he hadn't considered. He was bound to be wrong.

Bound to be. He cheered up a little, confident in his own awesome capacity for incompetence, and asked the security computer to activate a sweep search for Kryten and the Cat.

It found them in one of the engine rooms to the rear of the ship, frantically chasing around with a battalion of skutters, trying to re-start the engines.

Rimmer called for a voice link. 'Kryten – Lister's marooned on the ice planet. He's starving to death. We've got to get down and help him. What the smeg's happening?'

Kryten replied in a garbled falsetto before he was barged out of shot by the Cat, who was clearly impatient to deliver his own version of the facts.

'Gubudoobeedee,' he squeaked, his hands gesticulating wildly, like a deranged street drunk. 'Gadabadabadeebeedoobeedah. OK?'

'Speak slowly,' said Rimmer, as quick and high-pitched as he could. 'I have to speak fast and squeaky, and you have to speak slow and low. Otherwise we won't make sense to each other.'

Kryten blinked into the video shot, and spoke as slowly as he could. He still sounded like a man with a mouthful of helium, but at least now it was intelligible. 'Something is wrong,' he chirruped helpfully.

'Oh really?' Rimmer squeaked back sarcastically. 'How enlightening. It's Tuesday in here, Monday next door. and you think something is wrong.'

'What are you talking about?' Kryten said. 'It's Friday.'

He twisted the security camera so it pointed at the wall clock.

'Friday?' Rimmer squinted at the read-out. 'It's Monday next door, Tuesday in here, and Friday where you are.' He sat and thought. 'But which Friday? Is it last Friday, or next Friday?'

'It's this Friday,' said Kryten.

'What's the date?'

'Fifteenth.'

'So it's a week next Friday.'

There was a hiatus. Nobody could think of anything to say.

'I'm coming down,' Rimmer said, finally. 'I'll be there in a sec.'

'At last!' The Cat turned from testing the final piston housing and stood, hands on hips, in his red silk boilersuit with gold trimming. 'Where've you *been*, Buddy?'

'I ran all the way,' Rimmer panted. 'I can't have been more than five minutes.'

'You've been over a week.'

Rimmer glanced at the clock. It was Saturday the twenty-third.

Kryten's head poked round the corner of the piston housing. 'We're ready and primed,' he said. 'Let's start the engines.'

The three of them lumbered uneasily up the spiral staircase and into the Navicomp Suite.

Kryten stabbed in the start-up sequence, and the massive pistons smashed the engine into life. Kryten clapped his plastic hands in delight. 'We did it!'

'OK.' The Cat slid out of his silk boilersuit, revealing a quilted lamé jumpsuit underneath. 'Slip this baby into reverse and let's scoot.'

Kryten typed in the appropriate sequence, and the engine noise changed pitch, becoming a strangulated thudding whine. Three pairs of eyes fixed on the speed/bearing read-out. It scarcely changed.

'More power,' said the Cat. 'Get that pedal on the metal. Sluice that juice.'

'We're on full reverse thrust.'

The Cat shouldered Kryten out of the way and jabbed pointlessly at the controls. 'It cannot be, novelty condom head – we're still moving forwards.'

'Look,' Kryten pointed at the display. 'We're into the red. We're using all the power we've got.'

'It's true, then.' Rimmer slumped into the console chair.

'What's true?' said the Cat.

'What's true,' Rimmer looked up, red-eyed with fear, 'is that we're being sucked into a Black Hole.'

Part Three

Garbage world

ONE

Today was the day. Today was the big one.

John Ewe had been doing the Jovian run for the best part of twenty years. Not many people were prepared to spend their life ferrying human sewage from Jupiter's satellites all the way across the solar system and dropping it on the dump planet, but John Ewe actually enjoyed his work, and what's more, it paid well.

It wasn't just sewage that was disgorged on the dump planet, it was everything; all humankind's garbage – nuclear waste, chemical effluence, rotting foodstuffs, glass waste, waste paper; every kind of trash – all the unwanted by-products of three thousand years of civilization. But John Ewe specialized in sewage. He was the King of Crap. And right now he was sitting on top of two billion tons of it.

His tiny control dome, the only inhabitable section of the vast haulage ship, made up less than one per cent of the gigantic structure. The bulk of the craft was given over to the twin two-mile-long cylinders that stored the waste.

The ship's computer indicated they were about to go into orbit. Ewe climbed into his safety webbing and switched on the view screen.

The refuse ship powered through the thin atmosphere and hit the thick, choking black smog that spiralled up from the planet's surface. And there it was.

Garbage World.

Whole landmasses were given over to particular types of

waste. For twenty minutes the ship flew over a range of a dozen mountains composed entirely of discarded tin cans, so high the peaks were capped with snow. It passed over an island the size of the Malagasy Republic piled high with decomposing black bin bags. It flew over a fermenting sea, flaming with toxic waste. It skimmed over an entire continent of wrecked cars: thousands upon thousands of miles of rusting chassis. It crossed a desert; a vast featureless flatland of cigarette dimps.

And then it arrived at the continent for sewage.

This was the moment. The moment he'd been planning for almost two decades.

Like anyone else in a dull job, John Ewe made up games to help pass the time.

His game was graffiti.

And he was about to complete the biggest single piece of graffito ever attempted in the history of civilization.

It sprawled across a continent. It was visible from space. It was written in effluence, and it said: 'Ewe woz 'ere'.

Today he had the final two billion tons he required to complete the half-finished loop of the final 'e'.

The bay doors on the belly of the ship hinged open and the effluence poured down and splatted into place.

John Ewe unhooked himself from the safety harness and swaggered down the thin aisle, the cleft of his buttocks wobbling hairily over the top of his jeans. He flicked on the satellite link, and examined his masterpiece in its completed glory. He scratched his hairy shoulders and belched.

'Bewdiful.'

John Ewe was a colonial. He'd been born and raised on Ganymede, one of the moons that spun around Jupiter. He was aware that his ancestors had once lived here – in fact, they had orginated from the dump planet – but no one, no one at all had lived there for five or six generations. He felt no affinity for the world of his forebears, any more than Anglo-Saxons felt an affinity for Scandinavia.

Earth didn't really mean anything to Ewe – it was just there to be dumped on.

The mathematics were simple: civilization produces garbage; the greater the civilization, the greater the garbage – and humankind had become very civilized indeed.

Three hundred years after the invention of the lightbulb, they'd colonized the entire solar system. The solar system was soon jam-packed with civilization too, and humankind rapidly reached the point where there was so much indestructible garbage, there was nowhere left to put it.

Something had to be done. Firing the garbage willy-nilly off into space was cost-prohibitive. So the Inter-Planetary Commission for Waste Disposal conducted a series of feasibility studies, and they concluded that one of the nine planets of the solar system had to be given over to waste.

Delegates from all the planets and their satellites submitted tenders to lose the contract.

The Mercurian delegation pointed to their solar-energy plants, which provided cheap, limitless energy for the whole system.

The study group from Uranus hinged its case on its natural stores of mineral deposits.

Jupiter and its moons relied on their outstanding natural beauty.

Neptune built its case on famous planetary architecture – it had been terraformed to the highest specifications.

Saturn's rings, a massive tourist attraction, made that planet safe, and its network of moons, though often seedy and downmarket, generated a lot of business, merely because of their position along established trade routes.

Mars was the safest of all, because it was home to the wealthy. It was the chicest, most exclusive world in the planetary system, handy for commuting to other planets, yet far enough away from the riff-raff to be ideal for the mega-rich.

Venus took the Martian over-spill – the people who wanted to live on Mars, but couldn't quite afford it. Venus was full of people who wanted to be Martians, so much so they often quoted their address as 'South Mars' or 'Mars/Venus borders.' Still, it was a fairly wealthy planet, and the Venusians constituted a powerful political lobby.

And so it became a straight battle between Earth and Pluto. The Plutonian delegation made rather a weak case, drawing attention to their planet's erratic orbit and its position on the edge of the solar system.

The Earth delegation was beside itself with fury. Frankly, it was outraged that the planet that was mother to the human race, where life itself had been spawned and nurtured, was even being considered for such a putrid fate. It talked long and heatedly about how humankind had to remember its roots, and showed long, dull videos of Earth's past beauty. Of course, it conceded, the planet wasn't as pulchritudinous as it had once been. Yes, it agreed, it was now the most polluted planet in the solar system. True, most of the inhabitants had fled to the new terraformed worlds, and it was home, now, to only a handful of millions, too broke, too scared or too stupid to leave. But what about tradition, it argued? Earth had *invented* civilization. It had given civilization to the solar system. If civilization now turned round and literally dumped on Earth, what did that say about humankind?

And so it came to the vote.

The vote was telecast live to every terraformed world in the solar system. A jury on each of the worlds sat patiently through all nine presentations, and then allocated points, the lowest points going to the planet most favoured for the new mantle of Garbage World.

The show was broadcast from the French settlement of Dione, the Saturnian satellite. It was hosted by Avril Dupont, the greatly loved French TV star.

442

''Allo Mercury?'

Pause. Crackle. 'Hello, Avril.'

'Can you give us the votes of the Mercurian jury?'

'Here are the votes of the Mercurian jury. Pluto: two points.'

'Pluto, two points. *La Pluton, deux points.*'

'Neptune, seven points.'

'Neptune, seven points. *Le Neptune, sept points.*'

'Uranus, four points.'

'Uranus, four points. *L'Uranus, quatre points.*'

'Saturn, eight points.'

'Saturn, eight points. *Le Saturne, huit points.*'

'Jupiter, five points.'

'Jupiter, five points. *La Jupiter, cinque points.*'

'Mars, twelve points.'

'Mars, twelve points. *La Mars, douze points.*'

'Venus, ten points.'

'Venus, ten points. *La Vénus, dix points.*'

'Earth, no points.'

'Earth, no points. *La Terre, zéro points.*'

'And that concludes the voting of the Mercurian jury. Good night, Avril.'

And that was the best score Earth got.

It culled not one single vote.

At twenty past eleven, on 11 November the following year, the last shuttle-load of evacuees left for re-housing on Pluto, and the planet Earth was officially re-named 'Garbage World'.

The President of Callisto personally cut the ribbon of toilet paper, ceremonially deposited the first symbolic shovelful of horse manure in the centre of what once had been Venice and declared Garbage World open for business. The President and his aides dashed into the Presidential shuttle as the first wave of three hundred thousand refuse ships swooped down and dumped their stinking loads on the planet that was once called Earth.

The dumping areas were strictly regulated: North America, for instance, was bottles. Clear bottles on the west coast, brown bottles on the east and green in the centre. Australia was reserved for domestic waste: potato peelings, soiled paper nappies, used teabags, banana skins, squeezed toothpaste tubes. Japan became the graveyard of the motor car; from island to island, from tip to tail, from Datsuns to Chryslers, to forty-cylinder cyclotronic hover cars, dead, silent metal covered the land of the setting sun.

The Arctic Circle was allocated rotting foodstuffs, the Bahamas was home to old sofas and bicycle wheels, Korea took all broken electrical equipment.

Europe got the sewage.

And over the last twenty years, John Ewe had busied himself signing his name over the corner of that once-great continent.

John Ewe shut down the satellite link, and followed his hairy beer-belly back to the front of the ship. Before he could reach the safety webbing, a massive pocket of methane turbulence rocked the refuse craft and sent him staggering into the first-aid box. He fingered the gash that grinned bloodily on his brow and invented two new swear words. The methane storms had been getting worse over the past few years, and he knew he should have consulted the meteorological computer before he ventured from his safety harness.

As he lurched to his feet, a second methane blast hit the ship under its belly, sending him stumbling back down the narrow aisle. As he slithered helplessly backwards, his flailing arm caught the door-release mechanism, and the cockpit's emergency exit swung open.

His fat fingers scrambled for a hand-hold, but found nothing until he slid through the open doorway, and he grabbed the rim of the footledge.

For thirty seconds he dangled, screaming, over Europe.

Then he dangled no more.

He plunged from the yawing garbage ship, and drowned in his own signature.

'Ewe woz 'ere', it said. And it was right, 'e woz.

The unmanned craft hacked around wildly in the sudden turbulence, the autopilot stretched beyond its capacity. The methane storm whipped up to hurricane force and sucked the ship to the ground.

A continent of methane exploded.

The blast triggered off a thermo-nuclear reaction in a thousand discarded atomic-power stations, and the Earth tore itself from its orbit around the sun, and farted its way out of the solar system.

Two and a half thousand years of abuse were ended.

The Earth was free.

Free from humankind. Free from civilization.

When it was clear of the sun's influence, it froze in heatless space and bathed its wounds in a perennial Ice Age.

On it went, out of the solar system and into Deep Space, carving a path through the universe, looking for a new sun to call home.

TWO

Lister coughed himself awake. A gargantuan coughing fit forced his body into a ball and thrashed it about under the heavy quilting of the sleep sheet before his head finally emerged from under the covers, gasping for air.

Air, it turned out, was the last thing he wanted. It was thick and smoky and bitter to the taste. His hand scrambled blindly for the bunkside oxygen mask that dangled above the recessed sleeping couch. He held it to his face and sucked.

Gradually his vision cleared, and he peeked out into the murk. There was a hissing sound coming from the floor. Lister drew the blanket around him, knelt up and craned over the side of the couch to get a closer look. The whole of the steel-alloy deck was pitted with thin, deep, smoking holes, as if something were trying to burrow up into the craft from below.

As he watched, something flitted past his face, almost brushing his cheek, landed in a loud fizzle on the deck and started to tunnel patiently through the reinforced steel.

Lister snapped his head back into the shelter of the recess. His heart thumped a samba on the xylophone of his ribs. That could have been his head.

He ducked low so the edge of *Starbug*'s roof edged into his field of vision. Hollow metal stalactites hung down from the buckled structure, some of them dripping a clear, colourless liquid on to the '*bug*'s floor.

Lister shot back and huddled in the corner of the recess.

Acid rain.

But not normal acid rain – this was *acid* rain. Acid rain of such concentration it cut through high-density metal as if it were full-fat soft cheese. His eyes lit on what remained of the high-backed scanner scope chair. It was now a pile of steaming gloop. Only two nights earlier, he'd fallen asleep on that chair. That gloop could have been him.

It didn't make sense. Why hadn't the acid rain cut through the bunk roof? Why had that held out?

Lister looked up, and got his answer. It hadn't. The roof bulged crazily, like a balloon full of water, and stalactites of corrupted metal pointed their long, threatening fingers down towards him.

There was nowhere to go. No haven.

Whatever Lister decided to do, he had to do it fast. He grabbed his boots from the locker behind his head, and laced them frantically, keeping his eyes fixed on the ceiling. Suddenly the area of roof just above his head started to give way. Lister rolled off the bunk, taking the mattress with him, and swung into the bunk below.

Within minutes stalactites had begun to tongue down through the roof of the new bunk. He guessed that he had about two minutes before the acid came through.

But two minutes to do what? To go where? Up was unthinkable. Out? No way. No choice, then. Down.

He ripped at the wooden slats underneath the lower bunk's mattress. If only he could get down to the maintenance deck below, at least it would buy him some time. He piled the slats behind him and peered down into the hole.

Lister really didn't expect to find an access hatch leading straight down to the maintenance decks smack under the bunks, but it still surprised him when he didn't. He was shocked. He was offended. True, the chances of there being one were tiny – why would anyone in their right mind build an access hatch underneath two bunks? What for, apart from providing a handy escape route for any space-farer who happened to get caught in a particularly nasty downpour of acid rain? But on the other hand, there *had* to be one – otherwise there was no way out. Otherwise, he was dead. So when there wasn't one, frankly, he was out-raged. He was furious. There could have been a below-bunk access hatch for dozens of reasons. A long-forgotten disused cleaning hatch; an air-conditioning access point; a ventilation shaft – the craft was crammed full of them, why couldn't there be one here?

But there wasn't.

There was nothing but featureless flooring.

He scratched futilely at the smooth metal, then smashed three wooden slats to splinters without even marking the doubly-reinforced floor that separated him from the mainten-ance deck. Now what?

Lister jammed his back against the corner of the bunk and crammed his knees against his chest. He wrapped his knuckles around one of the wooden slats by his side, and jabbed it up into the metal base of the bunk above, at a forty-five degree angle from his body. Then he jabbed again. And again.

The slat slid through the softened steel, and the acid from the bunk above began to trickle down into the feet end of the lower bunk. Lister held the oxygen mask to his face and jabbed again, widening the drain hole above him.

He withdrew the blackened, smoking slat and jabbed again. More acid gushed in through the widening gap, melting its way towards the maintenance deck below.

There was nothing to do but wait and see which would give first – the base of the bunk above him, or the escape hole below.

There was a creaking sound, and the bunk ceiling lurched dangerously and ballooned down another two inches to-wards his head. He stabbed frantically at the floor, and wiggled the slat ferociously to increase the hole's diameter. Nine inches wide. Now, a foot. Still too small. Suddenly there was a screaming pain in his hand, in the fatty flesh between his thumb and forefinger. He held it up to his face. The acid had burnt straight through, leaving a smoking peephole. He could see through his hand.

The escape hole was fourteen, fifteen inches wide. He tossed the slat into the gap and waited for it to hit the deck below.

One little second.

Two little seconds.

Three little seconds.

Fou . . .

The wood hit the metal below.

Thirty or forty feet.

Without cushioning, a bone-breaking certainty.

He kicked the gap wider. His boot came away steaming and smouldering. The hole was three feet in diameter and growing.

He made his move. He wrapped the mattress he'd dragged from the upper bunk tightly around him, held the mattress from the lower bunk over his head, and leapt through the hole.

The lower mattress plugged the hole, giving him perhaps five seconds of protection as he plunged towards the pool of acid that was already working its way through the floor of the maintenance deck. He flung off the mattress that was curled around him and hurled it down to the smoking pool below. He landed on his back, winded, dazed and immobile. He looked up towards the ceiling, and saw three globules of acid dropping towards him.

He tried to twist right but his body refused to move. 'That was a hell of a fall,' it was saying. 'Let's rest here a while.'

Two of the drops cut pennycent holes in the mattress

centimetres from his groin. The third removed his left earlobe. Lister and his body had another meeting. Top of the agenda was a proposal to move, a.s.a.p. It was proposed by Lister, seconded by his body and the motion was carried by two votes to nil. He rolled on to his side as the temporary plug above finally gave and torrents of acid cascaded through the hole, crashing on to the mattress, barely a yard from his gasping, mono-lobed body.

He picked himself up, and started to stagger down the length of the maintenance deck, looking for something, anything, that might offer some form of protection. He ripped the first-aid kit from the wall and pulled out the bottle of medicinal alcohol. He poured a generous measure over the hole in his hand, dabbed his left ear and drank the rest.

Then he lumbered into the Engineering Supply Area. He slammed a pallet on to the forks of one of the three orange stacker trucks and piled it high with oxyacetylene canisters, blowtorches and welding gear.

He glanced up at the ceiling. It would hold for fifteen minutes. Twenty at best. After that there was nowhere else on board to shelter. There was no more down. The only way was out. Out in the acid storm.

For the next quarter of an hour he blowtorched steel doors from their hinges, ripped steel piping from the walls and welded together a jerry-built acid raincoat. He raced back into the engineering store and tried on the various welding helmets. He discovered that if he crammed his head into the smallest, he was then able to wear a medium size on top of it, and a large one on top of that.

In the howling, metallic silence imposed by three steel helmets, he climbed into the suit. Six feet of solid steel on top of him, plus his helmets, plus the metal-piping sleeves and trousers – this would give him at least fifteen minutes of protection while he scampered out of the craft and sought out some kind of refuge.

Only one problem.

He couldn't move.

He couldn't even nearly move.

Stupid.

Stupid, stupid, stupid.

How could he have wasted fifteen precious minutes constructing this immobile monstrosity, without realizing the damned thing was going to be too heavy to move?

He climbed out of the suit and kicked it.

Now he had a broken toe to add to his troubles.

He looked up at the ceiling. The stalactites were already forming.

He tottered over to the viewport window and stared out into the storm. He registered with a shock that the rain was local. Totally local. It just swirled around the small basin in which the *Starbug* had come to rest. Over the crest of the hill, the sky was clear. The crest of the hill was hardly five hundred yards away.

Surely he could get the damned thing to move five hundred yards. A third of a mile. Come *on*. Think.

His eyes swept the room

On the second pass, they stopped on the stacker truck.

Lister jumped into the driver's seat and started up the motor. He jabbed the truck's forks under the two arms of the suit, and pulled back the lift lever. Slowly, the truck hauled the suit off the ground.

He leapt down from the vehicle, raced back to the supply store and returned with a reel of steel cable. As the floor around him hissed and spluttered, he welded the cable to the stacker truck's twin joystick controls and fed it through the sleeves of the armour-plated raincoat.

He flipped the bay doors over to manual and typed in the opening code. They remained closed. He tried again. Nothing. Acid fizzled down the doorway. The electrics were shot to hell.

There was a rumble from the far end of the maintenance deck, and a whole twenty yard section of ceiling smashed to the floor.

Lister was completely unaware of the tears that coursed down his grease-streaked cheeks, and of the insane babble that chundered from his lips as he raced back and climbed into the suit. He yanked the left-hand cable, and his neck snapped forward as the stacker truck lurched back and reversed fifty yards, slamming into the rear bulkhead. The suit tottered on the forks.

If he fell now . . . if he fell and lay motionless on the floor as the acid swirled in from the deck above . . .

Gently, he tugged the right-hand cable, and the truck moved forward. He tugged again. The electric motor whined to maximum pitch. The truck gathered speed.

It screamed towards the bay doors, supporting Lister in his reinforced steel suit at the front.

Acid drizzled delta patterns down the bay doors as Lister and the stacker truck smashed through the weakened structure and out into the eye of the acid storm.

The truck's caterpillar tracks juddered over the basin's jagged terrain, gradually picking up the speed it had lost on impact with the doors.

When Lister came to, he was half way up the basin's incline. Over the peak of the hill before him, he could see the clear sky hanging a lazy blue over the next valley.

Two hundred yards to go.

He scanned the ground. Bizarrely, insanely, it seemed to be composed of broken bottles. He looked around. The whole of the mountain appeared to be glass. Millions upon millions of glass bottles, all shapes, all sizes, but only one colour – green. In fact, as he looked through the acid mist, he realized that all the mountains looming around him were likewise constructed of green bottles.

What was this place?

Overnight Ice Ages, acid rain that cut through steel, and a landscape made entirely of glass.

Nice place for a holiday.

There was a muffled bang from behind him, and the stacker truck jerked and stopped.

Lister craned round to see why. The truck was scarcely recognizable – a melting mess of metal and plastic. He tugged on the right-hand cable with idiot optimism. The cable snapped and slithered through the sleeve of his suit, gouging a thin red line of pain along the length of his arm.

He hung from the forks of the truck as the rain rodded down and bounced, sizzling, from his suit. Helpless and immobile, he swung like a giant metal pub sign.

He tried to lift his arms. Impossible. The suit was too heavy. So he just swung there, wondering how long it would take him to die when the rain eventually got through, and how much of him would be left for the others to find.

THREE

Rimmer, Kryten and the Cat disembarked from the shuttle-bus mid-afternoon the previous Tuesday and staggered surreally up the metal ramp to the Drive room.

'Look, stay calm,' said Rimmer, manically pacing up and down in front of the vast screen. 'It'll take Holly ten seconds to work out what to do, and then we'll be out of here.'

'Does anybody want toast?' came a small tinny voice.

They turned, and saw the Toaster perched on top of a stack of terminals.

'No!' they screamed in unison.

'How about a crumpet?'

Kryten tapped in Holly's activation sequence, and handed voice command over to Rimmer.

'On,' said Rimmer. 'Holly – we're being sucked into a Black Hole – how do we get out?'

The giant screen flitted and flickered, before Holly's image assembled in a mad, cubist parody of itself. His chin was where his forehead should be, his mouth was replaced by an ear and his nose pointed skywards on top of his balding pate.

'Jlkjhfsyuhjdk,' he said.

'What?'

'Mcujnkljfibnnbcbcy.'

'There's something wrong,' Rimmer yelled. 'Turn him off! We're wasting his run-time.'

Kryten slammed the flat of his palm on the keypad, and Holly fizzled away. 'What's wrong with him?'

Rimmer and the Cat shared shrugs.

'It's the dilation effect. His terminals are spread all over the ship, they're all operating in different time zones. While it's midnight Monday for his central processing unit, it's a week on Thursday for his Random Access Memory. Anybody fancy a muffin?'

'Will you shut up?' said Rimmer. 'What the smeg are we going to do?'

'What happens,' the Cat tilted his head to one side, 'if we get sucked into this Black Hole? Is that a bad thing?'

'A Black Hole is an unstable star that's collapsed into itself. Its gravitational pull is so enormous that nothing can escape – light, time, nothing. How about a potato cake?'

'Look, will you kindly shut your grill?' Rimmer spat. 'I'm trying to think.'

'Can't we just fly through it,' the Cat ventured, 'and out the other side?'

'Nice idea,' the Toaster scoffed. 'And perhaps we can stop off at the souvenir shop in the middle and buy various Black Hole memorabilia.'

'Black Holes have souvenir shops in the middle?' The Cat grinned hopefully.

'He's taking the smeg,' snapped Rimmer. 'Will you stop talking to that cheap piece of junk? We've got to work out how to get out of here.'

'Cheap!?' the Toaster snorted, 'I'm £19.99, plus tax!'

'There's no way out, is there?' said Kryten. 'We're going to duh duh duh duh duh duh duh duh . . .' he smacked his head into a monitor housing and cleared the seizure loop, '. . . die.'

'Not necessarily,' said the Toaster, with all the smugness he could muster.

'If you don't shut up,' Rimmer threatened, 'I'm going to unplug you.'

'You don't want to know how to get out of this mess, then?'

Rimmer spun on his heels. 'Oh, and you know, do you?'

The Toaster's browning knob spun from side to side. 'Maybe,' he said enigmatically. 'Who's for a toasted muffin?'

'How the smegging smeg would a Toaster know how to get out of a Black Hole?'

'Technically, we're not in a Black Hole. Not yet. We haven't passed the event horizon.'

'What's an event horizon?' asked the Cat.

'Let's start at the beginning.' The Toaster adjusted his bread width to maximum, and back again. 'A Black Hole isn't an object, it's a region – a rip in the fabric of space/time. It starts off as a massive sun. When the sun dies, the enormous gravitational pull at its centre drags all the matter in the star back into itself. A medium-sized sun becomes a neutron star – a star whose molecules are packed as tightly as possible. However, if the weight of the sun is great enough, it overrides the 'exclusion principle' which states that, in normal circumstances, two electrons can't occupy the same energy space, and so the star continues collapsing. Eventually the gravitational drag at the centre becomes so colossal, the escape velocity – the speed you have to achieve to get out – reaches 186,282 miles per second. Which is lightspeed. And since lightspeed is the speed limit for the universe, nothing can escape – not even light. It becomes a sort of giant galactic vacuum cleaner, sucking in everything in its range – even Time. That's why Time at the front of the ship is running more slowly than Time at the back. The closer you get to it, the more you feel the effects of its pull, and the event horizon is the point of no return. So.' He paused. 'Who's for a hot cross bun?'

Kryten shook his head. 'Did anyone follow that?'

'I was with it,' said the Cat, 'to the point where he said: "Let's start at the beginning." And I didn't pick it up again until he got to the hot cross bun part.'

Rimmer strode across to the Toaster. 'Explain this, mi-laddo: how does a novelty kitchen appliance suddenly get to know so much about Black Holes?'

'I have a voracious appetite for reading,' said the Toaster.

'Holly told you this, didn't he? After he got his IQ back, but before he turned himself off.'

The Toaster's grill glowed red. 'Maybe.'

'Did he happen to mention how to get out of one?'

'That depends,' said the Toaster.

'Depends on what?'

'Depends on whether or not anyone wants any toast.'

Twenty minutes later they sat in a horseshoe, munching their way through the towering piles of assorted toasted delights. Kryten, who had to eat Rimmer's share, was beginning to feel he needed to change his stomach bag, and the Cat was becoming quietly hysterical about what effect consuming thirty-four pieces of toast was going to have on his waistline.

'For godsakes, are you *insane*?' Rimmer snapped. 'How much toast are you expecting them to eat?'

'Here's how to get out of a Black Hole. Providing you accelerate into it, and achieve sufficient speed before you pass the event horizon, the additional acceleration provided by the gravitational pull means you can break the light barrier, loop round the singularity at the Black Hole's centre and be travelling fast enough to swoop out again.'

'I thought,' said Kryten through a mouthful of toast, 'that as soon as we pass the event horizon, we get crushed.'

'Not if we're travelling faster-than-light. We inherit a whole new set of physical laws.'

'So when we get out,' Rimmer frowned, 'we're travelling faster-than-light, yes?'

The Toaster inclined its bread-tray in a nod.

'How do we stop? Lister is stuck on that planet, starving

to death. If we finally draw to a halt a hundred and thirty galaxies south-sou'-west, that's not going to be tremendously helpful. Assuming Holly was right about all this and we survive, we've got to rescue him – how do we stop?'

'Well now,' the Toaster twirled his browning knob from side to side. 'Wouldn't you like to know?'

'Yes we would,' said the Cat politely.

'Well, for your part the answer's simple.'

'What?'

'Keep eating the toast.'

The Cat groaned and reached for his thirty-fifth slice.

FOUR

Lister tried to move his arm again. This time it moved. Not much, but a little. He tried it again. This time it moved a little more. His suit was melting. And the more it melted, the lighter it got. This was good, and this was bad.

It was good, because at least, at some point soon, he'd be mobile again, and able to make a break for the crest of the hill. It was bad because he had no idea whether or not he could get to the top of the hill before the suit melted completely.

He angled up his elbows so he slid from between the forks and crunched on to the broken glass of the incline.

He found he could lift his feet an inch or so off the ground, and he was able to make small, faltering steps forward. He began the slowest race of his life.

His thighs throbbed. His shoulders ached. With each step the suit got lighter and his pace got quicker. Lister lost all sense of his body. He was just a pair of lungs, scorched and straining. He struck for the top of the hill.

The suit was light, now. Frighteningly light. He felt almost naked. Then he realized, even if he got to the top, even if he scrambled free of the rain, the suit would still be melting – he still had to get it off.

And then it was over. He lunged over the brow and started clattering down the other side. Even as he fell he tugged at the inner straps of his suit, and hurled the smoking plates away. His fall was broken by a bank of bottles. There was no triumph. There was no joy, no celebration as he flung the final piece down the mountain, just a horrible aching weariness, and an irresistible desire to sleep. He stumbled along the glass mountain ridge and found a cave – hardly a cave, more a bolthole, no more than six feet deep and four feet high.

He crawled inside, curled up baby tight, and slept.

Less than twenty minutes later Lister woke up. The sound that roused him was the thick, wet sound of rainfall. He couldn't bear it. The acid storm must have moved across to this side of the valley.

He uncurled himself from his foetal position and shimmied on his bare elbows to the lip of the bolthole.

He was wrong – it wasn't acid rain.

But it wasn't normal rain, either.

It was black.

Torrents of thick black syrup drooled over the mountainside. Lister reached out a quivering hand and caught a glob of the viscous goo in his palm. He sniffed it. He tasted it. He spat it out.

Oil.

It was raining oil.

Still, Lister thought, oil rain was a damn sight better than acid rain. At least it wouldn't kill him. He felt quite cheered. Weatherwise, things were brightening up. Hell, if the trend continued, by evening it would probably be doing something as bland and normal as raining tomato soup, or snowing beach balls.

He crawled back into the shelter of his bolthole and tried to get some sleep. But he couldn't. Not even Lister could sleep through an earthquake. Especially when it was happening directly underneath him.

The ground sneered open, and a foot-wide chasm snaked towards him as he scrambled backwards out of the bolthole. He shielded his eyes from the lashing oil, and watched as zigzag splits powered across the splintering landscape. Millions of bottles crashed and tumbled into the ground's rumbling gullet.

Lister ran. He had no idea where he was running or whether there was any point. He leapt over sudden chasms, dodged past small avalanches of bottles, and scrambled and scraped his way to the top of the next peak.

The black sky hurled javelins of oil at his shivering, wretched body as he crumbled to his knees, and skidded and slithered into the next basin. The oil weighted his locks, and the wind whipped them across his face as oily fingers jabbed down his throat, forcing him to gag for air. Blind and choking, he staggered across the basin. He wiped the worst of the oil from his eyes with what remained of his T-shirt, and blinked up against the hammering rain. He wasn't alone. Looming on the horizon were the colossal silhouettes of five faces. Or, rather, five half-faces, which thrust out of the sea of garbage as if they were seeking one last breath before they were claimed by the refuse.

Lister knew them. He recognized them all. George Washington, Thomas Jefferson, Abraham Lincoln, Theodore Roosevelt and perhaps the greatest American President of all time, Elaine Salinger.

Lister hauled his aching body across the basin and took shelter under George Washington's nose. He knew where he was, now. Mount Rushmore. South Dakota.

This hell-hole of a planet, this uninhabitable pit of filth, was Earth.

Lister laughed. He'd made it. He was back home. He laughed too long and too hard, a dangerous laugh that danced with insanity. Everything that had kept him going, the goal that had given his life meaning, was suddenly, farcically, achieved.

This was Earth. He was home.

But what had happened? What had been done to the place?

The answer was fairly obvious even to a half-insane, sick, oil-sodden astro on the brink of starvation.

Earth had been turned into a garbage dump.

He had no idea what had torn it from its orbit and sent it hurtling to the outer reaches of the universe, but the fact that this was Earth, and it had been converted into a planet-sized refuse tip was undeniable.

But did that explain why the weather was haywire? Only partly. The more Lister thought about it, the more things seemed to click into place. Right from the moment he'd first arrived, from the moment he'd first emerged from *Starbug* and the arctic winds had whipped and toyed with him, whimsically changing direction every few seconds, tossing him up in the air and dashing his body into snow banks; right from that moment, the weather had been trying to kill him. There was the acid rain, the sizzling downpour which only fell in the basin where his ship had crashed. Then, after his miraculous escape to the bolthole, the quake had forced him out into the open, into the suffocating, cloying treacle of the oil storm.

Had exhaustion made him paranoid? Were his thoughts being twisted by hunger and fatigue?

Or was he right?

Was the Earth waging a war against him? Against him, personally?

But why?

If the Earth did have some kind of inexplicable, innate intelligence, why would it want to kill him? What had he ever done to the Earth? Why should it despise him?

Then he knew.

He'd done everything to Earth. He'd crucified it. He was a member of the human race, part of the species that had spread like bacteria over the planet; killing its rich, teeming life; consuming its wealth; finally rendering it fit only for use as a dumping ground for all humanity's garbage.

That's what he was: a single cell of bacteria. A plague germ. And the planet's auto-immune system was rejecting him.

No. The idea was preposterous. It was insane. Hunger and weariness were fuelling his paranoia. The Earth didn't have an intelligence. It didn't 'live'. It was a ball of stone.

He stood in the shelter of George Washington's left nostril and started to compose a list of humankind's many magnificent achievements. For some inexplicable reason, the first thing that popped into his addled head was the musical toilet-roll dispenser, before a sheet of lightning ignited the rain, sending a curtain of flame sweeping across the face of the mountain, scorching black all five presidents, and sending Lister hurtling back into the far recess of Washington's nasal passage.

A second sheet ignited, blasting Lister out of the nose, sending him scurrying across the mounds of garbage, which were alive with rivers of fire.

'Do it, then,' Lister screamed. 'Come on – kill me.' His fingers dug into the putrefying sludge and flung it skywards. 'Kill me! Come on, what are you waiting for?'

Surrounded by lakes of fire and exploding geysers of oil, Lister screamed and ranted at the Earth.

He ducked his head under his arm as two bursts of flaming rain strafed either side of the mound he was standing on.

Lister collapsed to his knees on the smouldering garbage. 'I could do something,' he sobbed. 'I could help. I could . . . If you let me live, I could start to make it right again. I could . . .' He blacked out.

As consciousness slowly percolated back into his body, he was aware of the rain. He groaned and raised his head. It was rain rain. Real rain. H_2O. The stuff of life.

He rolled on his back and opened his mouth. All around him, tails of smoke wriggled skyward from the few puddles of fire that still remained.

He drank in the rain. He let it cascade over him, cleansing his wounds, refreshing him, uplifting him. He'd rolled on to his belly to pick himself up, when he saw it.

Inches from where his right hand had fallen, out of the rubble, out of the garbage, out of the stinking mire, poked a single branch – a small, stunted tree with a crop of green berries.

Lister plucked off the fruit and started to eat. They were olives. He wept.

He cupped his hands and collected some rainwater which he sprinkled, tenderly, over the tree. It seemed a simple enough equation: if he looked after the olive tree, the olive tree would look after him.

He heard a movement in the rubble behind him. He turned. He wasn't the only living creature on the planet. There was at least one other. The creature joined him by the olive tree. It was one of the oldest of Earth's inhabitants. It had been there long before man, and would probably be there long after. It was a cockroach.

But a big cockroach.

A very big cockroach.

This cockroach could have played Nose Tackle for the London Jets in their all-time best season.

It was a mother of a cockroach.

This cockroach was eight feet long.

Lister moved slowly. Very slowly. He rocked back on his rump, drew his knees up to his chest, and with a sudden, swift movement brought both his boots down on the roach's side. There was a sickening thud, and the cockroach lay on its back, rocking helplessly, its mandibles opening and closing in shock.

Lister ferreted among the rubble for something lethal, and found a long thin shard of glass. He stood over the writhing beast, his hands raised over his head. The glass flashed down towards the soft underbelly.

Then he stopped.

He flung the glass blade away, then stooped and lifted the cockroach back on to its feet.

The cockroach made a series of curious clicking noises, but made no attempt to move away.

'Here,' Lister plucked an olive from the branch and held it out for the cockroach to take. 'I'm a reformed species. We're going straight. No more killing. Here. Take it.'

The giant insect ignored the olive. Instead, it nuzzled among the rubble and started to eat the garbage.

Lister sat there chewing his olives, watching the mammoth roach consume the refuse. It seemed like a hell of a good deal to him.

The meal over, Lister decided to head back to *Starbug*, to rake through the ruins and see if there was anything left he might salvage. As he walked across the rubble he realized the cockroach was following. He turned and made some shooing movements with his arms. The cockroach clicked and whistled and carried on following him. Lister broke into a trot. So did the cockroach.

Finally Lister slowed and stopped. The cockroach caught up with him, slithered to its belly, pushed its head in the crook of Lister's knees, and nudged the back of his legs. Lister stumbled and straightened, and tried to fend it off. The cockroach nudged again. Lister walked sideways, his arms out straight, trying to keep it at bay. The cockroach butted him a third time, and Lister fell full length across its back. It raised its belly from the ground and started to waddle forward.

It wanted to carry him.

And when an eight-foot cockroach wants to give you a ride, Lister reasoned, probably the smartest thing to do was to let it.

He changed his mind five seconds later. Just after he splayed his legs over its back, and tucked his fingers under the rim of its armour plating, the cockroach took off.

The view would probably have been staggering from two hundred feet, but you had to have your eyes open to appreciate it fully, and Lister had no intention of doing that.

He shouted and screamed and tried to steer the cockroach earthwards, but his benign captor had set its mind on its destination. It was taking him home to meet its folks.

Half-way up a tall bottle mountain, they landed.

The twenty or so members of the roach's clan surrounded them, whistling and clicking and rubbing their hindlegs together in insect delight.

Plainly, Lister was a hit.

One of the roaches retired to the back of the cave, and dragged a half-rotten sofa carcass to Lister's feet. The family looked on in mute anticipation.

Lister did something then he wouldn't have done in any other circumstances whatsoever. He started to eat a sofa.

This seemed to go down well. There was a cacophony of whirrs, clicks and whistles, and the cockroaches circled in delight.

'Well, it's been absolutely wonderful,' Lister found himself saying. 'Terrific place you've got here,' he said to the mother roach. 'And you serve a wicked rotting sofa. But I really must be going.' He nodded, threw in a few clicks and whistles for good measure, and climbed on the first roach's back. It waddled speedily down the length of the cave, and flung itself over the mountain side.

When Lister opened his eyes, he found to his alarm he was flying in formation, at the head of a swarm of cockroaches. Ten to his right, ten to his left. And as they flew down the middle of the valley, more and more were emerging from their caves, and taking up their place behind him.

He looked behind him at the swelling swarm of buzzing roaches and yelped like a bronco-busting rodeo star.

By the simple expedient of consuming a tiny portion of a

decomposing three-piece suite, Lister had been anointed King of the Cockroaches.

And together, Lister and his loyal subjects were going to start putting the planet back together again.

FIVE

The colossal cone-shaped jet housings on *Red Dwarf*'s under-belly screamed and whined in their losing battle against the irresistible drag of the Black Hole's gravitational pull. Sud-denly, as one, they ceased their pointless protestations and puttered into silence.

All resistance gone, the massive mining vessel catapulted into the blackness towards the event horizon. Lazily, the jet housings started to rotate – 45 degrees, 90 degrees, 120 degrees, until finally they had described a full half-circle. The rotation motors wound down, and the stabilizing bolts cracked loudly into place. All the while, the ship howled faster, ever faster towards the lightless unknown.

The jets fired up again. Thousands of hydrogen explosions harnessed the raw energy of the universe and thrust the ship forward, to the brink of demi-lightspeed, and beyond.

'Event horizon: two minutes and closing.' Kryten pulled the safety webbing over his shoulders and inflated his crash suit.

'Did I tell you about spaghettification?' said the Toaster.

The Cat lurched upright from the couch bolted to the corner of the anti-grav chamber. 'What's spaghettification?'

'I didn't mention it, then?'

'One minute fifty.'

'No you didn't. What is it?' said Rimmer.

'Well,' said the Toaster, 'when you enter a Black Hole, an effect takes place, called "spaghettification". I thought I'd mentioned it, but obviously I didn't. Anyway, just so you know, it'll happen fairly shortly.'

'One minute forty.'

The Cat lay back on the couch and stared up at the ceiling. 'So what the hell is it?'

'Spaghettification. Let me guess,' said Rimmer. 'I can see only two options: one – due to the bizarre effects of the intense gravitational pull, and because we're entering a region of time and space where the laws of physics no longer apply, we all of us inexplicably develop an irresistible urge to consume vast amounts of a certain wheat-based Italian noodle conventionally served with Parmesan cheese; or two – we, the crew, get turned into spaghetti. I have a feeling we can eliminate option one.'

'You're absolutely correct,' said the Toaster. 'You all become sort of spaghettified.'

'Forty seconds,' counted Kryten.

'Then what happens?'

'Well, then you become de-spaghettified,' said the Toaster, and added: 'hopefully. Holly was a bit vague about that part. Still, he didn't seem to think it was terribly important.'

'I get turned into spaghetti,' the Cat's eyebrows leapt to the top of his forehead, 'and that's not important?'

'Thirty seconds.'

The Cat tried vainly to lift his head from the cranium support – he had a major collection of dirty looks he wanted to sling at the Toaster – but G-force pinned him, immobile, to the couch, so he slung them at the ceiling instead. 'Is it too late to change this plan? I have no idea what well-dressed spaghetti is wearing this year.'

'Ten seconds.'

'Ten seconds?' Rimmer was equally immobile. 'What happened to twenty seconds?'

'I forgot to say twenty seconds,' Kryten apologised. 'I was listening to the Cat.' His eyes flitted to the scanner scope again. 'Oh, sorry – apologizing for not saying "twenty seconds" has now made me miss saying "five seconds".'

'So how long now?' yelled Rimmer.

'Err . . . no seconds,' said Kryten. And he was right.

The combination of jet thrust and gravitational pull forced *Red Dwarf* through the lightspeed barrier the moment it hit the event horizon. To all intents and purposes, the ship no longer existed in the universe of its origin. It shrugged off Newton, Einstein, Oppenheimer and Chien Lau, and subscribed to a completely new set of physical laws.

They were in the Black Hole, heading for its centre. Heading for the ring of light that swirled suicidally around the spinning singularity – the core of the dead star where all the matter sucked in by the Black Hole was compressed to infinity. And they were heading there at such a speed, they were overtaking light.

The Cat's body started to spill off the couch in every direction. Long, thin strands of what had formerly been him slithered across the floor and intertwined with the strands that had been Kryten and Rimmer and the Toaster. The anti-grav chamber became a sea of heaving, screaming, living linguini.

Everyone became part of everyone else.

They threaded together and formed a new whole. They weren't four, they were one. The particles that had once formed Rimmer's intelligence, in a blinding flash of empathetic insight, suddenly became aware of the desperate, monumental importance of toast. Instantaneously, the strands that had been the Toaster were conscious of the overriding necessity for dressing well and having a really terrific haircut. The vermicelli that was now the Cat tasted the feeling of being mechanical, and knew with unshakeable certainty that Silicon Heaven existed, and the best way to get there was through diligent hoovering. Simultaneously, the macaroni that was Kryten knew what it was like to be Rimmer. He understood what it was like to have had those parents, that childhood, that career, that life. It was impossible to scream, but that's what Kryten was trying to do.

The ship was no longer a ship, it was a huge tachyon, a superlight particle, howling through a universe outside our own. It was a pool, then a wave, then a ball, then a dot, then it had no shape – it just *was*.

The huge mound of spaghetti slithered across space/time and peered into the face of the spinning white disc.

'Look,' said a part of the spaghetti that was mostly Rimmer. In the centre of the spinning light were six inter-locking coils, like fibre optics, but of a size beyond size. The immense hollow cables twisted and undulated like the snakes on the Gorgons' heads. The tubes were of colours that had no meaning to the human eye. They spun and swirled in a timeless dance of beauty.

Not for the first time, Rimmer cursed himself for not bringing his camcorder. 'What is it?' he said, but before anyone could answer the ball of speed the ship had itself become slung around the singularity.

It bounced off the sudden cushion of anti-gravity it met there, then, like a swimmer who has dived too deep, lunged desperately for the surface, for the event horizon, for the known universe. It struck upwards, fighting off the gravity that tried to suck it back to its core at the speed of light.

Then the lightspeed drag of gravity cancelled out the lightspeed momentum of the ship, and *Red Dwarf* regained its physical form. Suddenly it was travelling at a relative speed of less than two hundred thousand miles an hour towards the event horizon. The metal of the bulkheads buckled and groaned. Leering cracks ripped through the metalwork and zigzagged insanely down the port side.

The ship started to slow.

Plasti-domes splintered and shattered. Steel mining rigs were wrenched protesting from the ship's back and swirled helplessly down into the singularity to be crushed into infinity.

Still the ship slowed.

The jet housings started to creak, and then, all over the vessel's belly, one by one, pinion rods snarled and snapped, and the housings came away and tumbled into the infinite abyss.

Still the ship slowed.

Half the propulsion jets were lost. Hydrogen fuel pumped from the jet carcasses and flooded into the relentless void. Like a harpooned whale, the wounded craft pitched wildly for the surface, for light, for life.

Slower still.

Another crop of housings moaned and warped and fell away.

Still slower.

And slower.

And slo–o–o–o–o–ower.

Relatively, the ship was moving at barely fifty miles an hour.

Then thirty.

Twenty.

Ten.

The Black Hole had just to claim one more jet housing to tip the balance, to drag the ship below lightspeed and trap it forever in its bleak embrace.

It didn't.

With the suddenness of an infant's birth scream, *Red Dwarf* exploded through the event horizon and into the known universe.

Free of the worst of the cloying quicksand grip of the dead star's interior, the limping vessel peaked back up to lightspeed for an instant of an instant before the final remnants of gravitational drag slewed it to a halt on the very periphery of the Black Hole's influence.

The de-spaghettified Cat looked down his body and checked it was all there. It seemed to be.

He unbuckled himself from the couch and stood on uneasy legs. 'Everyone OK?'

Kryten nodded, still too nauseous to speak.

'What was that?' said Rimmer. 'In the middle of the spinning light. Those tubes.'

'The Omni-zone,' said the Toaster. 'Holly predicted we'd find that. It confirms his theory.'

'What theory?'

'The theory that there are six other universes, and all their gateways converge at the centre of a singularity.'

'There are six other universes?' said Rimmer.

'So Holly reckoned,' said the Toaster. 'He also believed that our universe is the bad apple. It's the cock-up universe. Something went wrong with our Big Bang and made Time move in the wrong direction, that's why nothing makes sense.'

'I'll tell you something that *does* make sense,' The Cat staggered over to the Toaster. 'You made me eat seventy-three rounds of buttered toast. Check that: seven, three,' he slapped his rump. 'I feel like I'm carrying around a third buttock in my pants. And I just want you to know this – I want you to live with this for the rest of your life – you,' he jabbed the Toaster with his long-nailed forefinger, 'you make real lousy toast. It's cold, it's burnt, *and* it's soggy.'

The Toaster twirled his browning knob defiantly. 'Hey – what d'you expect for \$£19.99 plus tax? Conversation, quantum theory *and* good toast?'

SIX

The bulging, warped cargo-bay doors refused to yield to electronic command, but they did yield to the massive volley from the mining lasers, which ripped them from their hinges and sent them spinning off into space.

The two transport craft taxied along the take-off ramp and out through the yawning bay. They banked left and skirted *Red Dwarf*'s mangled hull, before swooping down into the planet's atmosphere.

When they hit the thick grey cloud bank, the craft peeled off. *White Giant*, with Rimmer and the Cat, took the northern hemisphere, and *Blue Midget*, piloted by Kryten and the Toaster, zoomed south.

Rimmer stared unblinking into the screen of the infra-red scanner scope as *White Giant* swept across the surface of the planet. 'What's happened to the snow? Where's the Ice Age gone?'

The Cat pushed aside the dangling furry dice and peered through the murk of the Drive window. 'What is all that stuff down there? That mountain – it's shining.'

Rimmer looked over his shoulder. 'Looks like glass.'

The Cat increased the magnification factor, and they stared at the mountain ranges of green bottles looming below them. 'Bottles? What is this place?'

Rimmer shrugged and turned back to the heat scanner. Nothing. He voice-activated the sonar scan for signs of movement. Still nothing. 'This is hopeless. We could fly around for years and not find him. One man on a planet this size? It's like looking for a needle in a haystack. No – it's worse. It's like trying to find a hidden can of lager at a student party.'

'If he's still alive, we'll find him. He'll have left some kind of signal.'

'Twenty-four days he's been down there. Twenty-four days without food. He may be too weak to signal.'

Kryten slipped *Blue Midget* into autodrive, and squeezed between the towering stacks of freshly baked bread that occupied eighty per cent of the living space in the craft's operational mid-section. He lifted the dozen or so brown loaves that covered the scanner screen, and piled them on top of a rack of pallets bulging with french sticks.

'Twenty-four days without food,' said the Toaster. 'I only pray we've brought enough bread.'

Kryten suppressed a sigh and wondered how he'd ever been persuaded to pair up with a novelty kitchen appliance.

For thirty-six hours they tracked back and forth across the surface of the planet, hoping for a heat reading on the infrared scan or some sign of movement from the sonar. At five o'clock, on the evening of the second day, they got one.

The signal originated from a small island, measuring barely sixty miles across, three thousand miles south of the equator. Small pockets of movement registered on the sonar. The infra-red confirmed life. Quite a lot of life.

Kryten looked at his watch, then spun off his ear, and spun it back on again, as was his habit when pensive. It wasn't possible to contact Rimmer and the Cat for another three hours. They were on different sides of the planet, and the only way to communicate was to bounce radio signals off the orbiting *Red Dwarf*, which was in the correct position just once every four hours. He looked at his watch again, tapped it several times, and made his decision.

Blue Midget's retro jets blasted deep smoking potholes into the island's swampy surface, and the landing legs telescoped down into the quagmire, sinking dozens of feet before they found purchase. The hatchway opened and Kryten leaned outside to scan the terrain. He sniffed gingerly at the air to sample the atmosphere for chemical analysis. Instantly, his olfactory system went into massive overload, and his nose exploded loudly.

He clucked impatiently, unscrewed the popped nose from his face and fished inside his utility pouch for a spare. He tore off the plastic packing and clicked it into place. He twisted the adjustment screw to turn the smell sense down to minimum and tentatively inhaled once more. His second nose went the way of the first. He had no more noses. He'd have to wait until he got back to *Red Dwarf*. In the meantime, he was noseless, which was probably just as well.

He staggered out on to the ramp and threw the hover dinghy into the steaming marsh, then ducked back into the craft to reappear with the Toaster strapped to his back.

'Careful!' yelled the Toaster. 'I'm only $£19.99. I'm not waterproof.'

A thought entered Kryten's CPU, but it was a very cruel thought, and unworthy of a mechanical, and not the kind of thought that would get him into Silicon Heaven, so he reluctantly dismissed it.

They sat in the hover dinghy, and Kryten checked the remote scanner. He wrenched back the joystick, and the dinghy rasped off, bouncing across the steaming swamp in the direction of the signal's source.

The Cat was beginning to panic. He'd gone almost two hours without a bath, or even a light shower. He was beginning to smell like a human. He snapped the controls over to automatic and shimmied off to the changing cubicle. 'I'm out of here, Buddy,' he said, and flicked quickly through his emergency travel wardrobe, which contained only his top one hundred indispensable suits, and selected his seventh new outfit of the afternoon.

Doing anything with the Cat was impossible. Rimmer looked up from his vigil at the scanner scope. 'Do you really, really, absolutely need another bath?'

The Cat didn't even consider the inquiry worthy of a reply. Human beings – what unhygienic, dirty, revolting little creatures they were. All their priorities were wrong: they had scant regard for relaxing and general quality snoozing time. Instead, they raced around, pell-mell, getting sweaty. It was no wonder they'd invented the wheel before they'd invented the twin-speed hairdrier with styling funnel. All their values were tip over tail. Still, what else could you expect from a race whose foremost scientists believed they evolved from slime? Ocean slime. They honestly held the opinion that their ancestors were mud. On the other hand, having spent some time with them, the Cat was inclined to agree.

He sculpted his face into an elegant sneer and disappeared into the shower cubicle.

The Cat was less than an hour into his ablutions when Rimmer spotted the *Starbug*.

'Look, there it is!'

The Cat dashed out of the cubicle, dripping underneath his bathrobe, his shower cap still in place.

'There!' Rimmer pointed at the magnified video image.

The Cat squelched into the Drive seat, looped *White Giant* over for an investigatory pass, and landed four hundred yards from the stricken craft.

Rimmer knew there was no one alive on board long before they scrambled over the dunes of glass and stood in front of the gutted *'bug*. The hatchway door was half-melted, and what was left was swinging creakily on one hinge. Inside, there was nothing; no fixtures, no fittings; just the rotting bulkhead. The roof was almost entirely missing, and cone-shaped holes gouged grotesque patterns in the three-foot-thick reinforced steel floor. The Cat curled a finger through a gap in the hull and pulled. A foot-square slab of metal came away easily and, when he tightened his fist, crumbled in his hand.

Rimmer looked down at the pile of ashes that lay on what remained of the sleeping couch.

'Found this on the Drive seat.' The Cat stood in the hatchway holding a melted fragment of Lister's leather deer-stalker.

'I've seen this before,' said Rimmer. 'One time on Callisto. Wiped out an entire settlement.'

'What is it?'

Rimmer looked up through the roof at the black knotted whisps of cloud threading across the grey sky. 'Acid rain,' he said, quietly.

Both of them knew they wouldn't find anything, but they decided to look around anyway. None of it made sense to Rimmer. He'd left Lister on an ice planet. Somehow, the ice had melted, exposing this strange terrain of geographical features apparently built from glass.

'Hey!'

Rimmer looked up. The Cat was standing high on a ridge overlooking the wreck of the *Starbug*.

'Look at this!' The Cat motioned for Rimmer to join him.

Rimmer picked his way up the jagged slope of the bottle mountain and looked down into the next basin.

Spread out below them were acres on acres of rich, verdant pasture land. Fields of wheat, fields of corn and fields of barley shimmered in the easy breeze of the sheltered valley. A long, thin stream of gurgling blue glinted its length. Trees, not very tall, but strong and young, sprouted in thick forests around the perimeter. And in the centre of the valley, in the heart of a vast olive grove, smoke curled from the chimney stack of a small homestead.

'There.'

Rimmer couldn't make out what the Cat was pointing at for some moments: his eyesight wasn't nearly as keen. Then he saw it. Distantly, in a thin rectangular patch of brown, a tiny figure was dragging a handmade plough across a half-furrowed field.

'It's Lister. It's got to be.'

They half slid, half tumbled down into the valley, and ran across the fields towards the figure. When they were two hundred yards away, they realized they were wrong. It was a human, but it wasn't Lister. It was an old man, grey-haired and slightly bent. More than a little hard of hearing, too, because he didn't respond to any of Rimmer's shouts until they were almost on him.

He swivelled and looked at them, his fingers toying idly with his long, braided silver beard. He had the strong muscle tone and weathered skin of a farmer who's spent a lifetime in the fields. He was fit and strong, but he had to be at least sixty, maybe more. He gazed at them for a while from under the thick, furry white caterpillars of his eyebrows, then he mopped his brow with a leathery forearm and turned back to his plough.

'Old man!' Rimmer panted. 'We're looking for someone.'

The man stopped, but didn't turn.

'A friend of ours. Crashed just over the hill.' The Cat pointed, but the old man didn't look. Instead, with his back still to them, he performed a passable impersonation of Rimmer's voice.

'I'll be back,' the old man said. 'Trust meeeeeee.' He turned and pulled off his cap. He swept a liver-spotted hand through the remaining wisps of silver on his pate.

Rimmer crooked his head to one side and studied the old

man's features. It was the eyes that gave it away. 'Lister?' he said, his eyes half-pinched in disbelief.

Lister shook his head. 'Where the smeg have you been?'

'We got here as quick as we could.'

'Quick?' Lister bellowed. *'Quick!?'* He rubbed his legs together and made a series of bizarre clicking noises with his tongue.

'It's only been sixteen days.' Rimmer looked at the old man Lister had become. 'My god – it must be the Time dilation.'

'The what?'

'The ship got stuck in a Black Hole. Time moves more slowly around a Black Hole. Relativity. From our point of view, you've only been away a couple of weeks.'

Lister snorted, showing a row of gnarled teeth. 'I've been here, on my own, waiting for you to bring me some food' – his eyes sparkled with fury – 'for the last thirty-four years. *Thirty-four smegging years.'*

Rimmer shook his head and tried to think of something adequate to say. All he could come up with was: 'Sorry.'

SEVEN

The Cat spun round, taking in the whole valley. 'You did all this yourself?'

Lister grunted.

'This was all garbage before, and you made it into this?'

Lister grunted again. He hadn't spoken much English for over a third of a century, and his conversation was sparse. He turned and squinted across the fields. Rimmer followed his sightline towards a herd of animals grazing at the very edge of the valley. They looked too small to be horses, but it was impossible to tell at this distance. Lister slid his two thumbs into his mouth and emitted a piercing, wavering whistle.

One of the herd looked up from its feeding, and broke into a trot. As they watched, the creature suddenly lifted off into the air and headed, skyborne, towards them.

The giant, eight-foot long cockroach landed neatly between the screaming Cat and the hysterical Rimmer. Its mandibles rubbed tenderly up the back of Lister's legs, and he patted its thorax fondly, cooing his strange clicks and whistles all the time.

'Yow! Warghh!' The Cat wriggled his body, as if shrugging off a thousand creeping bugs, while Rimmer convulsed quietly beside him.

'They eat all the garbage,' Lister said, as if this were some kind of explanation, and climbed on its back. 'Hop on.' He patted the cockroach's rump.

The Cat twisted and gyrated, scratching every spare inch of flesh. 'Yak! Wurghh! Yahhhh! It's a cockroach!'

'You expect us to sit on this thing?' Rimmer said, between heaves.

'It's six miles back to the house.'

'Six miles? Is that all?' Rimmer swept both his hands forward. 'You guys go on ahead. I feel like a jog.'

'What? No. I'm coming with you,' said the Cat, and went into another gyrating dance of revulsion.

The cockroach clicked and whistled and animatedly rubbed his bristling back legs together.

'He's getting upset,' said Lister. 'He thinks you don't like him.'

'Noooo.' The Cat laughed with false amusement. 'Where'd he get that idea? I think he's really cute. Cockroaches have always been my all-time favourite insects. In fact I have a pin-up of one in my locker. I especially love those black sticky hairs on the back of his legs, and that sort of slimy stuff that dribbles out of his mandibles. He's adorable! Waaarghhh.'

'Get on. You too.' Lister nodded at Rimmer.

They slung their legs over the roach's back, and it pattered along until it reached take-off speed, then fluttered noisily up into the sky.

'So,' said the Cat, holding on to the shell of the roach's abdomen, 'do we get an in-flight movie, or what?'

'What's that?' Rimmer pointed down at a field below them. There were no crops in the field, just yellow and white flowers which were arranged and planted to spell out two enormous letters; two 'K's.

'Jasmine,' said Lister, simply.

And Rimmer let it go at that.

Lister's home was made entirely of garbage. The walls were built from wastepaper, compressed into bricks that made them as hard as any wood. The roof slates were fashioned from beaten-out flattened bean tins, and the windows were the portholes taken from front-loading washing machines. Various tubes, pipes and cables ran to a tall tower some fifty feet away, which housed a configuration of mirrors that harnessed solar energy.

Besides the main house, there were a number of cockroach stables, and farm outhouses, which stored harvested crops, seeds and equipment.

As they walked across the courtyard, a number of young roaches flocked out excitedly to meet them. They yapped, clicked and whistled round Lister's ankles as he patted each of them and made his way to the main house.

The furnishings inside the dwelling were also constructed from unwanted refuse. There was a crude, but effective, central-heating system made out of old car radiators and exhaust pipes.

While Lister busied himself in the kitchen, Rimmer and the Cat sat on a remarkably comfortable sofa which was clearly three toilets lashed together, covered with bin liners stuffed with what turned out to be vacuum-cleaner fluff.

There was an elaborate hand-carved wooden mantelpiece over the stone hearth. It looked strangely incongruous in the jerry-built room. Above it hung an ornate gilt frame, which, at first glance appeared to be empty. Rimmer stood up and strode towards it. On closer inspection he found there was a picture in the middle of it. A less-than-passport-size photograph, which had been cut out of a *Red Dwarf* yearbook. Rimmer squinted and tried to make out the face. It was the photograph Lister always used to keep in his wallet. The one he didn't think Rimmer knew about. It was his only photograph of Kristine Kochanski, smiling her famous pinball smile. Rimmer shook his head. Lister was still hung up on a girl he'd dated for three weeks, several thousand epochs ago. His psyche had fantasized her as his mate in Better Than

Life, and now, after nearly forty years of solitude here on Garbage World, his memory still wasn't prepared to let her go.

Lister shuffled in from the kitchen, his wrinkled hands clutching a tray loaded with roughly thrown clay pots. He saw Rimmer looking at the thumbnail-size photograph in the frame that could have comfortably accommodated a couple of El Grecos and smiled. 'One day,' he said, 'I'll get her back.'

Rimmer and the Cat looked at the frail old man Lister had become and nodded in benign indulgence. It seemed fruitless to point out she'd died three million years previously, and even when she had been alive she'd been the one who broke off the relationship, dumping him for some guy who worked in Flight Navigation.

'One day,' he said again. And they nodded again.

Lister handed the Cat a mug of nettle tea and a plateful of juniper-and-dandelion stew, and sat down.

'So what happened?' said Rimmer. And Lister began to tell them. He told them pretty much everything, missing out only the olive-branch incident, the 'deal' he'd made with the planet, which, as the years had passed by, had begun to seem more and more like a dream, unreal, half-imagined.

'So what now?' asked the Cat, setting aside his still-full plate of juniper-and-dandelion stew, and his mugful of cold nettle tea. 'What are you going to do? Stay here, or come with us?'

'Both,' said Lister.

'Huh?'

'We're going to take Earth home. We're going to tow it back to the solar system.'

'We're what?' laughed the Cat.

'It's possible,' Lister said earnestly. 'I've been thinking about it for the last ten years.'

'So what are we going to do, exactly?' A patronizing smile rippled across Rimmer's face. 'Stretch a chain from the ship, and use Mount Everest as a tow hook? Then, maybe, stick a huge sign in Australia: "No hand signals: planet on tow"?'

'More or less,' said Lister, and he was perfectly serious. 'More or less.'

EIGHT

The giant roach circled *White Giant*, then landed deftly by its side. They dismounted, and as Rimmer and the Cat walked shakily up the embarkation ramp Lister fished in his coat pocket and fed the roach some decomposing insect paste.

The communications monitor in *White Giant*'s control room was flashing 'Incoming transmission – response required.'

Rimmer barked out the voice commands, and Kryten's face fizzed on to the screen. 'Ah! There you are. I've been trying to get through for two hours. I've found him.'

'*We* found him,' corrected the Toaster.

Rimmer frowned. 'Found who?'

'Queen Isabella of Spain,' said the Toaster, sarcastically. 'Who the smeg do you think?'

'Mr Lister,' Kryten said patiently. 'We've found Mr Lister.'

The Cat popped his head over Rimmer's shoulder. 'What? You mean you've found some sort of remains? A skeleton or something?'

'Read my lips,' said the Toaster, who didn't have any. 'We've found Lister. He's here. He's alive.'

'That's not possible.'

'Look.' Kryten swivelled the head of the transmission camera, so the figure lying on *Blue Midget*'s crash couch swung into view.

486

It *was* Lister.

Pasty and drawn – his complexion had a strange wax veneer, and there was an odd soulless quality to his eyes – but it was Lister.

At least, it looked like Lister, no older than the day Rimmer had left him marooned.

Rimmer stared at the screen, his face bunched like a ball of waste paper. Suddenly, a gnarled hand snaked past him and flicked off the transmission link.

Rimmer turned and looked into Lister's wizened old face.

The Cat backed up to the far bulkhead wall. 'What's going on here? Just who are you, Buddy?'

'I'm Lister,' said Lister, unsmiling.

'Then who the hell's that?' The Cat flung an elegant forefinger towards the screen. 'Benny Goodman and his Orchestra?'

'It's a Morph.'

'It's a what?'

'It's a Polymorph.'

NINE

The thing about human beings was this: human beings couldn't agree. They couldn't agree about anything. Right from the moment their ancestors first slimed out of the oceans, and one group of sludge thought it was better to live in trees while the other thought it blatantly obvious that the ground was the hip place to be. And they'd disagreed about pretty well everything else ever since.

They disagreed about politics, religion, philosophy – everything.

And the reason was this: basically, all human beings believed all other human beings were insane, in varying degrees.

This was largely due to a defective gene, isolated by a group of Danish scientists at the Copenhagen Institute in the late 1960s. This was a discovery which had the potential for curing all humankind's ills, and the scientists, naturally ecstatic, decided to celebrate by going out for a meal. Two of them wanted to go for a smorgasbord, one wanted Chinese cuisine, another preferred French, while the last was on a diet and just wanted to stay in the lab and type up the report. The disagreement blew up out of all proportion, the scientists fell to squabbling and the paper was never completed. Which was just as well in a way, because if it had been presented, no one would have agreed with it, anyway.

Small wonder, then, that *homo sapiens* spent most of their short time on Earth waging war against each other.

For their first few thousand years on the planet they did little else, and they discovered two things that were rather curious: the first was that when they were at war, they agreed more. Whole nations agreed that other nations were insane, and they agreed that the mutually beneficial solution was to band together to eliminate the loonies. For many people, it was the most agreeable period of their lives, because, apart from a brief period on New Year's Eve (which, incidentally, no one could agree the date of), the only time human beings lived happily side by side was when they were trying to kill each other.

Then, in the middle of the twentieth century, the human race hit a major problem.

It got so good at war, it couldn't have one anymore.

It had spent so much time practising and perfecting the art of genocide, developing more and more lethal devices for mass destruction, that conducting a war without totally obliterating the planet and everything on it became an impossibility.

This didn't make human beings happy at all. They talked about how maybe it was still possible to have a small, contained war. A little war. If you like, a warette.

They spoke of conventional wars, limited wars, and this insane option might even have worked, if only people could have agreed on a new set of rules. But, people being people, they couldn't.

War was out. War was a no-no.

And, like a small child suddenly deprived of its very favourite toy, the human race mourned and sulked and twiddled its collective thumbs, wondering what to do next.

Towards the conclusion of the twenty-first century, a solution was found. The solution was sport.

Sporting events were, in their way, little wars, and with war gone people started taking their sport ever more seriously. Scientists and theoreticians channelled their energies away from weaponry and into the new arena of battle.

And since the weapons of sport were human beings themselves, scientists set about improving them.

When chemical enhancements had gone as far as they could go, the scientists turned to genetic engineering.

Super sportsmen and women were grown, literally grown, in laboratory test-tubes around the planet.

The world's official sports bodies banned the new mutants from competing in events against normal athletes, and so a new, alternative sports body was formed, and set up in competition.

The GAS (Genetic Alternative Sports) finished 'normal' sport within two years. Sports fans were no longer interested in seeing a conventional boxing match, when they could witness two genetically engineered pugilists – who were created with their brains in their shorts, and all their other major organs crammed into their legs and feet, leaving their heads solid blocks of unthinking muscle – knock hell out of one another for hours on end in a way that normal boxers could only manage for minutes.

Basketball players were grown twenty feet tall.

Swimmers were equipped with gills and fins.

Soccer players were bred with five legs and no mouths, making after-match interviews infinitely more interesting. However, not all breeds of genetic athletes were accepted by the GAS and new rules had to be created after the 2224 World Cup, when Scotland fielded a goalkeeper who was a human oblong of flesh, measuring eight feet high by sixteen across, thereby filling the entire goal. Somehow they still failed to qualify for the second round.

American football provided the greatest variety of mutant athletes, each one specifically designed for its position. The Nose Tackle, for instance, was an enormous nose – a huge wedge of boneless flesh that was hammered into the scrimmage line at every play. Wide receivers were huge Xs – four long arms that tapered to the tiny waist perched on top of legs capable of ten-yard strides. The defensive line were even larger, specifically bred to secrete noxious chemicals whenever the ball was in play.

Genetic Alternative Sports were a huge hit, and the technological advancements spilled into other avenues of human life.

Cars were suddenly coming off the production line made from human mutations. Bone on the outside, soft supple flesh in the interior, and engines made from mutated internal organs – living cars, that drove themselves, parked themselves and never crashed. More importantly than that, they didn't rely on fossil fuels to run. All they required was carfood – a special mulch made from pig offal. Cars in the twenty-third century ran on sausages.

The trend spread. GELFs, Genetically Engineered Life Forms, were everywhere, and soon virtually every consumer product was made of living tissue. Gelf armchairs, which could sense your mood, and massage your shoulders when you were feeling tense, became a part of everyday life. Gelf vacuum cleaners, which were half kitchen appliance, half family pet, waddled around on their squat little legs, doing the household chores and amusing the children.

Finally, the bubble burst. The Gelfs rebelled, just as the Mechanoids had rebelled before them.

The unrest had been festering for half a century. The dichotomy was that, although Gelfs were created from human chromosomes, and therefore technically qualified as human, they had no rights whatsoever. Quite simply, they wanted to vote. And normal humans were damned if they were going to file into polling stations alongside walking furniture and twenty-feet tall athletic freaks.

The rebellion started in the Austrian town of Salzburg, when a vacuum cleaner and Gelf Volkswagen Beetle robbed a high street bank. They took the manager and a security guard hostage, agreeing to release them only if Valter Holman was brought to justice for murder.

Valter Holman had killed his armchair, and the whole of the Gelf community was up in arms, those that had arms, because the law courts refused to accept that a crime had been committed.

The facts in the case were undisputed. It was a crime of passion. Holman had returned home from work unexpectedly one afternoon to discover his armchair sitting on his naked wife. He immediately leapt to the right conclusion, and shot the chair as it hurriedly tried to wriggle back into its upholstery.

Finally the establishment capitulated, and Holman was brought to trial. After the two-day hearing the court ruled that since Holman would have to live out the rest of his life being known as the man who was cuckolded by his own furniture, he had suffered enough, and was given a six-month suspended sentence.

And so the Gelf War started.

And for a short time, humankind indulged in its favourite pastime. Humans versus man-made humans.

Armchairs and vacuum cleaners fought side by side with bizarrely shaped genetically engineered sports stars and living, breathing motor cars.

The Gelfs didn't stand a chance, and most of them were wiped out or captured. The few remaining went to ground, becoming experts in urban guerrilla warfare. For a short time, Gelf-hunters proliferated, and a rebel vacuum cleaner waddling frantically down a crowded street, pursued by a Gelf runner, became a common sight.

But it wasn't the Gelf resistance fighters who caused the problem. The problem was what to do with those who'd surrendered. Legally, killing them constituted murder, but equally, the authorities could hardly send them back into docile human service.

Fortunately the problem coincided with the nomination of Earth as Garbage World. All the captured Gelfs were dumped like refuse on the island of Zanzibar and left to die.

Most of them did. But not all. Some survived. Not the brightest, not even the biggest, just those best equipped to cope with the harsh rigours of living on a planet swamped in toxic waste and choking poisons. The ones who could endure the endless winter as Earth soared through the universe looking for its new sun. And gradually, a new strain of Gelf evolved.

A creature who could live anywhere. Even in the revolting conditions on Earth. A creature with a sixth sense – telepathy. A creature who was able to read its prey's mind, even through hundreds of feet of compacted ice. A creature with no shape of its own; whose form was dictated by the requirements of survival.

These were the polymorphs.

The shape-changers.

They didn't need food for survival.

They fed on other creatures' emotions. Their diet was fear, jealousy, anger . . .

And when no other creatures were left on the island of Zanzibar, they began to feed off each other.

Until finally, there were only a handful left.

TEN

The polymorph who'd assumed Lister's shape lay on the bunk, waiting for its energy to return after its metamorphosis, while Kryten and the Toaster stared at the suddenly blank screen.

'What've you done now? You've caused a malfunction.'

At the sound of the Toaster's tinny tones, Kryten's eyes rolled fully 720 degrees round in his head. 'The transmission stopped. It's nothing to do with me.'

'Why would the transmission suddenly stop? You must have pressed something. You must have pressed the wrong button.'

'I didn't press anything, they just stopped broadcasting.'

'Says you.'

Kryten had had it up to his stereophonic audial sensors with the Toaster. Frankly, old Talkie was beginning to get on Kryten's nipple nuts. Fourteen hours of bouncing around in the hover dinghy, scouring the swamps, with the Toaster navigating, had driven him to the very limits of his almost limitless patience.

Few relationships can survive the ordeal of travelling to an unknown destination over any kind of distance, with one driving and one reading the map. If Romeo and Juliet had ever been forced to jump in a family saloon and drive from Venice to Marbella, they would have split up long before they hit the Spanish border. Hopelessly lost, bawling and screaming in some deserted lay-by in the middle of God-knows-where, there'd have been no talk of suicide – they'd have been more than ready to murder each other.

And Kryten didn't have the advantage of being madly in love with the Toaster to start with. The sight of the Toaster didn't send his soul into rapture. He thought the Toaster was an infuriatingly perky little geek.

And that was before the journey.

Fourteen hours stuck together had not improved things, and, uncharacteristically, Kryten was beginning to have fantasies wherein he set about the Toaster with a petrol-powered chainsaw.

'No way would that screen have gone blank if I'd had anything to do with it,' the Toaster chirped. 'Absolutely no way.'

'Please. I'm trying to discover what's wrong.'

'I'll tell you what's wrong. You. You don't know what you're doing. You're a sanitation Mechanoid – bog-cleaning, that's all you're good for. You're a bog-bot. A lavvy droid. A mechanical basin bleacher.'

'Really?' Kryten's voice was dangerously quiet. 'And I suppose a novelty Toaster is infinitely better-equipped to cope with the complex communications system aboard this vessel?'

'Well, a certain so-called "novelty" Toaster certainly didn't do a half-bad job at getting us all out of a certain Black Hole I could mention.' The Toaster gave an arrogant twist of his browning knob.

Kryten discreetly crushed a small section of the console's façade, and continued trying unsuccessfully to restore the communication link with *White Giant*.

The pale waxy figure on the couch listened to them bickering. The words themselves meant nothing, but the shapes and colours of their emotions were new and exciting. As soon as its energy returned, it would feast.

*It had lived for so long on tiny morsels of insect emotion —
mainly fear — and the little snacks it managed to cannibalize from
weaker members of its species, that every shape change left it
drained and temporarily helpless.*

*And now the Shadow Time was almost on it. It would need
nourishment and sustenance if it was to survive the Aftering. It
didn't think these things. It simply knew them. It had no capacity
for abstract thought, it couldn't plan. It was a matter of instinct.
The instinct to survive, moment by moment, for as long as
possible.*

*But the water was helping. The cooling water on its brow was
helping its strength to return.*

Kryten dipped the cloth back in the water, then draped it
back over his patient's forehead. 'I don't know what's wrong
with the communication link. Still, that's not for you to
worry about. I'm sure they'll be in touch soon.' Kryten
tutted. Lister looked absolutely awful. 'Are you quite sure
there's nothing else I can do?'

'What he needs,' chipped in a tinny voice, 'is some nice,
hot . . .'

'No!' Kryten snapped.

'. . . tea. I was going to say "some nice, hot, sweet tea".
What did you think I was going to say?' said the Toaster.

And then the Shadow Time came, and with it, the pain.

Kryten was half-way back to the communication console
when Lister started convulsing. His back arched up off the
bed, and his limbs threshed uncontrollably in the crash
couch recess. Strange sounds, barely human, drove out of his
juddering throat.

'He's choking!' yelled the Toaster.

'I can see that!' said Kryten, hauling Lister into a sitting
position and slapping him on his back.

'Perhaps he's swallowed a fishbone!'

'Swallowed a what?'

'A fishbone. And you know what the cure is for a fishbone lodged in the throat.'

'What?'

'Dry toast! Oh, joy! I've waited for a moment like this all my life! Get me some bread!'

Kryten yanked a fire extinguisher off the wall and hurled it at the Toaster, catching it a glancing blow on its browning knob. The Toaster was temporarily stunned into silence, and Kryten went back to slamming the still-convulsing Lister between the shoulder blades.

And just when it seemed the convulsions could get no worse, they stopped. Something dislodged from Lister's throat, and fell into Kryten's outstretched palm.

'It's a piece of bubble-gum.' Kryten held out the small pink wad of gum for Lister to see.

Pale and sweating, the Lister morph sank back on to the couch, exhausted. Kryten dropped the gumball into a metal trash can, just as the communication screen crackled back to life.

'What's going on?' asked the Toaster.

Lines of silent machine code scrolled up the screen.

'It's machine code,' said the Toaster.

'Yes,' hissed Kryten, 'I'm perfectly well aware of that.'

'Why are they communicating in machine language?'

'I haven't the slightest clue.'

'No,' agreed the Toaster, 'you haven't, have you? D'you want me to translate it? I'm fairly fluent in machine code.'

'I can manage.'

'Well? What does it say?'

'If you can just give me half a second, I'll tell you.'

'Yes?'

'It says: 'Extreme danger. You have . . .' Kryten's voice tailed off.

'You have what?'

'Nothing.' Kryten's eyes flitted across the screen, absorbing the message.

'What d'you mean, "nothing"?'

Kryten craned round and looked at the figure on the couch. The lifeless milky eyes stared back at him.

'Come on – what d'you mean, "nothing"? There can't be five hundred lines of nothing on the screen.'

'I mean . . . I can't translate it,' Kryten lied. 'I don't know what it says.'

The Toaster sighed extravagantly, and turned, by flipping its bread-release lever rapidly up and down on the table top, to face the screen. 'Once more the cavalry, in the form of a handsome yet reasonably inexpensive red toasting machine, bugles over the hill to the rescue. The message,' it said, 'runs thus: "Extreme danger. You have on board a genetic mutation" . . .'

'Shut up.'

'. . . "It is not, repeat, not Lister" . . .'

'That's enough.'

'"Abandon your vessel" . . .'

'Quiet!'

'. . . "and engage self-destruct." Honestly, this is really easy. You'd have to be a moron not to be able to translate this. What's this next bit . . .?'

Before it could continue, Kryten had wrenched the two thin steel ashtrays from the arms of the relaxation chairs and hammered them into the Toaster's bread vents. It was silenced immediately.

The Lister creature on the couch swivelled upright and watched, expressionless, as Kryten sidled back towards the glass cabinet that contained the emergency fire axe.

Abandon ship? How could he abandon ship? They were no longer on Garbage World, they were in space, half-way back to *Red Dwarf*.

Something was happening. The shapes, the colours of the emotions of the prey were changing. The tall, thin one, the mobile one made of plastic and metal, was afraid. Very afraid.

Delicious.

Nurture the fear. Help it grow.

Then feast on its succulence.

Feast to gorging.

Must change.

Must change, to nurture the fear.

But weak.

Too weak to complete.

Kryten's elbow smashed into the glass casing behind him, and his hand found the grip of the fire axe. Then he froze.

It was a horrible sound. The most horrible sound Kryten had ever heard. Crunching bones and sickening wetness, and a scream that dipped all the way down to Hell.

Lister stopped being Lister and started to become something else. His body folded in on itself, and when it re-emerged it was inside out. The slimy, mucus-coated organs quivered and gurgled as the ribcage split open and a strange serpent-like suction head slithered out and began sliming across the floor towards Kryten's feet.

Kryten stood there, waxwork-still in terror, as the unspeakable appendage coiled itself up his legs. The rest of the creature lay writhing ecstatically on the floor: Lister from the shoulders up, blubbery gore below.

The grotesque tentacle wound its way effortlessly up Kryten's torso, and wrapped around his neck, until its drooling tip quivered inches from his lips.

It reared back, like a snake about to strike. The tentacle tip split and a pink, fleshy, pursed mouth flicked out and grinned.

Then there was a voice. It was high pitched and metallic. It was the Toaster.

'Hey, pal.'

The creature's mouth slowly turned towards the bright red plastic box on the table.

'Would you like a little toast?'

The Toaster jiggled its crumb tray, so that it toppled on to its front, then slammed down its bread-release lever. A red-hot metal ashtray skimmed through the air, slicing through the creature's tentacle. The severed appendage thrashed and flailed, spraying green gloop around the entire control room.

The part of the creature that was half Lister, half something else screeched with blind agony and lurched towards the Toaster.

'Hey – don't get angry. I have a slice for you, too.'

The second ashtray sizzled across the control room, ploughed through the neck of the Lister beast, decapitating it, silencing its inhuman shriek for ever.

The Toaster flipped back up on to its base, and said, in a voice as macho as its tinny larynx would allow: 'Was it something I said?' it burred. 'He seems a trifle cut up.'

Kryten slithered down the bulkhead wall, sat on the deck and groaned, a long, low grumble of a groan. This was possibly the worst thing that could have happened. Saved, yet again, by the Toaster. Now it would scale new peaks of obnoxiousness.

The Toaster was already in its stride. A little puff of smoke trilled from the top of its grill. 'Toast, quantum mechanics and now slimebeast-slayer. Not a bad buy for $£19.99, wouldn't you say?'

Without interrupting his groan, Kryten punched the re-heat button to take *Blue Midget* back to *Red Dwarf*, double speed.

ELEVEN

It was a strange feeling for Lister, staring down at his own dead features. He shook his head. 'It doesn't make sense — I don't understand how you managed to kill it so easy.'

'Hardly easy,' the Toaster objected. 'It was a *mano a mano*, ninja-type struggle, where a brave, rather ruggedly handsome red kitchen appliance finally managed to come out on top.'

Lister wasn't listening. His finger hovered over the fire button of his heavy-duty mining laser. 'It must have been weak.'

'Weak? It was on the brink of squeezing the very life out of a series 4000 Mechanoid. That's how weak it was. You just can't tolerate the thought that, yet again, your old buddy Talkie Toaster saved everybody's neck.'

'Why did it wait so long to feed? It doesn't make sense, none of it.'

'It didn't feed because it was engaged in a titanic battle *à morte* with a samurai toaster. It was too busy trying to dodge lethal discs of red-hot steel to be thinking about nosh time. Oh, you should have seen me, I was magnificent. I feinted right, I dodged left — I was ducking and diving, weaving and bobbing, and he didn't lay a sucker on me.'

Lister shook his head again, and clicked and whistled a cockroach expletive.

Kryten prodded the polymorph's remains with the shaft of his fire axe, and looked up at Lister. 'What I don't understand is why it looks thirty years younger than you do.'

'It read your mind. You were expecting to find me the same age as you left me. That was the only data it had. So it turned into what it knew you were looking for.'

Rimmer stood outside the hatchway on the embarkation ramp, still steadfastly refusing to enter *Blue Midget*. 'You've encountered these things before, then?' he called to Lister.

Lister nodded. 'Once. One of the scouting roaches brought one back to the valley. Wiped out half the settlement before we finally punched its card. After that we always kept lookouts, but no others ever showed up. I don't think they're that intelligent. They're like mynah birds – they copy things without really understanding what it is they're copying.'

'So what now, Mr Lister, sir?'

'I don't want to take any chances. I think we should shoot *Blue Midget* into space, and detonate the auto-destruct.'

'Destroy *Blue Midget*?' Rimmer's head leaned in through the hatchway. 'We've already lost *Starbug*. That leaves us with only one transport craft.'

'Rimmer – I know what these things can do.'

'It's dead! It can't do anything.'

'I know. But I want to get rid of it. Every last bit of the smegger. And the only way to be sure of that is to torch the ship.'

Rimmer continued his protests all the way to the Shuttle-Bay Launch Suite, but Lister was adamant; adamant and stubborn in a way he'd never been when he was younger. There was simply no arguing with him.

They were gone.
  It was safe now to move.
  Safe to change.

The wad of pink gum folded in on itself and began to fizzle

502

as it turned into a cloud of steam and floated out of the metal trash can towards the air lock. The steam wrapped itself into a ball and solidified into a round black stone. The stone clanked loudly as it hit *Blue Midget*'s deck, and rolled up against the air-lock door.

Then the stone became ice. And the ice became water. And the water tried to seep through the air-lock seal.

No way out.
Not here.

The water became steam again, and wafted around the craft's interior, looking for an exit.

Nothing. The whole craft was air-tight.

Then the engines rumbled, jets fired, and the vessel began to rise.

The steam floated up to the rear viewport window, became a fly and flung itself against the reinforced glass.

Blue Midget bucked and bobbled as its steering jets swung the craft round and aligned it with the damaged bay doors.

The fly became a feather and floated ineffectually against the glass. The feather became a bullet. Its rear-end ignited and it blasted against the glass, ricocheting back and tumbling once more to the deck.

It lay in silence.

It was young. It knew of no more shapes.

It needed more knowledge.

Something primeval inside it, some instinct it didn't understand told it to seek out the minds of its prey. The signals were weak – only just in range.

It searched through their memories, and changed into things it found there. Many things. And none of the shapes it became could get through the glass.

Blue Midget passed under the bay arch, and swept out into space.

And it was only then that the creature turned into the one thing that could pass through the glass.

A light beam.

It became a beam of light that flashed through the glass and streaked back through the open bay doors.

It was back.

Back on *Red Dwarf*.

It became a small puddle of water – the least demanding of all its shapes – and rested.

When its strength returned, it would feed.

It would feed well.

TWELVE

Kryten craned over the crumpled handwritten recipe sheet he'd been given by Lister. It was Lister's own concoction: 'shami kebabs diabolo', which he'd once claimed proudly had put Petersen in the medical unit for over a week. But surely there was some mistake. The amount of chilli peppers called for could have launched a three-stage Deep Space probe from Houston Mission Control to the outer reaches of the galaxy. This wasn't a shami kebab – it was a thermo-nuclear device.

Still, orders were orders. Kryten plugged the food-blending attachment into his groinal socket and thrust his hips towards the mixing-bowl. It was something of a design flaw with the series 4000 that the power socket was so indelicately placed. It looked particularly preposterous when-ever Kryten was called on to use the three-foot vacuum hose. He tugged his right ear and the blender whirred into life. He whistled happily and began mincing together the ingredients of the kebab.

Thin fast beads of water battered over Lister's body as he gloried in the warmth of the shower. He filled his cupped palm with a ludicrously generous amount of shampoo, and massaged it into his already well-lathered scalp.

Shampoo and soap were two of the luxuries he'd failed to duplicate adequately on Garbage World. For a third of a century he'd had to wash using salt. His attempts to make real soap by boiling decomposing vegetable fats had proved too revolting for words. He always ended up smelling worse after he'd bathed than before he'd started. He finally gave up his soap-making attempts when he noticed that the cockroaches had started avoiding him, and ever afterwards relied on salt.

He blinked through sudded eyes at his reflection in the cubicle's mirrored wall. He hadn't bothered with mirrors as a vanity device – he really had no desire to impress roaches with a well-groomed appearance – and all the mirrors and reflective surfaces he'd collected over the years were used to harness the sun's heat. It was strange having an old body; he still thought of himself as a permanent twenty-five.

Where did all the years go?

Who'd stolen that fabulous body he'd once had for a couple of months when he was eighteen? Who'd given him this one instead? OK, so it was pretty well preserved for its sixty-one years, and, curiously, it was fitter in many respects than it had been when he'd first arrived on Garbage World, thanks to all his labours in the field. But there was no getting away from it – he now lived in a body that was nine years away from being seventy.

Nearly seventy.

Soon he would have to face the fact that in all probability he would never play professionally for the London Jets.

He might not even live to see the conclusion of his plan to tow Earth back to its solar system.

He heard a voice through the shower's roar, and turned down the taps.

It was Kryten: 'Ready in two minutes, Mr Lister, sir.'

Lister smiled. He was two minutes away from his first shami kebab in three-and-a-half decades. He'd given up meat, of course, on Garbage World, and he had no regrets about that. But shami kebabs were something else. Fantasizing about this Indian *hors d'oeuvre* had kept him going when times had been rough.

And now he was going to have one.

He chuckled out loud, and began clicking and whistling an up-beat cockroach song as he rinsed the soap from his hair.

Kryten pulled on three sets of oven gloves, one on top of the other, and took the three sausage-shaped kebabs out of the oven. They looked innocent enough, but quite frankly he'd have felt safer handling them wearing an asbestos suit, preferably with long-range, remote-controlled mechanical arms.

These babies were hot.

He put the plate on the sleeping quarters' table and backed away nervously.

'Dinner is served, sir.'

'Just coming.'

As Kryten crossed the sleeping quarters, a small, brightly patterned beach ball bounced through the hatchway and into the room.

Kryten caught it on its fifth bounce, placed it on the table, next to Lister's kebabs, and went outside into the corridor to investigate.

There was no one there.

The corridor was empty.

Kryten ducked back into the sleeping quarters. Now the beach ball wasn't there either.

Kryten failed to notice that the three kebabs on the plate had become four.

'He-e-eyy!' Lister stepped out of the cubicle, tugging together the cords of his shower robe, 'Shami kebabs!' he orgasmed. 'Thirty-four years. I hope you haven't skimped on the old chillies, there, Kryters, old buddy, old pal.'

Lister sat down and prepared to eat. As his fork bore down towards his plate, one of the Indian sausages leapt out of the bed of lettuce and hurled itself around his throat. He catapulted back and crashed to the ground in his chair; his desperate fingers clawing at the choking kebab; his legs kicking and bucking.

Kryten turned from the wash basin at the sounds of Lister's agonized writhing.

He shook his head and tutted. 'Are you seriously telling me you like them *that* spicy?'

Lister gagged. His face started to blacken.

'*Far* too many chilli peppers,' Kryten clucked. 'Didn't I tell you?'

Lister's eyes bulged as he rolled over and over on the sleeping quarters' floor.

'And this is your idea of an enjoyable snack? It's sheer insanity.'

'The kebab,' Lister rasped, 'it's trying to kill me.'

'Well, I'm not the least bit surprised.'

Finally, Lister's clawing fingers found some purchase, and he ripped the lethal shami from his neck and slung it across the sleeping quarters.

He hunched, coughing and choking as it slid with snake speed underneath the bunks. 'Where'd it go?'

'Where did what go?'

'The polymorph! There's another polymorph!'

'What? Where?'

Lister staggered back against the bunks. 'I think it went under Rimmer's architect's desk.' He reached down and picked up his red boxer shorts from the floor and struggled into them. 'Come on, Kryten – we've got to get out of here.'

Lister grabbed a baseball bat from beside the bunk and started backing towards the hatchway.

There was a loud cracking sound, and Lister doubled up.

'Are you all right, sir?'

'Guhhhh!'

'What's the matter?'

'My . . . ah! . . . My boxers . . . aaah! . . . They're shrinking!' Lister staggered forward, his eyes double size with fear
as a second creak wrenched his body into spasm. 'The
polymorph! It's turned into a pair of boxers . . . getting
smaller . . . Ahhhh! No! God! Please! Please!'

Lister staggered and then toppled on to his back. 'Kryten
– help me! Please help me! My boxers – get them off – pull
them down! Please, God, I'm begging you.'

Kryten fell to his knees between Lister's splayed legs,
ripped open his shower robe, and tugged frantically at
Lister's boxer shorts.

Rimmer skidded into the quarters. 'What the hell's going
on?'

'Keep still, Mr Lister!'

'I can't stand it anymore. Get them off – please! Do it
now!'

'We need some kind of lubricant.' Kryten's eyes scanned
the room. 'Butter. I'll get some butter.'

'Anything! Anything! Just do it quick!'

Rimmer shook his head. He couldn't say he was totally
shocked. He wished he could, but he couldn't. He'd bonk
anything, Lister. Not even a male android was safe from his
vile appetites. And what was that dangling from Kryten's
groinal socket? A food blender? Oh, it brought tears to his
eyes just thinking about it.

With a final effort, Kryten ripped off Lister's tiny shorts
and stood up. The boxers were minute, doll size. Lister
scrambled backwards towards the hatchway. 'It's a
polymorph! Don't just stand there holding it! Get rid of the
smegger!'

Suddenly the tiny red shorts folded in on themselves, and
Kryten was holding the tail of a rat.

'Oh my God!' Lister's stomach surged for his throat. It
was a plague rat, two and a half feet long, not counting its
tail.

Lister hated rats.

Hated them.

And this one came from his nightmares: its razor-sharp yellow teeth, its black matted fur streaked with blood, its cold, dead eyes.

It wriggled, snapped and drooled as Kryten staggered towards him, still grimly holding it by its tail. 'What shall I do, sir? Where shall I put it.'

'Just get it out of here! Just get it away from me!'

Kryten swung the beast and flung it hard towards the bulkhead wall, but it twisted in the air, flipped back and changed direction. Lister watched in adrenalin-induced slow motion as the rat landed

on

his

FACE.

'Wuuuuhaaaaaaaaaaaahhhhhhhhhhh!' A voice Lister had never heard before screamed from deep inside him. He felt the rat's foetid breath crawl up into his nostrils.

'Oh my Guhhhhhhhhhnnnnnnnnnnnn!'

Then the most hideous, revolting, disgusting, foul, vile thing that had ever happened to Lister, happened to Lister.

Some of the rat's rabid spittle drooled into his gaping mouth.

'Oh, shiiiiiiiiiiiiirrrrrrhhhhhhhhggggggggggghhhhhh!'

Lister's fear was complete.

Terror pushed him to the very edge of insanity.

Then it happened.

The rat's head folded in on itself, split open and disgorged the polymorph's feeding tentacle. The slimy puckered mouth on the tip of the tentacle smacked on to Lister's head.

And the polymorph began to feed.

Kryten ripped the half-rat from Lister's face and pitched it against the bunkside wall. It squelched down the wall, leaving a trail of gloop and gore, and fell into the open laundry basket. Kryten launched himself across the quarters and slammed down the lid.

Lister rose from the floor and picked up the baseball bat. 'I hate rats.' He shuddered. 'They freak me out totally. They're my second all-time worst fear.'

Rimmer cleared his dry throat. 'What's your first?'

The metal lid blasted into the air, and a new form loomed out of the basket. Its head hung hugely above them. Mucus pulsed through the gaps in its armour-like endoskeleton. Its enormous jaws carried two hundred needle-sharp silver teeth, glistening with demonic slobber.

'This,' said Lister. 'This is my all-time worst fear.'

The creature's jaws opened to their limit, and a feeding tentacle shot out of its mouth and fastened on to Lister's head.

The half-sated polymorph completed its meal.

THIRTEEN

'So what are you saying?' The Cat frowned. 'This thing feeds off emotions?'

Kryten nodded. 'Exactly. It changes shape to provoke a negative emotion – in this case, fear. It took Mr Lister to the very limit of his terror, then sucked out his fear.'

'Then what happened?'

'It vanished. It turned into a cloud of steam and floated out of the room.'

The Cat looked down at Lister's inert form on the medical unit's biofeedback couch. 'Is he OK?'

'Apparently so. It's just he no longer has any sense of fear.'

Rimmer stopped pacing. 'The question is: what are we going to do?'

Lister's eyes flicked open, and he lurched upright on the couch. 'Well, I say let's get out there and twat it.'

'Lister, you're ill.' Rimmer started pacing again. 'Just leave this to us.'

Lister smacked his fist into his palm. 'I could have had it in the sleeping quarters, only it took me by surprise.'

'Lister – it turned into an eight-feet-tall armour-plated killing machine.'

'I've had bigger than him. They're all the same, these armour-plated killing machines. One good fist in the gob, they soon lose interest.'

'It's probably best you stay calm, sir,' said Kryten, soothingly. 'You've lost all sense of fear. You're not thinking rationally.'

'What's there to be scared of? If it wants a barny, we'll give it one. One swift knee in the happy sacs, it'll drop, like anyone else.'

'Fine,' Rimmer nodded. 'Well, we'll certainly bear that in mind when we're constructing our strategy.'

'I'll rip out its windpipe and whip it to death with the tonsil end.'

'Yes. Very good.' Rimmer caught Kryten's eye and nodded discreetly in the direction of the sedative cabinet.

'I'll shove my fist so far down its gob, I'll be able to pull the label off its underpants.'

Kryten pushed the syringe into Lister's arm.

Lister looked down at the hypodermic. 'What's that, pal? You starting trouble?'

'I'm sorry, Mr Lister, sir. It's just a little something to relax you.'

'Come on then, slags.' Lister lunged at him drunkenly. 'I'll have you all! One at a time or all together. Makes no odds to me. I'll ... I'll ...' Lister smiled as the sedative flushed into his bloodstream, and fell back on to the couch.

Rimmer sighed. 'Thank God for that. All right. As far as I can see, we've got two alternatives: one – we take this thing on, and we don't rest until it's dead. Or, two – we run away.' He hardly paused. 'Who's for two?'

'Sounds good to me,' voted Kryten.

'Always been my lucky number,' agreed the Cat.

Rimmer's plan was cowardly, but simple. They would go up to the supply deck, grab whatever they could fit into a supply wagon, load it on to *Blue Midget*, the one remaining shuttle craft, and get the hell out. Without emotions to feed on, the polymorph would eventually die. In the meantime they could survive on Garbage World for as long as necessary.

'What about him?' the Cat nodded at the snoring Lister.

'He'll only slow us down. We'll pick him up when we've got the supplies.'

They sealed the sedated Lister in the medical unit and started making their way up to the supply deck.

The mesh cage of the service lift juddered noisily to a stop three feet above the floor of the supply deck.

The Cat's boot democratically elected that Kryten should be first out. He went next, followed by Rimmer. Before them stretched the endless ranks of cargo crates – a huge regular matrix that covered almost twenty acres.

The Cat adjusted the strap of his backpack that powered the enormous bazookoid mining laser. 'Let's get this over with. This damn gun's destroying the line of my suit.'

Kryten trundled in the lead, nervously swinging his bazookoid at every imaginary sound. He'd never worn a grenade belt before, and he wasn't exactly in love with the way the grenades clanked noisily against his metal chest plate with each movement.

They turned left at the first intersection, and there, empty in the aisle, was a gleaming yellow supply truck. It looked brand-new.

Kryten unbuckled his grenade belt, set it down beside his mining laser and backpack, and started loading up the truck. The Cat's eyes scoured the gloom, but caught no movement. Rimmer stood, jiggling his right leg nervously, and occasionally clapping his hands to hurry Kryten along.

Twenty minutes later, the truck was full.

'Let's go!' Rimmer hissed, and Kryten and the Cat climbed up into the cab. Then something made Rimmer stop.

Something about that truck.

Too yellow. Too new. Too convenient.

He started backing away.

'Come on, Buddy, let's move it. Let's go, go, go!'

'There! Polymorph!' Rimmer's voice was barely audible. 'It's . . .'

The Cat swung out his mining laser. 'Where?'

'It's . . .' Rimmer could hardly speak with fear.

'Say it, dog breath. Where is it?'

'It's the truck! The polymorph is the supply truck!'

FOURTEEN

Kryten somersaulted backwards out of the cab and rolled down an aisle. The Cat's buttocks clenched so tightly they became a single ball, before he unfroze and launched himself after Kryten. As the Cat landed by his side, Kryten ripped a thermal grenade from his belt, twisted the detonator handle and bowled it under the cab.

The explosion flung the truck fully thirty feet in the air, and the blast debris rained down on top of them – tyres, engine parts, burnt-out chassis and broken windscreen glass. The Cat stood up and strode over the smouldering debris to the recess in the aisle where Rimmer was cowering. 'That supply truck . . .' he jabbed at Rimmer with the barrel of his bazookoid, '. . . the one we just spent twenty minutes loading with supplies, was, get this: a supply truck.'

Rimmer smiled contritely. 'Yes,' he agreed. 'I can see that now.'

'Twenty minutes we spent loading that thing. And now we've got to start all over . . .'

'There!' Rimmer cut across him. 'In the shadows!' He pointed past Kryten down the aisle. 'Something moved.'

'I think he's ruh-ruh-ruh-ruh-ruh-ruh . . .' Kryten whapped his head on the corner of a crate. 'I think he's right. The blast must have drawn it.'

'Set the bazookoids to heat-seeker. If there's anything out there, the laser bolts'll find it.'

Kryten and the Cat snapped the bazookoid control-setting

over to heat-seeker, braced themselves for the recoil and fired. Two blue balls screamed down the length of the aisle, and vanished into the distant murk.

They waited for the explosion, listening to the fading howl as the bolts sped harmlessly down towards the far end of the supply deck.

But the explosion didn't happen.

There was nothing there.

Rimmer felt the Cat's look. 'Sorry,' he held up his hands apologetically, 'my fault. False alarm.'

The laser bolts reached the end of the supply deck, flipped over like two Olympic swimmers and began powering back through the traces of their own tails.

The Cat was still berating Rimmer, when for the third time in as many minutes Rimmer pointed past him, and said, in the same fear-stricken voice: 'There!'

'What *now*?' the Cat snapped. 'You've got a bad case of the jitters, Buddy.'

Rimmer shook his head. The Cat sighed, turned and saw the bolts speeding back towards them.

'I don't understand it,' Rimmer said. 'Holograms don't produce heat, neither do Mechanoids. What are they homing in on?'

Rimmer and Kryten turned and looked at the Cat. The Cat said three words. The three words were: 'So long, guys.' He hoisted his bazookoid on to his shoulder, and he started to run.

The Cat knew he could move. Even with the weight of the backpack and the bazookoid; even with the rather impractical tight silver trousers, and the two inch cuban heels, he would still have put money on himself to out-run just about anything.

But the question was this: could he out-run two heat-seeking laser bolts? The honest truth was, he didn't know. He had no idea whether it was even possible to shake off two spinning bolts of death whose entire existence was dedicated to finding something that emitted heat, and blowing it up.

Still, he thought it would be a good idea to try.

So he did.

His neck craned back and his knees pistoned up and down, pumping so high they beat his chest with every step. He heard the bolts' distinctive *zhazhum* as they rounded the corner and ripped down the aisle in pursuit. At the next intersection he zigged left and zagged right. The sound of the bolts faded slightly – he could corner faster than they could. Hey! Things were looking up. Sure, they were faster than him on a straight, but if he kept turning, if he found enough corners, he could out-run these suckers until their power ran down.

He was feeling good, now. This wasn't going to be nearly as difficult as he expected. He came up to a maze of intersections, twisted left, right and left again. Behind him he heard the bolts overshoot a turn, and their low humming throb dimmed in volume. He'd bought himself a couple of seconds; seconds he badly needed. He pulled out a mirror and checked his hair. It was still perfect. He pulled out a small metal cylinder, freshened his breath, and took off again.

Another right, another left, another right.

And suddenly, he was in a straight.

A long narrow corridor lined with cargo crates. Three hundred yards without a turning in sight, and no exit – just a door at the very end of the corridor, marked 'lift'. The bolts rounded the bend behind him.

The confident grin dribbled off his face.

Then, the Cat did the most stupid thing possible: he stopped.

He planted both feet firmly on the grilled metal deck, and waited for the lasers to hit him. Half a second before they did, he climbed into the air, he kicked his legs above his head, and back-flipped his feline form over the sizzling bolts.

He watched them as they soared down the aisle before they corrected their course and curved back towards him.

He started to run.

He started to run straight at them. Two feet from impact, he launched himself upwards again and Fosbury-flopped over the deadly blue missiles.

Again they roared by underneath him and prepared to turn. He glanced down the aisle and started towards the lift.

The metal on his cuban heels spat sparks as he skidded up to the lift and slapped the lift call button and waited.

Nothing happened.

He slapped it again. The laser bolts streaked towards him.

He slapped it a third time, and the doors opened, but too late. He felt the bolts' heat on his face, and ducked – simultaneously slapping the 'door close' button.

The doors hammered shut, and trapped them.

The Cat peered in through the observation window and watched the bolts helplessly swirling around inside.

He pulled a tiny silver toothbrush out of his jacket pocket, and started to groom his eyebrows. 'You either got it, or you ain't. And you little blue guys – you ain't even close.'

He smelt the girl's perfume as she leaned over his shoulder. To the Cat's mind, she was the second most gorgeous thing he'd ever seen. Long black hair, short orange pvc suit, thigh-length boots and a whip. It was hard to stop his eyes from watering. Clearly, this girl had class.

She spoke. 'What are you looking for?'

'A mutant,' the Cat said, casually. 'It's dangerous.' His eyes half closed and his eyebrows smouldered above them. 'Can turn into anything.'

'Sounds pretty scary.'

A bravado snort jetted down the Cat's nostrils.

'Must take a pretty brave kind of guy to do this kind of work?'

'You think?'

'And smart. Bet you have to be smart, too.'

'Definitely. You've got to have your wits about you all the time – don't let up for one second, or it'll sneak up behind you and blip! you're dog meat.' They reached an intersection. The Cat held up his hand and leant out. When he was satisfied it was safe, he beckoned her forward with a nod of his head. 'Come on, baby.'

'Did anyone ever tell you you're quite a guy?'

The Cat shrugged. 'Not since this morning.'

'Smart, brave, handsome . . .' She ran her hand sensually down the curve of her hip. 'In fact, I think you're probably the best-looking guy I've ever seen.'

'Well,' he laughed, modestly. 'I didn't want to be the first to say it.'

'You know what I'd really like?' She tormented the button on his jacket with a long-nailed finger. 'I'd really like to make love to a guy like you.'

The Cat lost a short, one-sided struggle with a large, cheesy grin. 'We-e-ell. I'm sure I have a window in my schedule somewhere.' He raised his wrist, and looked at a watch that wasn't there. 'What are you doing in, say, ten seconds' time?'

'Nothing I couldn't cancel.'

The Cat leant into her. 'Hi. I'm the Cat.'

'Hi.' She leant back. 'I'm the genetic mutant.'

'Glad to know you,' the Cat leered. 'Jenny who?'

There was a revolting ripping of flesh, and the girl's head folded in on itself. From the mess of pink blubber, a feeding tentacle snaked out and hit the Cat between the eyes.

The polymorph suckled noisily as it feasted on the Cat's vanity.

FIFTEEN

Kryten heard the Cat's scream and doubled his pace. At top speed he could waddle at nearly twenty-five miles an hour, and he soon lost Rimmer in the maze of crates.

He came across the Cat lying groaning, barely conscious.

Kryten set down his bazookoid, and cradled the Cat's head in his hand. 'My goodness. Are you all right?'

The Cat moaned and blinked open his eyes. 'Don't worry about me, Bud – I'm nobody.'

Rimmer appeared around the corner. 'Is he dead?'

'Who cares?' said the Cat.

The Mechanoid shook his head. 'I think he's lost his vanity.'

Rimmer's eyes spat hate at Kryten. 'You've done it again, haven't you?'

'Done what, sir?' Kryten's plastoid brow crinkled into a frown.

'Failed. First, the *Nova 5*. Whose fault was it the ship crashed? Whose fault was it the crew died?'

'But that was . . .' Kryten stammered. 'I didn't . . . I was only trying to . . .'

'And who brought the polymorph aboard *Red Dwarf* in the first place?'

'Yes, but I didn't know. I . . .' Kryten's mouth yacked open and closed, but no sound came out.

'First Lister, now the Cat. You won't be happy till everyone's dead, will you?'

'Oh,' Kryten's voice cracked. 'Please . . .'

'Please what? We were supposed to stick together – you let the Cat run off alone.'

'But that wasn't . . .' he stuttered. 'I mean . . .'

'He trusted you. Now look at him.'

Kryten covered his face with his hands. 'Oh, goodness! I feel so . . . so . . . guilty.'

Rimmer smiled. Then his head collapsed in on itself and a green sucker ripped out from the slime and fastened on to Kryten's skull.

The real Rimmer skidded round the corner as the polymorph finished feeding on the Mechanoid's electronic emotion, and evaporated into a cloud of steam. 'What's going on? What's happened?'

Kryten turned to face him. 'The polymorph – it turned into you, then sucked away my guilt. I have lost the single emotion that prevents my transgressing the mores and manners of civilized society.'

'Come on – let's forget the supplies. We'll go back for Lister and just get the hell out of here.'

'Screw Lister,' said Kryten, flicking out a middle finger and jabbing it in the air. 'And quite frankly, Rimmer, screw you.'

SIXTEEN

Half-way back to the medical unit, something happened to Rimmer. They were speeding along one of the series of mile-long moving walkways, the Cat slugging from a bottle of cheap Tunisian whisky he'd smashed out of one of the dispensing machines, and Kryten was taking laser potshots at the advert boards that sped by, when Rimmer staggered and clutched his stomach.

Kryten shot out the mouth of a man advertising toothpaste, and turned, sniggering, to see Rimmer totter to his knees. 'What's the matter with you, groin-breath?'

'It's . . . inside me,' Rimmer gasped. 'The polymorph.'

'Oh, is that all?' Kryten tutted, and went back to his target practice.

The Cat blew his nose into his tie, and belched twice. 'Hoinnnnnnnnnnk. Huuuurp. Hurrrrrrp. How is that possible? It's not here.'

Kryten blasted the Kookie Kola Bear out of existence. 'It's broken into the hologram simulation suite, turned itself into electronic data and infiltrated his personality disk. Anyone whose brain wasn't constructed from discarded sphincter could work that one out.'

'You're right,' said the Cat, 'I'm a moron. I'm a nobody. I'm not fit to be alive.'

'Agreed,' Kryten nodded, and trained the barrel of his bazookoid on the Cat. 'Kiss your ass goodbye, Cat,' he said, and fired. There was a disappointing click, and the charge metre flashed: 'empty'. 'Damn,' said Kryten.

'Aw, hell,' said the Cat, 'I was really looking forward to being dead. I don't deserve any better.'

'Don't worry, I'll kill you later, when I get a new gun.'

'Well,' the Cat smiled gratefully, 'only if it's convenient. It's not worth putting yourself out for a useless piece of shit like me.'

Rimmer lay writhing on the floor as the polymorph wriggled through his databank, searching through his personality disk, trying to stimulate a new emotion to sample. Images jolted into Rimmer's brain. Memories, half-forgotten . . .

A hot summer day, waiting outside a cinema for a girl who doesn't turn up. Three hours, he's waited. Three hours. Boy, that makes him . . .

Putting together a cheap, self-assembly study desk with four missing screws, hammering his thumb with a wooden mallet. 'Smegging mallet!' . . .

A baby, now, five months old. He's dropped his teething ring, and no one picks it up. Can't they hear him screaming? Don't they know how badly he needs that teething ring? God, they really make you . . .

Twenty-four, and in the Space Corps. He's coming home on a weekend furlough, and he's stuck in a traffic jam for six hours. Six precious hours are totally wasted, and all the time he's getting more and more . . .

Now, ten. He wants to go to the Russian circus. Not much to ask. It's making a once-in-a-lifetime visit to his hometown. Every-one in his class has been, and then his parents say he can't go, because he didn't mow the lawn. Because he didn't mow their lousy, smegging lawn. Not fair! That really makes you . . .

He's thirty. He's opening a letter. '. . . failed to meet the required standard . . .' but he's worked harder than anyone. It makes him feel so damn . . .

Seventeen. And for the first time in his life, he brings a girl home to meet the family. Sunday afternoon, he chances into the greenhouse, and there she is, behind the tomato plants with his brother John. Would you believe it? Your own brother's got his tongue down your girlfriend's throat ... It really makes you angry!

Now he's fourteen. Boarding-school. Being beaten for talking during lunch. And all he said was 'pass the salt'. It makes him so angry!

Still in boarding-school, in the dormitory, and he's being beaten again, this time for snoring. Snoring in a dormitory is a beating offence? Snoring with malicious intent? And the thick rubber running-shoe slams against his thin cotton pyjamas, and how is that fair? And he's so frustrated and impotent and ... angry!

He's got an exam in the morning. He's thirty years old and he's got an exam in the morning. All his life, he's always seemed to have an exam in the morning. And those BASTARDS in room 1115 are having a smegging party, and how many times does he have to tell them he has an exam in the morning. And every time he tells them, what do they do? They turn the music UP!

And another letter. '... overlooked for promotion ...' for the sixth year on the run, overlooked for promotion. Have to wait yet another year and it's just not FAIR! It makes you so FURIOUS!

The countless frustrations of a lifetime welled up inside him until he felt he would burst.

Then he did.

Anger dragged a primal scream from his throat.

'Nooooooooooooooooooooooooooooooooooooooooooooooooo!'

And fifty-three decks above, in the hologram simulation suite, the polymorph devoured his anger.

Rimmer collapsed on to the moving walkway, panting, empty and drained of all his rage.

SEVENTEEN

Lister paced up and down the medical unit, swinging a baseball bat, his lip curled in a deranged snarl. He smashed the bat into a lab bench between Kryten and the Cat. 'It's war.'

Rimmer shook his head, and re-crossed his legs. 'Look, people,' he said with an even calmness, 'just because it's an armour-plated mutant killing machine that salivates unspeakable slobber, that doesn't mean it's a bad person.' He bit on the end of his pipe, which he'd requested from his hologrammatic accessory computer, along with a T-shirt printed with the words 'Give Quiche a Chance'. 'What we've got to do,' he continued serenely, 'is get it round a table, and put together a solution package, perhaps over tea and biscuits.'

'Look at him,' Kryten slid down from the lab bench. 'We can't trust his opinion – he has no anger – he's a total dork!'

'Good point, Kryten,' Rimmer said kindly. 'Let's take that on board, shall we?' He turned to Lister and smiled. 'David, do you have any suggestions you'd like to bring to this forum?'

'Yes, I have, actually, Arnold,' Lister mimicked. 'Why don't we go down to the ammunition store, get a nuclear warhead and then strap it to my head? I'll nut the smegger to oblivion.' To emphasize his point, the sixty-one-year-old man butted a metal panel on the wall, leaving a large indentation.

'Right. Well, that . . . that's very nice, David,' Rimmer

mumbled genially. 'But let's put that one on the back burner for a while, shall we? Cat, do you have a contribution?'

The Cat looked up from a wastebin he was scavenging through for food. 'Don't ask me my opinion. I'm nobody. Just pretend I'm not here.' He glugged noisily from a bottle of meths he'd found on one of the shelves and belched loudly.

Rimmer nodded benignly. 'That's lovely, thank you very much.'

'You guys are all insane,' the Toaster chirped from its vantage point at the back of the room. 'You're all emotional retards. This is a problem that calls for the leadership abilities of your old buddy, Talkie Toaster™ (patent applied for).'

There was an awkward pause. 'Well,' said Rimmer, finally. 'Moving on a step, and I hope no one thinks that I'm setting myself up as a sort of self-elected chairperson, just see me as a facilitator, Kryten, what's your view? Don't be shy.'

'Well, I think we should send Lister in as a decoy. And while it's busy eating him alive, we can creep up on it from behind and blast it into the stratosphere.'

'Good plan!' Lister punched the wall, breaking three of his fingers. 'That's the best plan yet. Let it get knackered out eating me to death, then you guys can catch it unawares.'

'Well, that's certainly an option, David, yes.' Rimmer sucked his pipe ferociously. 'But here's my proposal: let's get tough, the time for talking is over. Call it extreme, if you like, but I propose we hit it hard, and we hit it fast with a major, and I mean *major*,' he leaned forward, 'leaflet campaign. And while it's reeling from that, we follow up with a whist drive, a car-boot sale, some street theatre, and possibly even some benefit concerts.' Rimmer leaned back again. It was a radical course of action, and he just hoped he hadn't gone too far. He took a comforting suck from his hologrammatic pipe and carried on outlining his solution. 'Now, if that's not enough,' he said, almost crossly, 'I'm sorry, it's time for the T-shirts: "Mutants out"; "Chameleonic Life-forms? No thanks!" and if that doesn't get our message across, I don't know what will.'

Kryten rolled his eyes a full circle. 'Has anyone ever told you, Rimmer, that you are a disgusting, pus-filled bubo, who has all the wit, charm and self-possession of Jayne Mansfield *after* the car accident?'

The Toaster winced. 'Listen to me. You can't operate without fear, anger, guilt and vanity. They're all vital emotions that protect your personalities, and keep you sane.'

Kryten nodded, and walked over to the Toaster. He picked it up, jammed it into the waste-disposal unit, and turned on the grinder. There was a horrible sound of mashing metals. Kryten flicked the unit off, hauled out the flattened mess of components, and tossed them in the bin. 'He's had that coming for a long time,' he said, and stamped his foot into the bin.

'Goodness me,' said Rimmer, 'surely there was a non-violent solution to your differences with the Toaster. Why on earth didn't you try relationship counselling?'

Lister clubbed himself on the forehead with his baseball bat. 'Listen, you bunch of tarts: it's clobbering time. There's a body bag out there with that scudball's name on it, and I'm doing up the zip. Anyone who gets in my way gets a napalm enema.'

The Cat looked up from his bin. 'I think everybody's right, except me, so just forget I spoke, huh?'

Rimmer got to his feet. 'Er, I think we're all beginning to lose sight of the real issue here, which is what are we going to call ourselves?' He paused for suggestions. None came. 'I think it comes down to a choice between "The League Against Salivating Monsters", or, my own personal preference, which is the "Committee for the Liberation and Integration of Terrifying Organisms, and their Rehabilitation Into

Society".' He chewed his lip. 'Just one drawback with that – the abbreviation is Clitoris.'

'It needs killing.' Lister started rubbing some burnt cork over his face. 'If that means I have to sacrifice my life in some stupid, pointless way, then all the better.'

Kryten nodded. 'Yes. Why not? Even if it doesn't work, it'll still be a laugh.'

'Right, so let's cut all of this business,' Lister mimed a yacking mouth with his hand, 'and get on with it. Last one alive's a wet ponce,' he growled. 'Who's with me?'

Rimmer followed him to the hatchway. 'Well, the skutters won't have the protest posters ready till Thursday, but sometimes, I suppose, one just has to act spontaneously. OK, people – let's go.'

'Hey – I'm coming too,' the Cat staggered behind them. 'Maybe I can bum some money off it.'

Kryten took up the tail. Maybe if he handed the others over as hostages, the beast would let him go. He hoisted his bazookoid to waist level, and held the others in his field of fire. 'Move it, suckers.'

EIGHTEEN

It wasn't nearly as difficult as they expected, tracking down the polymorph – it had dined in rapid succession on a variety of emotions far richer than it was used to, and they found it lying bloated and half-asleep back down in the cargo bay.

It would have been easy to kill it then, as it lay, almost shapeless, a pulsating grey-green mush. But they couldn't agree on tactics.

The Cat wanted to throw himself on the creature's mercy. Lister wanted to strangle the mutant to death, as soon as anyone could locate its neck. Rimmer suggested they might offer it a number of concessions, including mutant crèche facilities, a chameleonic lifeform helpline and free travel passes for all slimebeasts; while Kryten refused to join in the discussion, and simply walked up and down one of the wide cargo aisles, happily and noisily evacuating his waste fumes, a practice Mechanoids normally perform in private.

As they stood over the slumbering polymorph, consumed by their pointless bickering, gradually the beast lumbered to awareness. Its primitive brain screamed for survival, and it was forced into a change. It scoured their minds for a shape to protect itself, a form that would be invulnerable while it regained its energy.

And it found one.

Before their eyes, the mound of blubber turned in on itself and rose up into the air, looming above their heads.

The polymorph turned into a tall, green, wrought-iron lamp post.

'Now, what do we do?' Lister nutted the post. 'How d'you fight a lamp post?'

'Hey,' Rimmer held up a conciliatory hand, 'just because it's a lamp post doesn't mean it hasn't got feelings. Isn't that right, big feller?' he said to the lamp post.

Kryten tried ripping off a volley of fire from his bazookoid. When the smoke finally cleared, the lamp post was scorched and a little blackened, but otherwise perfectly intact. 'Now what?'

'We just have to wait,' Lister snarled, 'until it turns into something we can kill.'

So they waited.

Two hours passed.

Two hours while the polymorph regained its strength, regained its energy.

'To hell with this,' said Kryten, finally. 'I'm going to loot the shops in the ship's shopping mall.' But as he made to leave there was a sickening squelching noise, and the lamp post began turning in on itself.

NINETEEN

So, how did he die?

The three surviving crew members would ask themselves the same questions over and over again during the weeks that followed.

Whose fault was it? Was there anything anyone could have done?

And the truth was: they would never know for sure.

He was dead, and that was the cold, hard fact.

There was no going back.

Now, they were three.

TWENTY

Lister charged the metamorphosing mass, trying to obliterate the beast before it completed its change. A tentacle whipped out of the blubber and tossed him effortlessly down the aisle. He smashed into a pile of crates, and lay, unconscious, in the timber rubble.

The other three fled down the corridor of packing cases, Kryten using the uncomplaining Cat as a shield.

The creature rose, shrieking, to become the mucus-pulsing, demonic beast of Lister's fear.

The Cat caught hold of Lister's collar, and Kryten dragged the two of them down the aisle. Kryten thumped down the bar on the emergency door with his hip, and they all fell backwards through it and began tumbling down a metal spiral staircase. They rolled out on to a white tiled floor, and found themselves in the pump room of the air-conditioning complex on the engineering deck.

Rimmer scampered down the staircase behind them, his eyes alight with fear.

They dragged themselves to their feet, and Kryten scoured the room for an exit.

There were no doors, or hatches.

They were at the very bottom of the ship.

Suddenly, iron girders and metal tiles began to rain down from the ceiling, and with a splintering of steel, the poly-morph dropped into the pump room.

Its black lips rolled back, exposing its glistening teeth, and it roared in demonic triumph.

Untempered by guilt, Kryten's heightened instinct for self-preservation overrode his fear. It didn't make sense – there had to be another way out; there was no room on the ship that had only one exit. There had to be a second door, or an airlock, or *something*.

He scanned the room again. Against the back wall was a disused pump unit, lying on its side. Kryten edged back towards it and dragged it away from the wall.

Behind it was an old service lift.

He jabbed the call button and heard the crashing of the gears as the motor ground into action, and the lift car began its creaking descent from perhaps twenty floors above.

A tentacle whiplashed out and coiled around Kryten's neck, hoisting him into the air as the lift juddered to a halt, and the doors sushed open.

Two blue shimmering balls hovered around the lift car. They spun end over end in tiny, menacing circles, before they shot out into the pump room. They streaked round the chamber before their tracking computers locked on to the hottest object in the room, and screeched down towards the target.

The polymorph simply disappeared. The short silence that followed the blast was broken by the sickening splatter of mucal debris and smouldering fragments of endoskeleton as the dead mutant's remains obeyed Newton.

Suddenly a swirling wind whipped all the papers in the pump room into a spiralling tornado. Then the wind divided into four frenzied twisters and blasted into each of the crew.

They each staggered back, filled by an energy and a force they had never experienced before.

When Kryten groped his way upright, he was whole again. His guilt had returned. 'How can you ever forgive me?' he moaned, wretchedly. 'Naturally, I'll commit suicide immediately.' He placed the muzzle of the bazookoid into his lipless mouth.

The Cat batted it away. 'Chill it, Buddy,' he said. 'We all did things back there we weren't proud of. Look at me.' He stood there in his ragged, stinking clothes, his hair matted and mangled. 'If I don't get a bath in the next thirty seconds, I'm going to have to resign my post as Most Handsome Guy on this ship.'

'The Toaster,' Kryten bleated, 'what did I do to the Toaster?'

'Lister?' Rimmer crouched over Lister's immobile form. 'Lister?' he called again.

Kryten hurried over and knelt by his side. He looked down at Lister's grey face.

'Is he OK?'

'He's had a heart attack.'

Kryten gently rolled Lister's head to one side, and felt the side of his neck for a pulse.

'Is he OK?' Rimmer said again.

Kryten reached forward and his open palm closed Lister's eyes.

Part Four

The end, and after

ONE

The funeral of the last remaining member of the human race was neither a solemn nor a sombre affair. Quite the opposite. Lister's favourite dance track, 'Born to Brutalize' thumped out of his old wax-blaster with such force it shook the coffin. Kryten, Rimmer and the Cat stood around the metal casket, wearing green Day-glo Deely-boppers, battery-propelled revolving bow-ties and yellow fishing waders, precisely as Lister had requested in his Last Will and Testament.

Rimmer had been present that drunken night Lister had decided to make a will. He'd scrawled his last wishes on a pair of his old boxers in red, indelible ink, and Rimmer ensured they followed the instructions to the last misspelt letter.

The Cat gently placed a sealed foil tray of chicken vindaloo by Lister's feet, followed by two spicy poppadoms and an onion salad. Kryten shuffled along behind him, and placed three six-packs of Leopard lager in the coffin, together with Lister's one and only photograph of Kristine Kochanski.

As 'Born to Brutalize' reached its climactic nuclear guitar solo, they sealed the casket lid and fired the coffin off into space.

''Bye, man,' said Rimmer quietly, and the three of them turned and shuffled sadly out of the waste-disposal bay.

★

Kryten busied himself setting the table for the wake. None of them felt much like drinking, but Lister had insisted they each consume an entire bottle of Cinzano Bianco. The menu was even more daunting: a triple fried-egg sandwich with chilli sauce and chutney, Lister's favourite snack.

'I suppose someone should tell Holly,' said Rimmer.

The Cat nodded.

Rimmer slouched off to the Drive room.

'On,' said Rimmer, and Holly's pixelized face materialized on to the screen. 'Sorry to bother you, Hol, but we've got some bad news.' He gazed down at the floor. 'It's Lister,' he said, eventually. 'He's dead.'

Holly nodded.

'I thought you'd want to know.'

'Yes.' Holly paused for two of his valuable remaining seconds. 'How?'

'Heart attack.' Rimmer sketched in the details.

Holly listened, and when Rimmer had finished, he simply said 'Oh,' and switched himself off.

Rimmer had passed under the Drive-room exit hatch and was half-way down the corridor before the noise started.

Printers printing.

He wheeled round and walked back into the Drive room.

Every single printer was churning out ream after ream of calculations and instructions.

Rimmer stood in the hatchway and his face yielded to a grin, which, in turn gave way to laughter. Not his normal hollow braying empty laughter, this was an altogether different noise. This was a noise his vocal cords had never been called on to make before.

It was the laughter of joy.

Kryten and the Cat were in the sleeping quarters, sifting through a stack of old photographs, when Rimmer poked his red face through the hatchway and said, breathlessly:

'Quick! Come on!' then vanished. By the time the Cat had sauntered over to the hatchway, Rimmer was two hundred and fifty yards down the corridor and still accelerating. They started after him.

Rimmer bounded down the emergency staircase four steps at a time, and carried on down the ship without a break, for thirty-two floors. He was moving so fast that several times even the Cat thought he'd lost him.

Finally Rimmer emerged on the shuttle deck, and streaked across the lined runway towards *White Giant*. By the time Kryten and the Cat hit the shuttle bay, Rimmer was high-stepping up the ship's embarkation ramp. He disappeared inside.

Seconds later the retros blasted into the ground, and the Cat and Kryten had to complete the last part of the journey through blinding, billowing white smoke.

They leapt on to the hovering embarkation ramp, and ran along its length as it began to retract into the craft. They stumbled inside, coughing and tear-blind, as the hatch slammed closed. They staggered towards the cockpit over skutters sorting through reams of computer print-out, as the transport craft's autopilot taxied it down the runway and out into space.

They listed into the cockpit section, where Rimmer stood impatiently jiggling his right leg, and flopped into the two Drive seats.

'What's happening, Buddy?'

'Where are we going?'

Rimmer's left arm snaked out, and pointed through the cockpit's viewscreen at a glimmering brown dot in the distance. 'Follow that coffin.'

The Cat flipped the controls to manual, and pressed the re-heat button.

White Giant burned across the blackness in pursuit of the slow-spinning casket.

TWO

Nothing.

At first, there was nothing.

Then.

Then there was something.

It was a light. A tiny shard of brilliance that shocked him with its suddenness.

Then.

Then there was nothing again.

There was no way of telling how long it lasted: nothing has no time.

Then the light again. And the light grew, and across the face of the light, dark shapes began to move.

He watched as the shapes became faces. Faces he didn't know. They were concerned faces; gentle, kindly. They made him feel safe.

Then he lost consciousness. But unconsciousness wasn't like nothing, it was studded with dreams. He dreamed of a garden, pungent with jasmine. He knew the garden. He knew it very well. But he had no idea where or when he knew it from.

Then pain.

Something imploded in his chest. He lurched upright, and there was a second implosion, and the pain was gone.

He drifted back off to sleep.

When he awoke, it was dusk. He was in a bed, with clean white cotton sheets tightly tucked into the sides. There was a green screen around the bed, so the rest of the room was obscured from him. By the bedside, on a cabinet, there was a huge vase full of jasmine, with some kind of greeting card nestling among the yellow flowers. His left arm, for some reason, felt weak and helpless, so he reached up with his right, and plucked the card from its place.

In the half-light his old eyes couldn't focus on the inscription. He replaced the card and, overcome with weariness, slid back into sleep.

When he woke again, he was moving. Fluorescent lights streaked past above him. He tried to raise his head, but a friendly hand patted it down again, as the hospital trolley raced along the white-tiled corridor. They burst through three sets of overlapping rubber doors, and suddenly they were outside in the biting wind of the cold winter air.

There was a jerk, and the stretcher was hoisted off the trolley. There was a commotion – people were shouting things he didn't understand, and all the time, the pain in his chest was getting worse. Two men ran with his stretcher and slid him into the back of a waiting ambulance. The doors slammed closed, and the ambulance screeched off.

'Where am I?' An oxygen mask loomed over him, and once again, he blacked out.

He came to as the ambulance doors swung open, and the same two men hauled his stretcher out of the vehicle, and set it down on a pavement, in the middle of a circle of people.

'What's happening?' he bleated pathetically. Gingerly, the two men eased him off the stretcher and placed him on the cold hard pavement.

One of them packed up the stretcher and dashed back with it to the ambulance, while the other twisted his leg so it folded under his body, then lifted up his head and slid his arm underneath it. The pain was unbearable, now.

He tilted his head weakly, and watched as the two men jumped into the ambulance, and reversed off into the busy traffic. He lay on his back, peripherally aware of the circle of onlookers. One of them, a woman, was talking, but she sounded vague and distant, and he couldn't make it out.

One by one the onlookers began to drift away, until, eventually, he was totally alone, lying in his unnatural pose on the pavement.

The pain reached a crescendo, and imploded in his chest. He jumped to his feet, staggered along a shop window, regained his balance, and started to walk slowly down the street.

The worst of the pain had subsided, just a sharp ache in his left arm remained, and his breathing was beginning to come more easily.

Half-dazed, he shuffled along the street, found a bench and sat down. After ten minutes, he didn't feel too badly at all, and decided to go for a coffee.

He found a café just a few shops down, and sat at one of the red plastic tables. Almost immediately, a waitress came over and set down a plate of money. Then she smiled at him, pleasantly and scurried off.

Soon after, she returned with some crockery: a cup, a saucer, and a plate. She put them on his table and went off to serve someone else.

The cup was dirty. It had a coffee ring around the top, and there was some half-dissolved sugar in the bottom. The plate was dirty, too. It was covered in crumbs, and in the middle there was a huge blob of mayonnaise.

He held up his hand to call back the waitress, but suddenly, he realized he was going to be sick. Liquid gushed up his throat, but he managed to catch it in the coffee cup.

But he hadn't been sick. He looked into the cup – it was half full of coffee. Then he was filled with panic again. This time, he definitely was going to be sick. He reached up to his mouth, and regurgitated a perfectly shaped triangular tuna and mayonnaise sandwich. Three other quarters followed in fast succession, along with a sliver of cucumber, a slice of tomato and a small portion of watercress.

'Help,' he said, quietly. His throat gurgled again, and he filled the coffee cup to the top.

He smelled the cup. It *was* coffee. Fresh. Steam was coming off it. He dipped his teaspoon in and swirled it around. When he brought the spoon out again, it was full of sugar. He tipped it into the sugar bowl, and looked around the café.

A large woman with two unruly children was mid-way through regurgitating an enormous chocolate éclair. On the next table, a man was jabbing a fork into his mouth, and pulling out french fries.

He looked over to the waitress, and watched as she flipped open the pedal bin, took out a handful of rib-bones, and arranged them on a large white plate. Then she served the bones to two teenage boys sitting at the counter.

He watched as the boys raised the bones to their mouths and began to fill them with meat.

The waitress swept over to his table and took away his sandwich and his coffee. She held the cup under a cappuccino machine, which sucked the liquid noisily up into its metal cylinder. Then she opened the sandwich, spooned the tuna and mayonnaise filling into a bowl, effortlessly scraped the bread clean of butter, and returned the bread to a large, uncut loaf.

He left the café, deciding he needed some fresh air.

All the traffic was going backwards.

What was this place? What was he doing here?

Almost every aspect of the city was strange and unfamiliar. He tramped around for twenty minutes, looking for a landmark, something he might recognize, but it was hopeless.

When he next looked around, he found he'd wandered off the main street, and was in a dimly lit alley. He felt panicked, and alone. Suddenly he heard urgent footsteps coming towards him from behind. Before he could turn, the man was on him, pressing him up against a wall, and holding a short silver knife against his throat.

Deftly the mugger fastened a watch around the old man's wrist, then slipped a wallet into the inside pocket of the old man's coat.

He watched bemused as the mugger flipped closed the blade of his knife, smiled with false charm and raced off down the alley.

'Help,' the old man said quietly. 'What's happening to me?'

He opened the wallet and looked inside. Astonishingly, his own photograph was in one of the credit card compartments. There was a driving licence, too. The name on the licence was: 'Retsil Divad'.

It took the old man a good ten minutes to realize the name was his.

Because, like everything else in this crazy place, his name was backwards.

THREE

Four thousand dull gunmetal-grey canisters lay stacked in neat ranks in the scoop room of *White Giant*'s cargo section.

'Here's some more,' said Kryten, as a fresh haul of canisters clattered down the chute. He read the numbers, and then one by one tossed them to the Cat, who began to pile them alongside the others.

'Has anyone even the vaguest, remotest idea what it is we're doing here?' asked Rimmer.

The Cat and Kryten grunted verbal shrugs. The truth was, none of them even pretended to begin to understand the list of instructions, data, formulae and coordinates Holly had left them. Not even the newly repaired Toaster claimed to understand this one. Although it was fair to say it wasn't in tip-top peak condition, despite the many hours Kryten had spent panel-beating its chrome cover, and reconstructing its mashed circuitry. Kryten wasn't exactly an expert when it came to Artificial Intelligence, and the Toaster wasn't all it might be in the sanity department.

In fact, for some reason, the Toaster now thought it was a moose.

It bellowed loudly from time to time, and occasionally threatened to charge them with its huge antlers, but otherwise it was harmless.

More canisters scuttled down the chute, and once again Kryten studied the numbers. 'Got it!' he squealed with delight, and clapped his hands.

The Cat began rotating his body from side to side, and pumping his hands so they circled over each other in front of his chest. 'Yes, yes, ye-ess!'

'Excellente!' grinned Rimmer.

'Mahooooooo!' bellowed the Toaster.

It had been easy enough collecting Lister's coffin and returning it to a stasis booth on *Red Dwarf*, but the second instruction was a little more bizarre. They had to locate a swarm of canisters floating through space at a certain set of coordinates, and bring aboard the one numbered '1121'. Holly had failed to mention there would be something in the region of ten thousand of these canisters, and the search had taken them the best part of five weeks.

'What next?' asked Rimmer, as he craned over Kryten's shoulder, trying to read the indecipherable machine code.

'I'm supposed to treat the canister; bombard it with X-rays, gamma rays – all kinds of stuff.'

'Then what?'

Kryten consulted Holly's sheet again. 'We take Lister's body on a little trip.'

'Where?'

'Through the Black Hole. Into the omni-zone. To a particular planet in Universe 3. Apparently, we're to bury him there.'

'Universe 3? What's so special about Universe 3?'

'Well, apart from the fact that it's almost a mirror image of our own universe, except that time moves backwards there,' Kryten said, 'there's nothing very special about it at all.'

The Cat shook the canister. 'What's this got to do with anything? What's in it?'

'I don't know,' Kryten flipped through the instructions. 'Maybe some chemical we have to use later.'

'I don't think so,' Rimmer tried to suffocate a smirk. 'I've got a pretty good idea what *is* in there, and I don't think you'll find it's a chemical.'

He raised an enigmatic eyebrow, and walked back to the cockpit, whistling happily.

FOUR

So time was running backwards. It had taken Lister a while to figure it out, but if he reversed the events of the day, it all seemed to come together. He'd walked down a dark alley, where a mugger had stolen his watch and his wallet. In a daze, he'd stumbled through the streets, until he came across a café where he'd had a coffee and something to eat to calm his nerves. Obviously it hadn't worked, because he'd gone out into the street, suffered a heart attack, and been rushed to hospital. After a few hours slipping in and out of consciousness, he'd suffered a second heart attack and died.

Except, of course, it had all happened backwards.

He looked at the address on his driving licence. A cab screeched up backwards beside him. He leaned in the window, accepted the fare and the tip from the cabbie and climbed in. Lister was about to attempt to read out the backwards address on his licence when the cab pulled off and began reversing through the streets at high speed.

The driver knew where he was going, which, when Lister thought about it, made some kind of sense. If everything was backwards, presumably, when they reached their destination, Lister would have to tell the driver where he picked him up.

His brain ached.

Suddenly, the cab stopped, caught up in traffic. Lister leant out of the window to see what was causing the jam. Three fire engines pulled up outside a ruined building. As the firemen uncoiled their hoses, the ruins began to smoulder. The hoses sucked giant jets of water out of the smoking rubble, and within minutes the ruins were a flaming orange inferno. When the blaze had reached its peak, the firemen put away their hoses and drove off with sirens blaring. The traffic began to shuffle past the fire. By the time Lister's cab had passed it, the fire was almost out. Where the ruins had been, there now stood a chic, new-looking office block.

Lister shook his head, and ducked back into the cab. There was a newspaper jammed down the side of the bench seat. He dug it out, and opened it out to the front page. Under the headline was a large photo of the blaze he'd just witnessed. This wasn't helping his brain-ache. Finally, he realized it must be an old newspaper, from the previous morning. In the backwards reality, obviously, news was reported before it happened.

A thought struck him, and he turned to the seirautibo column. And there he was: Retsil Divad. It took him a while to translate the accompanying text: 'David Lister, aged 61, joyfully brought to life on Thursday, the 21st, at eleven-thirty p.m. (see personal column).'

Lister feverishly ripped through the pages, and found the personal column. He traced his finger down the entries, and stopped when he found one that was printed forwards.

'Dave Lister,' it said. 'Sure everything will become clear to you. This was the only way. Obviously, can't be with you – everyone would get younger. Will pick you up in thirty-six years. Be at Niagara Falls, by the souvenir shop, at noon precisely. See you then. Good luck, from the *Red Dwarf* crew.'

They'd done it again. They'd marooned him in some insane part of the universe, expecting him to cope alone for the best part of forty years.

To do that once was bad enough. To do it twice – twice in consecutive lifetimes – that was sheer bad manners.

Lister was a social animal. He hated being alone. Always had done.

He looked out of the cab window.

It was beginning to rain.

There should have been a saxophone playing a wistful, melancholy blues number.

The rain swirled up from the wet pavements and hurled itself into the scowling clouds above.

Finally, the cab screeched to a start outside the address on the driving licence. He was home, whatever that meant. The taxi door flung itself open, and Lister climbed out.

He took the key from his wallet, walked up the path to the house and let himself in.

It was a big house. Whatever he was destined to do for a living, it looked like he was destined to do it pretty successfully. He walked into the first reception room. Framed photographs jostled for position on the old stone mantelpiece.

This was his life – the life he was about to lead in this strange reality in which he was an interloper.

Something in one of the photographs caught his eye, and he scrutinized the others more closely.

Impossible.

It just wasn't possible. Not even with an IQ of twelve thousand.

But the evidence was there, in the photographs. Somehow, Holly had done it.

But how?

Lister would have to wait thirty-six years to find out the answer.

He turned and watched the lace curtains fluttering in the breeze through the open french windows.

He crossed the room and stepped out into the garden.

At the end of the lawn an old woman in a wide-brimmed sun hat was clipping away at the jasmine borders. She looked up and saw him, and her face crinkled into her famous pinball smile.

Thirty-six years. They would grow young together. They had a whole new past to look forward to.

The old man's face crinkled into a smile of its own, and he started shuffling down the garden towards her.

BACKWORD

As creators of *Red Dwarf*, the most frequent question we're ever asked is, 'Don't you think it's cruel to keep a giraffe as a pet?', and the answer we always give is, 'Not if you live in a tall house.'

The second most frequent question is, 'Where did you get the idea for *Red Dwarf* from?' This is a very annoying question, because it ends on a preposition, and every good writer knows that's not something you should finish a sentence with. Dammit. The truth is, we don't know where the idea came from. If we did, we'd get another one.

All we can remember is it was some time in 1984, and hot, so it was probably summer. Searching through some old cardboard boxes, we found three things: 1) The beer mat on which the original idea was first mooted; 2) A sketch from the Radio 4 comedy series *Son Of Cliché* where the idea was first developed; and 3) The original curry-stained first draft of the TV pilot.

For those of you who are interested, those three things follow.

GRANT NAYLOR
Some time dull and overcast (probably autumn) 1992

The Beer Mat

Some time drunk and depressed, 1983

Dave Hollins – Space Cadet

Son of Cliché was a Radio 4 sketch show, starring Chris Barrie, Nick Maloney and Nick Wilton, produced by Alan Nixon, and was first broadcast in 1983.

Dave Hollins – Space Cadet became a regular feature during the third series in 1984, along with *Captain Invisible and the See-Thru Kid, Asso – Spanish Detective* and other such intellectual jewels.

Tape: Space music

ANNOUNCER: Dave Hollins – Space Cadet.

Tape: Space ship whooshes past

DAVE: This is Stellar Trader, Dave Hollins, calling Earth Com 597 beta 7. The rest of the crew are dead. Returning from a routine UEC mining expedition to Titan, we unwittingly took on board a strange chameleonic alien, who ruthlessly massacred the entire crew. Last time we invite him aboard. I alone escaped by placing myself in suspended animation for seven trillion years. Should have been two days but I overslept. According to Hab, the ship's computer, due to time dilation, I am now 140 gazillion light years from home, and that's not including the wait for the baggage carousel. My biggest problem is going Space crazy through loneliness. The only thing that keeps me sane is my collection of onions. To pass the time, I've decided to build an

android in the image of a woman. A perfectly functioning robot, capable of abstract thought and independent
decision making. The problem is – I don't know how.
God, I don't even know what to make the nose out of.
It's so depressing.

HAB: Hello, Dave.

DAVE: What is it, Hab?

HAB: The Melissa V is being tracked by two supra-light
speed pulsar fighters from Earth, representing the Norweb
Federation.

DAVE: Who's that?

HAB: The North Western Electricity Board.

DAVE: What do they want, Hab?

HAB: They want you for crimes against humanity, Dave.

DAVE: What?

HAB: Dave, remember when you left Earth, seven trillion
years ago? You left two half-eaten German sausages on a
plate in your kitchen.

DAVE: Oh, yeah, I remember.

HAB: Do you know what happens to sausages if you leave
them for seven trillion years?

DAVE: They go off?

HAB: Those sausages, Dave, now cover seven-eighths of the
Earth's surface.

DAVE: (*Pause*) Yuch.

HAB: Not only that – you also left £57.50 in your bank
account. The compound interest on that now means you
own 98 per cent of all the world's wealth. And because
you've hoarded it all for seven trillion years, nobody's got
any money except for you and Norweb.

DAVE: Why Norweb?

HAB: You left a light on in your bathroom. (*Pause*) Dave,
you've destroyed the world's economy, its ecology and
sent Humankind back to the Stone Age.

DAVE: Well, I'm sorry. I guess I just wasn't thinking straight.

Hab – you're the most intelligent machine ever built. What do I do?

HAB: One moment, Dave. I'll channel my run-time.

Tape: Long beep

HAB: I have it, Dave. Hide under the kitchen table and I'll tell them you're out.

DAVE: Hab – you've got to get me out of here.

HAB: Your only chance is somehow to find a disturbance in the fabric of Time – a sort of cross–dimensional temporal warp, which has the exact magnetic pull to convert you to anti-matter and reconstruct your carbon ions in your own spectral field . . .

DAVE: Oh look – there's one.

HAB: Have plotted a course, Dave. Hang on.

Tape: Weird space things happening

ANNOUNCER: Next week Dave returns to Earth to find the only survivors of a nuclear holocaust are fruit flies, beetles and PE teachers. Fruit flies are now the dominant species.

Tape: Space music

ANNOUNCER: Dave Hollins – Space Cadet.

Tape: Space ship whooshes off

Ends

Red Dwarf Pilot Script

Before we started writing the pilot script, we met Paul Jackson, then a TV producer, at the Latchmere pub in Battersea and outlined the idea. He remarked, prophetically, that the project would be difficult to sell.

Most TV executives, he explained, loathe, despise and revile Science Fiction. It's expensive, but looks cheap, the characters are usually lousy, and you always end up in a quarry in Wales pretending it's the planet Qweegle 7 in the star system Zzqqyzzqwykkk 5, running away from people dressed in Bacofoil suits from the star system Kkkywqzzyqqzz 15.

But it's not like that, we protested: it's *Steptoe and Son* in space on acid.

Whatever you do, he said, make it sound as ordinary and normal and accessible as possible, so those good old TV execs don't get scared.

Which is why, right from the opening stage direction, we took every opportunity to stress the ordinariness of the situation. We tried to give the impression that the whole thing could be filmed in BBC corridors and the BBC canteen, and we included only two model shots of the ship, tucked away in the last third of the show.

It still took three years to sell.

We wrote the script without a real cast in mind. At this stage we imagined a kind of English version of Christopher Lloyd (who was playing Reverend Jim in *Taxi*) as Lister, and an English Dan Aykroyd (as he was in *Trading Places*) as Rimmer.

Red Dwarf
A situation comedy in space
Draft One, August 1984

1. Film. Ship's corridor

Very ordinary. Could be the corridor in a TV company.

LISTER *and* RIMMER *are hard at work.* RIMMER *is removing circuit covers, making minor alterations with a circuit burner and replacing the cover on the wall.*

RIMMER *is a company man. Neatly dressed, slightly over-zealous crew-cut.* LISTER *is pushing a squeaky four-wheeled trolley. His hair sticks up madly. He's unshaven and sloppy. Stained T-shirt. Smoking.* RIMMER *finishes his panel and moves on.*

RIMMER: Lister, will you keep up?

LISTER *salutes and drags on his cigarette at the same time.*

LISTER: Yes, sir. Rimmer.

RIMMER *consults his clipboard.*

RIMMER: White corridor, Level Two. Good. That's the porous circuits.

They trundle off down the corridor.

2. Set. Section of white corridor

Set in the wall is a door marked 'Stasis'. It has a wheel lock and a viewing window.

RIMMER *is bending down to remove another panel.*

LISTER: Can I have a turn?

RIMMER: No.

LISTER: But I've been pushing the trolley all shift. Let me burn the circuits and you push the trolley.

RIMMER: Shut up, Lister. And that's an order.

LISTER: How about . . .

RIMMER: N–O spells no.

LISTER: No, listen. How about I take out one of the rivets, you take out the other one and burn the circuit, and I'll even still push the trolley. OK?

LISTER *smiles to tempt him with the deal.*

RIMMER: Look, Lister. As long as I'm Second Technician and you're just . . . what is it again?

LISTER: Captain.

RIMMER: *Third* Technician, you'll push the trolley, and I'll be the one who does everything else. Clear?

LISTER: Doesn't bother me.

RIMMER: Good.

LISTER: I'm not bothered.

RIMMER: Mmmm. Gives you a good feeling, removing a rivet. Mmmm. Oh. Good.

LISTER: It's a stupid job, anyway. I was talking to Chen, and he says the only reason they don't give it to the service droids is they don't want to waste their time.

RIMMER: That's a lie, Lister.

LISTER: No, it's not. You rank below all four of those service droids. Even the one that's broken.

RIMMER: Yes? Well not for long. Up. Up. Up. That's where I'm going.

LISTER: Not till you pass your Engineer's exam, and you won't do that, because you'll faint again.

Routed RIMMER *pretends he's just noticed* LISTER *smoking.*

RIMMER: Is that a cigarette you're smoking?

LISTER *looks at it.*

RIMMER: You realize I'm going to have to report you for this.

RIMMER *takes out his note pad, and writes in it.*

LISTER: I don't care.

TODHUNTER, *an officer, approaches.*

TODHUNTER: Rimmer? Lister?

RIMMER *salutes, smartly.*

RIMMER: Yes, Sir!
LISTER: Hi.
TODHUNTER: Rimmer, I'm just, uh, I'm just going through McIntyre's artefacts, and I see you filed . . . 247 complaints against Lister.
RIMMER: Yes, sir!
TODHUNTER: (*Reading*) 123 counts of insulting a superior officer. 39 counts of dereliction of duty. 86 counts of general insubordination. And one count of mutiny.
RIMMER: Yes, Sir!
TODHUNTER: Mutiny, Lister?
LISTER: I stood on his toe.
RIMMER: On purpose!
LISTER: By accident.
RIMMER: With both feet? How is it possible to get two big feet on one small toe by accident?
LISTER: Well, if you've got your toes pointed inwards, you . . .
RIMMER: I put it to you, Lister, you didn't stand on my toe at all – you stood on my entire foot! Thereby obstructing a superior officer in pursuit of vital duty.
LISTER: But the vital duty was preventing me from playing my guitar.

RIMMER: I removed the guitar, whereupon you leapt from the top bunk onto my right foot.

TODHUNTER: All right, that's enough . . .

RIMMER: If there had been a crisis situation, I would have had to carry out my duties hopping. Clearly putting the ship at risk. Clearly, therefore, mutiny.

TODHUNTER: Rimmer . . .

RIMMER: However, I don't intend to apply for the death penalty, because I'm not a vindictive man.

TODHUNTER: Finished?

RIMMER: Yes, sir.

TODHUNTER: There are 129 people aboard this ship. You Rimmer, are over one man. Why can't you get on?

LISTER: I try, sir. I'm not an insubordinate man by nature.

RIMMER: Yes, you are.

LISTER: I try and respect Rimmer, and everything, but it's not easy, because he's such a smeg head.

RIMMER: Did you hear that, sir? (*To* LISTER) Have you any conception of the penalty for calling a superior officer a 'smeg head'?

TODHUNTER: Rimmer – you *are* a smeg head.

TODHUNTER *starts to move off.*

RIMMER: You heard that, Lister. (*To* TODHUNTER) With respect, sir, your career is over! You're finished on this ship! You hear me? Finished.

3. Set. Drive room

The small control centre of the ship. Seven or eight people in uniform, with black armbands, standing sombrely in a horseshoe.
    TODHUNTER *comes in and takes up his place.*
    The CAPTAIN *speaks.*

CAPTAIN: We're all here today to pay our last respects to

George. (*Cough*) George McIntyre was an excellent officer and as good a friend as anyone could have. He was sixty-three, and in the prime of life, and he'll be missed more deeply and more completely than he could ever know. I now commend his ashes to the stars he loved so much. Goodbye, George, we'll miss you.

He produces a small tin, about the size of a Cadbury's Marvel tin, with a little Australian flag sticking out of the top of it. He puts the tin into a chute.

CAPTAIN: Start the tapes.

The strains of Stevie Wonder's 'Heaven is 10 zillion light years away'. The CAPTAIN *presses a button, and we hear the tin being shot into space.*

CAPTAIN: Everybody for sherry?

4. Set. Lister and Rimmer's sleeping quarters

Two bunkbeds. A large table, chairs, vid-screen, a porthole, a serving hatch for food. It's like a small bedsit.

We can still hear the music. The service has been relayed over the ship's vid-circuit.

LISTER *is looking out of the porthole.* RIMMER *is at the table with the book open, making notes on his arm.*

LISTER: There goes McIntyre.

He cranes his neck round to follow the can as it passes the ship. He waves.

LISTER: 'Bye, George. (*To* RIMMER) That was George.

RIMMER *leans over and turns the vid-screen off.*

LISTER: I was watching that.
RIMMER: Yes, well, I've got an exam tomorrow.

RIMMER *goes back to writing on his arm.*

LISTER: D'you mind if I play my guitar, Rimmer?

RIMMER: You touch that guitar and I'll remove the E-string and garotte you with it.

LISTER: Which E? Top E or bottom E?

RIMMER: What? What difference does it make?

LISTER: I haven't got a bottom E. I broke it eight months ago.

RIMMER: I thought you were going down to the bar to bum a drink or something?

LISTER: I don't know why you put yourself through this, Rimmer. You're only going to fail again.

RIMMER: No, I'm not.

LISTER: Yes, you are. You're just going to go in and write 'I AM A FISH' 400 times and faint again.

RIMMER: That's a lie.

LISTER: No, it's not. Petersen told me.

RIMMER: (*Mimics*) No, it's not. Petersen told me. What I did: I wrote a discourse on porous circuits which was just too radical for the examiners to accept.

LISTER: Yeah. You said you were a fish.

RIMMER *starts to roll up his trouser leg to write on his calf.*

RIMMER: God, I'll be glad to get out of here.

LISTER: Where are you going?

RIMMER: Out of this pit, and up the ziggurat. And the first step is when I pass that exam tomorrow.

LISTER: By cheating?

RIMMER: I'm not cheating. (*Points at his arm*) This is merely an aid to memory. It helps me marshal the facts already in my command.

LISTER: What does? Copying all the text books onto your body? Why don't you just hand your body in and let them mark that?

RIMMER: OK Modo – spell 'TITAN'. I've seen your report. You can't spell 'TITAN'. T-I-G-H-T-A-N. You're a nothing.

LISTER: I'm not a nothing. I've got a plan. I'm going to do two more trips, and I've been saving all my pay . . .

RIMMER: Since when?

LISTER: Since always. That's why I always wear this T-shirt. And I'm going to buy a little farm in Fiji, and I'm going to get a sheep and a cow and breed horses.

RIMMER: With a sheep and a cow?

LISTER: No, with horses and horses. The sheep and the cow are because I like them as animals.

RIMMER: On Fiji?

LISTER: Yeah.

RIMMER: Don't you know there's no animals on Fiji? And you know why? Because there's no grass on Fiji any more. What are you going to have – a sand farm?

LISTER: I don't care about the grass. I'll take my own. See? This is why I never talked about it. I knew you'd say something like this.

Attention-grabbing noise. We hear HOLLY *the ship's computer.*

HOLLY: The 'Welcome Back, George McIntyre' Reception is about to begin in the Refectory. George would like to invite everybody, especially those who weren't able to attend his funeral.

5. Film. The Refectory

A large, fairly modern canteen. Lots of people sitting at tables, facing the head table. The Reception Meal has just finished. A cake, in the shape of a cross, is in the centre of the head table. Seated either side of it are the CAPTAIN *and* GEORGE MCINTYRE, *who has a large 'H' on his forehead. The* CAPTAIN *stands and bangs his glass with a spoon for attention.*

CAPTAIN: Today is a day for both sadness and joy. Sadness for the passing away of George, and joy because George is back with us, albeit as a hologram. Some of you may not have travelled with a hologram before. And I ask you to treat him as a human being, because he is, in every respect, like George. He has George's personality, and George's knowledge and experience. Of course he can't touch anything, or lift anything, so I ask you to cooperate with his requests, and please take every care not to walk through him even when you are in a hurry. Thank you.

The CAPTAIN *sits. Applause.* GEORGE *stands up. He's normal, except for the 'H' on his forehead.*
Thumping on tables. Whoops. Cheers. Applause.

GEORGE: I want to thank everybody for giving me such a marvellous funeral. I've just seen the vid, and I want to thank the Captain for his beautiful eulogy. But I still don't know why he didn't use the one I wrote.

Huge laugh. Table banging. Spoons clinking against glasses. Shot of LISTER *absolutely falling about.*

GEORGE: This must be weird for everyone, but I don't want you to think of me as someone who's dead. More as someone who's no longer a threat to your wives.

Huge male laugh.

GEORGE: I think Joe knows what I'm talking about.

Shot of JOE *laughing harder than anyone.*

GEORGE: As you know, Holly's only capable of sustaining one hologram. So my advice to officers ranked higher than me is – don't die. Please.

Laugh.
Shot of LISTER *slapping his thigh.* RIMMER *revising his arm.*

GEORGE: But seriously, I'd like to thank you all for everything you've done today. I'm pretty sure it's what I would have wanted. Thank you.

He sits. Applause. Spoon banging. Feet stamping.
TODHUNTER *stands.*

TODHUNTER: Could the crew please be upstanding for the cutting of the cake.

Everyone stands.
The CAPTAIN *cuts the cross cake.* GEORGE'*s hologram is standing near him, to give the illusion that he's helping* TODHUNTER *raise his glass.*

TODHUNTER: Flight Coordinator George McIntyre.
ALL: George!

They drink. Applause. The CAPTAIN *cuts in . . .*

CAPTAIN: Just one thing before the disco. Holly tells me she's sensed a non-human life-form on board.
LISTER: It's Rimmer.
CAPTAIN: We don't know what it is – so be careful.
LISTER: I'm turning you in, Rimmer.

6. Set. Sleeping quarters

The next morning.
RIMMER *is up, and looks like he has been all night. He is dragging amateurishly on a cigarette, even though he doesn't smoke. He is in a T-shirt and shorts. All four limbs are covered in notation. He is mumbling to himself . . .*

RIMMER: CUTIE . . . CUTIE . . . Current Under Tension Is Equal . . . No. Current Under Tension Is Expandable . . . Current Under Tension Is Expendable? I don't know what this means. (*Looks at his arms*) I don't know what any of these notes mean. I've covered my entire body in gibberish.

He sits on his bed.

RIMMER: Come on. Relax. Relax. (*Pats his right calf*) This question is bound to come up. It always does. That's 20 per cent. They're bound to ask at least one of the forearms. So I have passed already. Anything on the left shin's a bonus. Oh, God.

LISTER *has woken up.*

LISTER: What time did you get to bed last night?
RIMMER: Two hours ago. I didn't get much sleep, though.

RIMMER *starts to pull on a one-piece baggy jumpsuit.*

RIMMER: I keep getting these complete blanks. I can't remember anything.
LISTER: F-I-S-H. That's how you spell fish. Then you just keel over. It'll all come back to you.

Attention-grabbing noise. The ship's computer speaks.

HOLLY: Entrants for the Engineer's examination now make their way to the Refectory.
LISTER: Good luck.
RIMMER: It's OK. I'm in control.

RIMMER *goes out of the door, and turns left.*
    LISTER *gets out of bed, goes to his locker and gets out a bottle of milk.* RIMMER *walks past the door, going in the opposite direction.* LISTER *shuts the door. He removes a grille from the wall. In the recess is a saucer. He bangs the saucer.*

LISTER: (*Calls*) Frankenstein. Frankenstein.

He puts down the saucer and pulls out a black cat.

LISTER: You're getting really big now. I hope it's not twins.

You already get all my milk ration. But when the baby comes, maybe we can give it water, and tell him it's milk. He's only a baby cat. He won't know. Hey. Do you want to see my pictures of Fiji again? You're going to like it there, Frankenstein.

He pulls a picture of Fiji from his top pocket, and points at it, pushing it into the cat's face.

LISTER: Look.

7. Film. The Refectory

Six or seven people are spread out on different tables, taking their Engineering exam. RIMMER *is rubbing his hands, nervously.*

TODHUNTER, *acting as supervisor, looks at his watch.*

TODHUNTER: OK, everybody. You've got three hours. You can turn over your papers and good luck.

RIMMER *whips over his paper and opens up the two-page booklet. As he scans the questions the blood drains slowly from his face. He checks the front to make sure it's the right subject. It is. He looks up for support. Surely everyone is equally baffled. No. Everyone is eagerly beavering away. He gets an idea. Obviously, it's not a two-page booklet, it's a four-page booklet. Two pages have stuck together containing all the questions he knows. He tries to prise open one page. No luck. Turns it upside-down . . . sideways.*

No.

That's just one page. These are the only questions. He wipes the sweat from his forehead, brushes his hands through his hair, and wipes his face. Composed, he finds one question with a technical term which he knows is on his right forearm. Surreptitiously, he places his hand on his wrist, and slowly moves it up his arm, lifting back his sleeve, and smudging all the ink with his sweaty hand. He looks at the illegible blue mess, then at his hand covered in ink. Then RIMMER *tries a chance in a million.*

He presses his inky hand onto his answer paper, and maybe, just maybe, it'll turn out as perfectly legible notes. No. It just looks like a smeary blue handprint. He smiles strangely, then stands, waves to TODHUNTER *and faints.*

8. Set. The Drive room

Five or six people, and the CAPTAIN. LISTER *comes in. He goes up to* KOCHANSKI, *a female navigating officer.*

LISTER: You asked to see me, sir?
KOCHANSKI: (*Laughs*) No, no. I'm not the Captain.
LISTER: Oh. I thought you got a promotion.
KOCHANSKI: No.
LISTER: (*Points*) What's this button for?
KOCHANSKI: Don't touch that.
LISTER: What? This button?

He presses it. Slowly, KOCHANSKI's *seat lowers to the floor.*

LISTER: Funny. It does that every time I press it. You should get it fixed.
CAPTAIN: Lister.
LISTER: (*Salutes*) Hi, sir.
CAPTAIN: Where's the cat?
LISTER: What?

They stare at one another.

LISTER: What cat?
CAPTAIN: Lister – not only are you so stupid you bring aboard an unquarantined animal, and jeopardize every man and woman on this ship, not only that, you take a photograph of yourself with the cat, and send it off to be processed in the ship's lab. Now, I'll ask you again. Have you got a cat?
LISTER: No.

The CAPTAIN *holds the photo right under* LISTER's *nose.*

CAPTAIN: Have you got a cat?

LISTER: Yes. That one.

CAPTAIN: Where'd you get it? Titan?

LISTER: Yes.

CAPTAIN: Don't you realize it could be carrying *anything*? You know what happened on the *Oregon* with the rabbits. A loose animal around this ship could do anything. He could get in the air vents, he could get into Holly. You know, a nibble here, a nibble there, before you know it, we're flying backwards. I want that cat, and I want it now.

LISTER: Just suppose I did have a cat. What would you do with Frankenstein?

CAPTAIN: I'd send it down to the ship's lab, and have it cut up and run tests on it.

LISTER: Would you put her together again when you'd finished?

CAPTAIN: Lister, the cat would be dead.

LISTER: Hmmm. What's in it for the cat?

CAPTAIN: Lister, give me the cat.

LISTER: It's not as easy as that. You see, me and the cat, we're going to have a baby cat. And, uh, we're going to live on a farm in Fiji with a sheep and a cow and three horses. Uh. It's my plan. And I can't . . . no one can spoil my plan. Not even you. And I respect you. Sir.

CAPTAIN: You want to be put in stasis for the rest of the trip? Lose eighteen months' wages?

LISTER: No.

CAPTAIN: D'you want to hand over the cat?

LISTER: No.

CAPTAIN: Choose.

9. Set. The corridor

LISTER *is being led to the stasis room by* TODHUNTER.

LISTER *is wearing an orange Hawaiian shirt, with a plastic garland of flowers around his neck. He is carrying a plastic coconut.*

TODHUNTER: Look, Lister ... Dave ... Nobody wants to go through with this.

LISTER: Don't worry. I'm OK.

TODHUNTER: Do you need anything.

LISTER: I've got everything I need. My flowers and my plastic coconut and my cassette of the *Magic Of Fiji*.

LISTER *pats his top pocket. Makes to go through the door.*

LISTER: Is this going to hurt?

TODHUNTER: Haven't you travelled interstellar?

LISTER: No.

TODHUNTER: You don't feel anything. The stasis room creates a static field of Time; just as x-rays can't pass through lead, Time can't penetrate a stasis field. Therefore, the temporal dimension is stripped away, so, although you exist, you don't exist in Time, and for you, Time itself doesn't exist.

LISTER: Simple as that, huh?

LISTER *steps in.*

TODHUNTER: OK. See you in eighteen months.

LISTER: Aloha.

TODHUNTER *closes the door.*

TODHUNTER: Holly. Activate the stasis field.

HOLLY: OK, Frank.

10. Model. Spaceship in space

We see the name Red Dwarf *printed over:*

> 'Approximately seven billion years later.'

11. Set. The corridor

We see LISTER *through the viewing window in the stasis room. The lights go on. Attention-grabbing noise.*

HOLLY: Good morning, Dave. It is now safe for you to emerge from stasis.

LISTER *steps out.*

LISTER: I only just got in.
HOLLY: Please proceed to the Drive room for debriefing.

LISTER *walks off down the corridor.*

12. Film. Empty corridor

LISTER *wandering down it.*

LISTER: Where is everybody, Holly?
HOLLY: They're dead, Dave.
LISTER: Who is?
HOLLY: Everybody.
LISTER: What? Captain Hollister?
HOLLY: Dead, Dave.
LISTER: What? Todhunter?
HOLLY: Dead, Dave.

13. Film. The Refectory

Deserted. LISTER *wandering through.*

LISTER: Selby?
HOLLY: Dave, they're all dead.
LISTER: Even Saunders?
HOLLY: Everybody is dead, Dave.
LISTER: Not Chen?
HOLLY: Dead, Dave.

LISTER *stops.*

LISTER: Rimmer?

HOLLY: He's dead, Dave.

LISTER: Wait. Are you telling me that everybody's dead?

14. Set. Drive room

Deserted. Several mounds of white dust are piled on chairs and on the floor. LISTER *comes in.*

LISTER: How?

HOLLY: The radioactive leak which killed Flight Co-ordinator McIntyre was inefficiently repaired. A drive plate blew, and the whole crew was subjected to a lethal dose of radiation before I could seal the area.

LISTER *brushes a pile of the dust from a chair, and sits, with his head in his hands.*

LISTER: This is terrible.

He looks around.

LISTER: And why is it so dirty around here?

Dips his fingers into a neat little pile of dust.

LISTER: What is this stuff?

He tastes it.

HOLLY: That is Flight Engineer Petersen.

He tastes it again. It's like someone's said, 'It's salmon' and he can't believe it.

LISTER: Olaf?

He tries to put the remaining dust back on the pile.

LISTER: I'm sorry, Olaf.

He points at the pile on the CAPTAIN'S *chair.*

LISTER: Who's that?

HOLLY: That's Captain Hollister.

Points at another pile.

LISTER: And that's Todhunter?

HOLLY: No, that's Second Technician Rimmer.

LISTER: (*Like he recognizes it*) Oh, yeah. What was he doing in the Drive room?

HOLLY: He was explaining to the Captain why he hadn't sealed the drive plate properly.

LISTER: So wait. How long was I in stasis?

HOLLY: It has taken approximately seven billion years for the radiation to reach its present background level.

LISTER: You mean I'm seven billion and forty-one years old? I don't feel it.

RIMMER *walks in, sporting a large 'H' on his forehead.*

RIMMER: Well, I hope you're happy now.

LISTER: Rimmer?

RIMMER: You certainly got what you wanted, didn't you?

LISTER: What did *I* do?

RIMMER: What did *you* do? If you hadn't kept that stupid cat, and you hadn't been sent to stasis, I would have had some help when I was mending that drive plate. And I wouldn't be dead. Dead.

LISTER: What does it feel like?

RIMMER: (*Shouts*) Terrible!

LISTER: No, I mean being a hologram.

RIMMER: Oh, great. I still have the same drives, the same feelings, the same emotions. But I can't touch anything. Never again will I be able to brush a rose against my cheek, cradle a laughing child, or interfere sexually with a woman.

LISTER: You never did any of those things anyway.

RIMMER: But I would have. One day. Murderer.

LISTER: It wasn't my fault. It was your fault. You didn't fix the drive plates.

RIMMER *points at his pile of dust*.

RIMMER: Is this me? Here?

LISTER: Yeah.

RIMMER: Me?

LISTER: You look . . . peaceful.

RIMMER: I look like soap powder.

LISTER: Come one, Rimmer. Look on the bright side.

RIMMER: The bright side? What bright side? I'm dead. I can't touch anything. And I'm alone in space with a man who talks like he's been hit on the head by a lightning bolt. WHERE'S THE BRIGHT SIDE??

LISTER: There's always a bright side.

RIMMER: Not this time. This time there's just a dark side, and another dark side.

LISTER: Well, maybe one of the dark sides is a bit brighter than the other dark side. Let's look at that side.

RIMMER: God, why couldn't you have died instead of me. There's no point in *me* dying. It's completely stupid.

LISTER: Well. You win some, you lose some.

RIMMER: Are you smoking? In the Drive room?

LISTER: Yeah. I stopped for quite a while, but I'm, back on them now.

RIMMER: You're on report, Lister.

Goes for his notebook. Realizes.

RIMMER: I can't write it down – I'll remember it.

LISTER: I know it's wrong to speak ill of the dead, Rimmer, but you're still a smeg head.

RIMMER: I'm a what?

LISTER: A smeg head.

RIMMER: Have you any conception of the penalty for calling a deceased superior officer a smeg head?

15. Set. Drive room

Cans piled like supermarket beans. LISTER *and* RIMMER, *wearing black armbands.* LISTER *still wearing his Hawaiian shirt.*

His hair is plastered down with water and soap, and he's wearing a black tie.

LISTER: Errm. I, uh, I've never, uh, been . . . (*Long pause*) . . . good with words. So if I say something wrong or stupid . . . I'm sorry. We're here today because the crew got wiped out. And uh, it beholds me . . .

RIMMER: Behoves.

LISTER: Yeah . . . to carry out this sad duty. I haven't got you here in any order, or anything, rank or whatever. I'm just going to pick a can, like a tombola, here, and I hope nobody minds.

He picks a canister. Reads it.

LISTER: Fourth Engineer Paul Allender. Uh. I didn't know you, Paul.

He puts the canister into the tube.

LISTER: I'm really sorry you're dead.

Slaps the button to shoot him into space. Gets another can.

LISTER: (*Reads*) Flight Organizer Jeremy Black.

Pops him into the tube.

LISTER: Ditto.

Slaps the button. Another can.

LISTER: Ah! Drive Officer Russell Farnworth. We only met once, Russ. It was in the Refectory, remember? And we had a conversation about bees. Never bumped into you again. But you were a fine officer. And, you knew a hell of a lot about bees.

Slaps the button. Another can.

RIMMER: Are you going to take this long on everybody?

LISTER: (*Reads*) Uh, Deck Sergeants Sam Murray and Rick Thesen. Uhm. Sam and Rick, we all knew how much you were in love and everything. So I've put you both in the same thing. And, uh, you'll be together now, for, uh, for ever. I thought you'd like it that way.

Puts the can in the tube.

RIMMER: They split up.

LISTER *pauses. Slaps the button.*

LISTER: They're back together now.

Another can.

LISTER: Second Technician Arnold Rimmer.

LISTER *stands there, desperately trying to think of something nice to say about him.*

RIMMER: (*Quietly*) May I . . .?
LISTER: OK.

RIMMER *steps forward. He is moved.*

RIMMER: There wasn't a single person aboard this ship who didn't have a special place in their heart for little Arnold Rimmer. He was an outstanding officer, who worked damn hard to better himself, but just didn't know exam technique. How should we best remember little Arnie? There are so many wonderful stories. (*Forces a laugh through his grief*) Ha. I remember one time. Arnie was in the Refectory, indulging in his favourite pastime of 'Elbow-Titting'. That's where you brush a woman's breast with your elbow and pretend it was an accident. (*Little laugh*) And, uh, when he did this to Lea, she punched him in the shoulder and said, 'Drop Dead'. So Arnie poured an entire jug of custard over her head and ran away. What a guy. But now it's over and . . . Arnie's dead . . . I'm dead . . . and . . . and . . . Excuse me.

RIMMER *runs out.* LISTER *presses the button. Looks through the pile for a particular can.*

LISTER: Uh, First Console Officer, Christine Kochanski. Uh. You didn't know this but I was in love with you. That's why I always used to make your chair go lower when I came into the Drive room. I kept on meaning to ask you out, Chrissie, but I was so scared you'd say 'no'. So I never did. I don't know what to say. Uh, you used to have a funny kind of squint when you were concentrating, that looked nice, and you had a nice laugh. You were going to wear a white dress and ride the horses, and I was going to take care of everything else. It was a good plan.

He puts her can gingerly into the tube, presses a button on a cassette tape and shoots out the can. Ridiculous Hawaiian steel-guitar music.

LISTER, *red-rimmed eyes, saluting. From the entrance to the Drive room, an incredibly smooth-looking black guy slinks in. He's wearing a grey silk suit.*

STRANGER: OK, I'm going to walk in here, this big room, and see if there's any food in it. How'm I looking?

Checks his appearance without breaking his stride.

STRANGER: Looking good.

Sidelong glance. Notices LISTER.

STRANGER: Uh-ho. Who's that? I'm going to pretend I didn't see him, and crouch behind this box . . .

Disappears behind computer.

STRANGER: . . . here.

LISTER *is watching, open-mouthed.*

STRANGER: OK. He can't see me, so he'll think I've disappeared. How's my hair? Hmmm. Maybe needs a little trim. OK, time for a peek.

LISTER *is craning his neck. The stranger's head appears round the side of the computer.*

STRANGER: Woh!

Head back down.

STRANGER: I don't know, but I think he knows I'm hiding here.

Lifts his head again.

LISTER: Who are you?
STRANGER: I'm embarrassed now. He's made me embarrassed. I'm going to comb my hair.

STRANGER *combs his hair.*

STRANGER: Hmmm. That's nice.
LISTER: Holly? Who is this?
HOLLY: Dave, during the radioactive crisis, your cat and her kittens were safely sealed in the hold. They have been breeding for seven billion years and have evolved into the life form now crouching behind the Navi-comp.
LISTER: Wait. Are you saying that man's a cat?
STRANGER: Don't want to lose face. So I'm going to pretend I dropped something behind this box, and I've been picking it up.

He emerges from behind the box, puts an imaginary something in his pocket and pats it.

LISTER: Hello, Cat.

STRANGER: I'm going to out-stare him.

Fixes LISTER *with a steely stare for about three seconds. Looks away.*

STRANGER: No I'm not. Instead, I'm going to clean my teeth.

Takes out a toothbrush and starts gently brushing his teeth.

LISTER: Uh . . . Are you hungry?

CAT *looks very unimpressed. Starts brushing his jacket with his toothbrush.*

LISTER: Come on, I'll get you some food.

LISTER *moves off.*

LISTER: Follow me.

LISTER *goes out.* CAT *yawns. Looks over to where* LISTER's *gone.*

CAT: Is he going that way? I was going that way.

Blinks out after LISTER. *Looks down at his jacket, brushes it.*

CAT: Woh! Crease!

16. Set. Sleeping quarters

Still sporting his Hawaiian shirt, LISTER *is getting a bowl of something from the food hatch.*
  The CAT *is stalking* RIMMER.

RIMMER: Stop it! Lister, tell him to stop it.

The CAT *is staring at* RIMMER *unblinkingly, enthralled.*

CAT: That's pretty. All those lights. How do they do that?
RIMMER: Get away from me. Shoo!

LISTER *approaches with the bowl.*

LISTER: He doesn't listen. Here Cat. Holly says you like this.

The CAT *looks at the bowl.*

CAT: Mmmm. Krispies.

LISTER *puts the bowl on the floor. The* CAT *picks it up and puts it on the table, and sits down.*

LISTER: Go on, Cat – eat it up.

LISTER *wiggles his tongue like a cat drinking milk. The* CAT *just looks at him. Then takes a silver spoon out of his top pocket, polishes it with his little hankie, and starts to eat demurely. His eyes darting from side to side, to check no one steals it back.*

RIMMER: I want this animal off the ship. I want him shot. I want him dissected and analysed.

LISTER: Where are all your catty friends, Cat?

LISTER *wiggles two fingers like cat ears.*

LISTER: Where are all the other little kitties?

The CAT, *still eating beautifully, dabs the corner of his mouth with his hankie.*

CAT: Mmmm. Good Krispies.

LISTER: Are they gone? Are they dead? Have they left you?

RIMMER: Who cares? He's a danger to this mission. It's your duty to dismember him.

LISTER: No. He's coming home with us. Aren't you, Cat?

RIMMER: Home? And where exactly is home supposed to be?

LISTER: Earth.

RIMMER: What makes you think there'll *be* any Earth? And

even if there is, look what's happened to a household pet in seven billion years. Can you imagine what mankind has evolved into? A super race. To them, you'll be the equivalent of the slime that first crawled out of the oceans.

LISTER: Well, I could smarten myself up a bit.

The CAT's *finished eating. He looks around, blinking. He's about to fall asleep. He takes out a clothes brush and starts brushing himself down.*

RIMMER: You're all that's left of the Human Race. We started with slime, and ended with slime. You haven't got a planet, you haven't got a species.

LISTER: I've been in tough spots before.

RIMMER: You modo! You're a dinosaur. You're extinct. You've got nothing.

LISTER: I've still got my guitar. I've still got ★

RIMMER: (*Shakes his head*) I hope no one ever finds us. They'll think we were all like this.

LISTER: And I've still got a cat! OK, he's not Frankenstein, but he's still a cat.

CAT: Did I hear Frankenstein? Is that what the monkey said, Frankenstein?

LISTER: Yeah – Frankenstein. She was your great grandmother or something.

CAT: The Holy Mother? I remember that stuff from school. Yeah. They tried to make you believe that. The virgin birth. Uh-oh, he's looking at me again.

CAT *whips out a cloth and starts polishing his shoes.*

LISTER: No, it wasn't a virgin birth. It was a big black Tom on Titan.

CAT: Frankenstein. Yeah. They made you learn that stuff. I

★ The rest of this line is missing.

remember. 'The Holy Mother, saved by Cloister the Stupid. Who gaveth of his life that we might live.'

LISTER: (*Very excited*) No, it's not Cloister − it's Lister! It's me! It's Lister the Stupid!

CAT: '. . . who shall return to lead us to Fuchal, the Promised Land.' Yeah. That was it.

LISTER: (*Jumping up and down and waving his arms about*) No, no! It's not Fuchal − it's Fiji! Fiji! She remembered! And I *have* returned! Look − here! Here I am! And I will − I will lead you to Fiji! That's where we're going! Holly − plot a course for Fiji. Look out, Earth − the slime's coming home!

Film. The ship in space

Hawaiian music. Titles.

'The Beginning.'

Discover more about our forthcoming books through Penguin's FREE newspaper...

READ MORE IN PENGUIN

In every corner of the world, on every subject under the sun, Penguin represents quality and variety – the very best in publishing today.

For complete information about books available from Penguin – including Puffins, Penguin Classics and Arkana – and how to order them, write to us at the appropriate address below. Please note that for copyright reasons the selection of books varies from country to country.

In the United Kingdom: Please write to *Dept. JC, Penguin Books Ltd, FREEPOST, West Drayton, Middlesex UB7 OBR*

If you have any difficulty in obtaining a title, please send your order with the correct money, plus ten per cent for postage and packaging, to *PO Box No. 11, West Drayton, Middlesex UB7 OBR*

In the United States: Please write to *Penguin USA Inc., 375 Hudson Street, New York, NY 10014*

In Canada: Please write to *Penguin Books Canada Ltd, 10 Alcorn Avenue, Suite 300, Toronto, Ontario M4V 3B2*

In Australia: Please write to *Penguin Books Australia Ltd, 487 Maroondah Highway, Ringwood, Victoria 3134*

In New Zealand: Please write to *Penguin Books (NZ) Ltd, 182–190 Wairau Road, Private Bag, Takapuna, Auckland 9*

In India: Please write to *Penguin Books India Pvt Ltd, 706 Eros Apartments, 56 Nehru Place, New Delhi 110 019*

In the Netherlands: Please write to *Penguin Books Netherlands B.V., Keizersgracht 231 NL–1016 DV Amsterdam*

In Germany: Please write to *Penguin Books Deutschland GmbH, Friedrichstrasse 10–12, W–6000 Frankfurt/Main 1*

In Spain: Please write to *Penguin Books S. A., C. San Bernardo 117–6° E–28015 Madrid*

In Italy: Please write to *Penguin Italia s.r.l., Via Felice Casati 20, I–20124 Milano*

In France: Please write to *Penguin France S. A., 17 rue Lejeune, F–31000 Toulouse*

In Japan: Please write to *Penguin Books Japan, Ishikiribashi Building, 2–5–4, Suido, Tokyo 112*

In Greece: Please write to *Penguin Hellas Ltd, Dimocritou 3, GR–106 71 Athens*

In South Africa: Please write to *Longman Penguin Southern Africa (Pty) Ltd, Private Bag X08, Bertsham 2013*

READ MORE IN PENGUIN

A SELECTION OF OMNIBUSES

The Cornish Trilogy   Robertson Davies

'He has created a rich oeuvre of densely plotted, highly symbolic novels that not only function as superbly funny entertainments but also give the reader, in his character's words, a deeper kind of pleasure – delight, awe, religious intimations, "a fine sense of the past, and of the boundless depth and variety of life"' – *The New York Times*

For Good or Evil: Collected Stories   Clive Sinclair

'An ever-changing kaleidoscope of character and scenery and time, some bewilderingly surreal, others starkly cold ... powerfully written, extremely clever and very unpleasant' – *The Times*

The Pop Larkin Chronicles   H. E. Bates

'Tastes ambrosially of childhood. Never were skies so cornflower blue or beds so swansbottom ... Life not as it is or was, but as it should be' – *Guardian*. 'Pop is as sexy, genial, generous and boozy as ever, Ma is a worthy match for him in these qualities' – *The Times*

The Penguin Book of British Comic Stories
Compiled by Patricia Craig

A rich blend of comic styles ranging from the sunny humour of Wodehouse and the droll comedy of Graham Greene to the grim irony of Fay Weldon and the inventive wit of Muriel Spark.

Lucia Victrix   E. F. Benson

Mapp and Lucia, *Lucia's Progress*, *Trouble for Lucia* – now together in one volume, these three chronicles of English country life will delight a new generation of readers with their wry observation and delicious satire.

READ MORE IN PENGUIN

A SELECTION OF OMNIBUSES

The Penguin Book of Modern Women's Short Stories
Edited by Susan Hill

'They move the reader to give a cry of recognition and understanding time and time again' – Susan Hill in the Introduction. 'These stories are excellent. They are moving, wise, and finely conceived ... a selection of stories that anyone should be pleased to own' – *Glasgow Herald*

Great Law-and-Order Stories
Edited and Introduced by John Mortimer

Each of these stories conjures suspense with consummate artistry. Together they demonstrate how the greatest mystery stories enthrall not as mere puzzles but as gripping insights into the human condition.

The Duffy Omnibus   Dan Kavanagh

Nick Duffy – bisexual ex-cop turned private detective – is on the loose, for four rackety adventures in the grimiest streets of old London town... 'Exciting, funny and refreshingly nasty' – *Sunday Times*

The Best of Roald Dahl   Roald Dahl

Twenty tales to curdle your blood and scorch your soul, chosen from his bestsellers *Over to You, Someone Like You, Kiss Kiss* and *Switch Bitch*. *The Best of Roald Dahl* is, quite simply, Roald Dahl at his sinister best!

The Rabbit Novels   John Updike

'One of the finest literary achievements to have come out of the US since the war ... It is in their particularity, in the way they capture the minutiae of the world ... that [the Rabbit] books are most lovable' – John Banville in the *Irish Times*

READ MORE IN PENGUIN

A SELECTION OF OMNIBUSES

Zuckerman Bound   Philip Roth

The Zuckerman trilogy – *The Ghost Writer*, *Zuckerman Unbound* and *The Anatomy Lesson* – and the novella-length epilogue, *The Prague Orgy* in a single volume. Brilliantly diverse and intricately designed, together they form a wholly original and richly comic investigation into the unforeseen consequences of art.

The Claudine Novels   Colette

Claudine at School, *Claudine in Paris*, *Claudine Married*, *Claudine and Annie*: seldom have the experiences of a young girl growing to maturity been evoked with such lyricism and candour as in these four novels. In the hands of Colette, Claudine herself emerges as a true original: first and most beguiling of the twentieth century's emancipated women.

The Summerhouse Trilogy   Alice Thomas Ellis

'The glitter comes from Alice Thomas Ellis's mastery in keeping just the right distance between tones and undertones … This is a dark comedy' – *Sunday Times*. 'Her style is succinct, her humour dry … unputdownable' – *Spectator*

The Complete Saki

Macabre, acid and very funny, Saki's work drives a knife into the upper crust of English Edwardian life. Here are the effete and dashing heroes, the tea on the lawn, the smell of gunshot, the half-felt menace of disturbing undercurrents … all in this magnificent omnibus.

The Best of Modern Horror
Edited by Edward L. Ferman and Anne Jordan

Encounter the macabre, the grotesque and the bizarre in this chilling collection of horror stories representing the cream of the infamous *Magazine of Fantasy and Science Fiction*.

READ MORE IN PENGUIN

A SELECTION OF OMNIBUSES

Italian Folktales Italo Calvino

Greeted with overwhelming enthusiasm and praise, Calvino's anthology is already a classic. These tales have been gathered from every region of Italy and retold in Calvino's own inspired and sensuous language. 'A magic book' – *Time*

The Penguin Book of Ghost Stories Edited by J. A. Cuddon

An anthology to set the spine tingling, from the frightening and bloodcurdling to the witty and subtle, to those that leave a strange and sinister feeling of unease and fear, including stories by Zola, Kleist, Sir Walter Scott, M. R. James, and A. S. Byatt.

The Collected Dorothy Parker

Dorothy Parker, more than any of her contemporaries, captured in her writing the spirit of the Jazz Age. Here, in a single volume, is the definitive Dorothy Parker: poetry, prose, articles and reviews. 'A good, fat book … greatly to be welcomed' – Richard Ingrams

Graham Greene: Collected Short Stories

The thirty-seven stories in this immensely entertaining volume reveal Graham Greene in a range of moods: sometimes cynical, flippant and witty, sometimes searching and philosophical. Each one confirms V. S. Pritchett's statement that Greene is 'a master of storytelling'.

The Stories of William Trevor

'Trevor's short stories are a joy' – *Spectator*. 'Trevor packs into each separate five or six thousand words more richness, more laughter, more ache, more multifarious human-ness than many good writers manage to get into a whole novel' – *Punch*

READ MORE IN PENGUIN

A CHOICE OF SCIENCE FICTION

The Penguin Science Fiction Omnibus Brian Aldiss (ed.)

An exciting collection of stories from some of the best-known, best-loved science fiction writers: J. G. Ballard, Harry Harrison, Isaac Asimov, Frederik Pohl, Arthur C. Clarke and dozens more...

Cat's Cradle Kurt Vonnegut

Vonnegut's relentlessly deadpan humour makes this novel of global destruction chilling and extraordinarily compelling. 'A major novelist and a major novel' – *Sunday Telegraph*

The Chrysalids John Wyndham

A terrifying story of conformity and deformity in a world paralysed by genetic mutation. The narrator of *The Chrysalids* is David, who can communicate with a group of other young people by means of 'thought shapes'. This deviation from a cruelly rigid norm goes unnoticed at first. But sooner or later the secret is bound to be discovered, and the results are violent ... and believable.

Tigana Guy Gavriel Kay

'Kay's brilliant and complex portrayal of good and evil ... will draw readers to this consuming epic' – *Publishers Weekly*. 'A huge book, packed with action. I enjoyed it all' – *The Times*. 'A boldly complex, intelligently articulated romance' – *USA Today*

READ MORE IN PENGUIN

A CHOICE OF SCIENCE FICTION

The Day of the Triffids John Wyndham

This superbly terrifying novel achieves a razor-edge balance between wry satire and dark tragedy. The story cuts deep into the imagination, leaving the reader shaken by its violent insights and intuitions.

Flatland Edwin A. Abbott

Humour, satire and logic combine in this brilliantly entertaining classic – a capricious mathematical fantasy of life in a sunless, shadowless, two-dimensional country. The narrator is A. Square, whose flat, middle-class life is suddenly given an exciting new shape by his encounter with a sphere, who introduces him to the joys and sorrows of the third dimension.

Citizen of the Galaxy Robert A. Heinlein

From that fateful day when Thorby was bought by the crippled beggar Baslim, his life changed dramatically. Treated with unaccustomed kindness, the young boy came to love the wise old man who was teaching him lessons which were to prove invaluable...

Better Than Life Grant Naylor
The sequel to the internationally bestselling *Red Dwarf*.

Lister, Rimmer, Cat and Kryten are trapped in the ultimate computer game: Better than Life. BTL transports you directly to a perfect world of your imagination, a world where you can enjoy fabulous wealth and unmitigated success. It's the ideal game with only one drawback – it's so good, it will kill you.

READ MORE IN PENGUIN

HUMOUR

Better than Life   Grant Naylor

The sequel to the internationally bestselling *Red Dwarf* finds Lister, Rimmer, Cat and Kryten trapped in the ultimate computer game: Better than Life. BTL transports you directly to a perfect world of your imagination, a world where you can enjoy fabulous wealth and un-mitigated success. It's the ideal game with only one drawback – it's so good, it will kill you…

The Quest for the Big Woof   Lenny Henry and Steve Parkhouse

What is the Big Woof? Perplexed by the question, and with a deadline to meet, Lenny Henry sets off to find the philosopher's stone that turns pain into laughter.

Be a Bloody Train Driver   Jacky Fleming

Jacky Fleming takes a wry, original look at women's (and girls') lives in these brilliantly funny cartoons.

Alex V: The Man with the Golden Handshake
Charles Peattie and Russell Taylor

Alex, hero of the *Independent*'s business pages, faces the ultimate in-dignity: not only has he been made redundant, but people seem to think he has hired his dinner jacket for the charity ball. Meanwhile, Greg, Alex's journalist brother, is roughing it in the desert reporting on the Gulf War … and claiming expenses for the Riyadh Hilton.

How to Become Ridiculously Well-Read in One Evening   E.O. Parrott

Contains some 150 succinct and entertaining encapsulations of the best-known books in the English language, including a few foreign works familiar to us in translation. 'Very funny. Well calculated to put all teachers of English Literature in their places' – John Mortimer